HER RESCUER

"You are hurt!" cried Diana. "Ah, sir, you are hurt for my sake!"

Diana slipped an arm under his shoulder and cast an anxious glance at the footman hurrying toward them.

"Quick!" she commanded. "Sir, you are faint! You must allow my servant to assist you to the coach."

Jack forced a smile.

"It is—nothing—I assure you—pray do not— I—" and he fainted comfortably away.

"Carry him into the coach!" ordered the girl. "Yes, lay him on the seat."

Diana studied the pale face lying against the dark cushions. The duel had set her every nerve tingling; she was filled with admiration for her preserver, and the sight of his sensitive, handsome countenance did nothing to dispel that admiration.

GEORGETTE HEYER
THE BLACK MOTH

BANTAM BOOKS · TORONTO · NEW YORK · LONDON

*This low-priced Bantam Book
has been completely reset in a type face
designed for easy reading, and was printed
from new plates. It contains the complete
text of the original hard-cover edition.*
NOT ONE WORD HAS BEEN OMITTED.

📖

THE BLACK MOTH
*A Bantam Book / published by arrangement with
E. P. Dutton & Company, Inc.*

PRINTING HISTORY
Dutton edition published February 1968
Bantam edition / May 1969
2nd printing .... May 1969   4th printing .. September 1971
3rd printing . November 1969   5th printing .... August 1976
6th printing

ISBN 0-553-02263-6

*Bantam Books are published by Bantam Books, Inc. Its trade-
mark, consisting of the words "Bantam Books" and the por-
trayal of a bantam, is registered in the United States Patent
Office and in other countries. Marca Registrada. Bantam
Books, Inc., 666 Fifth Avenue, New York, New York 10019.*

PRINTED IN THE UNITED STATES OF AMERICA

To
G.B.H.

Contents

THE
BLACK MOTH

Prologue

CLAD in his customary black and silver, with raven hair un-powdered and elaborately dressed, diamonds on his fingers and in his cravat, Hugh Tracy Clare Belmanoir, Duke of Andover, sat at the escritoire in the library of his town house, writing.

He wore no rouge on his face, the almost unnatural pallor of which seemed designedly enhanced by a patch set beneath his right eye. Brows and lashes were black, the former slanting slightly up at the corners, but his narrow, heavy-lidded eyes were green and strangely piercing. The thin lips curled a little, sneering, as one dead-white hand travelled to and fro across the paper.

". . . but it seems that the Fair Lady has a Brother, who, finding Me Enamoured, threw down the Gauntlet. I soundly whipt the presumptuous Child, and so the Affair ends. Now, as you, My dear Frank, also took some Interestt in the Lady, I write for the Express Purpose of informing You that at my Hands she has received no Hurt, nor is not like to. That I in part tell You that You shall not imagine Yr self in Honor bound again to call Me out, which purpose, an I mistake not, I yesterday read in Yr Eyes. I should be Exceeding loth to meet You a Second Time, when I should consider it my Duty to teach You an even severer Lesson than Before. This I am not Wishful of doing for the Liking I bear You.

"So in all Friendship believe me, Frank,

"Your most Obedient, Humble

"DEVIL."

His Grace of Andover paused, pen held in mid-air. A mocking smile dawned in his eyes, and he wrote again.

"In the event of any Desire on Yr Part to hazard Yr Luck with my late Paramour, Permit Me to warn You 'gainst the Bantam Brother, who is in Very Truth a Fire-Eater, and would wish to make of You, as of Me, one Mouthfull. I shall hope to see You at the Queensberry Rout on Thursday, when You may Once More strive to direct mine Erring Footsteps on to the Thorny Path of Virtue."

His Grace read the postscript through with another satisfied, sardonic smile. Then he folded the letter, and affixing a wafer, peremptorily struck the hand-bell at his side.

And the Honourable Frank Fortescue, reading the postscript half-an-hour later, smiled too, but differently. Also he sighed and put the letter into the fire.

"And so ends another *affaire*. . . . I wonder if you'll go insolently to the very end?" he said softly, watching the paper shrivel and flare up. "I would to God you might fall honestly in love—and that the lady might save you from yourself—my poor Devil!"

CHAPTER I

At the Chequers Inn, Fallowfield

CHADBER was the name of the host, florid of countenance, portly of person, and of manner pompous and urbane. Solely within the walls of the Chequers lay his world, that inn having being acquired by his great-grandfather as far back as the year 1667, when the jovial Stuart King sat on the English throne, and the Hanoverian Electors were not yet dreamed of.

A Tory was Mr. Chadber to the backbone. None so bitter 'gainst the little German as he, and surely none had looked forward more eagerly to the advent of the gallant Charles Edward. If he confined his patriotism to drinking success to Prince Charlie's campaign, who shall blame him? And if, when sundry Whig gentlemen halted at the Chequers on their way to the coast, and, calling for a bottle of Rhenish, bade him toss down a glass himself with a health to his Majesty, again who shall blame Mr. Chadber for obeying? What was a health one way or another when you had rendered active service to two of his Stuart Highness's adherents?

It was Mr. Chadber's boast uttered only to his admiring Tory neighbours, that he had, at the risk of his own life, given shelter to two fugitives of the disastrous 'Forty-five, who had come so far out of their way as quiet Fallowfield. That no one had set eyes on either of the men was no reason for doubting an honest landlord's word. But no one would have thought of doubting any statement that Mr. Chadber might make. Mine host of the Chequers was a great personage in the town, being able both to read and to write, and having once, when young, travelled as far north as London town, staying there for ten days and setting eyes on no less a person than the great Duke of Marlborough himself when that gentleman was riding along the strand on his way to St. James's.

Also, it was a not-to-be-ignored fact that Mr. Chadber's

home-brewed ale was far superior to that sold by the landlord
of the rival inn at the other end of the village.

Altogether he was a most important character, and no one
was more aware of his importance than his worthy self.

To "gentlemen born", whom, he protested, he could distin-
guish at a glance, he was almost obsequiously polite, but on
clerks and underlings, and men who bore no signs of afflu-
ence about their persons, he wasted none of his deference.

Thus it was that, when a little green-clad lawyer alighted
one day from the mail coach and entered the coffee-room at
the Chequers, he was received with pomposity and scarce-
veiled condescension.

He was nervous, it seemed, and more than a little worried.
He offended Mr. Chadber at the outset, when he insinuated
that he was come to meet a gentleman who might perhaps be
rather shabbily clothed, rather short of purse, and even of
rather unsavoury repute. Very severely did Mr. Chadber give
him to understand that guests of that description were entirely unknown at the Chequers.

There was an air of mystery about the lawyer, and it appeared almost as though he were striving to prove mine host.
Mr. Chadber bridled a little, and became aloof and haughty.

When the lawyer dared openly to ask if he had had any
dealings with highwaymen of late, he was very properly and
thoroughly affronted.

The lawyer became suddenly more at ease. He eyed Mr.
Chadber speculatively, holding a pinch of snuff to one thin
nostril.

"Perhaps you have staying here a certain—ah—Sir—Anthony—Ferndale?" he hazarded.

The gentle air of injury fell from Mr. Chadber. Certainly
he had, and come only yesterday a-purpose to meet his solicitor.

The lawyer nodded.

"I am he. Be as good as to apprise Sir Anthony of my arrival."

Mr. Chadber bowed exceeding low, and implored the lawyer not to remain in the draughty coffee-room. Sir Anthony
would never forgive him an he allowed his solicitor to await
him there. Would he not come to Sir Anthony's private parlour?

The very faintest of smiles creased the lawyer's thin face as
he walked along the passage in Mr. Chadber's wake.

He was ushered into a low-ceilinged, pleasant chamber looking out on to the quiet street, and left alone what time Mr. Chadber went in search of Sir Anthony.

The room was panelled and ceilinged in oak, with blue curtains to the windows and blue cushions on the high-backed settle by the fire. A table stood in the centre of the floor, with a white table-cloth thereon and places laid for two. Another smaller table stood by the fireplace, together with a chair and a stool.

The lawyer took silent stock of his surroundings, and reflected grimly on the landlord's sudden change of front. It would appear that Sir Anthony was a gentleman of some standing at the Chequers.

Yet the little man was plainly unhappy, and fell to pacing to and fro, his chin sunk low on his breast, and his hands clasped behind his back. He was come to seek the disgraced son of an Earl, and he was afraid of what he might find.

Six years ago Lord John Carstares, eldest son of the Earl of Wyncham, had gone with his brother, the Hon. Richard, to a card party, and had returned a dishonoured man.

That Jack Carstares should cheat was incredible, ridiculous, and at first no one had believed the tale that so quickly spread. But he had confirmed that tale himself, defiantly and without shame, before riding off, bound, men said, for France and the foreign parts. Brother Richard was left, so said the countryside, to marry the lady they were both in love with. Nothing further had been heard of Lord John, and the outraged Earl forbade his name to be mentioned at Wyncham, swearing to disinherit the prodigal. Richard espoused the fair Lady Lavinia and brought her to live at the great house, strangely forlorn now without Lord John's magnetic presence; but, far from being an elated bridegroom, he seemed to have brought gloom with him from the honeymoon, so silent and so unhappy was he.

Six years drifted slowly by without bringing any news of Lord John, and then, two months ago, journeying from London to Wyncham, Richard's coach had been waylaid, and by a highwayman who proved to be none other than the scapegrace peer.

Richard's feelings may be imagined. Lord John had been singularly unimpressed by anything beyond the humour of the situation. That, however, had struck him most forcibly, and he had burst out into a fit of laughter that had brought a lump into Richard's throat, and a fresh ache to his heart.

Upon pressure John had given his brother the address of the inn, "in case of accidents", and told him to ask for "Sir Anthony Ferndale" if ever he should need him. Then with one hearty handshake, he had galloped off into the darkness. . . .

The lawyer stopped his restless pacing to listen. Down the passage was coming the tap-tap of high heels on the wooden floor, accompanied by a slight rustle as of stiff silks.

The little man tugged suddenly at his cravat. Supposing— supposing debonair Lord John was no longer debonair? Supposing—he dared not suppose anything. Nervously he drew a roll of parchment from his pocket and stood fingering it.

A firm hand was laid on the door-handle, turning it cleanly round. The door opened to admit a veritable apparition, and was closed again with a snap.

The lawyer found himself gazing at a slight, rather tall gentleman who swept him a profound bow, gracefully flourishing his smart three-cornered hat with one hand and delicately clasping cane and perfumed handkerchief with the other. He was dressed in the height of the Versailles fashion, with full-skirted coat of palest lilac laced with silver, small-clothes and stockings of white, and waistcoat of flowered satin. On his feet he wore shoes with high red heels and silver buckles, while a wig of the latest mode, marvellously powdered and curled and smacking greatly of Paris, adorned his shapely head. In the foaming lace of his cravat reposed a diamond pin, and on the slim hand, half covered by drooping laces, glowed and flashed a huge emerald.

The lawyer stared and stared again, and it was not until a pair of deep blue, rather wistful eyes met his in a quizzical glance, that he found his tongue. Then a look of astonishment came into his face, and he took a half step forward.

"Master Jack!" he gasped. "Master—*Jack*!"

The elegant gentleman came forward and held up a reproving hand. The patch at the corner of his mouth quivered, and the blue eyes danced.

"I perceive that you are not acquainted with me, Mr. Warburton," he said, amusement in his pleasant, slightly drawling voice. "Allow me to present myself: Sir Anthony Ferndale, *à vous servir*!"

A gleam of humour appeared in the lawyer's own eyes as he clasped the outstretched hand.

"I think you are perhaps not acquainted with yourself, my lord," he remarked drily.

Lord John laid his hat and cane on the small table, and looked faintly intrigued.

"What's your meaning, Mr. Warburton?"

"I am come, my lord, to inform you that the Earl, your father, died a month since."

The blue eyes widened, grew of a sudden hard, and narrowed again.

"Is that really so? Well, well! Apoplexy, I make no doubt?"

The lawyer's lips twitched uncontrollably.

"No, Master Jack; my lord died of heart failure."

"Say you so? Dear me! But will you not be seated, sir? In a moment my servant will have induced the *chef* to serve dinner. You will honour me, I trust?"

The lawyer murmured his thanks and sat down on the settle, watching the other with puzzled eyes.

The Earl drew up a chair for himself and stretched his foot to the fire.

"Six years, eh? I protest 'tis prodigious good to see your face again, Mr. Warburton. . . . And I'm the Earl? Earl and High Toby, by Gad!" He laughed softly.

"I have here the documents, my lord. . . ."

Carstares eyed the roll through his quizzing glass.

"I perceive them. Pray return them to your pocket, Mr. Warburton."

"But there are certain legal formalities, my lord——"

"Exactly. Pray do not let us mention them!"

"But, sir!"

Then the Earl smiled, and his smile was singularly sweet and winning.

"At least, not until after dinner, Warburton! Instead, you shall tell me how you found me?"

"Mr. Richard directed me where to come, sir."

"Ah, of course! I had forgot that I told him my—*pied-à-terre* when I waylaid him."

The lawyer nearly shuddered at this cheerful, barefaced mention of his lordship's disreputable profession.

"Er—indeed, sir. Mr. Richard is eager for you to return."

The handsome young face clouded over. My lord shook his head.

"Impossible, my dear Warburton. I am convinced Dick never voiced so foolish a suggestion. Come now, confess! 'tis your own fabrication?"

Warburton ignored the bantering tone and spoke very deliberately.

"At all events, my lord, I believe him anxious to make—amends."

Carstares shot an alert, suspicious glance at him.

"Ah!"

"Yes, sir. Amends."

My lord studied his emerald with half-closed eyelids.

"But why—amends, Warburton?" he asked.

"Is not that the word, sir?"

"I confess it strikes me as inapt. Doubtless I am dull of comprehension."

"You were not wont to be, my lord."

"No? But six years changes a man, Warburton. Pray, is Mr. Carstares well?"

"I believe so, sir," replied the lawyer, frowning at the deft change of subject.

"And Lady Lavinia?"

"Ay." Mr. Warburton looked searchingly across at him, seeing which, my lord's eyes danced afresh, brim full with mischief.

"I am delighted to hear it. Pray present my compliments to Mr. Carstares and beg him to use Wyncham as he wills."

"Sir! Master Jack! I implore you!" burst from the lawyer, and he sprang up, moving excitedly away, his hands twitching, his face haggard.

My lord stiffened in his chair. He watched the other's jerky movements anxiously, but his voice when he spoke was even and cold.

"Well, sir?"

Mr. Warburton wheeled and came back to the fireplace, looking hungrily down at my lord's impassive countenance. With an effort he seemed to control himself.

"Master Jack, I had better tell you what you have already guessed. I know."

Up went one haughty eyebrow.

"You know what, Mr. Warburton?"

"That you are innocent!"

"Of what, Mr. Warburton?"

"Of cheating at cards, sir!"

My lord relaxed, and flicked a speck of dust from his great cuff.

"I regret the necessity of having to disillusion you, Mr. Warburton."

"My lord, do not fence with me, I beg! You can trust me, surely?"

"Certainly, sir."

"Then do not keep up this pretence with me; no, nor look so hard neither! I've watched you grow up right from the cradle, and Master Dick too, and I know you both through and through. I *know* you never cheated at Colonel Dare's nor anywhere else! I could have sworn it at the time—ay, when I saw Master Dick's face, I knew at once that he it was who had played foul, and you had but taken the blame!"

"No!"

"I know better! Can you, Master Jack, look me in the face and truthfully deny what I have said? Can you? Can you?"

My lord sat silent.

With a sigh, Warburton sank on to the settle once more. He was flushed, and his eyes shone, but he spoke calmly again.

"Of course you cannot. I have never known you lie. You need not fear I shall betray you. I kept silence all these years for my lord's sake, and I will not speak now until you give me leave."

"Which I never shall."

"Master Jack, think better of it, I beg of you! Now that my lord is dead——"

"It makes no difference."

"No difference? 'Twas not for his sake? 'Twas not because you knew how he loved Master Dick?"

"No."

"Then 'tis Lady Lavinia——"

"No."

"But——"

My lord smiled sadly.

"Ah, Warburton! And you averred you knew us through and through! For whose sake should it be but his own?"

"I feared it!" The lawyer made a hopeless gesture with his hands. "You will not come back?"

"No, Warburton, I will not; Dick can manage my estates. I remain on the road."

Warburton made one last effort.

"My lord!" he cried despairingly. "Will you not at least think of the disgrace to the name an you be caught?"

The shadows vanished from my lord's eyes.

"Mr. Warburton, I protest you are of a morbid turn of mind! Do you know, I had not thought of so unpleasant a contingency? I swear I was not born to be hanged!"

The lawyer would have said more, had not the entrance of a servant carrying a loaded tray, put an end to all private conversation. The man placed dishes upon the table, lighted candles, and arranged two chairs.

"Dinner is served, sir," he said.

My lord nodded and made a slight gesture toward the windows. Instantly the man went over to them and drew the heavy curtains across.

My lord turned to Mr. Warburton.

"What say you, sir? Shall it be burgundy or claret, or do you prefer sack?"

Warburton decided in favour of claret.

"Claret, Jim," ordered Carstares, and rose to his feet.

"I trust the drive has whetted your appetite, Warburton, for honest Chadber will be monstrous hurt an you do not justice to his capons."

"I shall endeavour to spare his feelings," replied the lawyer with a twinkle, and seated himself at the table.

Whatever might be Mr. Chadber's failings, he possessed an excellent cook. Mr. Warburton dined very well, beginning on a fat duck, and continuing through the many courses that constituted the meal.

When the table was cleared, the servant gone, and the port before them, he endeavoured to guide the conversation back into the previous channels. But he reckoned without my lord, and presently found himself discussing the Pretender's late rebellion. He sat up suddenly.

"There were rumours that you were with the Prince, sir."

Carstares set down his glass in genuine amazement.

"I?"

"Indeed, yes. I do not know whence the rumour came, but it reached Wyncham. My lord said nought, but I think Mr. Richard hardly credited it."

"I should hope not! Why should they think me turned rebel, pray?"

Mr. Warburton frowned.

"Rebel, sir?"

"Rebel, Mr. Warburton. I have served under his Majesty."

"The Carstares were ever Tories, Master Jack, true to their rightful king."

"My dear Warburton, I owe nought to the Stuart princes. I was born in King George the First's reign, and I protest I am a good Whig."

Warburton shook his head disapprovingly.

"There has never been a Whig in the Wyncham family, sir."

"And you hope there never will be again, eh? What of Dick? Is he faithful to the Pretender?"

"I think Mr. Richard does not interest himself in politics, sir."

Carstares raised his eyebrows, and there fell a silence.

After a minute or two Mr. Warburton cleared his throat.

"I—I suppose, sir—you have no idea of—er—discontinuing your—er—profession?"

My lord gave an irrepressible little laugh.

"Faith, Mr. Warburton, I've only just begun!"

"Only—— But a year ago, Mr. Richard——"

"I held him up? Aye, but to tell the truth, sir, I've not done much since then!"

"Then, sir, you are not—er—notorious?"

"Good gad, no! Notorious, forsooth! Confess, Warburton, you thought me some heroic figure? 'Gentleman Harry', perhaps?"

Warburton blushed.

"Well, sir—— I—er—wondered."

"I shall have to disappoint you, I perceive. I doubt Bow Street has never heard of me—and—to tell the truth—'tis not an occupation which appeals vastly to my senses."

"Then why, my lord, do you continue?"

"I must have some excuse for roaming the country," pleaded Jack. "I could not be idle."

"You are not—compelled to—er—rob, my lord?"

Carstares wrinkled his brow inquiringly.

"Compelled? Ah—I take your meaning. No, Warburton, I have enough for my wants—now; time was—but that is past. I rob for amusement's sake."

Warburton looked steadily across at him.

"I am surprised, my lord, that you, a Carstares, should find it—amusing."

John was silent for a moment, and when he at length spoke it was defiantly and with a bitterness most unusual in him.

"The world, Mr. Warburton, has not treated me so kindly that I should feel any qualms of conscience. But, an it gives you any satisfaction to know it, I will tell you that my robberies are few and far between. You spoke a little while ago of my probable—ah—fate—on Tyburn Tree. I think you need not fear to hear of that."

"I—— It gives me great satisfaction, my lord, I confess," stammered the lawyer, and found nothing more to say. After a long pause he again produced the bulky roll of parchment and laid it down before the Earl with the apologetic murmur of:

"Business, my lord!"

Carstares descended from the clouds and eyed the packet with evident distaste. He proceeded to fill his and his companion's glass very leisurely. That done, he heaved a lugubrious sigh, caught Mr. Warburton's eye, laughed in answer to its quizzical gleam, and broke the seal.

"Since you *will* have it, sir—business!"

*   *   *   *   *

Mr. Warburton stayed the night at the Chequers and travelled back to Wyncham next day by the two o'clock coach. He played piquet and écarté with my lord all the evening, and then retired to bed, not having found an opportunity to argue his mission as he had hoped to do. Whenever he had tried to turn the conversation that way he had been gently but firmly led into safer channels, and somehow had found it impossible to get back. My lord was the gayest and most charming of companions, but talk "business" he would not. He regaled the lawyer with spicy anecdotes and tales of abroad, but never once allowed Mr. Warburton to speak of his home or of his brother.

The lawyer retired to rest in a measure reassured by the other's good spirits, but at the same time dispirited by his failure to induce Carstares to return to Wyncham.

Next morning, although he was not up until twelve, he was before my lord, who only appeared in time for lunch, which was served as before in the oak parlour.

He entered the room in his usual leisurely yet decided

fashion and made Mr. Warburton a marvellous leg. Then he
bore him off to inspect his mare, Jenny, of whom he was in-
ordinately proud. By the time they returned to the parlour
luncheon was served, and Mr. Warburton realised that he had
scarcely any time left in which to plead his cause.

My lord's servant hovered continually about the room,
waiting on them, until his master bade him go to attend to
the lawyer's valise. When the door had closed on his retreating form, Carstares leaned back in his chair, and, with a
rather dreary little smile, turned to his companion.

"You want to reason with me, I know, Mr. Warburton,
and, indeed, I will listen an I must. But I would so much
rather that you left the subject alone, believe me."

Warburton sensed the finality in his voice, and wisely
threw away his last chance.

"I understand 'tis painful, my lord, and I will say no more.
Only remember—and think on it, I beg!"

The concern in his face touched my lord.

"You are too good to me, Mr. Warburton, I vow. I can
only say that I appreciate your kindness—and your forbear-
ance. And I trust that you will forgive my seeming churlish-
ness and believe that I am indeed grateful to you."

"I wish I might do more for you, Master Jack!" stammered
Warburton, made miserable by the wistful note in his favourite's voice. There was no time for more; the coach already
awaited him, and his valise had been hoisted up. As they
stood together in the porch, he could only grip my lord's
hand tightly and say good-bye. Then he got hurriedly into the
coach, and the door was slammed behind him.

My lord made his leg, and watched the heavy vehicle move
forward and roll away down the street. Then with a stifled
sigh he turned and walked towards the stables. His servant
saw him coming and went at once to meet him.

"The mare, sir?"

"As you say, Jim—the mare. In an hour."

He turned and would have strolled back.

"Sir—your honour!"

He paused, looking over his shoulder.

"Well?"

"They're on the look-out, sir. Best be careful."

"They always are, Jim. But thanks."

"Ye—ye wouldn't take me with ye, sir?" pleadingly.

"Take you? Faith, no! I've no mind to lead you into danger. And you serve me best by remaining to carry out my orders."

The man fell back.

"Ay, sir; but—but——"

"There are none, Jim."

"No, sir—but ye *will* have a care?"

"I will be the most cautious of men." He walked away on the word, and passed into the house.

In an hour he was a very different being. Gone was the emerald ring, the foppish cane; the languid air, too, had disappeared, leaving him brisk and businesslike. He was dressed for riding, with buff coat and buckskin breeches, and shining top boots. A sober brown wig replaced the powdered creation, and a black tricorne was set rakishly atop.

He stood in the deserted porch, watching Jim strap his baggage to the saddle, occasionally giving a curt direction. Presently Mr. Chadber appeared with the stirrup-cup, which he drained and handed back with a word of thanks and a guinea at the bottom.

Someone called lustily from within, and the landlord, bowing very low, murmured apologies and vanished.

Jim cast a last glance at the saddle-girths, and, leaving the mare quietly standing in the road, came up to his master with gloves and whip.

Carstares took them silently and fell to tapping his boot, his eyes thoughtfully on the man's face.

"You will hire a coach, as usual," he said at length, "and take my baggage to——" (He paused, frowning)—"Lewes. You will engage a room at the White Hart and order dinner. I shall wear—apricot and—h'm!"

"Blue, sir?" ventured Jim, with an idea of being helpful.

His master's eyes crinkled at the corners.

"You are a humorist, Salter. Apricot and cream. Cream? Yes, 'tis a pleasing thought—cream. That is all—Jenny!"

The mare turned her head, whinnying as he came towards her.

"Good lass!" he mounted lightly and patted her glossy neck. Then he leaned sideways in the saddle to speak again to Salter, who stood beside him, one hand on the bridle.

"The cloak?"

"Behind you, sir."

"My wig?"

"Yes, sir."

"Pistols?"

"Ready primed, sir."

"Good. I shall be in Lewes in time for dinner—with luck."

"Yes, sir. Ye—ye will have a care?" anxiously.

"Have I not told you?" He straightened in the saddle, touched the mare with his heel, and bestowing a quick smile and a nod on his man, trotted easily away.

CHAPTER II

My Lord at the White Hart

"SIR ANTHONY FERNDALE" sat before the dressing-table in his room at the White Hart, idly polishing his nails. A gorgeous silk dressing gown lay over the back of his chair, and, behind him, Jim was attending to his wig, at the same time hovering anxiously over the coat and waistcoat that were waiting to be donned.

Carstares left off polishing his nails, yawned, and leaned back in his chair, a slim graceful figure in cambric shirt and apricot satin breeches. He studied his cravat for some moments in the mirror, and lifted a hand to it. Salter held his breath. With extreme deliberation the hand moved a diamond and emerald pin the fraction of an inch to one side, and fell to his side again. Salter drew a relieved breath, which brought his master's eyes round to himself.

"No trouble, Jim?"

"None at all, sir."

"Neither had I. 'Twas most surprisingly easy. The birds had no more fight in them than sparrows. Two men in a coach—one a bullying rascal of a merchant, the other his clerk. Gad! but I was sorry for that little man!" He paused, his hand on the rouge pot.

Salter looked an inquiry.

"Yes," nodded Carstares. "Very sorry. The fat man would appear to bully and browbeat him after the manner of his kind; he even blamed him for my advent, the greasy coward! Yes, Jim, you are right—he did not appeal to me, my M. Fudby. So—" ingenuously, "I relieved him of his cash-box and two hundred guineas. A present for the poor of Lewes."

Jim jerked his shoulder, frowning.

"If ye give away all ye get, sir, why do ye rob at all?" he asked bluntly.

His whimsical little smile played about my lord's mouth.

" 'Tis an object for my life, Jim; a noble object. And I be-

14

lieve it amuses me to play Robin Hood—take from the rich
to give to the poor," he added, for Salter's benefit. "But to
return to my victims—you would have laughed had you but
seen my little man come tumbling out of the coach when I
opened the door!"

"Tumble, sir? Why should he do that?"

"He was at pains to explain the reason. It seems he had
been commanded to hold the door to prevent my entering—
so when I jerked it open, sooner than loose his hold, he fell
out on to the road. Of course, I apologised most abjectly—
and we had some conversation. Quite a nice little man. . . .
It made me laugh to see him sprawling on the road, though!"

"Wish I could have seen it, your honour. I would ha' liked
fine to ha' been beside ye." He looked down at the lithe form
with some pride. "I'd give something to see ye hold up a
coach, sir!"

Haresfoot in hand, Jack met his admiring eyes in the glass,
and laughed.

"I make no doubt you would. . . . I have cultivated a superb voice, a trifle thick and beery, a little loud, perhaps—ah,
something to dream of o' nights! I doubt they do, too," he
added reflectively, and affixed the patch at the corner of his
mouth.

"So? A little low, you think? But 'twill suffice—— What's
toward?"

Down below in the street there was a great stirring and
bustling: horses' hoofs, shouts from the ostlers, and the sound
of wheels on the cobble-stones. Jim went to the window and
looked down, craning his neck to see over the balcony.

" 'Tis a coach arrived, sir."

"That much had I gathered," replied my lord, busy with
the powder.

"Yes, sir. O lord, sir!" He was shaken with laughter.

"What now?"

" 'Tis the curiousest sight, sir! Two gentlemen, one fat and
t'other small! One's all shrivelled-looking, like a spider, while
t'other——"

"Resembles a hippopotamus—particularly in the face?"

"Well yes, sir. He do rather. And he be wearing purple."

"Heavens, yes! Purple, and an orange waistcoat!"

Jim peered afresh.

"So it is, sir! But how did you know?" Even as he put the
question, understanding flashed into Jim's eyes.

"I rather think that I have had the honour of meeting these gentlemen," replied my lord placidly. "My buckle, Jim. . . . Is't a prodigious great coach with wheels picked out in yellow?"

"Ay, your honour. The gentlemen seem a bit put out, too."

"That is quite probable. Does the smaller gentleman wear somewhat—ah—muddied garments?"

"I can't see, sir; he stands behind the fat gentleman."

"Mr. Bumble Bee. . . . Jim!"

"Sir!" Jim turned quickly at the sound of the sharp voice.

He found that my lord had risen, and was holding up a waistcoat of pea-green pattern on a bilious yellow ground, between a disgusted finger and thumb. Before his severe frown Jim dropped his eyes and stood looking for all the world like a schoolboy detected in some crime.

"You put this—this monstrosity—out for *me* to wear?" in awful tones.

Jim eyed the waistcoat gloomily and nodded.

"Yes, sir."

"Did I not specify cream ground?"

"Yes, sir. I thought—I thought that 'twas cream!"

"My good friend, it is—it is—I cannot say what it is. And pea-green!" he shuddered. "Remove it."

Jim hurried forward and disposed of the offending garment.

"And bring me the broidered satin. Yes, that is it. It is particularly pleasing to the eye."

"Yes, sir," agreed the abashed Jim.

"You are excused this time," added my lord, with a twinkle in his eye. "What are our two friends doing?"

Salter went to the window.

"They've gone into the house, sir. No, here's the spider gentleman! He do seem in a hurry, your honour!"

"Ah!" murmured his lordship. "You may assist me into this coat. Thanks."

With no little difficulty, my lord managed to enter into the fine satin garment, which, when on, seemed moulded to his back, so excellently did it fit. He shook out his ruffles and slipped the emerald ring on to his finger with a slight frown.

"I believe I shall remain here some few days," he remarked presently. "To—ah—allay suspicion." He looked across at his man as he spoke, through his lashes.

It was not in Jim's nature to inquire into his master's affairs, much less to be surprised at anything he might do or say. He was content to receive and promptly execute his orders, and to worship Carstares with a dog-like devotion, following blindly in his wake, happy as long as he might serve him.

Carstares had found him in France, very down upon his luck, having been discharged from the service of his late master owing to the penniless condition of that gentleman's pocket. He had engaged him as his own personal servant, and the man had remained with him ever since, proving an invaluable acquisition to my Lord John. Despite a singularly wooden countenance, he was by no means a fool, and he had helped Carstares out of more than one tight corner during his inglorious and foolhardy career as highwayman. He probably understood his somewhat erratic master better than anyone else, and he now divined what was in his mind. He returned that glance with a significant wink.

" 'Twas them gentlemen ye held up to-day, sir!" he asked, jerking an expressive thumb towards the window.

"M'm. Mr. Bumble Bee and friend. It would almost appear so. I think I do not fully appreciate Mr. Bumble Bee. I find his conduct rather tiresome. But it is just possible that he thinks the same of me. I will further my acquaintance with him."

Jim grunted scornfully, and an inquiring eye was cocked at him.

"You do not admire our friend? Pray, do not judge him by his exterior. He may possess a beautiful mind. But I do not think so. N-no, I really do not think so." He chuckled a little. "Do you know, Jim, I believe I am going to enjoy myself to-night!"

"I don't doubt it, your honour. 'Twere child's play to trick the fat gentleman."

"Probably. But it is not with the fat gentleman that I shall have to deal. 'Tis with all the officials of this charming town, an I mistake not. Do I hear the small spider returning?"

Salter stepped back to the window.

"Ay, sir—with three others."

"Pre-cisely. Be so good as to hand me my snuff-box. And my cane. Thank you. I feel the time has now come for me to put in an appearance. Pray, bear in mind that I am new

come from France and journey by easy stages to London.
And cultivate a stupid expression. Yes, that will do excellently."

Jim grinned delightedly; he had assumed no expression of
stupidity, and was consequently much pleased with this pleasantry. He swung open the door with an air, and watched "Sir
Anthony" mince along the passage to the stairs.

In the coffee-room the city merchant, Mr. Fudby by name,
was relating the story of his wrongs, with many an impressive
pause, and much emphasis, to the mayor, town-clerk, and
beadle of Lewes. All three had been fetched by Mr. Chilter,
his clerk, in obedience to his orders, for the bigger the audi-
ence the better pleased was Mr. Fudby. He was now enjoying
himself quite considerably, despite the loss of his precious
cash-box.

So was not Mr. Hedges, the mayor. He was a fussy little
man who suffered from dyspepsia; he was not interested in
the affair, and he did not see what was to be done for Mr.
Fudby. Further, he had been hailed from his dinner, and he
was hungry; and, above all, he found Mr. Fudby very unat-
tractive. Still, a highroad robbery was serious matter enough,
and some course of action must be thought out; so he listened to the story with an assumption of interest, looking exceedingly wise, and, at the proper moments, uttering sounds
betokening concern.

The more he saw and heard of Mr. Fudby, the less he
liked him. Neither did the town-clerk care for him. There
was that about Mr. Fudby that did not endear him to his fel-
low-men, especially when they chanced to be his inferiors in
the social scale. The beadle did not think much about anything. Having decided (and rightly) that the affair had nothing whatever to do with him, he leaned back in his chair and
stared stolidly up at the ceiling.

The tale Mr. Fudby was telling bore surprisingly little resemblance to the truth. It was a much embellished version, in
which he himself had behaved with quite remarkable gallantry. It had been gradually concocted during the journey to
Lewes.

He was still holding forth when my lord entered the room.
Carstares raised his glass languidly to survey the assembled
company, bowed slightly, and walked over to the fire. He
seated himself in an armchair and took no further notice of
anybody.

Mr. Hedges had recognised at a glance that here was some *grand seigneur* and wished that Mr. Fudby would not speak in so loud a voice. But that individual, delighted at having a new auditor, continued his tale with much relish and in a still louder tone.

My lord yawned delicately and took a pinch of snuff.

"Yes, yes," fussed Mr. Hedges. "But, short of sending to London for the Runners, I do not see what I can do. If I send to London, it must, of course, be at your expense, sir."

Mr. Fudby bristled.

"At *my* expense, sir? Do ye say at *my* expense? I am surprised! I repeat—I am surprised!"

"Indeed, sir? I can order the town-crier out, describing the horse, and—er—offering a reward for the capture of any man on such animal. But—" he shrugged and looked across at the town-clerk—"I do not imagine that 'twould be of much use—eh, Mr. Brand?"

The clerk pursed his lips and spread out his hands.

"I fear not; I very much fear not. I would advise Mr. Fudby to have a proclamation posted up round the country." He sat back with the air of one who has contributed his share to the work, and does not intend to offer any more help.

"Ho!" growled Mr. Fudby. He blew out his cheeks. "'Twill be a grievous expense, though I suppose it must be done, and I cannot but feel that if it had not been for your deplorably cowardly conduct, Chilter—yes, cowardly conduct I say—I might never have been robbed of my two hundred!" He snuffled a little, and eyed the flushed but silent Chilter with mingled reproach and scorn. "However, my coachman assures me he could swear to the horse again, although he cannot remember much about the man himself. Chilter! How did he describe the horse?"

"Oh—er—chestnut, Mr. Fudby—chestnut, with a half-moon of white on its forehead, and one white foreleg."

Jack perceived that it was time he took a hand in the game. He half turned in his chair and levelled his quizzing-glass at Mr. Chilter.

"I beg your pardon?" he drawled.

Mr. Fudby's eyes brightened. The fine gentleman was roused to an expression of interest at last. He launched forth into his story once more for my lord's benefit. Carstares eyed him coldly, seeing which, Mr. Hedges came hurriedly to the rescue.

"Er—yes, Mr. Fudby—quite so! Your pardon, sir, I have not the honour of knowing your name?"

"Ferndale," supplied Jack, "Sir Anthony Ferndale."

"Er—yes——" Mr. Hedges bowed. "Pray pardon my importuning you with our——"

"Not at all," said my lord.

"No—quite so—— The fact is, these—er—gentlemen have had the—er—misfortune to be waylaid on their journey here."

Sir Anthony's glass was again levelled at the group. His expression betokened mild surprise.

"All these gentlemen?" he inquired blandly. "Dear, dear!"

"Oh, no, no, no, sir! Not all! Only Mr.—er——"

"Fudby," said that worthy, and discovered that Sir Anthony was bowing frigidly. At once he rose and, resting his knuckles on the table before him, bent his body slowly and painfully. Sir Anthony inclined his head, whereupon, to the delight of all the rest, Mr. Fudby bowed again with even greater stateliness than before. Mr. Hedges observed Sir Anthony's lips to twitch convulsively. He waited for Mr. Fudby to subside, and then continued:

"Yes—Mr. Fudby and Mr.——"

"My clerk!" snapped Fudby.

Sir Anthony favoured Mr. Chilter with his peculiarly sweet smile, and turned again to Mr. Hedges.

"I see. A *daylight* robbery, you say?"

"Broad daylight!" boomed Mr. Fudby.

"Er—yes, yes," interposed the mayor, fearing a fresh outbreak from that quarter. "I wonder if you have seen anything of such an animal as Mr.—er—Chilter—described?"

" 'Tis a most extraordinary thing," said Carstares slowly, "but I have just bought such an one." He glanced round with an inquiring smile and one eyebrow lifted.

"Well!" ejaculated Mr. Fudby. "Well!"

"Dear me, sir, what a strange coincidence! May I ask where you bought it, and from whom?"

"She has not been in my possession over two hours. I bought her from an out-at-elbows ruffian, on my way hither. I thought at one time that 'twas strange that the man should possess such a mare—pure bred, I vow—and wondered why he was so eager to be rid of her."

"He was eager because he knew he would be recognised by her," explained Mr. Fudby kindly.

"Without doubt. Perhaps you would like to see her? I will
send my man——"

"Oh no, no!" cried the mayor. "We would not dream of so
inconveniencing you——"

" 'Twere a pleasure," bowed Jack, devoutly hoping that
Mr. Fudby would not require to see Jenny, who, he felt sure,
would betray him by her very evident affection.

"No, no, Sir Anthony, 'tis quite unnecessary, I assure you,
but I thank you for all that. Mr. Fudby, if you would describe the man himself, I will see to the proclamation."

"Describe him, Chilter!" ordered Mr. Fudby, who was becoming rather grumpy.

Mr. Chilter smiled suddenly.

"Certainly, sir!" he said with alacrity. " 'Twas a great ruf-
fianly fellow, monstrous tall——"

"How tall?" interrupted the town-clerk. "Six feet?"

"Oh, quite!" lied Mr. Chilter. "And fat."

Jack's shoulders shook.

"Fat, you say?" he asked gently.

"Very fat," affirmed Mr. Chilter. "And prodigious rough,
swearing dreadfully in his speech."

"You could not see his face, I suppose?"

Mr. Chilter hesitated.

"I could see his mouth and chin," he said, "and I remarked
a long scar running from his under-lip to the—er—bottom of
his face."

Involuntarily Carstares' hand caressed his perfectly smooth
chin. Either the little clerk was a born romancer, or for some
reason or other he did not want the highwayman to be taken.

"Well, Sir Anthony?" the mayor was saying. "Does that
description fit your man?"

My lord frowned thoughtfully.

"Tall," he said slowly, "and fat—you said fat, I think, Mr.
Chilter?"

Rather anxiously Mr. Chilter reiterated this statement.

"Ah! And with a long scar—yes, that is undoubtedly he.
Furthermore," he added audaciously, "he has a squint in his
left eye. 'Tis a most ill-favoured rogue in all."

"It would appear so, Sir Anthony," remarked the mayor
drily. He did not in the least believe the story of the squint,
and imagined that the fine court gentleman was amusing himself at their expense. Nevertheless, he had no intention of re-
monstrating; the sooner he could withdraw from this very

tiresome affair the better. So he gravely took down all the absurd particulars, remarked that the man should be easy to find, and made ready to depart.

The town-clerk rose, and tapped the beadle on the shoulder, whereupon that worthy, with a grunt, abandoned his pose of masterly inactivity and followed the mayor out of the room.

Mr. Fudby rose.

"I doubt I shall never see my money again," he said pettishly. "If you, Chilter, had not been so——"

"Allow me to offer you some snuff, Mr. Chilter," interposed my lord gently, extending his jewelled box. "Doubtless, sir, you would wish to see my mare?"

"I know nought of horses," snorted Mr. Fudby. " 'Tis my clerk who appears to have remarked all the details." He sneered terrifically.

"Then pray, do me the honour of walking as far as the stables, Mr. Chilter. 'Twere as well to be certain about the mare. Mr.—ah—Fudby, your servant."

*   *   *   *   *

"And now, Mr. Chilter, I have a grudge against you," said Carstares, as they walked across the little garden.

"Me, sir? Oh——er——have you, Sir Anthony?"

He looked up and perceived that the gentleman was laughing.

"Yes, Mr. Chilter, a very serious grudge: you have described me as fat!"

Chilter nearly fainted.

"*You*, sir," he gasped, and stared in amazement.

"Also that I swear dreadfully in my speech, and that I have a scar running from my mouth to my chin."

Mr. Chilter stood stock-still in the middle of the path.

"It was you, sir, all the time? *You* held us up? Were *you* the man who wrenched open the door?"

"I was that infamous scoundrel. I beg leave once more to apologise for my carelessness in opening that same door. Now tell me, why did you take such pains to throw dust in their sleepy eyes?"

They resumed their walk slowly. The little clerk flushed.

"I scarce know, sir, save that I—that I liked you, and—and——"

"I see. 'Twas prodigious good of you, Mr. Chilter. I wonder if there is anything that I can do to show my gratitude?"

Again the clerk flushed and lifted his head proudly.

"I thank you, sir, but there is nought."

By now they had reached the stable. Carstares opened the door and they entered.

"Then will you accept this in token of my regard, sir?"

Mr. Chilter gazed at the emerald ring that glowed and winked at him from the palm of my lord's hand. He looked up into the blue eyes and stammered a little.

"Indeed, sir—I—I——"

" 'Tis honestly come by!" pleadingly. "Come, Mr. Chilter, you'll not hurt my feelings by refusing? You will keep it in remembrance of a man—a fat man, Mr. Chilter—who rudely jerked you on to the road?"

The clerk took it with unsteady fingers.

"I thank you most——"

"Nay, I beg of you. 'Tis I thank you for aiding me so kindly. . . . Come and see my Jenny! Well, lass?" For the mare at the first sound of his voice had turned in her loose-box, and was whinnying and pawing the ground eagerly.

"I do not understand, sir, anything: how it is that you are a highwayman, or why you have honoured me with your confidence—why you should trust me. But—thank you."

As he spoke, Mr. Chilter placed his hand in my lord's, and for the second time in his life, felt the pressure of those firm, kindly fingers.

*   *   *   *   *

"Why, your honour! Ye've lost your emerald!"

"No, Jim. I gave it away."

"Ye—ye *gave* it away, sir?"

"M'm. To the small spider."

"B-but——"

"And he called me fat, too."

"Called ye fat, sir?" asked the man, bewildered.

"Yes. Very fat. By the way, let me tell you that I bought Jenny at Fittering to-day from the naughty ruffian who waylaid Mr. Bumble Bee." He proceeded to give Jim a sketch of what had transpired below. When he had finished the man shook his head severely.

"I doubt ye'll never learn wisdom, sir," he scolded.

"I? What have I done?"

"What did ye want to tell it all to the spider man for, sir? 'Twas most incautious of ye. Like as not, he'll split to the fat gentleman, and we'll have the whole town at our heels."

"Which just shows all you know of the small spider," replied his master calmly. "Hand me the powder."

CHAPTER III

Introducing the Hon. Richard Carstares

WYNCHAM! A stately old house with mullioned windows, standing high on its stone terraces, half-covered by creepers; a house surrounded by lawns, rolling down on the one side to a river that rippled and murmured its way along beneath overhanging trees and a blue sky, over boulders and rocks, so clear and sparkling that the myriad pebbles could be seen deep down on its bed.

In the other direction, the velvet lawns stretched away till they met the orchards and the quiet meadowland.

On two sides the house had its terraces, very white in the sunshine, with stone steps leading down to a miniature lake where water-lilies grew, and where the tiny fish darted to and fro unconcernedly.

Flagged walks there were, running between flower beds a riot of colour, and solemn old trees that had stood there through all the years. Cool woodland lay beyond the little river, carpeted with dark moss, where in spring the primroses grew. So thick was the foliage of the trees that the sun but penetrated in uneven patches.

Up the terrace walls crept roses, yellow and red, pink and white, and tossed their trailing sprays across the parapet. Over the walls of the house they climbed, mingling with purple clematis, jasmine, and sickly honeysuckle. The air was heavy with their united perfumes, while, wafted from a bed below, came the smoky scent of lavender.

The old house seemed half asleep, basking in the sunlight. Save for a peacock preening its feathers on the terrace steps, there was no sign of life. . . .

The old place had harboured generations of Carstares. Earl had succeeded Earl and reigned supreme, and it was only now that there was no Earl living there. No one knew where he was. Scarce a month ago one died, but the eldest son was not there to take his place. For six years he had been absent,

25

and none dared breathe his name, for he disgraced that name, and the old Earl cast him off and forbade all mention of him. But the poor folk of the countryside remembered him. They would tell one another tales of his reckless courage; his sweet smile and his winning ways; his light-heartedness and his never-failing kindness and good-humour. What a rider he was! To see him sit his horse! What a swordsman! Do ye mind the time he fought young Mr. Welsh over yonder in the spinney with half the countryside watching? Ah, he was a one, was Master Jack! Do ye mind how he knocked the sword clean out o' Mr. Welsh's hand, and then stood waiting for him to pick it up? And do ye mind the way his eyes sparkled, and how he laughed, just for the sheer joy o' living?

Endless anecdotes would they tell, and the old gaffers would shake their heads and sigh, and long for the sight of him again. And they would jerk their thumbs towards the Manor and shrug their old shoulders significantly. Who wanted Mr. Richard for squire? Not they, at least. They knew he was a good squire and a kindly man, but give them Master John, who would laugh and crack a joke and never wear the glum looks that Mr. Richard affected.

In the house, Richard Carstares paced to and fro in his library, every now and again pausing to glance wretchedly up at the portrait of his brother hanging over his desk. The artist had managed to catch the expression of those blue eyes, and they smiled down at Richard in just the way that John was always wont to smile—so gaily, and withal so wistfully.

Richard was twenty-nine, but already he looked twice his age. He was very thin, and there were deep lines on his good-looking countenance. His grey eyes bore a haunted, care-worn look, and his mouth, though well-shaped, was curiously lacking in determination. He was dressed soberly, and without that touch of smartness that had characterised him six years ago. He wore black in memory of his father, and it may have been that severity, only relieved by the lace at his throat, that made his face appear so prematurely aged. There was none of his brother's boyishness about him; even his smile seemed forced and tired, and his laughter rarely held merriment. . . .

He pulled out his chronometer, comparing it with the clock on the mantelpiece. His pacing took him to the door, and almost nervously he pulled it open, listening.

No sound came to his ears. Back again, to and fro across the room, eagerly awaiting the clanging of the bell. It did not come, but presently a footfall sounded on the passage without, and someone knocked at the door.

In two strides Richard was by it, and had flung it wide. Warburton stood there.

Richard caught his hand.

"Warburton! At last! I have been waiting this hour and more!"

Mr. Warburton disengaged himself, bowing.

"I regret I was not able to come before, sir," he said primly.

"I make no doubt you travelled back as quickly as possible —come in, sir."

He led the lawyer into the room and shut the door.

"Sit down, Warburton—sit down. You—you found my brother?"

Again Warburton bowed.

"I had the felicity of seeing his lordship, sir."

"He was well? In good spirits? You thought him changed —yes? Aged perhaps, or——"

"His lordship was not greatly changed, sir."

Richard almost stamped in his impatience.

"Come, Warburton, come! Tell me everything. What did he say? Will he take the revenues? Will he——"

"His lordship, sir, was reluctant to take anything, but upon maturer consideration, he—ah—consented to accept his elder son's portion. The revenues of the estate he begs you will make use of."

"Ah! But you told him that I would touch nought belonging to him?"

"I tried to persuade his lordship, sir. To no avail. He desires you to use Wyncham as you will."

"I'll not touch his money!"

Warburton gave the faintest of shrugs.

"That is as you please, sir."

Something in the suave voice made Richard, from his stand by the desk, glance sharply down at the lawyer. Suspicion flashed into his eyes. He seemed about to speak, when Warburton continued:

"I believe I may set your mind at rest on one score, Mr. Carstares: his lordship's situation is tolerably comfortable. He has ample means."

"But—but he lives by—robbery!"

Warburton's thin lips curled a little.

"Does he not?" persisted Carstares.

"So he would have us believe, sir."

" 'Tis true! He—waylaid me!"

"And robbed you, sir?"

"Rob me? He could not rob his own brother, Warburton!"

"Your pardon, Mr. Carstares—you are right: his lordship could not rob a brother. Yet have I known a man do such a thing."

For a long minute there was no word spoken. The suspicion that had dwelt latent in Carstares' eyes sprang up again. Some of the colour drained from his cheeks, and twice he passed his tongue between his lips. The fingers of his hand, gripping a chair-back, opened and shut spasmodically. Rather feverishly his eyes searched the lawyer's face, questioning.

"John told you—told you——" he started, and floundered hopelessly.

"His lordship told me nothing, sir. He was singularly reticent. But there was nothing he could tell me that I did not already know."

"What do you mean, Warburton? Why do you look at me like that? Why do you fence with me? In plain words, what do you mean?"

Warburton rose, clenching his hands.

"I know you, Master Richard, for what you are!"

"Ah!" Carstares flung out his hand as if to ward off a blow.

Another tense silence. With a great effort Warburton controlled himself, and once more the mask of impassivity seemed to descend upon him. After that one tortured cry Richard became calm again. He sat down; on his face a look almost of relief, coming after a great strain.

"You learnt the truth . . . from John. He . . . will expose me?"

"No, sir. I have not learnt it from him. And he will never expose you."

Richard turned his head. His eyes, filled now with a species of dull pain, looked full into Warburton's.

"Oh?" he said. "Then you . . . ?"

"Nor I, sir. I have pledged my word to his lordship. I would not speak all these years for your father's sake—now it is for his." He choked.

"You . . . are fond of John?" Still the apathetic, weary voice.

"Fond of him——? Good God, Master Dick, I love him!"

"And I," said Richard, very low.

He received no reply, and looked up.

"You don't believe me?"

"Once, sir, I was certain of it. Now——!" he shrugged.

"Yet 'tis true, Warburton. I would give all in my power to undo that night's work."

"You cannot expect me to believe that, sir. It rests with you alone whether his name be cleared or not. And you remain silent."

"Warburton, I—— Oh, do you think it means nothing to me that John is outcast?"

Before the misery in those grey eyes some of Warburton's severity fell away from him.

"Master Richard, I want to think the best I can of you. Master Jack would tell me nothing. Will you not—can you not explain how it came that you allowed him to bear the blame of your cheat?"

Richard shuddered.

"There's no explanation—no excuse. I forced it on him! On Jack, my brother! Because I was mad for love of Lavinia —— Oh, my God, the thought of it is driving me crazed! I thought I could forget; and then—and then—I met him! The sight of him brought it all back to me. Ever since that day I have not known how to live and not shriek the truth to everyone! And I never shall! I never shall!"

"Tell me, sir," pleaded Warburton, touched in spite of himself.

Richard's head sunk into his hands.

"The whole scene is a nightmare. . . . I think I must have been mad. . . . I scarce knew what I was about. I——"

"Gently, sir. Remember I know hardly anything. What induced you to mark the cards?"

"That debt to Gundry. My father would not meet it; I had to find the money. I could not face the scandal—I tell you I was mad for Lavinia! I could think of nought else. I ceased to care for John because I thought him in love with her. I could not bear to think of the disgrace which would take her from me. . . . Then that night at Dare's. I was losing; I knew I could not pay. Gad! but I can see my notes of hand under Milward's elbow, growing . . . growing.

"Jack had played Milward before me, and he had won. I remember they laughed at him, saying his luck had turned at last—for he always lost at cards. Milward and I played with the same pack that they had used. . . . There was another table, I think. Dare was dicing with Fitzgerald; someone was playing faro with Jack behind me. I heard Jack say his luck was out again—I heard them laugh. . . . And all the time I was losing . . . losing.

"The pin of my cravat fell out on to my knee. I think no one saw it. As I picked it up the thought that I should mark the cards seemed to flash into my mind—oh, it was despicable, I know! I held the ace of clubs in my hand: I scratched it with that pin—in one corner. It was easily done. By degrees I marked all four, and three of the kings.

"No one noticed, but I was nervous—I dared do no more. I replaced that pin. Soon I began to win—not very much. Then Tracy Belmanoir came across the room to watch our play. From that moment everything seemed to go awry. It was the beginning of the trouble.

"Tracy stood behind me—watching. . . . I could feel him there, like some black moth, hovering. . . . I don't know how long he stayed like that—it seemed hours. I could feel his eyes. . . . I could have shrieked—I'll swear my hands were trembling.

"Suddenly he moved. I had played the ace of hearts. He said: 'One moment!' in that soft, sinister voice of his.

"Milward was surprised. I tried to tell myself that Devil had noticed nothing. . . . The mark on that card was so faint that I could scarce see it myself. I thought it impossible that he, a mere onlooker, should discover it. He stepped forward. I remember he brushed my shoulder. I remember how the light caught the diamonds he was wearing. I think my brain was numbed. I could only repeat to myself: 'Extravagant Devil! Extravagant Devil!' and stare at those winking jewels. Then I thought: 'He is Lavinia's brother, but I do not like him; I do not like him . . .'—little foolish things like that— and my throat was dry—parched.

"He bent over the table . . . stretched out his white, white hand . . . turned over the ace . . . lifted his quizzing glass . . . and stared down at the card. Then he dropped the glass and drew out his snuff-box. . . . It had Aphrodite enamelled on the lid. I remember it so distinctly. . . . I heard Tracy ask

Milward to examine the ace. I wanted to spring up and strangle him. . . . I could scarce keep my hands still." Richard paused. He drew his hand across his eyes, shuddering.

"Milward saw the scratch. He cried out that the cards were marked! Suddenly everyone seemed to be gathered about our table—all talking! Jack had his hand on my shoulder; he and Dare were running through the pack. But all the while I could look at no one but Tracy—Andover. He seemed so sinister, so threatening, in those black clothes of his. His eyes were almost shut—his face so white—— And he was looking at me! He seemed to be reading my very soul. . . . For an instant I thought he knew! I wanted to shout out that he was wrong! I wanted to shriek to him to take his eyes away! Heaven knows what I should have done! . . . but he looked away—at Jack, with that sneering smile on his damned mask of a face! I could have killed him for that smile! I think Jack understood it—he dropped the cards, staring at Tracy.

"Everyone was watching them . . . no one looked at me. If they had they must surely have learnt the truth; but they were hanging on Andover's lips, looking from him to Jack and back again. . . . I remember Fitzgerald dropped his handkerchief—I was absurdly interested in that. I was wondering why he did not pick it up, when Andover spoke again. . . . 'And Carstares' luck turned . . . ?' Like that, Warburton! With just that faint, questioning in his voice.

"Before Jack could speak there was an outcry. Dare cried 'Shame!' to Andover. They laughed at him, as well they might. But I saw them exchange glances—they were wondering. . . . It was suspicious that Jack should have had that run of luck—and that he should lose as soon as he left that table.

"Milward—poor, silly Milward—gaped at Tracy and stuttered that surely 'twas another pack we had used. I could hardly breathe! Then Andover corrected him—— How did he *know*? No one else remembered, or thought of noticing—only he! . . .

"I can see Jack now, standing there so stiffly, with his head thrown up, and those blue eyes of his flashing.

" 'Do I understand you to accuse me, Belmanoir?' he said. Oh, but he was furious!

"Tracy never said a word. Only his eyes just flickered to my face and away again.

"Jack's hand was gripping my shoulder hard. I could feel his anger. . . . Dare called out that the suggestion was preposterous. That John should cheat!

"Tracy asked him if the cards were his. Gad! I can hear his soft, mocking voice now!

"Dare went purple—you know his way, Warburton.

" 'Opened in your presence on this table!' he cried.

" 'By Carstares!' smiled Tracy.

"It was true. But why should Tracy remember it, and none other? They stared at him, amazed. Dare turned to Jack for corroboration. He nodded. I think he never looked haughtier.

"You know how fond of Jack Dare was? He tried to bluster it off—tried to get control over the affair. It was to no avail. We were puppets, worked by that devil, Belmanoir! One man managing that ghastly scene. . . . He pointed out that only three of us had used that pack: Jack, Milward and I.

"Jack laughed.

" 'Next you will accuse Dick!' he snapped scornfully.

" 'One of you, certainly,' smiled Andover. 'Or Milward.'

"Then everyone realised that one of us three must have marked the cards. Milward was upset, but no one suspected him. It was Jack—or me.

"As long as I live I shall never forget the horror of those moments. If I were exposed it meant the end of everything between Lavinia and me. I tell you, Warburton, I would have committed any sin at that moment! Nothing would have been too black—I could not bear to lose her. You don't know what she meant to me!"

"I can guess, sir," said the lawyer, gravely.

"No, no! No one could imagine the depths of my love for her! I think not even Jack. . . . I felt his hand leave my shoulder. . . . The truth had dawned on him. I heard the way the breath hissed between his teeth as he realised. . . . Somehow I got to my feet, clutching at the table, facing him. I don't excuse myself—I know my conduct was beyond words dastardly. I looked across at him—just said his name, as though I could scarce believe my ears. So all those watching thought. But Jack knew better. He knew I was imploring him to save me. He understood all that I was trying to convey to him. For an instant he stared at me. I thought—I thought—God forgive me, I prayed that he might take the blame on himself. Then he smiled. Coward though I was, when I saw that hurt, wistful little smile on his lips, I nearly blurted out the whole truth. Not quite. . . . I suppose I was too mean-spirited for that.

"Jack bowed to the room and again to Dare. He said: 'I owe you an apology, sir.'

"Dare sprang forward, catching him by the shoulder—crying out that it could not be true! When Jack laughed—he fell away from him as from the plague. And all of them! My God, to see them drawing away—not looking at Jack! And Jack's face—growing paler and harder . . . every moment. . . . All his friends . . . turning their backs to him. Davenant—even Jim Davenant walked away to the fireplace with Evans.

"I could not look at Jack. I dared not. I could not go to him—stand by him! I had not the right. I had to leave him there—in the middle of the room—alone. The awful hurt in his eyes made me writhe. The room was whirling round—I felt sick—I know I fell back into my chair, hiding my face. I hardly cared whether they suspected me or not. But they did not. They knew how great was the love between us, and they were not surprised that I broke down.

"I heard Andover's soft voice . . . he was telling some tale to Dare. Oh, they were well-bred those men! They skimmed over the unpleasant little episode—ignored Jack!

"Jack spoke again. I could guess how bravely he was keeping a proud front. I know word for word what he said: 'Mr. Dare, your Grace, Gentlemen—my apologies for being the cause of so unpleasant an incident. Pray give me leave.'

"They paid no heed. I heard him walk to the door—heard him open it. I could not look at him. He—he paused . . . and said just one word: 'Dick!' quite softly. Heaven knows how I got to him! I know I overturned my chair. That drew Dare's attention. He said: 'You are not going, Dick?' I shouted 'Yes,' at him, and then Jack took my arm, leading me out.

"And—and all he said was: 'Poor old Dick!'. . . He—he had no word of blame for me. He would not allow me to go back and tell the truth—as I would have done. Ay, Warburton, when Jack called me to him, I could have cried it aloud—but—he would not have it. . . . He said: 'For Lavinia's sake.' . . ."

Warburton blew his nose violently. His fingers were trembling.

"You know what happened afterwards. You know how my father turned Jack out penniless—you know how his friends shunned him—you know my poor mother's grief. And you know that he went away—that we could not find him when —my mother died. . . . His last words to me—were: 'Make Lavinia—happy—and try to forget—all this.' Forget it! Heavens! Try as I might, I could hear nothing further of him until two months ago, when he—waylaid me. Then I was half-dazed at the suddenness of it. He—he grasped my hand—and —laughed! It was so dark, I could scarce see him. I only had time to demand his address, and then—he was off—galloping away over the heath. I think—even then—he bore no malice."

"He does not now!" said Warburton sharply. "But, Master Dick, if all this is true, why do you not even now clear him? Surely——"

Richard turned his head slowly.

"Now I may not drag my wife's name through the mud. By clearing him—I ruin her."

Warburton could find nothing to say. Only after some time did he clear his throat and say that he was honoured by Carstares' confidence.

"You—ah—you dwell on the part played by his Grace on that evening. Surely your—shall we say—overwrought imagination magnified that?"

Richard was disinterested.

"I suppose so. Mayhap 'twas his extraordinary personality dominating me. He cannot have pulled the wires as I thought he did. Not even Belmanoir could make me act as I did. But —but at the time I felt that he was pushing—pushing—compelling me to accuse Jack. Oh, doubtless I was mad!"

Warburton eyed the dejected figure compassionately. Then he seemed to harden himself and to regain some of his lost primness of manner.

"You—ah—you are determined not to accept the revenues, sir?"

"I have not yet sunk so low, Mr. Warburton."

"His lordship leaves Wyncham and all appertaining to it at your disposal. He would be grieved at your refusal."

"I will not touch it."

The lawyer nodded.

"I confess, Mr. Carstares, I am relieved to hear you say that. It will not be necessary again to communicate with his

Her face clouded over instantly, and the full-lipped mouth drooped petulantly.

"He has seen him."

"Oh?" She made the word twice its length, and filled it with disinterest.

"Yes. Jack will have none of it. He asks me to be his steward and to use Wyncham as I will. He is very generous."

"Yes, oh yes. And you will, Richard?"

He ignored the question.

"He—Warburton—says he is not much changed."

"Oh?" Again the long-drawn monosyllable, accompanied by a tiny yawn.

"He says he does not think—Jack—bears me ill-will——" He paused, as if expecting her to speak, but she was absorbed in arranging two flowers—culled from a bowl at her side—at her breast, and took no notice. Carstares turned his head away wearily.

"If it were not for you, my dear, I would tell the truth. I believe I shall go crazed an I do not."

"Dick!" . . . She dropped the flowers on the floor and thought no more about them. "Dick!"

"Oh, you need have no fear! I do not suppose," bitterly, "that I have the courage to face them all now—after six years."

Lavinia moved restlessly, brushing her hand along the couch.

"You will not do it, Richard? Promise? You *will* not? I could not bear the disgrace of it; promise me you will never do it?"

"No," he said slowly, not looking at her. "No, I cannot promise that."

She sprang to her feet, flinging her broidery from her carelessly, and waved fierce, agitated little hands.

"That means you will do it. You *want* to disgrace me! You do not *care* how you hurt me by holding this threat over my head so cruelly! You——"

"Lavinia, for heaven's sake!" he implored, pushing back his chair. "Calm yourself!" He knew she was about to fly into one of her sudden passions, and frowned with acute vexation.

"I will not! Oh yes, yes! You think me a shrew! I know! I know! But you need not frown on me, sir, for you are worse! No, I will not hush. I am a horrid woman, but you are a cheat—a cheat—a cheat!"

Carstares strode over to her.

"Lavinia!"

"No—no! Leave me alone! You make me miserable! You refuse me everything that I want most, and then you threaten to disgrace me——"

"That is untrue!" cried Richard, goaded into replying. "I will not promise, that is all. What have I refused you that was within my means to give you? God knows you try your best to ruin me——"

"There! There! 'Tis *I* who am to blame! Pray, did you not induce my lord to leave his money to John when you knew he would have willed it all to you an you had kept silence? You took no thought to me——"

"For heaven's sake, Lavinia, be still! You do not know what you are saying!"

She pressed her hands to her hot cheeks.

"No—I am unreasonable! I know it, but don't *tell* me so, for I cannot bear it! And don't look reproach at me, Richard! You drive me mad, I tell you!" She was sweeping up and down the room like some caged animal, lashing herself to a worse fury.

"Say something, Richard! *Do* something! Don't stand there so quietly! Oh, you should never have married me! I displease you, and you make me worse; and you do not see how 'tis that I cannot live without pleasure, and money! I am despicable? Yes, yes, but what are you? Oh, why did you tell me you cheated *after* you had wedded me?" Angry sobs escaped her; her handkerchief was in shreds upon the floor.

Carstares turned his back to her, that she might not see how she had contrived to hurt him, and the movement drove her to fresh fury.

"Don't do that! Don't! Don't! You make me worse by your dreadful silence! Oh, if you really loved me!"

"You cannot doubt that!" he cried out, wheeling suddenly round. "You know how I love you! Don't you?" He gripped her by the shoulders and swung her to face him.

She trembled and gave a sobbing little laugh. As suddenly as it had come, her anger left her.

"Oh, yes, yes! You do love me, Dicky?" She twined her arms about his neck and shrank closer.

"God help me, yes!" he groaned, thrusting her away. "And you—you care for no one save yourself!"

"No! No!" she cried, pressing up to him again. "Do not

say that, Dick. Indeed, I love you, but I cannot live without gaiety—you know I cannot. Oh, I do not doubt but what I am very selfish, but 'tis the way I am fashioned, and I cannot change my nature. And now I have hurt you, and I did not mean to! I did not mean to!"

"My dear, I know you did not; but try to be less a child, I beg of you! You are so uncontrolled, so——"

"I knew you would say that," she answered in a dead voice. "You do not understand me. You expect me to be good, and patient, and forbearing, and I tell you 'tis not in my nature."

"But, Lavinia, you can control your passions," he said gently.

"No! I cannot! We Belmanoirs—as God made us, so we are—and He made us spendthrift, and pleasure-loving, and mad!" She walked slowly to the door. "But you do not understand, and you try to make me staid, and thoughtful, and a good mother, when I am dying for *life*, and excitement, and care not that for housewifery!" She opened the door slowly. "And now my head aches, and you look grave and say 'tis my wicked temper, when I want you to be sorry, and to be ready to do anything to comfort me. Why can you not take me to London, when you know how I long to be there, instead of in this gloomy house with nought to do, save mind my child and my needle? I am so tired of it all! So very tired of it all!" She could have left the room then, but he detained her.

"Wait, Lavinia! You say you are unhappy?"

She released the door handle and fluttered her hands expressively.

"Unhappy? No, I am dull. I am ill-tempered. I am discontented. I am aught you please, so do not be sad, Richard. I cannot bear you to be solemn. Oh, why do we quarrel?" With one of her impulsive movements she was again at his side, with her beautiful face upturned. "Love me, Richard! Take me to London and never mind an I *do* squander your money. Say you do not care! Say that nothing matters so long as I am happy! Why do you not say it? Does anything matter? Don't be prudent, Dicky! Be wild! Be reckless! Be anything rather than grave and old!" Her arms crept up to his coaxingly. "Take me to London!"

Carstares smoothed the soft hair back from her forehead, very tenderly, but his eyes were worried.

"My dear, I will take you, but not just yet. There is so much to be done here. If you will wait a little longer——"

"Ah, if I will wait! If I will be patient and good! But I cannot! Oh, you don't understand, Dicky—you don't understand!"

"I am sorry, dear. I promise I will take you as soon as possible, and we will stay as long as you please."

Her arms fell away.

"I want to go now!"

"Dear——"

"Very well—very well. We will go presently. Only don't reason with me."

He looked at her concernedly.

"You are overwrought, my love—and tired."

"Yes," she agreed listlessly. "Oh yes; I will go now and rest. Forgive me, Dick!" She kissed her finger-tips and extended them to him. "I will be good one day." She turned and hurried out of the room and up the stairs, leaving the door open behind her.

Richard stayed for a moment looking round at the signs of her late presence. Mechanically he stooped to pick up her embroidery and the pieces of her handkerchief. The two flowers were broken off short, and he threw them away. Then he left the room and went out on to the sunny terrace, gazing across the beautiful gardens into the blue distance.

Across the lawn came a child of four or five, waving a grimy hand.

"Father!"

Richard looked down on him and smiled.

"Well, John?"

The boy climbed up the terrace steps, calling his news all the way.

" 'Tis Uncle Andrew, sir. He has rid over to see you, and is coming through the garden to find you."

"Is he? Has he left his horse at the stables?"

"Ay, sir. So I came to tell you."

"Quite right. Will you come with me to meet him?"

The little rosy face lighted up with pleasure.

"Oh, may I?" he cried and slipped his hand in Richard's.

Together they descended the steps and made their way across the lawn.

"I have run away from Betty," announced John with some

pride. "There's Uncle Andrew, sir!" He bounded away towards the approaching figure.

Lord Andrew Belmanoir was Richard's brother-in-law, brother to the present Duke. He came up with John in his arms and tumbled him to the ground.

"Good day, Dick! 'Tis a spoilt child you have here!"

"Ay. He is but now escaped from his nurse."

"Splendid! Come, John, you shall walk with us, and we'll confound fat Betty!" He slipped his arm through Richard's as he spoke. "Come, Dick! There's a deal I have to say to you." He grimaced ruefully.

The child ran on ahead towards the woods, a great bull-mastiff at his heels.

"What's to do now?" asked Richard, looking round into the mobile, dissipated countenance.

"The devil's in it this time, and no mistake," answered his lordship with a rueful shake of his head.

"Debts?"

"Lord, yes! I was at Delaby's last night, and the stakes were high. Altogether I've lost about three thousand—counting what I owe Carew. And devil take me an I know where 't's to come from! Here's Tracy turned saint and swears he'll see me damned before he hands me another penny. I doubt he means it, too."

Tracy was the Duke. Richard smiled a little cynically; he had already had to lend his Grace a thousand guineas to pay off some "trifling debt".

"He means it right enough. I believe it would puzzle him to find it."

"Do you say so? Why, 'tis impossible man! Tracy was in town scarce a fortnight since, and he had a run of the devil's own luck. I tell you, Dick, I saw him walk off with a cool five thousand one night! And then he denies me a paltry three! Lord, what a brother! And all with the air of an angel, as if *he* had never lost at dice. And a homily thrown in! Anyone would think I had cheated, instead of—ahem! . . . Dick, I'm confoundedly sorry! Damned thoughtless of me— never thought about Jo—— about what I was saying—— I'm a fool!" For Richard had winced.

"You cannot help that," he said, forcing a laugh. "Have done with your apologies, and continue."

They had come to the stream by now, and crossed the little bridge into the wood.

"Oh, there's not much more. 'Tis only that something must be done, for Carew won't wait, and stap me if I'd ask him, the lean-faced scarecrow!—so I came to you, Dick."

He let go Richard's arm and flung himself down on a fallen tree-trunk, regardless of velvet and laces.

"You're a good fellow, and you don't lecture a man as Tracy does, devil take him! And you play high yourself, or you did, though 'tis an age since I saw you win or lose enough to wink at. And, after all, you're Lavvy's husband, and—oh, damn it all, Dick, 'tis monstrous hard to ask you!"

Carstares, leaning against a tree, surveyed the youthful rake amusedly.

" 'Tush, Andrew!" he reassured him. "You're welcome to ask, but the Lord knows where I'm to find it! Gad, what a life! Here's Lavinia keeps buying silks, and I don't know what all, and——"

"She was ever a spendthrift jade," said Andrew with a mighty frown.

Richard laughed at him.

"You're a thrifty fellow yourself, of course!"

Andrew looked round for something to throw at him, and finding nothing, relapsed once more into the deepest despondency.

"You're in the right of't. We're a worthless lot. 'Tis the old man's blood in us, I doubt not, with a smattering of her Grace. You never knew my mother, Richard. She was French —Lavvy's the spit of her. There's Tracy—stap me, but Tracy's the very devil! Have you ever seen a face like his? No, I'll swear you've not! What with his sneering mouth and his green eyes—oh, 'tis enough to make a fellow go to the dogs to have a brother like it, 'pon my soul it is? Ay, you laugh, but I tell you 'tis serious!"

"Ay, go on!"

"Well next there's Bob—damn it all, but I'm sorry for Bob! 'Tis a beggarly pittance they give one in the army, and he was never one to pinch and scrape. Well, as I say, there's Bob, and I never see him, but what it's: 'Lend me a hundred, Andy!' or the like. And all to buy his mistress some gewgaw. That's what sickens me! Why, Bob's for ever in some scrape with a petticoat, and as for Tracy! Gad, how they can! Then there's Lavinia, but I should think you know her by now, and lastly, there's your humble servant. And I tell you, Dick, what with the racing, and the cards, and the bottle, I shall be a ruined man before you can turn round! And the pother is I'll never be any different. 'Tis in the blood, so where's the use in trying?" He made a rueful grimace, and rose. "Come on, young rip! We're going back."

John, engaged in the task of hunting for tadpoles in the water some yards distant, nodded and ran on.

"I fear my lady is indisposed," said Richard hesitatingly. "You wished to see her?"

Andrew winked knowingly.

"Tantrums, eh? Oh, I know her. No, I do not care an I do not see her; 'tis little enough she cares for me, though she's as thick as thieves with Tracy—oh, ay, I'll be dumb."

They walked slowly back to the house, Andrew, silent for once, twirling his gold-mounted cane.

"You shall have the money, of course. When do you want it?" said Richard presently.

" 'Pon honour, you're a devilish good fellow, Dick! But if 'tis like to put you to any——"

"Nonsense. When do you need it?"

"I should pay Carew as soon as may be. Markham can wait over if——"

"No, no! Wednesday?"

" 'Twill do excellently well. Dick, you're a——"

"Oh, pshaw! 'Tis nought. I want your opinion on the bay mare I bought last week. You'll maybe think her a trifle long in the leg, but she's a fine animal."

John had run indoors, and the two men proceeded to the stables alone, Andrew discoursing all the way, recounting for his brother-in-law's benefit the choicest morsels of scandal that were circulating town at the moment. That his auditor but attended with half an ear affected him not at all; he never paused for an answer, and, in any case, was far too good-natured to care if he received none.

By the time they had duly inspected the mare, and walked back to the house, it was nearly four o'clock, and, not altogether to Carstares' surprise, Lavinia was awaiting them on the terrace, clad in a totally different gown, and with her hair freshly arranged and curled.

" 'Twould appear that Lavinia has recovered," remarked Andrew as they mounted the steps. "She was ever thus—not two minutes the same. Well, Lavvy?"

"Well, Andrew?" She gave him a careless hand to kiss, but smiled sweetly up at her husband. "My headache is so much better," she told him, "and they said that Andrew was come to see you. So I came downstairs." She turned eagerly to her brother. "Tell me, Andrew, is Tracy at home?"

"Lord, yes! He arrived yesterday, devil take him! Do you want him?"

"Oh, yes," she nodded. "I want to see him again. I've not set eyes on him for an age. I want you to take me back with you."

"Surely, my dear, 'tis a trifle late in the day for such a drive?" demurred Richard, trying to conceal his annoyance. "Can you not wait until to-morrow?"

"Faith, you'll have to, Lavvy, for I'll not take you to-day, that's certain. I'm riding to Fletcher's when I leave here. Tracy can visit you to-morrow an he chooses."

"Will he?" she asked doubtfully.

Andrew clapped his hand to his vest pocket. "If I had not forgot!" he exclaimed. "I've a letter from him for you. He intends waiting on you to-morrow, in any case. Lord, what it is to have a scatter brain like mine!" He pulled a handful of papers from his pocket and selected one, sealed, and addressed in a sloping Italian handwriting.

Lavinia pounced upon it joyfully, and tore it open. Andrew restored the rest of the documents to his pocket with yet another rueful laugh.

"Duns, Richard! Duns!"

"Give them to me," answered the other, holding out his hand.

"Oh, no! But many thanks, Dick. These are quite unimportant."

"Why not pay them all, and start afresh?" urged Carstares.

"Lord, no! Why, I should be so damned elated that before the day was out there'd be a score of fresh debts staring me in the face!"

"Let me lend you a thousand to begin on? Could you not keep out of debt?"

"I keep out of debt? Impossible! Don't look so solemn, Dick; I told you 'twas in the blood. We never have a penny to bless ourselves with, but what's the odds? I shall have a run of luck soon—a man can't always lose. Then I shall be able to repay you, but, of course, I shan't. It'll all go at the next table. I know!" He spoke so ingenuously that Richard could not be angry with him. There was a certain frankness about him that pleased, and though he might be spendthrift

and heedless, and colossally selfish, Richard felt a genuine affection for him. He would have liked to argue the point further, but Lavinia came forward, refolding her letter.

"Tracy is coming to-morrow afternoon," she told her husband. " 'Twill be prodigiously agreeable, will it not?"

He assented, but with a lack of warmth that did not fail to
strike her ears.

"And he will stay to dine with us!" she cried challengingly.

"Certainly, my love."

"Look pleased, Dicky, look pleased! Why don't you like
Tracy? He is my own brother; you *must* like him!"

"Of course I like him, Lavinia. Pray, do not be foolish."

"Oh, I am not! Don't be cross, Dicky dear!"

"Well, if you like him, I'm surprised," broke in Andrew. "I
can't bear him! Ay, flash your eyes at me, Lavvy; I don't
mind."

Lavinia opened her mouth to retaliate, but Richard hastily
interposed. Their bickering was more than he could bear, and
he never understood how Lavinia could stoop to quarrel with
the boisterous youth, who tried so palpably to rouse her.

He bore them both off to the house, feeling much like a
nursemaid with two recalcitrant children.

CHAPTER V

His Grace of Andover

LADY LAVINIA dressed herself with even more than her usual care next afternoon, and well-nigh drove her maid distracted by her flashes of temper and impatient, contradictory orders. So lengthy was the toilet that she was only just in her boudoir when his Grace of Andover was announced. She had no time to tell the footman that she would receive his Grace, for almost before the words were out of James' mouth, he stood bowing in the doorway, sure of his welcome.

He was curiously like his sister, this man, and at the same time curiously unlike. Hers were the high cheek-bones and pinched, aristocratic nostrils, but the mouth with its thin lips, and the heavy-lidded green eyes were totally different. His Grace's brows slanted up at the corners, and his eyes, though piercing and bright, were constantly veiled by the black-lashed lids. He wore his own black hair, unpowdered, and that, together with the black and silver garments that he always affected, greatly enhanced the natural pallor of his countenance. Altogether it was a very striking figure that stood just before the closed white door and bowed to my lady.

Lavinia took an eager step towards him, swinging her pearl-grey brocades.

"Oh, Tracy!" she cooed, holding out both hands.

His Grace advanced into the room and bent low over them.

"I rejoice to find you within, Lavinia," he said, a faint tinge of sarcasm running through his smooth tones. "As you perceive, I rode over." He made a gesture towards his high boots with their wicked-looking spurs. "No doubt Andrew forgot to give you my letter?"

"No," she said, slipping her hand in his arm. "He remembered in time, and—oh, Tracy, I was so vastly delighted to have it!"

46

"I am indeed honoured," he replied. "I am come on a sufficiently important matter."

"Oh!" She pulled her hand away disappointedly. "Money!"

"You are really wonderful, my dear. As you so crudely remark—money! Will you not be seated?"

She sank down on the couch dejectedly and watched him take a chair opposite her.

"Your most noble lord and master lent me a trifling sum the other day, but very trifling. I am, as usual, hard-pressed. And that young fool Andrew must needs fall into debt."

My lady opened wide her eyes in surprise.

"Do you tell me you need money from Richard to pay Andrew's debts?" she asked, frankly incredulous.

"I do not. Is it likely? The remark was purely by the way."

"Well, in any case, Andrew borrowed three thousand from poor Dick only yesterday. I know, because I heard him speak of it."

His Grace raised his black brows in patient exasperation.

"How unnecessary of Andrew! And how typical! So 'poor Dick' has been squeezed already?"

"Don't speak like that, Tracy!" she cried. "Dicky is good to me!" She met his piercing look unflinchingly.

"Now this becomes interesting," drawled the Duke. "Since when have you come to that conclusion? And why this sudden loyalty?"

"I have *always* been loyal to him, Tracy! You know I have! I worry him—and indeed he is very forbearing."

"But how charming of him!"

"No, do not sneer, Tracy! He has promised to take me to London for the whole winter——"

His Grace leant back in his chair again.

"Now I understand," he said placidly. "I was at a loss before."

" 'Tis not that, Tracy! Indeed I realise how kind he is to me. And we have quarrelled again. We are always quarrelling, and I know 'tis all my fault."

"What a comfortable conviction, my dear!"

"No, no! 'Tis not comfortable, Tracy! For somehow I cannot change my disposition, though I *mean* to be patient and sweet. Tracy, I hate Wyncham!"

"You hate Wyncham? There was a time——"

"I know, I know! But I never meant to live here always like this! I want to go to London!"

"I thought you said you were going?"

"Yes, I am! But I want to go with someone who is gay—not—not——"

"In fact, you want distraction, and not with the amiable Richard? Well, I can conceive that life with him might prove uninspiring. Safe, my dear, but not exciting."

"I knew you would understand! You see, he does not like me to play at cards, because I cannot stop! And he cannot see how 'tis that I care nought for what he calls 'home-life' when there are routs, and the play, and *real* life. He—he is so—so—so *staid,* Tracy, and careful!"

"A good trait in a husband, Lavinia," replied his Grace cynically. " 'Tis because I do not possess it that I am single now."

Her lips curled scornfully at this, for well she knew her brother.

"No, Tracy, that is not so! It is because you are a devil! No woman would marry you!"

"That is most interesting, my dear," purred his Grace. "But pray strive to be a little more original. Continue your analysis of Richard's sterling character."

" 'Tis only that we are so different," she sighed. "I always desire to do things quickly—if I think of something, I want it at once—at once! You know, Tracy! And he likes to wait and think on it, and—oh, 'tis so tiresome, and it puts me in a bad humour, and I behave like a hysterical bourgeoise!" She got up swiftly, clasping her nervous little hands. "When he speaks to me in that gentle, reasoning way, I could scream, Tracy! Do you think I am mad?" She laughed unmusically.

"No," he replied, "but the next thing to it: a Belmanoir. Perhaps it was a pity you ever married Richard. But there is always the money."

"There is not," she cried out sharply.

"Not? What mean you?"

"Tracy, 'tis of this that I wanted to speak! You think my lord left his money to Dick?"

"Certainly. He should be stupendously wealthy."

"He is not!"

"But, my good girl, the revenue must be enormous. He has the land, surely?"

"No! No! He has not the land! Oh, but I am angry whenever I think on it! He induced my lord to leave it to John. *He* has but his younger son's portion!"

"I still fail to understand. You informed me that the Earl left all to Richard?"

"He changed his will, Tracy!"

"He—changed—his—will! Then, my dear, must you have played your cards very badly!"

" 'Twas not my fault, Tracy—indeed 'twas not! I knew nought until the will was read. Richard never spoke a word to me about it! And now we are comparatively poor!" Her voice trembled with indignation, but his Grace only whistled beneath his breath.

"I always knew, of course, that Dick was a fool, but I never guessed how much so till now!"

At that she flared up.

"He is not a fool! He is an honest man, and 'tis we—*we*, I tell you—who are mean and despicable and mercenary!"

"Undoubtedly, Lavinia, but pray do not excite yourself over it. I suppose he is still devoted to that young hothead?"

"Yes, yes—'tis all Jack, Jack, Jack, until I am sick to death of the sound of his name—and——" She broke off, biting her lips.

"And what?"

"Oh, nought! But 'tis all so disagreeable, Tracy!"

"It certainly is slightly disturbing. You had better have chosen John, in spite of it all, it seems."

She stamped angrily.

"Oh, where's the good in being flippant?"

"My dear Lavinia, where's the good in being anything else? The situation strikes me as rather amusing. To think of the worthy Richard so neatly overturning all my plans!"

"If it had not been for you, I might never have married him. Why did you throw them both in my way? Why did I ever set eyes on either?"

"It should have been a good match, my dear, and, if I remember rightly, no one was more alive to that fact than yourself."

She pouted angrily and turned her shoulder to him.

"Still," he continued reflectively, "I admit that for the smart lot we are, we do seem rather to have bungled the affair."

Lavinia swept round upon him.

"Oh, do you care no more than that? How can you be so casual! Does it affect you not at all?"

He wrinkled his thin nose expressively.

"I shall not weep over it, Lavinia, but 'tis a plaguey nuisance. But we must see what can be done. And that brings me back to the original subject. Despite these upsetting revelations, I still require that money."

"Oh, dear! How much must you have, Tracy?"

"Five hundred might suffice."

"Tracy, do not the estates bring in anything?" she asked petulantly. "And Andrew told us you had a run of marvelous luck not a fortnight since?"

"Since then, my dear, I have had three runs of marvelous ill-luck. As to the estates, they are mortgaged up to the hilt, as you very well know. What little there is is between three. And Robert is extravagant."

"I hate Robert!"

"I am not partial to him myself, but it makes no odds."

"I wish he might die!—oh no, no! Now I am become ill-natured again—I don't wish it—only I am so tired of everything. You shall have that money as soon as possible; but be careful, Tracy—please be careful! 'Tis not easy to get money from Dick!"

"No, I should imagine not. However, we have managed rather well up to the present, take it all in all."

"Up to the present he has had all the money he wanted. My lord denied him nought!"

"Well, 'tis unfortunate, as I said before, but it must be endured. Where is Dick?"

"I know not. You will stay to dinner, Tracy?"

"Thank you. I shall be charmed."

"Yes, yes—oh, how prodigiously pleasant it is to see you again! Soon I shall come to Andover. Will you let me stay a few days?"

"The question is, will Richard allow you to stay so long in my contaminating presence?"

"Richard would never keep me away, Tracy!" she replied proudly. "He *could* not. Oh, why is it that I don't love him more! Why do I not care for him as much as I care for you even?"

"My dear Lavinia, like all Belmanoirs, you care first for yourself and secondly for the man who masters you. That, alas! Richard has not yet succeeded in doing."

"But I *do* love Richard. I do, I do, yet——"

"Exactly. 'Yet——!' The 'grand passion' has not yet touched you, my dear, and you are quite self-absorbed."

"Self-absorbed! Those are hard words."

"But not too hard for the case. You think solely of yourself, your own pleasure, your own character, your own feelings. If you could cast yourself into the background a little, you would be less excitable and considerably less discontented."

"How dare you, Tracy! Pray, what of you? Are you so selfless?"

"Not at all. I am precisely the same. I was merely suggesting that you might be happier an you could depose 'self'."

"You had best do the same yourself!"

"My dear Lavinia, when I feel the need of greater happiness, I most undoubtedly shall. At present I am quite content."

"You are unkind!" she protested. "And you sneer at me."

"Pray accept my heartfelt apologies! You shall come to Andover if the worthy Richard permits."

Her face cleared as by magic.

"Oh, Tracy! Oh, I am so desirous to be gay once more! I cannot even receive now, on account of this mourning! But when I am at Andover—oh, we well not worry over anything, and I can be bad-tempered without feeling that someone is being hurt by me! Oh, come to Dicky at once—at once!"

He rose leisurely.

"I can imagine that you try Richard's patience somewhat," he remarked. "Happily, your impetuosity in no way disturbs me. We will go in search of Richard."

Half-way down the great staircase she perceived her husband, and flew to meet him.

"Richard, I was coming in search of you! Tracy has invited me to Andover for a week—he purposes to ask several people to stay, and there will be parties—and entertainment! You will let me go? Say yes, Dicky—say yes, quickly!"

Carstares bowed to his Grace, who stood watching them from the stairs. The bow was returned with exaggerated flourish. Carstares looked down at his wife.

"So soon, Lavinia?" he remonstrated, and indicated her mourning. She shook his hand off impatiently.

"Oh, Dicky, does it matter? What can it signify? I do not ask you to come——"

"No," he said half-sadly, half-amusedly. "I notice that, my dear."

"No, no! I did not mean to be unkind—you must not think that! You *don't* think it, do you, Dick?"

"Oh, no," he sighed.

"Good Dicky!" She patted his cheek coaxingly. "Then, you will allow me to go—ah, but yes, yes, you must listen! You know how dull I am, and how silly—'tis because I need a change, and I *want* to go to Andover. I *want* to go!"

"Yes, dear, I know. But my father is not yet dead six weeks, and I cannot think it seemly——"

"Please, Dick, please! Please do not say no! 'Twill make me so unhappy! Oh, you will not be so unkind? You will not forbid me to go?"

"I ask you not to, Lavinia. If you need a change, I will take you quietly to Bath, or where you will. Do not pain me by going to Andover just now."

"Bath! Bath! What do I want with Bath at this time of the year? Oh, 'tis kind in you to offer, but I want to go to Andover! I want to see all the old friends again. And I want to get away from everything here—'tis all so gloomy—after—after my lord's death!"

"Dearest, of course you shall go away—but if only you would remember that you are in mourning——"

"But 'tis what I wish to forget! Oh, Dicky, don't, don't, don't be unkind."

"Very well, dear. If you must go—go."

She clapped her hands joyfully.

"Oh thank you, Dicky! And you are not angry with me?"

"No, dear, of course not."

"Ah! Now I am happy! 'Tis sweet of you, Dicky, but confess you are secretly thankful to be rid of me for a week! Now are you not?" She spread out her fan in the highest good-humour and coquetted behind it. Richard was induced to smile.

"I fear I shall miss you too sadly, dear."

"Oh!" She dropped the fan. "But think how you will look forward to seeing me again, and I you. Why, I shall be so thankful to be back after a week away, that I shall be good for months!"

His face lightened, and he caught her hands in his.

"Darling, if I thought you would miss me——!"

"But of course I shall miss you, Dick—oh, *pray*, mind my frock! Shall I not miss him, Tracy?"

Richard suddenly remembered his brother-in-law's presence. He turned and went to the foot of the stairs.

"So you are determined to wrest my wife from me?" he smiled.

Tracy descended leisurely, opening his snuff-box.

"Yes, I require a hostess," he said. "And I have"—he paused—"induced her to honour Andover with her presence. Shall we have the felicity of seeing you at any time?"

"I thank you, no. I am not, you will understand, in the mood for the gaiety for which my poor Lavinia craves."

The Duke bowed slightly, and they all three went out on to the terrace, Lavinia laughing and talking as Richard had not heard her laugh or talk for days. She was the life and soul of the little dinner-party, flirting prettily with her husband and exerting herself to please him in every way. She had won her point; therefore she was in excellent spirits with all the world, and not even the spilling of some wine on her new silk served to discompose her.

CHAPTER VI

Bath: 29 Queen Square

THE autumn and the winter passed smoothly, and April found the Carstares installed at Bath, whither Lady Lavinia had teased her husband into going, despite his desire to return to Wyncham and John. She herself did not care to be with the child, and was perfectly content that Richard should journey occasionally to Wyncham to see that all was well with him.

On the whole, she had enjoyed the winter, for she had induced Richard to open Wyncham House, Mayfair, the Earl's town residence, where she had been able to hold several entirely successful routs, and many select little card-parties. Admirers she had a-many, and nothing so pleased her vain little heart as masculine adulation. Carstares never entered his home without stumbling against some fresh flame of hers, but as they mostly consisted of what he rudely termed the lap-dog type, he was conscious of no jealous qualms, and patiently submitted to their inundation of his house. He was satisfied that Lavinia was happy, and, as he assured himself at times when he was most tried, nothing else signified.

The only flaw to Lavinia's content was the need of money. Not that she was stinted, or ever refused anything that he could in reason give her; but her wants were never reasonable. She would demand a new town chariot, upholstered in pale blue, not because her own was worn or shabby, but because she was tired of its crimson cushions. Or she would suddenly take a fancy to some new, and usually fabulously expensive toy, and having acquired it, weary of it in a week.

Without a murmur, Richard gave her lap-dogs (of the real kind), black pages, jewels, and innumerable kickshaws, for which she rewarded him with her brightest smiles and tenderest caresses. But when she required him to refurnish Wyncham House in the style of the French Court, throwing away all the present Queen Anne furniture, the tapestries and the

countless old trappings that were one and all so beautiful and
so valuable, he put his foot down with a firmness that surprised her. Not for any whim of hers was Jack's house to be
spoiled. Neither her coaxing nor her tears had any effect
upon Richard and when she reverted to sulks, he scolded her
so harshly that she was frightened, and in consequence silenced.

For a week she thought and dreamt of nothing but gilded
French chairs, and then abruptly, as all else, the fancy left
her, and she forgot all about it. Her mantua-maker's bills
were enormous, and caused Richard many a sleepless night,
but she was always so charmingly penitent that he could not
find it in his heart to be angry; and, after all, he reflected, he
would rather have his money squandered on her adornment
than on that of her brothers. She was by turns passionate and
cold to him: one day enrapturing him by some pretty bland-
ishment, the next snapping peevishly when he spoke to her.

At the beginning of the season he dutifully conducted her
to routs and *bals-masqués*, but soon she began to go always
with either Andrew or Robert, both of whom were in town,
and whose casual chaperonage she much preferred to Richard's solicitous care. Tracy was rarely in London for more
than a few days at a time, and the Carstares, greatly to Richard's relief, saw but little of him. Carstares disliked Colonel
Lord Robert Belmanoir, but the Duke he detested, not only
for his habitual sneer towards him, but for the influence that
he undoubtedly held over Lavinia. Richard was intensely jealous of this, and could sometimes hardly bring himself to be
civil when his Grace visited my lady. Whether justly or not,
he inwardly blamed Tracy for all Lavinia's crazy whims and
periodical fits of ill-temper. It did not take his astute Grace
long to discover this, and with amused devilry he played
upon it, encouraging Lavinia in her extravagance, and making a point of calling on her whenever he was in town.

Carstares never knew when not to expect to find him there;
he came and went to and from London with no warning
whatsoever. No one ever knew where he was for more than a
day at a time, and no one was in the least surprised if he
happened to be seen in London when he should, according to
all accounts, have been in Paris. They merely shrugged their
shoulders, and exchanged glances, murmuring: "Devil Belmanoir!" and wondering what fresh intrigue he was in.

So altogether Richard was not sorry when my lady grew

suddenly sick of town and was seized with a longing for Bath. He had secretly hoped that she might return to Wyncham, but when she expressed no such wish, he stifled his own longing for home, shut up the London house, and took her and all her baggage to Bath, installing her in Queen Square in one of the most elegantly furnished houses in the place.

Lady Lavinia was at first charmed to be there again, delighted with the house, and transported over the excellencies of the new French milliner she had discovered.

But the milliner's bills proved monstrous, and the drawing-room of her house not large enough for the routs she contemplated giving. The air was too relaxing for her, and she was subject to constant attacks of the vapours that were as distressing to her household as they were on herself. The late hours made her head ache as it never ached in London, and the damp gave her a cold. Furthermore, the advent of an attractive and exceedingly wealthy little widow caused her many a bitter hour, to the considerable detriment of her good-temper.

She was lying on a couch in her white and gilt drawing-room one afternoon—alas! the craze for French furniture was o'er—smelling-bottle in hand and a *bona fide* ache in her head, when the door opened and Tracy walked into the room.

"Good heavens!" she said faintly, and uncorked her salts.

It was his Grace's first appearance since she had come to Bath, and the fact that he had politely declined an invitation that she had sent to him still rankled in her mind. He bowed over the limp hand that she extended, and looked her up and down.

"I regret to find you thus indisposed, my dear sister," he said smoothly.

"'Tis nought. Only one of my stupid headaches. I am never well here, and this house is stuffy," she answered fretfully.

"You should take the waters," he said, scrutinising, through his eyeglass, the chair to which she had waved him. "It has an unstable appearance, my dear; I believe I prefer the couch." He moved to a smaller sofa and sat down.

"Pray, how long have you been in Bath?" she demanded.

"I arrived last Tuesday week."

Lady Lavinia started up.

"Last Tuesday week? Then you have been here ten days and not visited me until now!"

He appeared to be examining the whiteness of his hands through the folds of black lace that drooped over them.

"I believe I had other things to do," he said coolly.

A book of sermons that she had been trying to peruse slid to the ground as Lavinia jerked a cushion into place.

"And you come to me when it suits you? How could you be so unkind as to refuse my invitation?" There was a rising, querulous note in her voice which gave warning of anger.

"My dear Lavinia, if you exhibit your deplorable temper to me, I shall leave you, so have a care. I thought you would understand that your good husband's society, improving though it may be, would be altogether too oppressive for my taste. In fact, I was surprised at your letter."

"You might have come for my sake," she answered peevishly, sinking back again. "I suppose you have been dancing attendance on the Molesly woman? Lud! but I think you men have gone crazed."

Understanding came to his Grace, and he smiled provokingly.

"Is that what upsets you? I wondered."

"No, 'tis not!" she flashed. "And I do not see why you should think so! For my part, I cannot see that she is even tolerable, and the way the men rave about her is disgusting! Disgusting! But 'tis always the same when a woman is unattached and wealthy. Well! Well! Why do you not say something? Do you find her so lovely?"

"To tell the truth, my dear, I have barely set eyes on the lady. I have been otherwise engaged, and I have done with all women, for the time, save one."

"So I have heard you say before. Do you contemplate marriage? Lud! but I pity the girl." She gave a jeering little laugh, but it was evident that she was interested.

His Grace was not in the least ruffled.

"I do not contemplate marriage, Lavinia, so your sympathies are wasted. I have met a girl—a mere child, for sure—and I will not rest until I have her."

"Lord! Another farmer's chit?"

"No, my dear sister, not another farmer's chit. A lady."

"God help her! Who is she? Where does she live?"

"She lives in Sussex. Her name I shall not tell you."

Her ladyship kicked an offending cushion on to the floor, and snapped at him.

"Oh, as you please! I shall not die of curiosity!"

"Ah!" The cynical lips curled annoyingly, and Lady Lavinia was seized with a mad desire to hurl her smelling-bottle at him. But she knew that it was worse than useless to be angry with Tracy, so she yawned ostentatiously, and hoped that she irritated him. If she did, she got no satisfaction from it, for he continued, quite imperturbably:

"She is the daintiest piece ever a man saw, and I'll swear there's blood and fire beneath the ice!"

"Is it possible the girl will have none of your Grace?" wondered Lavinia in mock amazement, and had the pleasure of seeing him frown.

The thin brows met over his arched nose, and the eyes glinted a little, while she caught a glimpse of cruel white teeth closing on a sensual under-lip. She watched his hand clench on his snuff-box, and exulted silently at having roused him. It was a very brief joy, however, for the next moment the frown had disappeared, the hand unclenched, and he was smiling again.

"At present she is cold," he admitted, "but I hope that in time she will become more plastic. I think, Lavinia, I have some experience with your charming, if capricious sex."

"I don't doubt you have. Where did you meet this perverse beauty?"

"In the Pump Room."

"Lud! Pray, describe her."

"I shall be delighted. She is taller than yourself, and dark. Her hair is like a dusky cloud of black, and it ripples off her brow and over her little ears in a most damnably alluring fashion. Her eyes are brown, but there are lights in them that are purest amber, and yet they are dark and velvety——"

My lady had recourse to the smelling-bottle.

"But I perceive I weary you. A man in love, my dear Lavinia——"

She was up again at that.

"In love? You? Nonsense! Nonsense! Nonsense! You do not know what the word means. You are like a—like a fish, with no more of love in you than a fish, and no more heart than a fish, and——"

"Spare me the rest, I beg. I am very clammy, I make no

doubt, but you will at least accord me more brain than a fish?"

"Oh, you have brain enough!" she raged. "Brain for evil! I grant you that!"

"It is really very kind of you——"

"The passion you feel now is not *love*. It is—it is——"

"Your pardon, my dear, but at the present moment I am singularly devoid of all strenuous emotions, so your remark is——"

"Oh, Tracy, Tracy, I am even quarrelling with you!" she cried wretchedly. "Oh, why?—why?"

"You are entirely mistaken, my dear. This is but the interchange of compliments. Pray, do not let me hinder you in the contribution of your share!"

Her lip trembled.

"Go on, Tracy, go on."

"Very well. I had described her eyes, I think?"

"Very tediously."

"I will strive to be brief. Her lips are the most kissable that I have ever seen——"

"And, as you remarked, you have experience," she murmured.

He bowed ironically.

"Altogether she's as spirited a filly as you could wish for. All she needs is bringing to heel."

"Does one bring a filly to heel? I rather thought——"

"As usual, my dear Lavinia, you are right: one does not. One breaks in a filly. I beg leave to thank you for correcting my mixed metaphor."

"Oh, pray do not mention it."

"I will cease to do so. She needs breaking in. It should be amusing to tame her."

"Should it?" She looked curiously at him.

"Vastly. And I am persuaded it can be done. I will have her."

"But what if she'll none of you?"

Suddenly the heavy lids were raised.

"She will have no choice."

Lady Lavinia shivered and sat up.

"La, Tracy! Will you have no sense of decency?" she cried. "I suppose," she sneered, "you think to kidnap the girl?"

"Exactly," he nodded.

She gasped at the effrontery of it.

"Heavens, are you mad? Kidnap a lady! This is no peasant girl, remember. Tracy, Tracy, pray do not be foolish! How *can* you kidnap her?"

"That, my dear, is a point which I have not yet decided. But I do not anticipate much trouble."

"But goodness gracious me! has the child no protectors? No brothers? No father?"

"There is a father," said Tracy slowly. "He was here at the beginning of their stay. He does not signify, and, which is important, he is of those that truckle. Were *I* to make myself known to him, I believe I might marry the girl within an hour. But I do not want that. At least—not yet."

"Good God, Tracy! do you think you are living in the Dark Ages? One cannot do these things now, I tell you! Will you not at least remember that you represent our house? 'Twill be a pretty thing an there is a scandal!" She broke off helplessly and watched him flick a remnant of snuff from his cravat.

"Oh, Tracy! 'Tis indeed a dangerous game you play. Pray consider!"

"Really, Lavinia, you are most entertaining. I trust I am capable of caring for myself and mine own honour."

"Oh, don't sneer—don't sneer!" she cried. "Sometimes I think I quite hate you!"

"You would be the more amusing, my dear."

She swept the back of her hand across her eyes in a characteristic movement.

"How cross I am!" she said, and laughed waveringly. "You must bear with me, Tracy. Indeed, I am not well."

"You should take the waters," he repeated.

"Oh, I do!—I do! And that reminds me that I must look for your beauty."

"She is not like to be there," he answered. " 'Tis only very seldom that she appears."

"What! Is she then *religieuse*?"

"*Religieuse!* Why, in heaven's name?"

"But not to walk in the Rooms——!"

"She is staying here with her aunt, who has been ill. They do not mix much in society."

"How very dreadful! Yet she used to walk in the Rooms, for you met her there?"

"Yes," he admitted coolly. " 'Tis for that reason that she now avoids them."

"Oh, Tracy, the poor child!" exclaimed his sister in a sudden fit of pity. "How can you persecute her, if she dislikes you?"

"She does not."

"Not! Then——"

"Rather, she fears me. But she is intrigued, for all that. I persecute her, as you call it, for her own (and my) ultimate good. But they quit Bath in a few days, and then, *nous verrons!*" He rose. "What of Honest Dick?"

"Don't call him by that odious name! I will not have it!"

"Odious, my dear? Odious? You would have reason an I called him *Dis*honest Dick."

"Don't! Don't!" she cried, covering her ears.

His Grace laughed softly.

"Oh, Lavinia, you must get the better of these megrims of yours, for there is nought that sickens a man sooner, believe me."

"Oh, go away!—go away!" she implored. "You tease me and tease me until I cannot bear it, and indeed I do not *mean* to be shrewish! Please go!"

"I am on the point of doing so, my dear. I trust you will have in a measure recovered when next I see you. Pray bear my respects to Hon—to the Honourable Richard."

She stretched out her hand.

"Come again soon!" she begged. "I shall be better to-morrow! 'Tis only to-day that my head aches till I could shriek with the worry and the pain of it! Come again!"

"Unfortunately I anticipate leaving Bath within a day or two. But nothing would have given me greater pleasure than to comply with your wishes." He kissed her hand punctiliously, and took his leave. At the door he paused, and looked back mockingly. "By the way—her name is—Diana." He bowed again and swept out, as Lavinia buried her face in the cushions and burst into tears.

It was thus that Richard found her, twenty minutes later, and his concern was so great that it in part restored her spirits, and she spent a quiet and, for him, blissful evening, playing at piquet.

In the middle of a game she suddenly flung down her hand and caught at his wrist.

"Dicky, Dicky—I will go home!"

"Go home? What do you mean? Not——"

"Yes, yes—Wyncham! Why not?"

"My dear, do you mean it?" His voice quivered with joyful surprise, and the cards slipped from his hands.

"Yes, I mean it! But take me quickly before I change my mind! I can sleep at Wyncham, and here I lie awake all night, and my head aches. Take me home and I will try to be a better wife! Oh, Dicky, have I been tiresome and exacting? I did not mean to be! Why do you let me?" She came quickly round the table and knelt at his side, giving no heed to the crumpling of her billowing silks. "I have been a wicked, selfish woman!" she said vehemently. "But indeed I will be better. You must not *let* me be bad—you *must* not, I tell you!"

He flung his arm about her plump shoulders and drew her tightly to him.

"When I get you home at Wyncham, I promise you I will finely hector you, sweetheart," he said, laughing to conceal his deeper feelings. "I shall make you into a capital housewife!"

"And I will learn to make butter," she nodded. "Then I must wear a dimity gown with a muslin apron and cap. Oh, yes, yes—a dimity gown!" She sprang up and danced to the middle of the room. "Shall I not be charming, Richard?"

"Very charming, Lavinia!"

"Of course! Oh, we will go home at once—at once! But first I must procure some new gowns from Marguérite!"

"To make butter in, dear?" he protested.

She was not attending.

"A dimity gown—or shall it be of tiffany with a quilted petticoat? Or both?" she chanted. "Dicky, I shall set a fashion in country toilettes!"

Dicky sighed.

CHAPTER VII

Introducing Sundry New Characters

NOT twenty minutes' walk from Lady Lavinia's house in Queen Square resided a certain Madam Thompson—a widow —who had lived in Bath for nearly fifteen years With her was staying Miss Elizabeth Beauleigh and her niece, Diana. Madam Thompson had been at a seminary with Miss Elizabeth when both were girls, and they had ever afterwards kept up their friendship, occasionally visiting one another, but more often contenting themselves with the writing of lengthy epistles, full of unimportant scraps of news and much gossip, amusing only to Miss Elizabeth's side, and on the widow's uninteresting and rambling.

It was a great joy to Madam Thompson when she received a letter from Miss Beauleigh begging that she and her niece might be allowed to pay a visit to her house in Bath, and to stay at least three weeks. The good lady was delighted at having her standing invitation at last accepted, and straightway wrote back a glad assent. She prepared her very best bedchamber for Miss Beauleigh, who, she understood, was coming to Bath principally for a change of air and scene after a long and rather trying illness.

In due course the two ladies arrived, the elder very small and thin, and birdlike in her movements; the younger moderately tall, and graceful as a willow tree, with great candid brown eyes that looked fearlessly out on to the world, and a tragic mouth that belied a usually cheerful disposition, and hinted at a tendency to look on the gloomy side of life.

Madam Thompson, whose first meeting with Diana this was, remarked on the sad mouth to Miss Elizabeth, or Betty as she was more often called, as they sat over the fire on the first night, Diana herself having retired to her room.

Miss Betty shook her head darkly and prophesied that her precious Di would one day love some man as no man in *her* opinion deserved to be loved!

"And she'll have love badly," she said, clicking her knit-ting-needles energetically. "*I* know these temperamental chil-dren!"

"She looks so melancholy," ventured the widow.

"Well there you are wrong!" replied Miss Betty. " 'Tis the sunniest-tempered child, and the sweetest-natured in the whole wide world, bless her! But I don't deny that she can be miserable. Far from it. I've known her weep her pretty eyes out over a dead puppy even! But usually she is gay enough."

"I fear this house will be dull and stupid for her," said Madam Thompson regretfully. "If only my dear son George were at home to entertain her——"

"My love, pray do not put yourself out! I assure you Diana will not at all object to a little quiet after.the life she has been leading in town this winter with her friend's family."

Whatever Diana thought of the quiet, she at least made no complaint, and adapted herself to her surroundings quite con-tentedly.

In the morning they would all walk as far as the Assembly Rooms, and Miss Betty would drink the waters in the old Pump Room, pacing sedately up and down with her friend on one side and her niece on the other. Madam Thompson had very few acquaintances in Bath, and the people she did know were all of her own age and habits, rarely venturing as far as the crowded fashionable quarter; so Diana had to be content with the society of the two old ladies, who gossiped happily enough together, but whose conversation she could not but find singularly uninteresting.

She watched the *monde* with concealed wistfulness, seeing Beau Nash strut about among the ladies, bowing with his ex-treme gallantry, always impeccably garbed, and in spite of his rapidly increasing age and bulk still absolute monarch of Bath. She saw fine painted madams in enormous hoops, and with their hair so extravagantly curled and powdered that it appeared quite grotesque, mincing along with their various cavaliers; elderly beaux with coats padded to hide their shrunken shoulders, and paint to fill the wrinkles on their faces; young rakes; stout dowagers with their demure daugh-ters; old ladies who had come to Bath for their health's sake; titled folk of fashion, and plain gentry from the country—all parading before her eyes.

One or two young bucks tried to ogle her, and received such indignant glances from those clear eyes, that they never dared annoy her again, but for the most part no one paid any heed to the unknown and plainly clad girl.

Then came his Grace of Andover upon the stage.

He drew Diana's attention from the first moment that he entered the Pump Room—a black moth amongst the gaily-hued butterflies. He had swept a comprehensive glance round the scene and at once perceived Diana. Somehow, exactly how she could never afterwards remember, he had introduced himself to her aunt and won that lady's good will by his smoothness of manner and polished air. Madam Thompson, who, left to herself, never visited the Assembly Rooms, could not be expected to recognise Devil Belmanoir in the simple Mr. Everard who presented himself.

As he had told his sister, Diana was cold. There was something about his Grace that repelled her, even while his mesmeric personality fascinated. He was right when he said that she feared him; she was nervous, and the element of fear gave birth to curiosity. She was intrigued, and began to look forward to his daily appearance in the Pump Room with mingled excitement and apprehension. She liked his flattering attention, and his grand air. Often she would watch him stroll across the floor, bowing to right and left with that touch of insolence that characterized him, and rejoiced in the knowledge that he was coming straight to her, and that the painted beauties who so palpably ogled and invited him to their sides could not alter his course. She felt her power with a thrill of delight, and smiled upon Mr. Everard, giving him her hand to kiss, and graciously permitting him to sit with her beside her aunt. He would point out all the celebrities of town and Bath for her edification, recalling carefully chosen and still more carefully censored anecdotes of each one. She discovered that Mr. Everard was an entertaining and harmless enough companion, and even expanded a little, allowing him a glimpse of her whimsical nature with its laughter and its hint of tears.

His Grace of Andover saw enough to guess at the unsounded depths in her soul, and he became lover-like. Diana recoiled instinctively, throwing up a barrier of reserve between them. It was not what he said that alarmed her, but it was the way in which he said it, and the vague something in the purring, faintly sinister voice that she could not quite define, that made her heart beat unpleasantly fast, and the blood rush to her temples. She began first to dread the morn-

ing promenade, and then to avoid it. One day she had a
headache; the next her foot was sore; another time she
wanted to work at her fancy stitchery, until her aunt, who
knew how she disliked her needle, and how singularly free
from headaches and all petty ailments she was wont to be,
openly taxed her with no longer wishing to walk abroad.

They were in the girl's bedroom at the time, Diana seated
before her dressing-table, brushing out her hair for the night.
When her aunt put the abrupt question she hesitated, caught
a long strand in her comb, and pretended to be absorbed in
its disentanglement. The clouds of rippling hair half hid her
face, but Miss Betty observed how her fingers trembled, and
repeated her question. Then came the confession. Mr. Everard was unbearable; his attentions were odious; his continued
presence revolting to Mistress Di. She was afraid of him,
afraid of his dreadful green eyes and of his soft voice. She
wished they had never come to Bath, and still more that they
had not met him. He looked at her as if—as if—oh, in short,
he was hateful.

Miss Betty was horrified.

"You cannot mean it! Dear, dear, dear! Here was I
thinking what a pleasant gentleman he was, and all the time
he was persecuting my poor Di, the wretch! *I* know the type,
my love, and I feel inclined to give him a good piece of my
mind!"

"Oh, no—no!" implored Diana. "Indeed, you must do no
such thing, Auntie! He had said nought that I could possibly
be offended at—'tis but his *manner,* and the—and the way he
looked at me. Indeed, indeed, you must not!"

"Tut, child! Of course I shall say naught. But it makes me
so monstrous angry to think of my poor lamb being tor-
mented by such as he that I declare I could tear his eyes out!
Yes, my dear, I could! Thank goodness we are leaving Bath
next week!"

"Yes," sighed Diana. "I cannot help being glad, though
Madam Thompson is very amiable! 'Tis so very different
when there is no man with one!"

"You are quite right, my love. We should have insisted on
your father's staying with us instead of allowing him to fly
back to his fusty, musty old volumes. I shall not be so foolish
another time, I can assure you. But we need not go to the
Assembly Rooms again."

"I need not go," corrected Diana gently. "Of course you and Madam Thompson will continue to."

"To tell the truth, my love," confessed Miss Betty, "I shall not be sorry for an excuse to stay away. 'Tis doubtless most ill-natured of me, but I cannot but think that Hester has altered sadly since last I saw her. She is always talking of sermons and good works!"

Diana twisted her luxuriant hair into a long plait, and gave a gurgling little laugh.

"Oh, Auntie, is it not depressing? I wondered how you could tolerate it! She is so vastly solemn, poor dear thing!"

"Well," said Miss Betty charitably, "she has seen trouble, has Hester Thompson, and I have my doubts about this George of hers. A worthless young man, I fear, from all accounts. But, unkind though it may be, I shall be glad to find myself at home again, and that's the truth!" She rose and picked up her candle. "In fact, I find Bath not half so amusing as I was told 'twould be."

Diana walked with her to the door.

" 'Tis not amusing at all when one has no friends; but last year, when my cousins were with us and papa took a house for the season on the North Parade, 'twas most enjoyable. I wish you had been here, instead of with that disagreeable Aunt Jennifer!"

She kissed her relative most affectionately and lighted her across the landing to her room. Then she returned to her room and shut the door, giving a tired little yawn.

It was at about that moment that his Grace of Andover was ushered into the already crowded card-room of my Lord Avon's house in Catharine Place, and was greeted with ribald cries of "Oho, Belmanoir!" and "Where's the lady, Devil?"

He walked coolly forward into the full light of a great pendant chandelier, standing directly beneath it, the diamond order on his breast burning and winking like a living thing. The diamonds in his cravat and on his fingers glittered every time he moved, until he seemed to be carelessly powdered with iridescent gems. As usual, he was clad in black, but it would have been difficult to find any other dress in the room more sumptuous or more magnificent than his sable satin with its heavy silver lacing, and shimmering waistcoat. Silver lace adorned his throat and fell in deep ruffles over his hands, and in defiance of Fashion, which decreed that black alone should be worn to tie the hair, he displayed long silver ribands, very striking against his unpowdered head.

He raised his quizzing glass and looked round the room with an air of surprised hauteur. Lord Avon, leaning back in his chair at one of the tables, shook a reproving finger at him.

"Belmanoir, Belmanoir, we have seen her and we protest she is too charming for you!"

"In truth, we think we should be allowed a share in the lady'th thmileth," lisped one from behind him, and his Grace turned to face dainty, effeminate little Viscount Fotheringham, who stood at his elbow, resplendent in salmon-pink satin and primrose velvet, with skirts so full and stiffly whale-boned that they stood out from his person, and heels so high that instead of walking he could only mince.

Tracy made a low leg.

"Surely shall you have a share in her smiles an she wills it so," he purred, and a general laugh went up which caused the fop to flush to the ears, as he speedily effaced himself.

He had been one of those who had tried to accost Diana, and gossip-loving Will Stapley, with him at the time, had related the story of his discomfiture to at least half-a-dozen men, who immediately told it to others, vastly amused at the pertinacious Viscount's rebuff.

"What was it Selwyn said?" drawled Sir Gregory Markham, shuffling cards at Lord Avon's table.

Davenant looked across at him inquiringly.

"George? Of Belmanoir? When?"

"Oh, at White's one night—I forget—Jack Cholmondely was there—he would know; and Horry Walpole. 'Twas of Devil and his light o' loves—quite apt, on the whole."

Cholmondely looked up.

"Did I hear my name?"

"Ay. What was it George said of Belmanoir at White's the night Gilly made that absurd bet with Ffolliott?"

"When Gilly—oh, yes, I remember. 'Twas but an old hexameter tag, playing on his name: *'Est bellum bellis bellum bellare puellis.'* He seemed to think it a fitting motto for a ducal house."

There was another general laugh at this. Markham broke in on it:

"Who is she, Tracy?"

His Grace turned.

"Who is who?" he asked languidly.

Lord Avon burst out laughing.

"Oh, come now, Belmanoir, that won't do! It really will not! Who is she, indeed!"

"Ay, Belmanoir, who is the black-haired beauty, and where did you find her?" cried Tom Wilding, pressing forward with a glass in one hand and a bottle of port in the other. "I thought you were captivated by Cynthia Evans?"

Tracy looked bewildered for the moment and then a light dawned on him.

"Evans! Ah, yes! The saucy widow who lived in Kensington, was it not? I remember."

"He had forgotten!" cried Avon, and went off into another of the noisy laughs that had more than once caused Mr. Nash to shudder and to close his august eyes. "You'll be the death of me, Devil! Gad! but you will!"

"Oh, I trust not. Thank you, Wilding." He accepted the glass that Tom offered, and sipped delicately.

"But you've not answered!" reminded Fortescue from another table. He dealt the cards round expertly. "Is it hands off, perhaps?"

"Certainly," replied his Grace. "It generally is, Frank, as you know."

"To my cost!" was the laughing rejoinder, and Fortescue rubbed his sword arm as if in memory of some hurt. "You pinked me finely, Tracy!"

"Clumsily, Frank, clumsily. It might have been quicker done."

The Viscount, who had been a second at the meeting, tittered amiably.

"Neatetht thing I ever thaw, 'pon my honour. All over in leth than a minute, Avon. Give you my word!"

"Never mind, you had fought Devil, Frank? What possessed you?"

"I was more mad than usual, I suppose," replied Fortescue in his low, rather dreamy voice, "and I interfered between Tracy and his French singer. He objected most politely, and we fought it out in Hyde Park."

"Gad, yes!" exclaimed his partner, Lord Falmouth. "Why, I was Devil's second! But it was ages ago!"

"Two years," nodded Fortescue, "but I have not forgotten, you see!"

"Lord, I had! And 'twas the funniest fight I ever saw, with

you as furious as could be and Devil cool as a cucumber. You were never much of a swordsman, Frank, but that morning you thrust so wildly that stap me if I didn't think Devil would run you through. 'Stead of that he pinks you neatly through the sword-arm, and damme if you didn't burst out laughing fit to split! And then we all walked off to breakfast with you, Frank, as jolly as sandboys. Heavens, yes! That was a fight!"

"It was amusing," admitted Tracy at Fortescue's elbow. "Don't play, Frank."

Fortescue flung his cards face downwards on the table. "Curse you, Tracy, you've brought bad luck!" he said entirely without rancour. "I had quite tolerable hands before you came."

"Belmanoir, I will thtake my chestnut mare 'gaintht your new grey," lisped the Viscount, coming up to the table, dice-box in hand.

"Stap me, but that is too bad!" cried Wilding. "Don't take him, Devil! Have you seen the brute?"

The four players had finished their card-playing and were quite ready for the dice.

"Trust in your luck, Belmanoir, and take him!" advised Pritchard, who loved hazarding other men's possessions, but kept a tight hold on his own.

"Ay, take him!" echoed Falmouth.

"Don't," said Fortescue.

"Of course I shall take him," answered his Grace tranquilly. "My grey against your chestnut and the best of three. Will you throw?"

The Viscount rattled his box with a flourish. Two threes and a one turned up.

With a hand on Fortescue's shoulder, and one foot on the rung of his chair, Tracy leaned forward and cast his own dice on to the table. He had beaten the Viscount's throw by five. The next toss Fotheringham won, but the last fell to his Grace.

"Damnathion!" said the Viscount cheerfully. "Will you thtake your grey againtht my Terror?"

"Thunder and turf, Fotheringham! You'll lose him!" cried Nettlefold warningly. "Don't stake the Terror!"

"Nonthenth! Do you take me, Belmanoir?"

"Certainly," said the Duke, and threw.

"Oh, an you are in a gaming mood, I will play you for the

right to try my hand with the dark beauty!" called Markham across the room.

"Against what?" asked Fortescue.

"Oh, what he wills!"

The Viscount had cast and lost, and his Grace won the second throw.

"It appears my luck is in," he remarked. "I will stake my beauty against your estates, Markham."

Sir Gregory shook his head, laughing.

"No, no! Keep the lady!"

"I intend to, my dear fellow. She is not your style. I begin to wonder whether she altogether suits my palate." He drew out his snuff-box and offered it to his host, and the other men finding that he was proof against their railing, allowed the subject to drop.

In the course of the evening his Grace won three thousand guineas—two at ombre and one at dice—lost his coveted grey hunter and won him back again from Wilding, to whom he had fallen. He came away at three o'clock in company with Fortescue, both perfectly cool-headed, although his Grace, for his part, had imbibed a considerable quantity of burgundy, and more punch than any ordinary man could take without afterwards feeling very much the worse for wear.

As my Lord Avon's door closed behind them, Tracy turned to his friend:

"Shall we walk, Frank?"

"Since our ways lie together, yes," replied Fortescue, linking his arm in the Duke's. "Down Brock Street and across the Circus is our quickest way."

They strolled down the road for a few moments in silence, passing a linkman on the way. Fortescue bade him a cheery good-night, which was answered in a very beery voice, but the Duke said nothing. Frank looked into his dark-browed face thoughtfully.

"You've had the luck, to-night, Tracy."

"Moderately. I hoped entirely to repair last week's losses."

"You are in debt, I suppose?"

"I believe so."

"To what extent, Tracy?"

"My dear fellow, I neither have, nor wish to have, the vaguest notion. Pray do not treat me to a sermon!"

"I shall not. I've said all I have to say on the subject."

"Many times."

"Yes—many times. And it has had no more effect upon you than if I had not spoken."

"Less."

"I daresay, I wish it were not so, for there's good in you somewhere, Tracy."

"By what strange process of reasoning do you arrive at that?"

"Well," said Fortescue laughing, "there's nearly always some good in the very worst of men. I count on that—and your kindness to me."

"I should be interested to know when I have been kind to you—beyond the time when I was compelled to teach you to leave me and my affairs alone."

"I was not referring to that occasion," was the dry answer. "I had not seen your act in that light. I meant well over the episode."

"You could not damn yourself more effectually than by saying that," said his Grace calmly. "But we wander from the point. When have I done you an act of kindness?"

"You know very well. When you extricated me from that cursed sponging-house."

"I remember now. Yes, that *was* good of me. I wonder why I did it?"

" 'Tis what I want to know."

"I suppose I must have had some sort of an affection for you. I would certainly never have done such a thing for any-one else."

"Not even for your own brother!" said Frank sharply.

They had crossed the Circus and were walking down Gay Street now.

"Least of all for them," came the placid response. "You are thinking of Andrew's tragic act? Most entertaining, was it not?"

"You evidently found it so."

"I did. I wanted to prolong the sensation, but my esteemed brother-in-law came to the young fool's rescue."

"Would you have assisted him?"

"In the end I fear I should have had to."

"I believe there must be a kink in your brain!" cried Fortescue. "I cannot else account for your extraordinary conduct!"

"We Belmanoirs are all half-mad," replied Tracy sweetly, "but I think that in my case it is merely concentrated evil."

"I will not believe it! You have shown that you can behave differently! You do not try to strip me of all I possess—why all those unfortunate youths you play with?"

"You see, you possess so little," the Duke excused himself. "Neither do you sneer at me in your loathsome fashion. Why?"

"Because I have hardly ever any desire to. I like you."

"Tare an' ouns! you must like someone else in the world besides me?"

"I can think of no one. And I do not exactly worship the ground *you* tread on. The contemplation of my brothers appals me. I have loved various women, and shall no doubt love many more——"

"No, Tracy," interposed Fortescue, "you have never loved a woman in your life. 'Tis that that might save you. I do not allude to the lustful passion you indulge in, but real love. For God's sake, Belmanoir, live clean!"

"Pray do not distress yourself, Frank. I am not worth it."

"I choose to think that you are. I cannot but feel that if you had been loved as a boy—— Your mother——"

"Did you ever see my mother?" inquired his Grace lazily.

"No—but——"

"Have you ever seen my sister?"

"Er—yes——"

"In a rage?"

"Really, I——"

"Because, if you have, you have seen my mother. Only she was ten times more violent. In fact, we were a pleasant party when we were all at home."

"I understand."

"Good Gad! I believe you are sorry for me?" cried Tracy scornfully.

"I am. Is it a presumption on my part?"

"My dear Frank, when I am sorry for myself you may be sorry too. Until then——"

"When that day comes I shall no longer pity you."

"Very deep, Frank! You think I shall be on the road to recovery? A pretty conceit. Luckily, the happy moment has not yet come—and I do not think it is like to. We appear to have arrived."

They were standing outside one of the tall houses where Fortescue lodged. He turned and grasped his friend's shoulders.

"Tracy, give up this mad life you lead! Give up the women and the drink, and the excessive gaming; for one day, believe me, you will overstep yourself and be ruined!"

The Duke disengaged himself.

"I very much object to being man-handled in the street," he complained. "I suppose you still *mean* well. You should strive to conquer the tendency."

"I wonder if you know how insolent is your tone, Belmanoir?" asked Fortescue steadily.

"Naturally. I should not have attained such perfection in the art else. But pray accept my thanks for your good advice. You will forgive me an I do not avail myself of it, I am sure. I prefer the crooked path."

"Evidently," sighed the other. "If you will not try the straight and narrow way, I can only hope that you will fall very deeply and very honestly in love; and that the lady will save you from yourself."

"I will inform you of it when it comes to pass," promised his Grace. "And now good-night!"

"Good-night!" Frank returned the low bow with a curt nod. "I shall see you to-morrow—that is, this morning—at the Baths?"

"Sufficient unto the day is the evil thereof," was the smiling rejoinder. "Sleep soundly, Frank!" He waved an ironic farewell and crossed the road to his own lodgings, which stood almost directly opposite.

"And I suppose *you* will sleep as soundly as if you had not a stain on your conscience—and had not tried your uttermost to alienate the regard of the only friend you possess," remarked Frank bitterly to the darkness. "Damn you, Tracy, for the villain you are!" He walked up the steps to his own front door and turned the key in the lock. He looked over his shoulder as a door slammed across the street. "Poor Devil!" he said. "Oh, you poor Devil!"

CHAPTER VIII

The Biter Bit

WITH John Carstares the winter had passed quite uneventfully. He continued his highway robbery, but he made two bad blunders—not from the point of view of a thief, but from that of the gentleman in him. The first was when he stopped an opulent-looking chariot, which he found to contain two ladies, their maid and their jewels, and the second when the occupant of a large travelling coach chanced to be an old gentleman who possessed far greater courage than physical strength. On the first occasion my lord's dismay had been ludicrous, and he had hastily retired after tendering a naïve apology. The old gentleman in the second episode had defied him so gallantly that he had impulsively offered the butt end of one of his pistols. The old man was so surprised that he allowed the weapon to fall to the ground, where it exploded quite harmlessly, sending up a cloud of dust and smoke. Carstares then begged his pardon most humbly, assisted him back into his coach, and rode off before the astonished Mr. Dunbar had time to collect his wits.

The robbing was not carried out in a very scientific manner, for, as has been seen, Carstares could not bring himself to terrorise women or old men, and there only remained the young and the middle-aged gentlemen, one of whom Jack offered to fight for the possession of his jewels. His challenge was promptly accepted by the man, who happened to possess a strong sense of humour, and probably saw a chance of saving his belongings in the offer. He had been speedily worsted, but Carstares was so pleased with a particularly neat thrust which he had executed, that he forwent half the booty, and the pair of them divided the contents of the jewel-box by the roadside, the sporting gentleman keeping his most valued belongings and giving Jack the surplus. They parted on the very best of terms, and all Carstares got out of the episode was a little sword practice and a few trinkets.

When May came he was patrolling the west side of Sussex, beyond Midhurst, not because he thought it a profitable part, but because he knew and loved the country. One late afternoon towards the end of the month he rode gaily into one of the small villages that nestle amongst the Downs, and made his way down the quaint main street to the George Inn, where he drew rein and dismounted. At his call an aged ostler hobbled out of a side door, chewing an inevitable straw, and after eyeing the newcomer and his steed for an appreciable length of time, evidently decided that they were worthy of his attention, for he came forward, remarking that it had been a pleasant day.

Carstares agreed with him, and volunteered the information that it would be another fine day to-morrow, if the sunset were to be trusted. To this the ostler replied that he, for one, never trusted to no red sunsets, and added darkly that there warn't nothing so deceitful to his manner o' thinking. He'd known it be such a red sunset as never was, and yet be a-pouring with rain all next day. . . . Should he take the mare?

Carstares shook his head.

"No, I thank you. I remain here but a few moments. I doubt she's thirsty though—eh, Jenny?"

"Water, sir?"

"For her, yes. For myself I fancy a tankard of your home-brewed ale. Stand, Jenny!" He turned away and walked up the steps to the inn door.

"Be you a-going to leave her there, sir—a-standing all by herself?" inquired the man, surprised.

"Why, yes! She's docile enough."

"Well! Seems to me a risky thing to leave a hoss—and a skittish hoss at that—a-standing loose in the road. Ye won't be tying her to a post, master?"

Carstares leaned his arms on the balustrade and looked down at them.

"I will not. She'd be very hurt at such treatment, wouldn't you, lass?"

Jenny tossed her head playfully, as if in agreement, and the ostler scratched his head, looking from her to my lord:

"A'most seems as if she understands what you be a-saying to her, sir!"

"Of course she understands! Don't I tell you 'tis a clever

little lady? If I call her now she'll come up these steps to me, and not all the ostlers in Christendom could stop her."

"Don't'ee go for to do it, sir!" urged the old man, backing. "She must be uncommon fond o' ye?"

"She'd be a deal fonder of you if you'd fetch her a drink," hinted Jack broadly.

"Ay, sir! I be a-going this werry instant!" And with many an anxious glance over his shoulder at the perfectly quiet mare, he disappeared through an open doorway into the yard.

When Carstares, tankard of ale in hand, emerged from the inn and sat himself down on one of the benches that stood against the wall, the mare was drinking thirstily from a bucket which the ancient one held for her.

" 'Tis a wunnerful fine mare, sir," he remarked at length, after a careful inspection of her points.

Carstares nodded pleasantly, and surveyed Jenny through half-shut eyes.

"I think so every time I look at her," he said.

"I should think she could get a bit of a pace on her, sir? Mebbe ye've tried her racing?"

"No, she wasn't brought up to that. But she's fast enough."

"Ay, sir. No vices?"

"Lord, no!"

"Don't kick neither?"

"Not with me."

"Oh! they allus knows who'll stand it and who won't."

Jack drained his tankard, and setting it down on the bench beside him, rose to his feet.

"She'd not dream of kicking a friend. Jenny!"

The ostler watched her pick her way towards her master, coquetting with her head, and sidling round him in the most playful manner possible. A slow smile dawned on the man's face.

"Ah, it be a purty sight to watch her—so it be!" he said, and received a guinea from Jack, who never tired of listening to praise of his beloved Jenny.

Carstares remounted, nodded farewell to the ostler, and rose leisurely on down the street, soon branching off to the right into a typical Sussex lane, where he trotted between uneven hedges. sweet with blossom and with May, and placid fields rolling away on either side, upwards until they merged into the undulating hills, barely discernible in the gloom, that are the downs. It was a wonderfully calm evening, with only a gentle west wind blowing, and the moon already shining faintly in the dark sky. There was nothing beyond the sound of the mare's hoofs to break the beautiful stillness of it all.

He rode for some way without meeting a soul, and when at the end of an hour someone did chance along the road it was only a labourer returning home to his supper after a long day in the fields. John bade him a cheery good evening and watched him pass on down the road humming.

After that he met no one. He rode easily along for miles, into the fast-gathering darkness. He was frowning as he rode, thinking.

Curiously enough, it was on his penniless days in France that his mind dwelt this evening. He had resolutely thrust that dark time behind him, determined to forget it, but there were still days when, try as he might, he could not prevent his thoughts flying back to it.

With clenched teeth he recalled the days when he, the son of an Earl, had taught fencing in Paris for a living. . . . Suddenly he laughed harshly, and at the unusual sound the mare pricked up her ears and sidled uneasily across the road. For once no notice was taken of her, and she quickened her pace with a flighty toss of her head. . . .

He thought how he, the extravagant John, had pinched and scraped and saved rather than go under; how he had lived in one of the poorer *quartiers* of the city, alone, without friends —nameless.

Then, cynically now, he reviewed the time when he had taken to drinking, heavily and systematically, and had succeeded in pulling himself up at the very brink of the pit he saw yawning before him.

Next the news of his mother's death. . . . John passed over that quickly. Even now the thought of it had the power of rousing in him all the old misery and impotent resentment.

His mind sped on to his Italian days. On his savings he had travelled to Florence, and from there he went gradually south, picking up all the latest arts and subtleties of fence on the way.

The change of scene and of people did much to restore his spirits. His devil-may-care ways peeped out again; he started to gamble on the little money he had left. For once Fortune proved kind; he doubled and trebled and quadrupled the con-

tents of his purse. Then it was that he met Jim Salter, whom
he engaged as his servant. This was the first friend since he
had left England. Together they travelled about Europe, John
gambling his way, Jim keeping a relentless hand on the ex-
chequer. It was entirely owing to his watchfulness and care
that John was not ruined, for his luck did not always hold
good, and there were days when he lost with distressing stead-
iness. But Jim guarded the winnings jealously, and there was
always something to fall back on.

At last the longing for England and English people grew so
acute that John made up his mind to return. But he found
that things in England were very different from what they
had been abroad. Here he was made to feel acutely that he
was outcast. It was impossible to live in town under an assumed name, as he would like to have done, for too many
people knew Jack Carstares, and would remember him. He
saw that he must either live secluded, or—and the idea of becoming a highwayman occurred to him. A hermit's existence
he knew to be totally unsuited to a man of his temperament,
but the free, adventurous spirit of the road appealed to him.
The finding of his mare—J. the Third, as he laughingly
dubbed her—decided the point; he forthwith took on himself
the rôle of quixotic highwayman, roaming his beloved South
Country, happier than he had been since he first left England;
bit by bit regaining his youth and spirits, which last, not all
the trouble he had been through had succeeded in
extinguishing. . . .

Clip-clap, clip-clop. . . . With a jerk he came back to earth
and reined-in his mare, the better to listen.

Along the road came the unmistakable sound of horses'
hoofs, and the scrunch-scrunch of swiftly-revolving wheels on
the sandy surface.

But now the moon was right out, but owing to the fact that
she was playing at hide-and-seek in and out of the clouds, it
was fairly dark. Nevertheless, Jack fastened his mask over his
face with quick, deft fingers, and pulled his hat well over his
eyes. His ears told him that the vehicle, whatever it was, was
coming towards him, so he drew into the side of the road,
and taking a pistol from its holster, sat waiting, his eyes on
the bend in the road.

Nearer and nearer came the horses, until the leader swung
round the corner. Carstares saw that it was an ordinary travelling chariot, and levelled his pistol.

"Halt, or I fire!" He had to repeat the command before it was heard, and to ride out from the shadow of the hedge.

The chariot drew up and the coachman leaned over the side to see who it was bidding them to stop in so peremptory a manner.

"What d'ye want? Who are ye? Is there naught amiss?" he cried testily, and found himself staring at a long-nosed pistol.

"Throw down your arms!"

"I ain't got none, blast ye!"

"On your honour?" Jack dismounted.

"Ay! Wish I had, and I'd see ye damned afore I'd throw 'em down!"

At this moment the door of the coach opened and a gentleman leapt lightly down to the road. He was big and loose-limbed as far as Carstares could see, and carried himself with an easy grace.

My lord presented his pistol.

"Stand!" he ordered gruffly.

The moon peeped coyly out from behind a cloud and shed her light upon the little group as if to see what all the fuss was about. The big man's face was in the shadow, but Jack's pistol was not. Into its muzzle the gentleman gazed, one hand deep in the pocket of his heavy cloak, the other holding a small pistol.

"Me very dear friend," he said in a rich brogue, "perhaps ye are not aware that that same pistol ye are pointing at me is unloaded? Don't move; I have ye covered!"

Jack's arm fell to his side, and the pistol he held clattered to the ground. But it was not surprise at Jim's defection that caused him that violent start. It was something far more overwhelming. For the voice that proceeded from the tall gentleman belonged to one whom, six years ago, he had counted, next to Richard, his greatest friend on earth.

The man moved a little, and the moonlight shone full on his face, clearly outlining the large nose and good-humoured mouth, and above, the sleepy grey eyes. Miles! Miles O'Hara! For once Jack could find nothing amusing in the situation. It was too inconceivably hideous that he should meet his friend in this guise, and, further, be unable to reveal himself. A great longing to tear off his mask and to grasp Miles' hand assailed him. With an effort he choked it down and listened to what O'Hara was saying:

"If ye will be so kind as to give me your word of honour

ye'll not be afther trying to escape, I should be greatly obliged. But I tell ye first that if ye attempt to move, I shall shoot."

Jack made a hopeless gesture with his hand. He felt dazed. The whole thing was ridiculous; how Miles would laugh afterwards. He went cold. There would be no "afterwards". . . . Miles would never know. . He would be given over to the authorities, and Miles would never know that he had helped Jack Carstares to the scaffold . . . Perhaps, too, he would not mind so very much, now that he, Jack, was so disgraced. One could never tell; even if he risked everything now, and told his true identity, Miles might turn away from him in disgust, Miles, who could never stoop to a dishonourable act. Carstares felt that he would bear anything sooner than face this man's scorn. . . .

"Never tell me 'tis a dumb man ye are, for I heard ye shout meself! Do ye give me your word of honour, or must I have ye bound?"

Carstares pulled himself together and set his teeth as he faced the inevitable. Escape was impossible; Miles would shoot, he felt sure, and then his disguise would be torn away and his friend would see that Jack Carstares was nothing but a common highwayman. Whatever happened, that must not be, for the sake of the name and Richard. So he quietly held out his hands.

"Ay, I give you my word, but ye can bind me if ye choose." It was his highwayman voice: raucous, and totally unlike his own.

But O'Hara's eyes were fixed on the slender white hands held out to him. In his usual haphazard fashion, Jack had quite forgotten to grime his hands. They were shapely and white, and carefully manicured.

Miles took either wrist in his large hands and turned them palm upwards in the moonlight.

"Singularly white hands ye have, for one in your profession," he drawled, and tightened his hold as Jack tried to draw them away. "No, ye do not! Now be so good as to step within, me friend."

Jack held back an instant.

"My mare?" he asked, and O'Hara noted the anxiety in his voice.

"Ye need not be after worrying about her," he said. "George!"

The footman sprang forward.

"Yessir."

"Ye see that mare? I want ye to ride her home. Can ye do it?"

"Yessir."

"I doubt it," murmured Jack.

So did Jenny. She refused point blank to allow this stranger to mount her. Her master had left her in one spot, and there she would stand until he chose to bid her move. In vain did the groom coax and coerce. She ran round him and seemed a transformed creature. She laid her ears flat and gnashed at the bit, ready to lash out furiously at the first opportunity.

Jack watched the man's futile struggles with the ghost of a smile about his lips.

"Jenny!" he said quietly, and O'Hara looked round at him sharply, frowning. Unconsciously he had spoken naturally, and the voice was faintly familiar.

Jenny twitched the bridle from the perspiring groom and minced up to the prisoner.

"Would ye allow me to have a hand free—sir?" he asked. "Mebbe I can manage her."

Without a word Miles released him, and he caught the bridle, murmuring something unintelligible to the now quiet animal.

O'Hara watched the beautiful hand stroke her muzzle reassuringly, and frowned again. No ordinary highwayman this.

"Mount her now, will 'ee?" Jack flung at the groom, and kept a warning hand on the rein as the man obeyed. With a final pat he turned away. "She'll do now, sir."

O'Hara nodded.

"Ye've trained her well. Get in, please."

Jack obeyed, and in a minute or two O'Hara jumped in after him, and the coach began to move forward.

For a while there was silence, Carstares keeping himself well under control. It was almost unbearable to think that after this brief drive he would never set eyes on his friend again, and he wanted so badly to turn and grasp that strong hand. . . .

Miles turned in his seat and tried to see the masked face in the darkness.

"Ye are a gentleman?" he asked, going straight to the point.

Jack was prepared for this.

"Me, sir? Lor' no, sir!"

"I do not believe ye. Don't be forgettin' I've seen your hands!"

"Hands, sir?" in innocent bewilderment.

"Sure, ye don't think I'd be believing ye an ordinary rogue, with hands like that?"

"I don't rightly understand ye, sir?"

"Bejabbers then, ye'll be understanding me to-morrow!"

"To-morrow, sir?"

"Certainly. Ye may as well tell me now as then. I'm not such a daft fool as I look, and I know a gentleman when I see one, even an he does growl at me as you do!" he chuckled. "And I'd an odd feeling that I knew ye when ye spoke to the mare. I'd be loth to send a friend to the gallows."

How well Jack knew that soft, persuasive voice. His hands clenched as he forced himself to answer:

"I don't think I've ever seen ye afore, sir."

"Maybe ye have not. We shall see to-morrow."

"What do ye mean by to-morrow, sir?" ventured Carstares uneasily.

"Sure, ye will have the honour of appearing before me, me friend."

"Before *you*, sir?"

"Why not! I'm a Justice of the Peace, heaven save the mark!"

There was a breathless pause, and then at last the funny side of it struck Jack, and his shoulders shook with suppressed laughter. The exquisite irony of it was almost too much for him. He, the Earl of Wyncham, was to be formally questioned by his friend St. Miles O'Hara, J.P.!

"What ails ye now, man? Ye find it amusing?" asked Miles, surprised.

"Oh, Lud, yes!" gasped Jack, and collapsed into his corner.

CHAPTER IX

Lady O'Hara Intervenes

LADY O'HARA found that her big, indolent husband was unusually silent next morning at breakfast. She had not been married long enough to consent to being practically ignored, no matter what the time of day, but she had been married quite long enough to know that before she took any direct action against him, she must first allow him to assuage his appetite. Accordingly she plied him with coffee and eggs, and with a satisfied and slightly motherly air, watched him attack a sirloin of beef. She was a pretty, bird-like little lady, with big eyes, and soft brown curls escaping from under a demure but very becoming mob cap. She measured five foot nothing in her stockings, and was sometimes referred to by her large husband as the Midget. Needless to say, this flippant appellation was in no wise encouraged by the lady.

She decided that Miles had come to the end of his repast, and, planting two dimpled elbows on the table, she rested her small chin in her hands and looked across at him with something of the air of an inquisitive kitten.

"Miles!"

O'Hara leaned back in his chair, and at the sight of her fresh prettiness his brow cleared and smiled.

"Well, asthore?"

A reproachful finger was raised and a pair of red lips pouted adorably.

"Now, Miles, confess you've been vastly disagreeable this morning. Twice have I spoken to you and you've not troubled to answer me—nay, let me finish! And once you growled at me like a nasty bear! Yes, sir, you did!"

"Did I now, Molly? 'Tis a surly brute you're after thinking me, then? Troth, and I've been sore perplexed, me dear."

Lady O'Hara got up and sidled round to him.

"Have you so, Miles?"

He flung an arm about her and drew her on to his knee.

"Sure, yes, Molly."

"Well then, Miles, had you not better tell me what it is that troubles you?" she coaxed, laying a persuasive hand on his shoulder.

He smiled up at her.

" 'Tis just an inquisitive puss you are!"

Again the pout.

"And ye should not pout your pretty lips at me if ye are not wanting me to kiss them!" he added, suiting the action to the word.

"But of course I do!" cried my lady, returning the kiss with fervour. "Nay, Miles, tell me."

"I see ye mean to have the whole tale out of me, so——"

"To be sure I do!" she nodded.

He laid a warning finger on her lips and summoned up a mighty frown.

"Now will ye be interrupting, me lady?"

Not a whit abashed, she bit the finger, pushed it away, and folding her hands in her lap, cast her eyes meekly heaven-wards.

With a twinkle in his own eyes the Irishman continued:

"Well, alanna, ye must know that yesterday evening I was at Kilroy's on a matter of business—and that reminds me, Molly, we had a hand or two at faro and the like before I left, and I had very distressing luck——"

On a sudden my lady's demure air vanished.

"Is that so, Miles? I make no doubt the stakes were prodigious high? Pray, how much have you lost?"

"Whisht, darlin', 'tis a mere trifle, I assure you. . . . Well, as I was saying, on me way home, what should happen but that we be held up by one of these highwaymen——"

My lady's eyes widened in horror, and two little hands clutched at his coat.

"Oh, Miles!"

His arm tightened round her waist.

"Sure, asthore, I'm still alive to tell the tale, though 'tis not far I'll be getting with you interrupting at every moment!"

"But, Miles, how terrible! You might have been killed! And you never told me! 'Twas monstrous wicked of you, darling!"

"Faith, Molly, how should I be telling you when 'twas yourself that was fast asleep? Now will you whisht?"

She nodded obediently, and dimpled.

"Well, as I say, here was this man standing in the road, pointing his pistol at me. But will ye believe me, my love, when I tell you that same pistol was as empty as—my own?" Here he was shaken with laughter. "Lud, Molly, 'twas the drollest thing! I had me pistol in me hand, knowing 'twas unloaded, and wondering what the devil, saving your presence, was to be next, when the idea struck me that I should try to bluff me fine sir. So I cried out that his pistol was unloaded, and completely took him by surprise! Sure he hadn't time to ask himself how the devil I should be knowing that! He dropped it on the road. Afther——"

"Miles, you are becoming very Irish!"

"Never say so, alanna. *After* that 'twas simple enough, and me lord gave in. He held out his hands for me to bind—and here's where 'tis puzzling, Molly—I saw that they were a prodigious sight too white and fine for an ordinary highwayman. So I taxed him with it——"

" 'Twas a gentleman in disguise! How splendid, Miles!"

"Will ye hold your tongue, asthore, and not be spoiling me story on me?"

"Oh, indeed I am sorry! I will be good!"

"—— and he started and seemed monstrous put out. What's more, me dear, I heard him speak to his mare in an ordinary, gentleman's voice. Molly, ye never saw the like of that same mare! The sweetest——"

"Pray, never mind the mare, dear! I am all agog to hear about the gentleman-highwayman!"

"Very well, me love, though 'twas a prodigious fine mare —When I heard him speak, it flashed across me brain that I knew him—no, ye don't, Molly!" His hand was over her mouth as he spoke, and her eyes danced madly. "But I could not for the life of me think where I had heard that voice: 'twas but the one word I heard him speak, ye understand, and when I held his wrists I felt that 'twas no stranger. And yet 'tis impossible. When I got him within the coach——"

"How imprudent! He might have——"

"Whisht now! When I got him within the coach I tried to worm his identity out of him, but 'twas to no avail. But when I told him he would have to appear before me to-day, he went off into a fit of laughing, till I wondered what he was at, at all. And not another word could I get out of him after beyond 'Yes, sir,' and 'No, sir'. Still, I felt that 'twas a gentleman all the same, so I——"

He was enveloped in a rapturous embrace.

"You dear Miles! You let him escape?"

"Sure, alanna, is it meself that would be doing the like? And me a Justice of the Peace withal? I told them not to handcuff me lord."

"Oh, I do so wish you had let him escape! But if 'tis really a gentleman, you will?"

"I will not then, asthore. I'll be sending him to await the Assizes."

"You are very cruel. then."

"But, me darlin'———"

"And I wish to get off your knee."

He drew her close.

"I'll see what can be done for your protégé, Molly. But don't be forgetting he tried to kill the only husband you have!" He watched the effect of this with that humorous twinkle in his eye. But my lady was not to be put off.

"With an empty pistol? Fie on you, Miles! And may I hide behind the screen while you question him?"

"Ye may not."

"But I wish so much to see him!"

O'Hara shook his head with an air of finality she knew full well. However easy-going and good-natured her husband might be, there were times when he was impervious to all blandishments. So after darkly hinting that she would be nearer than he imagined, she gave up the contest to go and visit young Master David in his nursery.

*   *   *   *   *

For some time in lock-up Carstares had cudgelled his brain to think out a possible mode of escape next day, but try as he might he could light on nothing. If only Miles were not to question him! It was hardly likely that he would be allowed to retain his mask, yet therein lay his only chance of preserving his incognito. He prayed that by some merciful providence O'Hara would either fail to recognise him or would at least pretend that he did not. Having decided that there was nothing further to be done in the matter he lay down on his extremely hard pallet, and went to sleep as if he had not a care in the world.

Next morning, after a long and wordy argument with the

head gaoler on the subject of masks, he was haled in triumph
to the house.

As the little cavalcade was about to ascend the steps that
led to the front door, my Lady O'Hara came gaily forth carrying a basket and a pair of scissors, and singing a snatch of
song. At the sight of the highwayman the song broke off and
her red lips formed a long-drawn "Oh!" She stood quite still
on the top step, gazing down at my lord. The two gaolers
stood aside to allow her to come down, just as a greyhound
darted up the steps and flung itself against her in an exuber-
ance of joy. My lady, none too securely balanced, reeled; the
basket fell from her arm, her foot missed the next step, and
she tumbled headlong down. But in the flash of an eyelid
Carstares had sprung forward and received her in his arms.
He lowered her gently to the ground. "I trust you are not
hurt, madam?" he asked, and retrieved her basket, handing it
to her.

Molly took it with a smile.

"I thank you sir, not at all; though I fear I should have
injured myself quite considerably had you not been so swift
in catching me. 'Twas most kind of you, I am sure!" She extended her small hand, and her eyes devoured him.

For a moment my lord hesitated, and then, sweeping off
his hat, he bowed low over the hand.

" 'Twas less than nothing, madam," he said in his own cultivated voice. "I beg you will dismiss it from your mind." He
straightened himself as the gaolers came forward, and put on
his hat again.

Lady O'Hara stepped aside and watched them disappear
into the house. Her cheeks were rather flushed, and her eyes
suspiciously bright. Suddenly she nodded her head decisively,
and throwing away her luckless basket, hurried across the
lawn and entered the house through a long window.

My lord was conducted to the library, where O'Hara sat
awaiting him, and slouched forward with his hands thrust
deep into his pockets and his hat still on his head.

The head gaoler eyed him gloomily, and looked pained
when Carstares with studied boorishness leaned carelessly
against a fine carved table.

"We 'ave refrained from 'andcuffin' pris'ner, sir, at your
horders," he said, in a tone that warned O'Hara that should
harm come of it, on his head be the blame.

Miles nodded.

"Quite right," he said pleasantly, and glanced at the cloaked and masked figure before him with more suspicion than ever.

"But I regrets to 'ave to report very hobstinate be'aviour on part of pris'ner, sir," added the gaoler impressively.

"Indeed?" said Miles gravely. "How so?"

Jack controlled an insane desire to laugh, and listened to the gaoler's complaint.

"You see the pris'ner, sir, with that great mask on 'is face? Afore we set out to come 'ere, I told 'im to take it hoff. And 'e refoosed, sir. Seeing as 'ow you gave no horders, I did not force 'im to hobey."

"Ah! . . . Your name, please?"

"John Smith, sir," answered Carstares promptly and hoarsely.

O'Hara wrote it down with a sceptical smile on his lips that Jack did not quite like.

"Perhaps ye will have the goodness to unmask?"

There was a momentary silence.

"Why, sir, I thought ye might allow me to keep it on?"

"Did ye now? I will not be allowing any such thing."

"But, sir——"

" 'Tis impossible. Off with it!"

"Sir——"

"If ye don't take it off, I shall ask these men to assist ye," warned Miles.

"May I not speak with ye alone, sir?" pleaded Jack.

By now O'Hara was greatly intrigued.

"Ye may not. Unmask!" He was leaning half across the table, his eyes fixed on Jack's face.

With a quaint little laugh that made O'Hara's brows contract swiftly, my lord shrugged his shoulders French fashion and obeyed. The mask and hat were tossed lightly on to the table, and Miles found himself gazing into a pair of blue eyes that met his half defiantly, half imploringly. He drew in his breath sharply and the thin ivory rule he held snapped suddenly between his fingers. And at that crucial moment a door behind him that had stood ajar was pushed open, and my Lady O'Hara came tripping into the room.

The two goalers and her husband turned at once to see who it was, while Jack, who had recognised her, but had not the least idea who she was, fell to dusting his boots with his handkerchief.

O'Hara rose, and for once looked severe.

"What——" he began, and stopped, for without so much as a glance at him, my lady ran towards the prisoner, crying:

"Harry! Oh, Harry!"

Jack gathered that he was the person addressed, and instantly made her an elaborate leg.

The next moment she was tugging at the lapels of his coat, with her face upturned to his.

"Harry, you WICKED boy!" she cried, and added beneath her breath: "My name is Molly!"

A laugh sprang to my lord's eyes and his beautiful smile appeared.

In a stupefied fashion O'Hara watched him steal an arm about her waist, and place a hand beneath her chin. The next instant a kiss was planted full on the little lady's lips, and he heard Jack Carstares' voice exclaim:

"Fie on you, Molly, for a spoil-sport! Here had I fooled Miles to the top of my bent—and 'pon rep! he scarce knows me yet!"

My lady disengaged herself, blushing.

"Oh, Miles, you do know Harry—my cousin Harry?"

O'Hara collected his scattered wits and rose nobly to the occasion.

"Of course I do, me dear, though at first he gave me such a shock, I was near dumbfounded. Ye are a mad, scatter-brained fellow to play such a thrick upon us, devil take ye!" He laid his hands on Jack's shoulders. "Pray, what did ye do it for, boy?"

Jack's brain worked swiftly.

"Why, Miles, never tell me you've forgot our wager! Did I not swear I'd have you at a disadvantage—to be even with your for that night at Jasper's? But what must you do but see my pistol was unloaded and make me lose my wager! Still, 'twas worth that and a night in gaol to see your face when I unmasked!"

O'Hara shook him slightly, laughing, and turned to the two amazed gaolers. The senior gaoler met his humorous glance with a cold and indignant stare, and gave a prodigious sniff.

"Me good fellows," drawled Miles, "I'm mighty sorry ye've been worried over me young cousin here. He's fooled us all it appears, but now there's nought to be done in the matter, though I've a mind to send him to await the next sessions!" He slipped a guinea into each curiously ready palm, and replied to the head gaoler's haughty bow with a pleasant nod. In silence he watched them leave the room shaking their heads over the incomprehensible ways of the gentry. Then he turned and looked across at Carstares.

CHAPTER X

Lady O'Hara Retires

FOR a long minute silence reigned, all three actors in the little comedy listening to the heavy footsteps retreating down the passage, Carstares with one arm still around my lady's waist and a rather strained look on his face. Molly instinctively felt that something beyond her ken was in the air, and glanced fearfully up at the white face above her. The expression in the blue eyes fixed on her husband made her turn sharply to look at him. She found that he was staring at my lord as though he saw a ghost. She wanted to speak, to relieve the tension, but all words stuck in her throat, and she could only watch the *dénouement* breathlessly. At last O'Hara moved, coming slowly toward them, reading John's countenance. Some of the wonder went out of his face, and, as if he sensed the other's agony of mind, he smiled suddenly and laid his hands once more on the straight, stiff shoulders.

"Jack ye rascal, what do ye mean by hugging and kissing me wife under me very eyes?"

Molly all at once remembered the position of her "Cousin Harry's" arm, and gave a little gasp, whisking herself away.

My lord put out his hands and strove to thrust his friend off.

"Miles, don't forget—don't forget—what I am!"

The words were forced out, but his head was held high.

"Tare an' ouns, man! And is it meself that'll be caring what ye may or may not be? Oh, Jack, Jack, I'm so pleased to see ye, that I can scarce realise 'tis yourself I am looking at! When did ye come to England, and what-a-plague are you doing in that costume?" He jerked his head to where John's mask lay, and wrung the hand he held as though he would never stop.

"I've been in England a year. As to the mask——!" He shrugged and laughed.

Lady O'Hara pushed in between them.

"But please I do not understand!" she said plaintively.

Carstares bowed over her hand.

"May I be permitted to thank you for your kindly intervention, my lady? And to congratulate Miles on his marriage?"

She dimpled charmingly and curtsied. Her husband caught her round the waist.

"Ay, the saucy minx! Oh, me cousin Harry, forsooth! If it had been anyone but Jack I should be angry with ye, asthore, for 'twas a wicked thrick to play entirely!"

She patted his hand and smiled across at Jack.

"Of course, I would never have done such a forward thing had I not known that he was indeed a gentleman—and had he not saved me from sudden death!" she added as an afterthought.

Miles looked sharply round at her and then at Carstares.

"What's this?"

"My lady exaggerates," smiled my lord. " 'Tis merely that I had the honour to catch her as she fell down the steps this morning."

O'Hara looked relieved.

"Ye are not hurt, alanna?"

"Gracious, no! But I had to do something to show my gratitude—and I was sure that you would never expose *my* fraud—so I——— But," as a sudden thought struck her, "you seem to *know* my highwayman!"

"Sure an' I do, Molly. 'Tis none other than Jack Carstares of whom ye've often heard me speak!"

She turned round eyes of wonderment upon my lord.

"Can it be—is it possible that you are my husband's dearest friend—Lord John!"

Jack flushed and bowed.

"I was once—madam," he said stffly.

"Once!" she scoffed. "Oh, if you could but hear him speak of you! But I'll let you hear him speak *to* you, which perhaps you'll enjoy more. I know you've a prodigious great deal to say to one another, so I shall run away and leave you alone." She smiled graciously upon him, blew an airy kiss to her husband and went quickly out of the room.

Carstares closed the door behind her and came back to O'Hara, who had flung himself back into his chair, trying, manlike, to conceal the excitement he was feeling.

"Come, sit ye down, Jack, and let me have the whole story!"

My lord divested himself of his long cloak and shook out his hitherto tucked-up ruffles. From the pocket of his elegant scarlet riding coat he drew a snuff-box, which he opened languidly. With his eyes resting quizzically on O'Hara's face, he took a delicate pinch of snuff and minced across the room.

Miles laughed.

"What's this?"

"This, my dear friend, is Sir Anthony Ferndale, Bart.!" He bowed with great flourish.

"Ye look it. But come over here, Sir Anthony Ferndale, Bart., and tell me everything."

Jack perched on the edge of the desk and swung his leg.

"Well really, I do not think there is much to tell that you do not already know, Miles. You know all about Dare's card-party, for instance, precisely six years ago?"

" 'Tis just exactly what I do not know!" retorted O'Hara.

"You surprise me! I thought the tale was rife."

"Now, Jack, will ye have done drawling at me? Don't be forgetting I'm your friend——"

"But are you? If you know the truth about me, do you feel inclined to call me friend?"

"There never was a time when I would not have been proud to call ye friend, as ye would very well have known, had ye been aught but a damned young hothead! I heard that crazy tale about the card-party, but do ye think I believed it?"

"It was the obvious thing to do."

"Maybe, but I fancy I know ye just a little too well to believe any cock-and-bull story I'm told about ye. And even if I had been fool enough to have believed it, do ye think I'd be going back on ye? Sure, 'tis a poor friend I'd be!"

Jack stared down at the toe of his right boot in silence.

"I know something more than we guessed happened at that same party, and I have me suspicions, but 'tis your affair, and whatever ye did ye had your reasons for. But, Jack, why in the name of wonder must ye fly off to the devil alone knows where, without so much as a good-bye to anyone?"

Carstares never raised his eyes from the contemplation of that boot. He spoke with difficulty.

"Miles—in my place—would you not have done the same?"

"Well——"

"You know you would. Was it likely that I should inflict myself on you at such a time? What would you have thought of me had I done so?"

O'Hara brought his hand down smartly on the other's knee.

"I'd have thought ye less of a young fool! I would have gone away with ye, and nothing would have stopped me!"

Jack looked up and met his eyes.

"I know," he said. " 'Twas the thought of that—and—and —I could not be sure. Last night—last night—I was horribly afraid. . . ."

The hand on his knee tightened.

"Ye foolish boy! Ye foolish boy!"

Bit by bit he drew the story of the past six years out of Carstares, and though it was a very modified version, Miles understood his friend well enough to read between the lines.

"And now," said Jack, when the recital was over, "tell me about yourself. When did you marry the attractive lady whom I have just been kissing?"

"Ye rogue! I married Molly three years ago. 'Tis a real darling she is, isn't she? And upstairs there's a little chap— your godson."

"You lucky fellow! My godson, you say! Could you not find anyone more worthy for that? I want to see him."

"So ye shall presently. Have ye seen Richard?"

"A year ago I held up his coach. 'Twas dark, and I could scarce see him, but I thought he seemed aged."

"Aged! Ye wouldn't be afther knowing him! 'Tis an old man he is. Though I swear 'tis no wonder with that hussy about the house! Lord, Jack, you were well out of that affair with your ladyship!"

Carstares nursed his foot reflectively.

"Lavinia? What ails her?"

"Nought that I know of, save it be her shrewish temper. 'Tis a dog's life she leads poor Dick."

"Do you mean to say she does not love Dick?"

"I cannot say—sometimes she's as affectionate as you please, but at others she treats him to a fine exhibition of rage. And the money she spends! Of course, she married him for what she could get. There was never anything else to count with her."

Jack sat very still.

"And anyone but a young fool like yourself would have seen that!"

A gleam of amusement shot into the wistful blue eyes.

"Probably. Yourself, for instance?"

O'Hara chuckled.

"Oh, ay, I knew! 'Twas the money she was after all along; and now there's not so much, it seems, as Dick won't touch a penny that belongs to you."

"M'm. Warburton told me. Foolish of him."

A grunt was the sole response.

Jack's eye narrowed a little as he gazed out of the window.

"So Lavinia never cared? Lord, what a mix-up! And Dick?"

"I'm afraid he still does."

"Poor old Dick! Devil take the woman! Does she bully him? I know what he is—always ready to give in."

"I am not so sure. Yet I'll swear if 'twere not for John his life would be a misery. He misses you, Jack."

"Who is John?"

"Did not Warburton tell you? John is the hope of the house. He's four and a half, and as spoilt a little rascal as you could wish for."

"Dick's child? Good Lord!"

"Ay, Dick's child and your nephew." He broke off and looked into the other's face. "Jack, cannot this mystery be cleared up? Couldn't ye go back?" He was clasping Jack's hand, but it was withdrawn, and the eyes looking down into his were suddenly bored and a little cold.

"I know of no mystery," said Carstares.

"Jack, old man, will ye be afther shutting me out of your confidence?"

A faint, sweet smile curved the fine lips.

"Let us talk of the weather, Miles, or my mare. Anything rather than this painful subject."

With an impatient movement O'Hara flung back his chair and strode over to the window with his back to my lord. Jack's eyes followed him seriously.

"If ye cannot trust me, sure I've no more to say, thin!" flashed O'Hara. "It seems ye do not value your friends too highly!"

My lord said never a word. But the hand that rested on the desk clenched suddenly. O'Hara wheeled about and came back to his side.

"Sure, Jack, I never meant that! Forgive me bad temper!"

Carstares slipped off the table and straightened himself, linking his arm in the Irishman's.

"Whisht, Miles, as you'd say yourself," he laughed, "I know that. 'Tis not that I don't trust you, but——"

"I understand. I'll not ask ye any more about it at all. Instead, answer me this: what made ye come out with unloaded pistols?"

The laugh died out of Carstares' face.

"Oh, just carelessness!" he answered shortly, and he thought of the absent Jim with a tightening of the lips.

" 'Twas that very reason with meself thin!"

Jack stared at him.

"Miles, don't tell me yours were unloaded, too?"

" 'Deed an' they were! Ecod, Jack! 'tis the best joke I've heard for a twelvemonth." They both started to laugh. "Sure 'twas bluff on my part, Jack, when I told ye yours was unloaded. And me lady was determined to set you free from the moment I told her all about it this morning. We were sure ye were no ordinary highwayman, though I was a fool not to have known ye right away. But now I have found ye out, ye'll stay with us—Cousin Harry?"

"I cannot thank you enough, Miles, but I will not do that. I must get back to Jim."

"And who the devil is Jim?"

"My servant. He'll be worried nigh to death over me. Nay, do not press me, I could not stay here, Miles. You must see for yourself 'tis impossible—Jack Carstares does not exist; only Anthony Ferndale is left."

"Jack, dear man, can I not——"

"No, Miles, you can do nothing, though 'tis like you to want to help, and I do thank you. But—oh well! . . . What about my mare?"

"Plague take me if I'd not forgotten! Jack, that scoundrel of mine let her strain her fetlock. I'm demmed sorry."

"Poor Jenny! I'll swear she gave him an exciting ride, though."

"I'll be trying to buy her off ye, Jack, if I see much of her. 'Tis a little beauty she is."

"I'm not selling, though I intended to ask you to keep her, if——"

A quick pressure on his arm arrested him.

"That will do! I'm too heavy for her anyway."

"So was that devil of a groom you put on her."

"Ay. I'm a fool."

"I always knew that."

"Whisht now, Jack! Ye'll have to take one of my nags while she heals, if ye won't stay with us. Can ye trust her to me for a week, do ye suppose?"

"I don't know. It seems as though I must—oh, I retract, I retract. You are altogether too large, the day is too hot, and my cravat too nicely tied—— Egad, Miles! I wish—oh, I *wish* we were boys again, and—— Yes. When may I see your son and heir?"

"Sure, ye may come now and find Molly, who'll be aching for the sight of you. Afther you, Sir Anthony Ferndale, Bart.!"

CHAPTER XI

My Lord Turns Rescuer
and Comes Nigh Ending His Life

LATE that afternoon Carstares left Thurze House on one of his friend's horses. He waved a very regretful farewell to O'Hara and his lady, promising to let them know his whereabouts and to visit them again soon. O'Hara had extracted a solemn promise that if ever he got into difficulties he would let him know:

"For I'm not letting ye drift gaily out of me life again, and that's flat."

Jack had assented gladly enough—to have a friend once more was such bliss—and had given Miles the name of the inn and the village where he would find him, for O'Hara had insisted on bringing the mare over himself. So Carstares rode off to Trencham and to Jim, with the memory of a very hearty handshake in his mind. He smiled a little as he thought of his friend's words when he had shown himself reluctant to give the required promise:

"Ye obstinate young devil, ye'll do as I say, and no nonsense, or ye don't leave this house!"

For six years no one had ordered him to obey; it had been he who had done all the ordering. Somehow it was very pleasant to be told what to do, especially by Miles.

He turned down a lane and wondered what Jim was thinking. That he was waiting at the Green Man, he was certain, for those had been his orders. He was annoyed with the man over the incident of the pistols, for he had inspected them and discovered that they were indeed unloaded. Had his captor been other than O'Hara, on whom he could not fire, such carelessness might have proved his undoing. Apart from that, culpable negligence always roused his wrath. A rather warm twenty minutes was in store for Salter.

For quite an hour Carstares proceeded on his way with no mishaps nor adventures, and then, suddenly, as he rounded a corner of a deserted road—little more than a cart-track—an extraordinary sight met his eyes. In the middle of the road stood a coach, and by it, covering the men on the box with two large pistols, was a seedy-looking ruffian, while two others were engaged in what appeared to be a life-and-death struggle at the coach door.

Jack reined in his horse and rose in his stirrups to obtain a better view. Then his eyes flashed, and he whistled softly to himself. For the cause of all the turmoil was a slight, graceful girl of not more than nineteen or twenty. She was frenziedly resisting the efforts of her captors to drag her to another coach further up the road. Jack could see that she was dark and very lovely.

Another, elderly lady, was most valiantly impeding operations by clawing and striking at one of the men's arms, scolding and imploring all in one breath. Jack's gaze went from her to a still, silent figure at the side of the road in the shadow of the hedge, evidently the stage-manager. "It seems I must take a hand in this," he told himself, and laughed joyously as he fixed on his mask and dismounted. He tethered his mount to a young sapling, took a pistol from its holster, and ran softly and swiftly under the lea of the hedge up to the scene of disaster, just as the man who covered the unruly and vociferous pair on the box made ready to fire.

Jack's bullet took him neatly in the neck, and without a sound he crumpled up, one of his pistols exploding harmlessly as it fell to earth.

With an oath the silent onlooker wheeled round to face the point of my lord's gleaming blade.

Carstares drew in his breath sharply in surprise as he saw the white face of his Grace of Andover.

"Damn you!" said Tracy calmly, and sprang back, whipping out his own rapier.

"Certainly," agreed Jack pleasantly. "On guard, M. le Duc!"

Tracy's lips curled back in a snarl. His eyes were almost shut. Over his shoulder he ordered curtly:

"Keep watch over the girl. I will attend to this young jackanapes."

On the word the blades clashed.

Jack's eyes danced with the sheer joy of battle, and his point snicked in and out wickedly. He knew Tracy of old for an expert swordsman, and he began warily.

The girl's persecutors retained a firm hold on either arm,

but all their thoughts were centered on the duel. The men on the box got out their blunderbuss, ready to fire should the need arise, and the girl herself watched breathlessly, red lips apart, and eyes aglow with fright, indignation, and excitement. As for the old lady, she positively bobbed up and down shrieking encouragement to Carstares.

The blades hissed continuously against one another; time after time the Duke thrust viciously, and ever his point was skilfully parried. He was absolutely calm, and his lips sneered. Who it was that he was fighting, he had not the faintest idea; he only knew that his opponent had recognised him and must be speedily silenced. Therefore he fought with deadly grimness and purpose. Carstares, on the other hand, had no intention of killing his Grace. He had never liked him in the old days, but he was far too good-natured to contemplate any serious bloodshed. He was so used to Tracy's little affairs that he had not been filled with surprise when he discovered who the silent figure was. He did not like interfering with Belmanoir, but, on the other hand, he could no more stand by and see a woman assaulted than he could fly. So he fought on with the idea of disarming his Grace, so as to have him at a disadvantage and to be able to command his withdrawal from the scene. Once he feinted cleverly, and lunged, and a little blood trickled down over the Duke's hand. No sign made Belmanoir, except that his eyelids flickered a moment and his play became more careful.

Once the Duke thrust in tierce and Jack's sword arm wavered an instant, and a splash of crimson appeared on his sleeve. He, for the most part, remained on the defensive, waiting for the Duke to tire. Soon his Grace's breath began to come unevenly and fast, and beads of moisture started on his forehead. Yet never did the sneer fade nor his temper go; he had himself well in hand, and although his face was livid, and his brain on fire with fury, no trace of it showed itself in his sword-play.

Then Carstares changed his tactics, and began to put into practice all the arts and subtleties of fence that he had learnt abroad. He seemed made of steel and set on wires, so agile and untireable was he. Time after time he leapt nimbly aside, evading some wicked thrust, and all the while he was driving his Grace back and back. He was not panting, and now and again he laughed softly and happily. The blood from the wound on his arm was dripping steadily on the ground, yet it seemed to Tracy to affect him not at all. But Jack himself knew that he was losing strength rapidly, and must make an end.

Suddenly he feinted, and fell back. Tracy saw his advantage and pressed forward within the wavering sword-point.

The next instant his sword was whirled from his grasp, and he lay on the ground, unhurt but helpless, gazing up at the masked face and at the shortened rapier. How he had been thrown he did not know, but that his opponent was a past master in the art of fence he was perfectly sure.

My lord gave a little chuckle and twisted a handkerchief about his wounded arm.

"I am aware, m'sieur, that this is most unusual—and, in duels—forbidden. But I am sure milor' will agree that the circumstances are also—most unusual—and the odds—almost overwhelming!" He turned his head to the two men, one of whom released his hold on the girl's arm and started forward.

"Oh, no!" drawled my lord, shaking his head. "Another step and I spit your master where he lies."

"Stand," said his Grace calmly.

"*Bien!* Throw your arms down here at my feet, and—ah —release Mademoiselle!"

They made no move to obey, and my lord shrugged deprecatingly, lowering his point to Tracy's throat.

"*Eh bien!*"

They still hesitated, casting anxious glances at their master.

"Obey," ordered the Duke.

Each man threw down a pistol, eyeing Jack furtively, while the girl ran to her aunt, who began to soothe and fuss over her.

Jack stifled a yawn.

"It is not my intention to remain here all night. Neither am I a child—or a fool. *Dépêchez!*"

Belmanoir saw that the coachman had his blunderbuss ready and was only too eager to fire it, and he knew that the game was up. He turned his head towards the reluctant bullies who looked to him for orders.

"Throw down everything!" he advised.

Two more pistols and two daggers joined their comrades.

"A thousand thanks!" bowed my lord, running a quick eye over the men. "M. le Duc, I pray you be still. Now, you with the large nose—yes, *mon ami,* you—go pick up the pistol our defunct friend dropped."

The man indicated slouched over to the dead body and flung another pistol on to the heap.

My lord shook his head impatiently.

"Mais non. Have I not said that I am not entirely a fool? The unexploded pistol, please. You will place it here, *doucement.* Very good."

His eye travelled to the men on the box. The coachman touched his hat and cried:

"I'm ready, sir."

"It is very well. Be so good as to keep these gentlemen covered, but do not fire until I give the order. And now, M. le Duc, have I your parole that you will return swiftly from whence you came, leaving this lady unmolested, an I permit you to rise?"

Tracy moved his head impatiently.

"I have no choice."

"Monsieur, that is not an answer. Have I your parole?"

"Yes, curse you!"

"But certainly," said Jack politely. "Pray rise."

He rested his sword-point on the ground, and watched Tracy struggle to his feet.

For an instant the Duke stood staring at him, with face slightly out-thrust.

"I almost think I know you," he said softly, caressingly.

Jack's French accent became a shade more pronounced.

"It is possible. I at least have the misfortune to know monsieur by sight."

Tracy ignored the insult, and continued very, very silkily:

"One thing is certain: I shall know you again—if I meet you!"

Even as the words left his mouth Jack saw the pistol in his hand and sprang quickly to one side, just in time to escape a shot that would have gone straight through his head. As it was, it caught him in his left shoulder.

"Do not fire!" he called sharply to the coachman, and bowed to his Grace. "As I was saying, m'sieu—do not let me detain you, I beg."

The Duke's green eyes flashed venom for a minute, and then the heavy lids descended over them again, and he returned the bow exaggeratedly.

"*Au revoir,* monsieur," he smiled, and bent to pick up his sword.

"It will—not be necessary for—m'sieu to—take his sword," said Jack. "I have a—desire to keep—it as a—souvenir. Yes."

"As you will, monsieur," replied Tracy carelessly, and walked away to his coach, his men following close on his heels.

My lord stood leaning heavily on his sword, watching them go, and not until the coach had swung out of sight did he give way to the weakness that was overwhelming him. Then he reeled and would have fallen, had it not been for two cool hands that caught his, steadying him.

A tremulous, husky voice sounded in his ears:

"You are hurt! Ah, sir, you are hurt for my sake!"

With a great effort Jack controlled the inclination to swoon, and lifted the girl's hand shakily to his lips.

"It is a—pleasure—mademoiselle," he managed to gasp. "Now—you may—I think—proceed in safety."

Diana slipped an arm under his shoulder and cast an anxious glance at the footman, hurrying towards them.

"Quick!" she commanded. "Sir, you are faint! You must allow my servant to assist you to the coach."

Jack forced a smile.

"It is—nothing—I assure you—pray do not—I——" and he fainted comfortably away into stout Thomas's arms.

"Carry him into the coach, Thomas!" ordered the girl. "Mind his arm, and—oh! his poor shoulder. Aunt, have you something to bind his wounds with?"

Miss Betty hurried forward.

"My darling child, what an escape! The dear, brave gentleman! Do have a care, Thomas! Yes, lay him on the seat."

My lord was lowered gently on to the cushions, and Miss Betty fluttered over to him like a distracted hen. Then Diana told Thomas to take charge of my lord's horse that they could see, quietly nibbling the grass further down the road, stooped and picked up his Grace of Andover's sword, with its curiously wrought hilt, and jumped into the coach to help Miss Betty to attend to Jack's wounds.

The slash on the arm was not serious, but where the pistol had taken him was very ugly-looking. While she saw to that, Miss Betty loosened the cravat and removed my lord's mask.

"Di, see what a handsome boy 'tis! The poor brave gentleman! What a lucky thing he came up! If only this bleeding would stop!" So she ran on, hunting wildly for her salts.

Diana looked up as her aunt finished, and studied the pale face lying against the dark cushions. She noted the firm, beautifully curved mouth, the aristocratic nose and delicately pencilled eyebrows, with a little thrill. The duel had set her every nerve tingling; she was filled with admiration for her preserver, and the sight of his sensitive, handsome countenance did nothing to dispel that admiration.

She held the salts to his nostrils and watched eagerly for some sign of life. But none was forthcoming, and she had to be content with placing cushions beneath his injured shoulder, and guarding him as best she might from the jolts caused by the uneven surface of the road.

Miss Betty bustled about and did all she could to stanch the bleeding, and when they had comfortably settled my lord, she sat down upon the seat opposite and nodded decisively.

"We can do no more, my dear—but, yes—certainly bathe his forehead with your lavender water. Dear me, what an escape! I must say I would never have thought it of Mr. Everard! One would say we were living in the Stone Age! The wretch!"

Diana shuddered.

"I knew he was dreadful, but never *how* dreadful! How can he have found out when we were to leave Bath—and why did he waylay us so near home? Oh, I shall never be safe again!"

"Nonsense, my dear! Fiddlesticks! You saw how easily he was vanquished. Depend upon it, he will realise that he has made a bad mistake to try to abduct you, and we shall not be worried with him again."

With this comfortable assurance, she nodded again and leant back against the cushions, watching her niece's ministrations with a professional and slightly amused air.

CHAPTER XII

My Lord Dictates a Letter and Receives a Visitor

MY LORD came sighing back to life. He opened his eyes wearily, and turned his head. A faint feeling of surprise stole over him. He was in a room he had never been in before, and by the window, busy with some needlework, sat a little old lady who was somehow vaguely familiar.

"Who—are—you?" he asked, and was annoyed to find his voice so weak.

The little lady jumped, and came across to him.

"Praise be to God!" she ejaculated. "Likewise, bless the boy! The fever is passed." She laid a thin hand on his brow, and smiled down into his wondering eyes.

"As cool as a cucumber, dear boy. What a mercy!"

It was a long time since anyone had called Jack dear, or boy. He returned the smile feebly and closed his eyes.

"I—do not—understand—anything," he murmured drowsily.

"Never trouble your head then. Just go to sleep."

He considered this gravely for a moment. It seemed sensible enough, and he was so very, very tired. He shut his eyes with a little sigh.

*   *   *   *   *

When he awoke again it was morning of the next day, and the sun streamed in the window, making him blink.

Someone rustled forward, and he saw it was the lady who had called him dear and bidden him go to sleep.

He smiled and a very thin hand came out of the bedclothes.

"But who are you?" he demanded a little querulously.

Miss Betty patted his hand gently.

"Still worrying your poor head over that? I am Di's Aunt Betty—though, to be sure, you don't know who Di is!"

106

Remembrance was coming back to my lord.

"Why—why—you are the lady in the coach!—Tracy—I remember!"

"Well, I know nought of Tracy, but I'm the lady in the coach."

"And the other——"

"That was Diana Beauleigh, my niece—the pet. You will see her when you are better."

"But—but—where am I, madam?"

"Now don't get excited, dear boy!"

"I'm thirty!" protested Jack with a wicked twinkle.

"I should not have thought it, but thirty's a boy to me, in any case!" retorted Miss Betty, making him laugh. "You are in Mr. Beauleigh's house—Di's father, and my brother. And here you will stay until you are quite recovered!"

Jack raised himself on his elbow, grimacing at the pain the movement caused him.

"Egad, madam! have I been here long?" he demanded.

Very firmly was he pushed back on to his pillows.

"Will you be still? A nice thing 'twould be if you were to aggravate that wound of yours! You will have been here a week to-morrow. Bless my heart, what ails the boy!" For Jack's face took on an expression of incredulous horror.

"A *week*, madam? Never say so!"

" 'Tis as true as I stand here. And a nice fright you have given us, what with nearly dying, and raving about your Dicks and your Jims!"

My lord glanced up sharply.

"Oh! So I—talked?"

"Talk? Well, yes, if you can call that mixture of foreign jargon talking. Now you must be still and wait till the doctor comes again."

For a while Carstares lay in silence. He thought of Jim and smiled a little. "I could not have thought of a better punishment had I tried," he told himself, and then frowned. "Poor fellow! He'll be off his head with fright over me. Miss—er—Betty?"

"Well, and are you not asleep yet?"

"Asleep, madam? Certainly not!" he said with dignity. "I must write a letter."

" 'Deed, an' you shall not!"

"But I must! 'Tis monstrous important, madam."

She shook her head resolutely.

"Not until Mr. Jameson gives permission," she said firmly.

Jack struggled up, biting his lip.

"Then I shall get up!" he threatened.

In an instant she was by his side.

"No, no! Now lie down and be good!"

"I will not lie down and be good!"

"Then I shan't let you touch a pen for weeks!"

Jack became very masterful and frowned direfully upon her.

"Madam, I insist on being allowed to write that letter!"

"Sir, I insist on your lying down!"

He controlled a twitching lip.

"Woe betide you unless you bring me pen and paper, Miss Betty!"

"But, dear boy, reflect! You could not use your arm."

"I will use it!" replied Jack indomitably, but he sank back on the pillows with his eyes closed and a tiny furrow of pain between his straight brows.

"I told you so!" scolded Miss Betty, not without a note of triumph in her voice, and proceeded to rearrange the disorderly coverlet.

The blue eyes opened wide, pleadingly.

"Madam, indeed 'tis very important."

She could not withstand that look.

"Well," she compromised, "I'll not let you write yourself, that's certain——but could you not dictate to me?"

Jack brightened, and caught her hand to his lips.

"Miss Betty, you are an angel!" he told her.

"Ah, now, get along with you!" She hurried away to fetch paper and ink.

When she returned she found him plucking impatiently at the sheet, and frowning.

"I am ready," she said.

"Thank you, madam. 'Tis very kind in you——"

"Nonsense!"

He laughed weakly.

"I want to write to my servant, to bid him bring my baggage to the nearest inn——"

"That will I not! I shall tell him to bring it here."

"But, Miss Betty, I cannot possibly trespass upon——"

"Will you have done? Trespass indeed!"

"I perceive I shall be much put upon," sighed Jack, and watched her lightning smile.

"You BOY! Will you dictate?"

"Very well, ma'am. No, I have changed my mind. I'll have it writ to a friend, please: 'Dear Miles. . . . True to my promise . . . I write to you. . . . In case . . . you should be worried . . . over my disappearance . . . be it known . . . that I am at—' pray, madam, where am I?"

"Horton Manor, Littledean," she replied, writing it down.

"Thank you. 'I had the misfortune to injure my shoulder in a——' "

" 'And arm,' " put in the scribe, inexorably.

" 'And arm, in a fight . . . and a certain very . . . kind lady—' "

"I refuse to write that rubbish! 'One of the ladies whom I rescued——' "

"Good heavens, madam, you've not put that?" cried Jack horrified.

She smiled reassuringly.

"I have not. I have put: 'My nurse is writing this for me.' "

"Madam, you are of a teasing disposition," reproved my lord. "M—yes—'When you take Jenny—over to Trencham . . . will you please tell Jim . . . to bring my baggage . . . here at once?' Have you that, Miss Betty?"

"Yes."

" 'Remember me to Lady . . . Molly, I beg . . . and accept my apologies . . . and thanks.' " He paused. "Will you sign it J.C. please, and address it to Sir Miles O'Hara, Thurze House, Maltby?"

"Sir Miles O'Hara! Is he your friend, Mr.—Mr.—I do not know your name."

"Car——" began Jack, and stopped, biting his lip. "Carr," he continued imperturbably, "John Carr. Do you know O'Hara, Miss Betty?"

"Me? No! Will he come to see you, do you think?"

"If you let him in, madam!"

"Gracious! Well, well! I'll tell Thomas to ride over with this at once."

"Miss Betty, you are marvellously good. I vow I can never thank——"

"Bless the boy! And what about yourself, pray? I shudder to think of what might have happened to Di if you had not come up! 'Tis we can never thank you enough."

Jack reddened boyishly and uncomfortably.

"Indeed, you exaggerate——"

"Tut, tut! Well, go to sleep, and never worry about any-thing till I return. And you won't try and get up?"

He shook with laughter.

"I swear I will not! Even an you never return, I will lie here, wasting away——" But he spoke to space, for with a delighted laugh she had left the room.

It was not until late that afternoon that O'Hara arrived, and he was conducted, after a brief conversation with Diana and her father, to my lord's room, where Miss Betty received him with her cheery smile and jerky curtsey.

"You'll not excite Mr. Carr?" she said, but was interrupted by my lord's voice from within, weak but very gay.

"Come in, Miles, and never listen to Miss Betty! She is a tyrant and denies me my wig!"

O'Hara laughed in answer to Miss Betty's quizzical smile, and strode over to the bed. He gripped my lord's thin hand and frowned down at him with an assumption of anger.

"Young good-for-nought! Could ye find nought better to do than to smash yourself up and well-nigh drive your man crazy with fright?"

"Oh, pshaw! Did you find Jim?"

O'Hara looked round and saw that Miss Betty had discreetly vanished. He sat gingerly down on the edge of the bed.

"Ay. I took the mare over as soon as I had your letter—and a fine scare you gave me, Jack, I can tell you! She recognized him, and I accosted him."

"I'll swear you did not get much satisfaction from Jim!" said my lord. "Did he look very foolish?"

"To tell ye the truth, I thought the man was half daft, and wondered whether I'd been after making a mistake. But in the end I got him to believe what I was trying to tell him, and he has taken the mare, and will bring your baggage along this evening. By the way, John, I told him of our little meeting, and of your pistols being unloaded. He said 'twas his fault, and ye never saw aught to touch his face! Put out was not the word for it."

"I suppose so. Look here, Miles, this is a damned funny affair."

"What happened to you exactly?"

" 'Tis what I am about to tell you. After I had left you, I rode on quite quietly for about an hour, and then came upon

Miss Beauleigh's coach stopped by three blackguards who were trying to drag her to another coach belonging to the gentleman who conducted the affair. So, of course, I dismounted, and went to see what was to be done."

"You *would* be after poking your nose into what didn't concern ye. Four men, and ye had the audacity to tackle them all? 'Tis mad ye are entirely!"

"Of course if you had been in my place you would have ridden off in another direction——or aided the scoundrels?" was the scathing reply.

O'Hara chuckled.

"Well, go on, Jack. I'm not saying I don't wish I had been with ye."

" 'Twould have been superb. I suppose Miss Beauleigh has told you most of the tale, but there is one thing that she could not have told you, for she did not know it: the man I fought with was Belmanoir."

"Thunder and turf! Not the Duke?"

"Yes. Tracy."

"Zounds! Did he know ye?"

"I cannot be certain. I was masked, of course, but he said he thought he did. 'Twas at that moment he fired his pistol at me."

"The dirty scoundrel!"

"M'm——yes. 'Tis that which makes me think he did not know me. Damn it all, Miles, even Tracy would not do a thing like that!"

"Would he not? If ye ask me, I say that Tracy is game enough for any kind of devilry."

"But, my dear fellow, that is too black! He could not try to kill in cold blood a man he had hunted with, and fenced with ——and——and——no man could!"

O'Hara looked extremely sceptical.

"Because ye could not yourself, is not to say that a miserable spalpeen like Belmanoir could not."

"I don't believe it of him. We were always quite friendly ——if it had been Robert now—— But I am not going to believe it. And don't say anything to these people, O'Hara, because they do not know Devil. I gather from what Miss Betty says, that he calls himself Everard. He met the girl—Diana —at Bath; you know his way. She'd none of him: hence the abduction."

"Heavens, but 'tis a foul mind the man's got!"

"Where women are concerned, yes. Otherwise—'tis not such a bad fellow, Miles."

"I've no use for that kind of dirt myself, Jack."

"Oh, I don't know. I daresay we are none of us exactly saints." He changed the subject abruptly. "How is Jenny?"

"Rather off her feed; missing you, I expect. I left her with your man. He should be arriving soon, I should think. I don't fancy he'll waste much time."

"Neither do I. Poor fellow, he must have worried terribly over his worthless master."

"Sure, his face was as white as your own when I told him ye were wounded!"

Carstares turned his head quickly.

"What's this about my face? Just be so kind as to hand me that mirror, Miles."

O'Hara laughed and obeyed, watching my lord's close scrutiny of his countenance, with some surprise.

"Interesting pallor, my dear friend, interesting pallor. Nevertheless, I am glad that Jim is on his way." He met O'Hara's eyes as he looked up, and his lips quivered irrepressibly.

"You think me very vain, Miles?"

"Is it a pose of yours, John? Is it Sir Anthony Ferndale, Bart.?"

"No. I believe it is myself. You see, when one has but one's self to live for and think for—one makes the most of one's self! Hence my vanity. Take the mirror away, please—the sight of my countenance offends me!"

"Sure, ye are free with your orders, me lord!" said O'Hara, putting the glass down on the table. "And, while I think of it —what might your name be now?"

"John Carr—a slip of the tongue on my part, stopped in time. I heard my mentor returning—and—Miles!"

"Well?"

"Come again!"

"Come again! My dear boy, ye'll be sick of the sight of me soon! I shall be here every day."

"Thanks! It will take a good deal to sicken me, I think." He bit his lip, turning his head away as Miss Betty came into the room.

"I'm afraid that you ought to leave my patient now, Sir Miles," she said. "He has had enough excitement for one day, and should sleep." She glanced at the averted head inquiringly. "I doubt he is tired?"

Jack turned and smiled at her.

"No, Miss Betty, I'm not. But I know you will refuse to believe me."

"My dear boy, do you know you have black lines beneath your eyes?"

"More remarks about my face!" he sighed, and glanced at O'Hara, who had risen.

"You are quite right, Miss Beauleigh, I must go. May I come again to-morrow?"

"Surely," she beamed. "We shall be delighted to welcome you."

O'Hara bent over the bed.

"Then *au revoir*, Jack. My lady sent her love to her 'Cousin Harry'—the saucy puss!"

"Did she? How prodigious kind of her, Miles! And you'll give her mine, and kiss her——"

"Yes?" said O'Hara with dangerous calm. "I'll kiss her what?"

"Her hand for me!" ended Carstares, bubbling over. "Good-bye, and thank you——"

"That will suffice!" said Miles, cutting him short.

He bowed to Miss Betty and left the room.

The business-like little lady fluttered over to the bedside and rearranged the pillows.

"Well, and are you satisfied?"

"Madam, most extraordinarily so, I thank you. I shall be getting up soon."

"H'm!" was all she vouchsafed, and left him to his meditations.

As she had foreseen, he dozed a little, but his shoulder would not allow him to sleep. He lay in a semi-comatose condition, his eyes shut, and a deep furrow, telling of pain, between his brows.

The sound of a shutting door made him open his eyes; he turned his head slightly and saw that Jim Salter was standing in the middle of the room looking at him anxiously.

My lord returned his gaze crossly, and Jim waited for the storm to break.

Carstares' heart melted, and he managed to smile.

"I'm monstrously glad to see you, Jim," he said.

"You—you can't mean that, sir! 'Twas I left your pistols unloaded."

"I know. Damned careless of you, but it's the sort of thing I should do myself, after all."

Jim advanced to the bedside.

"Do you mean you forgive me, sir?"

"Why, of course! I could not have fired on my best friend in any case."

"No, sir, but that don't make it any better."

"It doesn't, of course, and I was rather annoyed at the time —Oh, devil take you, Jim, don't look at me like that! I'm not dead yet!"

"If—if you had been killed, sir—'twould have been my fault."

"Rubbish! I'd a sword, hadn't I? For heaven's sake don't worry about it any more! Have you brought all my baggage?"

"Yes, sir. It shan't occur again, sir."

"Certainly not. Jenny is well?"

"Splendid, sir. Will you still trust me with your pistols, sir?"

Carstares groaned.

"Will you have done? 'Twas an accident, and I have forgotten it. Here's my hand on it!" He grasped Jim's as he spoke, and seemed to brush the whole subject aside.

"Have you disposed of that horrible coat you tried to make me wear the other day?"

"I gave it to the landlord, sir."

"I should have burned it, but perhaps he liked it."

"He did, sir. Will you try to go to sleep now?"

"If you had a shoulder on fire and aching as mine does, you wouldn't ask such a ridiculous question," answered Jack snappishly.

"I'm sorry, sir. Is there aught I can do?"

"You can change the bandages, if you like. These are prodigious hot and uncomfortable."

Without another word Salter set about easing his master, and he was so painstaking and so careful not to hurt the ugly wound, and his face expressed so much concern, that Carstares controlled a desire to swear when he happened to touch a particularly tender spot, and at the end rewarded him with a smile and a sigh of content.

"That is much better," he said. "You have such a light touch, Jim."

The man's face reddened with pleasure, but he said nothing, and walked away to the window to draw the curtains.

CHAPTER XIII

My Lord Makes His Bow

AFTER Jim's arrival my lord recovered quickly, each day making great progress, much to the doctor's satisfaction, who never tired of telling Mr. Beauleigh and Miss Betty that it was entirely owing to his treatment that the patient had recovered at all. As his idea of treatment mainly consisted of copiously bleeding John, which process Miss Betty very soon put an end to, he and she had many arguments on the subject, in which he was completely routed. She held that Mr. Carr was well on the strength of her nursing and his own constitution—and very probably she was right. In any case, hardly a fortnight after O'Hara's first visit, my lord was standing before his mirror, surveying himself, with his head speculatively on one side and a worried look in his eyes. Salter watched him anxiously, knowing this to be a critical moment. His master was somewhat of an enigma to him; the important things in life never appeared to affect him, but over a question of two cravats as opposed to each other, or some equally trivial matter, he would become quite harassed.

After contemplating his appearance for several moments, Carstares frowned and looked over his shoulder.

"I have changed my mind, Jim. I will wear blue after all."

Salter sighed despairingly.

"Ye look very well in what ye have on, sir," he grunted.

Jack sat down obstinately.

"I have conceived a dislike—nay, a veritable hatred—for puce. I will wear blue."

"Now, sir, do ha' done changing your clothes! Ye'll be tired out before ever ye get downstairs, and ye know what the doctor said."

My lord consigned the doctor and his words of wisdom to a place of great heat.

"Ay, sir, but——"

"The doctor is a worthy individual, Jim, but he knows

116

even less of the art of dressing than you do. He does not understand the soul-agony of a man who makes his first appearance in puce."

"But——"

"The blue coat laced with gold."

"Sir——"

"I order it! I insist; the blue coat or nought!"

"Very well, sir." Resignedly Jim walked to the cupboard.

When at length his lordship was dressed to his entire satisfaction it was midway through the hot June afternoon, and Miss Betty was tapping at the door, wishing to know whether Mr. Carr was coming down, or whether he was not.

Carstares shifted his sling, and taking up his hat, moved just a little shakily to the door.

Salter opened it, and cast a triumphant glance at Miss Betty, as though he was showing off all my lord's graces. He proffered an arm.

"Shall I help ye, sir?"

Miss Betty curtsied low.

"La, Mr. Carr!"

John bowed profoundly.

"Give ye good ken, madam," he said. "I am just about to descend. Thank you, Jim." He leaned heavily on the man's arm.

Miss Betty walked round him admiringly.

"Lud! 'Tis mighty elegant, I vow! But I protest, I am shy!"

"Egad, Miss Betty! and why?"

"You are not so young as I imagined," she replied candidly.

"Bear in mind, madam, that I never sought to deceive you. I am an aged man."

"Thirty!" she scoffed, and went on ahead. "Come, child, and mind the first step!"

At the bottom of the staircase stood Mr. Beauleigh, a man of medium height, thin-lipped and grey-eyed. He came forward with one hand outstretched.

"I am delighted to see you so much better, sir. I trust your shoulder no longer pains you?"

My lord pushed Jim gently to one side and placed his hand in Mr. Beauleigh's.

"I thank you, sir, it is almost well. But for Miss Betty, who, I fear, has the makings of a true tyrant, I should not wear this obnoxious sling."

Mr. Beauleigh smiled a little.

"Ah, yes, she keeps us all in order, does Betty. Pray, will you not walk a little in the garden? There are chairs on the lawn—and here is my daughter."

He waved to the door, and Carstares, turning, beheld Diana.

She stood framed by the dark wood, gowned in amber silk, with old lace falling from her elbows and over the bosom of her dress. Her hair was dark as night, with little tendrils curling over her broad, white brow. One rolling curl fell over her shoulder, the rest were gathered up under a small lace cap, which was secured by means of a riband passed beneath her chin.

Jack gazed, and gazed again, and in her turn Diana studied him with wide brown eyes of almost childlike innocence. Then her lids fluttered and curling lashes veiled the glorious depths, as a slow blush mounted to her cheeks.

My lord recovered his manners and made his most approved leg as her father presented him.

"My love, this is Mr. Carr——"

Diana sank into a curtsey.

"——and, Mr. Carr, this is my daughter, Diana."

"I am delighted to make Miss Beauleigh's acquaintance," said John, and raised her hand to his lips.

The delicate, tapering fingers trembled a little in his hold, and tremulous lips parted in the shyest and most adorable smile that he had ever seen.

"Indeed, sir, we are already acquainted. I am not like to forget my rescuer."

"I am happy to think that I was able to be of some service to you, mademoiselle. Believe me, it was an honour to fight in your cause." His eyes were on the facinating dimple that played about her mouth.

" 'Tis very kind of you to say so, sir. I fear we greatly incommoded you—and——" She made a gesture towards his sling.

"That, mademoiselle, is less than nothing. All the obligation is on my side."

Miss Betty bustled forward.

"Now that will do! I never heard such a foolish set of compliments! You are looking tired, Mr. Carr; come into the garden and rest."

Salter stepped forward, but Diana stayed him with uplifted finger.

"If Mr. Carr will accept my arm?" she hazarded.

Jack flushed.

"Indeed, no, Miss Beauleigh—I can——"

"Oh, tut-tut!" cried Miss Betty. "Have done dilly-dallying! Take him out, Di!"

Mr. Beauleigh had already disappeared. His world lay in his library, and he was never far from it for any length of time. Now he had seized the moment when his sister was not looking to withdraw quietly, and, when she turned round, she was only in time to see the library door close softly.

"Your papa has gone again," she remarked to her niece. "What a trying man he is, to be sure!"

She followed the pair out on to the lawn, and helped to make Carstares seat himself in a long chair under a great elm. A cushion was placed under his wounded shoulder and another at his back.

"And are you sure that you are quite comfortable?" inquired Miss Betty, anxiously bending over him.

Jack laughed up at her.

"Quite right, thank you, madam. But where will you sit?"

"I shall sit in this chair, and Di will sit on a cushion"—throwing one down—"at my feet—so."

"I see that you are all ruled with a rod of iron, mademoiselle," he said, and watched the dimple tremble into being.

"Indeed, yes, sir. 'Tis very sad."

Miss Betty chuckled, and unrolled a packet of silks which she threw into her niece's lap.

"Will you have the goodness to sort those for me, love?" she asked, taking out her embroidery.

"Pray allow me to assist!" pleaded John.

Diana rose and planted her cushion down beside his chair. She then knelt down upon it and emptied the multi-coloured strands on to his knee.

"Very well! You must be very careful to separate the different pinks, though. See, we will have the rose here, the salmon here, the deeper rose here, the pale pink over there, and the reds—there is no more room—we will put the reds in this paper."

"Certainly," agreed Carstares. "Are we to leave the other colours until the pinks are sorted?"

She nodded and bent her head over the silks.

"Is Sir Miles coming this afternoon, Mr. Carr?"

"Why, yes, Miss Betty—now you mention it, I remember that he is. Miss Beauleigh, I defy you to put that one on the rose pile; 'tis a shade too deep."

"I am sure 'tis not! Where is one to compare with it?"

Carstares produced a long thread and held it next to hers. The two heads were bent close over it. Diana sighed.

"You are right; I can just see the difference. But 'tis *very* slight!"

Miss Betty peeped over their shoulders.

"Gracious, what an eye you must have! I can detect no difference." Her eye ran along the row of silks laid out on my lord's white satin leg.

"Mr. Carr," said Diana suddenly, "I want to ask you something—something that has been puzzling me."

"Faith, what is it, Miss Beauleigh?"

"Just this: why did you call Mr. Everard M. le Duc?"

There was a tiny pause. My lord looked down into the gold-flecked eyes and frowned a little.

"Did I call him that?"

"Yes, I remember it distinctly. Was it just—a manner of speaking?"

"Just a manner of speaking. . . . You may call it that, mademoiselle. Do you not think that he looks rather ducal?"

"I tried not to think of him at all. I hate him!"

"Almost I begin to pity this Mr. Everard," quoth Jack.

The dimple peeped out.

"Then 'tis most ungallant of you, sir!" she reproved. "Do you know Mr. Everard?"

"I have certainly seen him before, madam."

Diana sat back on her heels and eyed him wonderingly.

"I believe you do not wish to answer me," she said slowly. "Tell me, is 'Everard' that man's real name?"

My lord twisted the ring on his finger uneasily. He did not feel himself at liberty to expose Belmanoir, and if he should reveal his true identity, it was quite possible that Mr. Beauleigh might seek him out, in which case he himself might be recognised. He looked up.

"Pardon me, mademoiselle, but whence this cross-examination?"

Diana nodded placidly.

"I thought you would refuse, but I have discovered something that will confound you, sir!" She rose to her feet. "I will go and get it." She walked gracefully towards the house, and my lord watched her go.

"Now *I* am going to ask a question," broke in Miss Betty's voice.

He threw out an imploring hand.

"Madam, I beg you will consider my feeble condition! Am I fit to bear the strain, think you?"

"I do!—Is it usual for gentlemen to ride masked, as you were?"

At that he laughed.

"No, madam, but for the gentlemen of the High Toby, it is *de règle*."

She paused, with her needle held in mid-air:

"Now, what mean you by that?"

"Just that I am a common highwayman, Miss Betty."

She stared at him for a moment, and then resumed her work.

"You look it."

John cast a startled glance down his slim person.

"Is that so, madam? And I rather flattered myself I did not!"

"I was only laughing at you. You do not expect me to believe that fabrication—surely?"

"I fear I do," he sighed. " 'Tis very true, alack!"

"Oh, indeed? Also a friend of Sir Miles O'Hara, *J.P.*—and of Mr. Everard?"

"At least the last-named is not an acquaintance to be proud of," he retorted.

"Perhaps not. My Di says he is some great gentleman."

"I perceive that your Di is by nature suspicious. Why does she think that?"

"You will see. Di, love, here is Mr. Carr trying to make me believe that he is a highwayman!"

Diana came up to them smiling.

"I fear he teases you, aunt. Do you remember this, sir?" Into Jack's hands she put his Grace of Andover's sword.

Carstares took it, surprised, and glanced casually at the hilt. Then he started up.

"Why, 'tis his sword. And I thought 'twas left on the roadside. Can it be—did *you* bring it, mademoiselle?"

She dropped him a curtsey and laughed.

"You are surprised, sir? You demanded the sword, so I

naturally supposed that you required it. Therefore I brought
it home."

" 'Twas monstrous thoughtful of you then. I dared not
hope that it had not been forgotten. I am very grateful——"

"Then pray show your gratitude by sitting down again!"
advised the elder Miss Beauleigh. "Remember that this is
your first day up, and have a care!"

John subsided obediently, turning the sword over in his
hands.

Diana pointed to the wrought gold hilt with an accusing
finger.

"An I mistake not, sir, that is a coronet."

My lord's eyes followed the pink-tipped finger and rested
wrathfully upon the arms of Andover. It was like Tracy to
flaunt them on his sword-hilt, he reflected.

"It certainly has that appearance," he admitted cautiously.

"Also, those are not paste, but real diamonds, and that is a
ruby."

"I do not dispute it, madam," he answered meekly.

"And I believe that that big stone is an emerald."

"I am very much afraid that it is."

"An expensive toy!" she said, and looked sharply at him.

"Ornate, I agree, but as true a piece of steel as ever I saw,"
replied my lord blandly, balancing the rapier on one finger.

"A very expensive toy!" she repeated sternly.

John sighed.

"True, madam—true." Then with a brightened air: "Perhaps Mr. Everard has expensive tastes?"

"It is very possible. And I think that Mr. Everard must
have been more than a simple country gentleman to indulge
those tastes."

Carstares bit his lip to hide a smile at the thought of Tracy
in the light of a simple country gentleman, and shook his
head sadly.

"Do you infer that he came by this sword dishonestly,
madam?"

The dimple quivered and was gone.

"Sir, I believe that you are playing with me," she said with
great dignity.

"Madam, I am abashed."

"I am very glad to hear it, then. I infer that Mr. Everard
was something more than he pretended to be."

"In truth, a sorry rogue to deceive a lady."

"And I want to know if I am right. Is he, perhaps, some grand gentleman?"

"I can assure you, madam, that there is very little of the gentleman about Mr. Everard."

Miss Betty began to laugh.

"Have done, my dear! 'Tis of no avail, and 'tis impolite to press Mr. Carr too hard."

Diana pouted.

"He is monstrous provoking, I think," she said, and eyed him reproachfully.

"I am desolated," mourned Jack, but his eyes danced.

"And now you are laughing!"

"But then, mademoiselle, so are you!"

She shook her head, resolutely repressing the dimple.

"Then I am inconsolable."

The brown eyes sparkled and her lips parted in spite of her efforts to keep them in a stern line.

"Oh, but you are ridiculous!" she cried, and sprang to her feet. "And here is Sir Miles!"

O'Hara came across the lawn towards them, bowed to the ladies, and glanced inquiringly from one to the other.

"Is it a joke ye have?" he asked.

Diana answered him.

"Indeed no, sir. 'Tis Mr. Carr who is so provoking."

"Provoking, is it? And what has he been doing?"

"I'll tell you the whole truth, Miles," interposed the maligned one. " 'Tis Mistress Diana who is so inquisitive!"

"Oh!" Diana blushed furiously. "I protest you are unkind, sir!"

"Sure, 'tis no gentleman he is, at all!"

" 'Twas on the subject of gentlemen that we——"

"Quarrelled," supplied her aunt.

"Disagreed," amended his lordship.

"Disagreed," nodded Diana. "I asked him whether Mr. Everard was not some grand gentleman, and he evaded the point."

"I vow 'tis slander!" cried Jack. "I merely said that Everard was no gentleman at all."

"There! And was not that evading the point, Sir Miles?"

"Was it? Sure, I'm inclined to agree with him."

"I declare you are both in league against me!" she cried, with greater truth than she knew. "I mean, was he perhaps a *titled* gentleman?"

"But how should Jack know that?"

"Because I am sure he knows him—or, at least, of him." '

"Listen, Mistress Di," broke in my lord, shooting a warning glance at O'Hara. "I will tell you all about Mr. Everard, and I hope you will be satisfied with my tale." He paused and seemed to cudgel his brain. "First he is, of course, titled—let me see—yes, he is a Duke. Oh, he is certainly a Duke—and I am not sure but what he is royal—he——"

"Now you are ridiculous!" cried Miss Betty.

"You are very teasing," said Diana, and tried to frown. "First you pretend to know nothing about Mr. Everard, and then you tell me foolish stories about him. A duke, indeed! I believe you *really* do know nothing about him!"

As Carstares had hoped, she refused to believe the truth.

"He is playing with ye, child," said O'Hara, who had listened to Jack's tale with a face of wonder. "I warrant he knows no Everard—eh, Jack?"

"No, I cannot say that I do," laughed his lordship.

"But—but—you said——"

"Never mind what he said, Miss Di. 'Tis a scurvy fellow he is."

She regarded him gravely.

"Indeed, I almost think so."

But the dimple peeped out for all that! The next instant it was gone, and Diana turned a face of gloom to her aunt, pouting her red lips, adorably, so thought my lord.

"Mr. Bettison," she said in accents of despair.

At these mystic words, Jack saw Miss Betty frown, and heard her impatient remark: "Drat the man!"

He looked towards the house, and perceived a short, rather stout, young man to be walking with a peculiar strutting gait towards them. The boy was good-looking, Carstares acknowledged to himself, but his eyes were set too close. And he did not like his style. No, certainly he did not like his style, nor the proprietary way in which he kissed Diana's hand.

"How agreeable it is to see you again, Mr. Bettison!" said Miss Betty with much affability. "I declare 'tis an age since we set eyes on you!"

"Oh, no, Aunt," contradicted Diana sweetly. "Why, it was only a very short while ago that Mr. Bettison was here, *surely*!" She withdrew the hand the young man seemed inclined to hold fast to, and turned to John.

"I think you do not know Mr. Bettison, Mr. Carr?" she

said. "Mr. Bettison, allow me to present you to Mr. Carr. Sir Miles I think you know?"

The squire bowed with a great deal of stiff hostility. Carstares returned the bow.

"You will excuse my not rising, I beg," he smiled. "As you perceive—I have had an accident."

Light dawned on Bettison. This was the man who had rescued Diana, confound his impudence!

"Ah, yes, sir! Your arm, was it not? My faith, I should be proud of such a wound!"

It seemed to Carstares that he smiled at Diana in a damned familiar fashion, devil take his impudence!

"It was indeed a great honour, sir. Mistress Di, I have finished sorting your green silks."

Diana sank down on the cushion again, and shook some more strands out on to his knee.

"How quick you have been! Now we will do the blue ones."

Bettison glared. This fellow seemed prodigious intimate with Diana, devil take him! He sat down beside Miss Betty, and addressed my lord patronisingly.

"Let me see—er—Mr. Carr. Have I met you in town, I wonder? At Tom's, perhaps?"

This country bumpkin *would* belong to Tom's, reflected John savagely, for no reason at all. Aloud he said:

"I think it extremely unlikely, sir. I have been abroad some years." .

"Oh, indeed, sir? The "grand tour", I suppose?"

Mr. Bettison's tone was not the tone of one who supposes any such thing.

John smiled.

"Not this time," he said, "that was seven years ago."

Mr. Bettison had heard rumours of this fellow who, it was murmured, was nought but a common highwayman.

"Really? After Cambridge, perhaps?"

"Oxford," corrected Carstares gently.

Curse his audacity! thought Mr. Bettison.

"Seven years ago—let me think. George must have been on the tour then—Selwyn, I mean, Miss Beauleigh."

Jack, who had made the tour with several other young bucks fresh down from college, accompanied as far as Paris by the famous wit himself, held his peace.

Mr. Bettison then launched forth into anecdotes of his own

tour, and seeing that his friend was entirely engrossed with
Miss Diana and her silks, O'Hara felt it incumbent on him to
draw the enemy's fire, and, taking his own departure, to bear
the squire off with him. For which he received a grateful
smile from my lord, and a kiss blown from the tips of her
fingers from Mistress Di, with whom he was on the best of
terms.

CHAPTER XIV

Mistress Diana Is Unmaidenly

THE idyllic summer days passed quickly by, and every time that my lord spoke of leaving, the outcry was so indignant and so firm that he hastily subsided and told himself he would stay just another few days. His shoulder, having mended up to a certain point, refused quite to heal, and exertion brought the pain back very swiftly. So his time was for the most part spent with Mistress Di out of doors, helping her with her gardening and her chickens—for Diana was an enthusiastic poultry farmer on a small scale—and ministering to her various pets. If Fido had a splinter in his paw, it was to Mr. Carr that he was taken; if Nellie, the spaniel, caught a live rabbit, Mr. Carr would assuredly know what to do with it, and the same with all the other animals. The young pair grew closer and closer together, while Miss Betty and O'Hara watched from afar, the former filled with pride of her darling, and satisfaction, and the latter with apprehension. O'Hara knew that his friend was falling unconsciously in love, and he feared the time when John should realise it. He confided these fears to his wife, who, with young David, was staying at her mother's house in Kensington, in a long and very Irish letter. She replied that he must try and coax my lord into coming to stay with them, when her charms would at once eclipse Mistress Diana's, though to be sure, she could not understand why Miles should not wish him to fall in love, for as he well knew, 'twas a prodigious pleasant sensation. If he did not know it, then he was indeed most disagreeable. And had he ever heard of anything so wonderful?—David had drawn a picture of a horse! Yes, really, it was a horse! Was he not a clever child? Further, would her dearest Miles please come and fetch her home, for although Mamma was prodigious amiable, and wanted her to stay several weeks, she positively could not live without her husband an instant longer than was necessary!

As soon as O'Hara read the last part of the letter he brushed Carstares and his love affairs to one side, and posted straight to London to obey the welcome summons.

Bit by bit my lord discovered that he was very much in love with Diana. At first his heart gave a great bound, and then seemed to stop with a sickening thud. He remembered that he could not ask her to marry him, disgraced as he was, and he immediately faced the situation, realising that he must go away at once. His first move was to Mr. Beauleigh, to tell him of his decision. On being asked why he must so suddenly leave Horton House, he explained that he loved Diana and could not in honour speak of love to her. At which Mr. Beauleigh gasped and demanded to know the reason. Carstares told him that he was by profession a highwayman, and watched him bridle angrily. Before so agreeable and so smiling, Mr. Beauleigh now became frigidly polite. He quite understood Mr. Carr's position, and—er—yes, he honoured him for the course on which he had decided. But Mr. Beauleigh was very, very cold. Carstares gave Jim orders to pack immediately, that he might depart next day, and reluctantly informed Miss Betty of his going. She was startled and bewildered. She had imagined that he would spend all June with them.—Circumstances, he regretted, willed otherwise. He should always remember her great kindness to him, and hoped that she would forgive the brusque nature of his departure.

When he told Diana her eyes opened very wide and she laughed, pointing an accusing finger at him.

"You are teasing, Mr. Carr!" she cried, and ran into the house.

That evening Miss Betty confirmed Jack's words, and seeing the hurt look in the girl's eyes, wisely held her peace.

Next morning in the pleasance Diana came across my lord, and went up to him, gravely questioning.

"You are really leaving us to-day, Mr. Carr?"

"I am afraid I must, Mistress Di."

"So suddenly? Then you were not teasing yesterday?"

"No, mademoiselle—I was not. I fear I have tarried too long, taking advantage of your kindness."

"Oh, no, no!" she assured him. "Indeed, you have not! Must you *really* go?"

Looking down into her big eyes, John read the answering

love in them, and grew pale. It was worse to think that she cared, too. If only he thought she was indifferent, parting would not seem so unbearable.

"Mademoiselle—you overwhelm me—I must go."

"Oh, but I am sorry. Your being here has been such a pleasure! I——" She stopped, and looked away across the flowers.

"You?" prompted Jack before he could check himself.

With a tiny laugh she brought her gaze back.

"I am sorry you must leave us, naturally."

She sat down beneath an arbour of roses, and patted the place beside her invitingly, with just the same unconscious friendliness that she had always shown him. My lord stayed where he was, with one hand on a tree trunk and the other fidgeting with his quizzing glass.

"Mistress Di—I think it only right that I should tell you what I have told your father, and what I told your aunt some time ago, when she refused to believe me. To some extent I am here under false pretences. I am not what you think me."

Diana laced and unlaced her fingers, and thought that she understood.

"Oh, no, Mr. Carr!"

"I am afraid yes, mademoiselle. I am—a common felon . . . a highwayman!" He bit the words out, not looking at her.

"But I knew that," she said softly.

"You *knew* it?"

"Why, yes! I remember when you told Aunt Betty."

"You believed me?"

"You see," she apologised, "I always wondered why you were masked."

"And yet you permitted me to stay——"

"How silly of you, Mr. Carr! Of course I do not care what what you are! I owe so much to you!"

He wheeled round at that, and faced her.

"Madam, I can bear anything rather than gratitude! It is only that which has made you tolerate me all this time?"

Her fingers gripped one another.

"Why, sir—why, sir——"

The flame died out of his eyes, and he drew himself up stiffly, speaking with a curtness that surprised her.

"I crave your pardon. I should be whipped at the cart-tail for asking such an impertinent question. Forget it, I beg."

Diana looked up at the stern face, half amazed, half affronted.

"I do not think I quite understand you, sir."

"There is nought to understand, mademoiselle," he answered with dry lips. " 'Twere merely that I was coxcomb enough to hope that you liked me a little for mine own sake."

She glanced again at his averted head with a wistful little smile.

"Oh!" she murmured. *"Oh!"*—and—"It is very dreadful to be a highwayman!" she sighed.

"Yes, mademoiselle."

"But surely you could cease to be one?" coaxingly.

He did not trust himself to answer.

"I know you could. Please do!"

"That is not all," he forced himself to say. "There is worse."

"Is there?" she asked wide-eyed. "What else have you done, Mr. Carr?"

"I—once——" heavens, how hard it was to say! "I once . . . cheated . . . at cards." It was out. Now she would turn from him in disgust. He shut his eyes in anticipation of her scorn, his head turned away.

"Only *once*?" came the soft voice, filled with awed admiration.

His eyes flew open.

"Mademoiselle——!"

She drooped her head mournfully.

"I'm afraid I always cheat," she confessed. "I had no idea 'twas so wicked, although Auntie gets very cross and vows she will not play with me."

He could not help laughing.

" 'Tis not wicked in you, child. You do not play for money."

"Oh, did you?"

"Yes, child."

"Then that *was* horrid of you," she agreed.

He stood silent, fighting the longing to tell her the truth.

"But—but—do not look so solemn, sir," the pleading voice went on. "I am sure you must have had a very strong excuse?"

"None."

"And now you are letting it spoil your life?" she asked reproachfully.

"It does not wait for my permission," he answered bitterly.

"Ah, but what a pity! Must one moment's indiscretion interfere with all else in life! That is ridiculous. You have—what is the word—expiated! yes, that is it—expiated it, I know."

"The past can never be undone, madam."

"That, of course, is true," she nodded, with the air of a sage, "but it can be forgotten."

His hand flew out eagerly and dropped back to his side. It was hopeless. He could not tell her the truth and ask her to share his disgrace; he must bear it alone, and, above all, he must not whine. He had chosen to take Richard's blame and he must abide by the consequences. It was not a burden to be cast off as soon as it became too heavy for him. It was for ever—for ever. He forced his mind to grasp that fact. All through his life he must be alone against the world; his name would never be cleared; he could never ask this sweet child who sat before him with such a wistful, pleading look on her lovely face, to wed him. He looked down at her sombrely, telling himself that she did not really care: that it was his own foolish imagination. Now she was speaking: he listened to the liquid voice that repeated:

"Could it not be forgotten?"

"No, mademoiselle. It will always be there."

"To all intents and purposes, might it not be forgotten?" she persisted.

"It will always stand in the way, mademoiselle."

He supposed that mechanical voice was his own. Through his brain thrummed the thought: "It is for Dick's sake . . . for Dick's sake. For Dick's sake you must be silent." Resolutely he pulled himself together.

"It will stand in the way—of what?" asked Diana.

"I can never ask a woman to be my wife," he replied.

Diana wantonly stripped a rose of its petals, letting each fragrant leaf flutter slowly to the ground.

"I do not see why you cannot, sir."

"No woman would share my disgrace."

"No?"

"No."

"You seem very certain, Mr. Carr. Pray have you asked the lady?"

"No, madam." Carstares was as white as she was red, but he was holding himself well in hand.

"Then——" the husky voice was very low, "then—why don't you?"

The slim hand against the tree trunk was clenched tightly, she observed. In his pale face the blue eyes burnt dark.

"Because, madam, 'twere the action of a—of a——"

"Of a what, Mr. Carr?"

"A cur! A scoundrel! A blackguard!"

Another rose was sharing the fate of the first.

"I have heard it said that some women like—curs, and—and—and scoundrels; even blackguards," remarked the provocative voice. Through her lashes its owner watched my lord's knuckles gleam white against the tree-bark.

"Not the lady I love, madam."

"Oh? But are you sure?"

"I am sure. She must marry a man whose honour is spotless; who is not—a nameless outcast, and who lives—not—by dice—and highway robbery."

He knew that the brown eyes were glowing and sparkling with unshed tears, but he kept his own turned inexorably the other way. There was no doubting now that she cared, and that she knew that he did also. He could not leave her to think that her love had been slighted. She must not be hurt, but made to understand that he could not declare his love. But how hard it was, with her sorrowful gaze upon him, and the pleading note in her voice. It was quivering now:

"Must she, sir?"

"Yes, madam."

"But supposing—supposing the lady did not care? Supposing she—loved you—and was willing to share your disgrace?"

The ground at her feet was strewn with crimson petals, and all around and above her roses nodded and swayed. A tiny breeze was stirring her curls and the lace of her frock, but John would not allow himself to look, lest the temptation to catch her in his arms should prove too great for him. She was ready to give herself to him; to face anything, only to be with him. In the plainest language she offered herself to him, and he had to reject her.

"It is inconceivable that the lady would sacrifice herself in such a fashion, madam," he said.

"Sacrifice!" She caught her breath. "You call it that!"

"What else?"

"I . . . I . . . I do not think that you are very wise, Mr.

Carr. Nor . . . that you . . . understand women . . . very well. She might not call it by that name."

"It would make no difference what she called it, madam. She would ruin her life, and that must never be."

A white rose joined its fallen brethren, pulled to pieces by fingers that trembled pitifully.

"Mr. Carr, if the lady . . . loved you . . . is it quite fair to her—to say nothing?"

There was a long silence, and then my lord lied bravely.

"I hope that she will—in time—forget me," he said.

Diana sat very still. No more roses were destroyed; the breeze wafted the fallen petals over her feet, lightly, almost playfully. Somewhere in the hedge a bird was singing, a full-throated sobbing plaint, and from all around came an incessant chirping and twittering. The sun sent its bright rays all over the garden, bathing it in gold and happiness; but for the two in the pleasance the light had gone out, and the world was very black.

"I see," whispered Diana at last. "Poor lady!"

"I think it was a cursed day that saw me come into her life," he groaned.

"Perhaps it was," her hurt heart made answer.

He bowed his head.

"I can only hope that she will not think too hardly of me," he said, very low. "And that she will find it in her heart to be sorry—for me—also."

She rose and came up to him, her skirts brushing gently over the grass, holding out her hands imploringly.

"Mr. Carr . . ."

He would not allow himself to look into the gold-flecked eyes. . . . He must remember Dick—his brother Dick!

In his hand he took the tips of her fingers, and bowing, kissed them. Then he turned on his heel and strode swiftly away between the hedges towards the quiet woods, with a heart aflame with passion, and with rebellion and impotent fury. He would go somewhere quite alone and fight the devil that was prompting him to cry the truth aloud and to throw aside his burden for love, forgetting duty.

But Diana remained standing among the scattered flowers, very still, very cold, with a look of hopeless longing in her eyes and a great hurt.

CHAPTER XV

O'Hara's Mind Is Made Up

JIM SALTER folded one of my lord's waistcoats and placed it carefully in an open valise; then he picked up a coat, and spread it on the bed preparatory to folding it in such wise that no crease should afterwards mar its smoothness. All about him my lord's clothing was strewn; Mechlin ruffles and cravats adorned one chair, silk hose another; gorgeous coats hung on their backs; shoes of every description, red-heeled and white, riding boots and slippers, stood in a row awaiting attention; wigs perched coquettishly on handy projections, and piles of white cambric shirts peeped out from an almost finished bag.

Jim laid the coat tenderly in the valise, coaxing it into decorous folds, and wondering at the same time where his master was. He had been out all the morning, and on his return had looked so ill that Jim had been worried, and wished that they were not leaving Horton House quite so soon. A little while ago my lord had been closeted with his host; Jim supposed he must be still there. He reached out his hand for another waistcoat, but before his fingers had touched it, he stopped, and lifted his head, listening. Hasty, impetuous footsteps sounded on the stairs, and came furiously along the corridor. The door was twisted open, and my lord stood on the threshold. Jim scanned the tired face anxiously, and noted with a sinking heart that the blue eyes were blazing and the fine lips set in a hard, uncompromising line. The slender hand gripping the door-handle twitched in a way that Jim knew full well; evidently my lord was in an uncertain mood.

"Have you finished?" rapped out Carstares.

"Not quite, sir."

"I wish to leave this year, and not next if 'tis all the same to you!"

"Yes, sir. I didn't know you was in a hurry, sir."

There was no reply to this. My lord advanced into the

room and cast one glance at his scattered baggage and another all round him.

"Where is my riding dress?"

Jim shivered in his luckless shoes.

"I—er— 'tis packed, sir. Do ye want it?"

"Of course I want it! Do you suppose that I am going to ride in what I have on?"

"I rather thought ye were driving, your honour."

"I am not. The scarlet suit at once, please."

He flung himself down in a chair before his dressing-table and picked up a nail-file.

Salter eyed his reflection in the glass dismally, and made no movement to obey. After a moment my lord swung round.

"Well! What are you standing there for? Didn't you hear me?"

"Ay, sir, I did, but—your pardon, sir—but do ye think 'tis wise to ride to-day for—for the first time?"

The file slammed down on to the table.

"I am riding to Horley this afternoon!" said his master dangerously.

" 'Tis a matter of fifteen miles or so, your honour. Hadn't ye better——"

"Damn you, Jim, be quiet!"

Salter gave it up.

"Very well, sir," he said, and unearthed the required dress. "I'll see the baggage goes by coach, and saddle the mare and Peter."

"Not Peter. You go in the coach."

"No, sir."

"What!"

My lord stared at him. There had been a note of finality in the respectful tone. My lord became icy.

"You forget yourself, Salter."

"I ask your pardon, sir."

"You will travel in charge of my things, as usual."

Jim compressed his lips, and stowed a shoe away in one corner of the bag.

"You understand me?"

"I understand ye well enough, sir."

"Then that is settled."

"No, sir."

My lord dropped his eye-glass.

"What the devil do you mean—'No sir?' "

"I ask your pardon, sir, an I presume, but I can't and won't let ye ride alone with your wound but just healed." There was not a hint of defiance or impertinence in the quiet voice, but it held a great determination.

"You won't, eh? Do you imagine I am a child?"

"No, sir."

"Or unable to take care of myself?"

"I think ye are weaker than ye know, sir."

"Oh, you do, do you?"

Jim came up to him.

"Ye'll let me ride with ye, sir? I won't trouble ye, and I can ride behind, but I can't let ye go alone. Ye might faint—sir——"

"I can assure you I am not like to be a pleasant companion!" said Carstares with a savage little laugh.

"Why, sir, I understand there's something troubling ye. Will ye let me come?"

My lord scowled up at him, then relented suddenly.

"As you please."

"Thank ye, sir." Salter returned to his packing, cording one bag and placing it near the door, and quickly filling another. The piles of linen grew steadily smaller until they disappeared, and he retired into a cupboard to reappear with a great armful of coats and small-clothes.

For a long while my lord sat silent staring blankly before him. He walked to the window and stood with his back to the room, looking out, then he turned and came back to his chair. Jim, watching him covertly, noted that the hard glitter had died out of his eyes, and that he looked wearier than ever.

Carstares studied his nails for a moment in silence. Presently he spoke:

"Jim."

"Yes, sir?"

"I shall be—going abroad again shortly."

If Carstares had remarked that it was a fine day the man could not have shown less surprise.

"Shall we, sir?"

John looked across at him, smiling faintly.

"You'll come, Jim?"

"I would go anywhere with ye, sir."

"And what about that little girl at Fittering?"

Salter blushed and stammered hopelessly.

"My dear fellow, since when have I been blind? Did you think I did not know?"

"Why, sir—well, sir—er—yes, sir!"

"Of course I knew! Can you leave her to come with me?"

"I couldn't leave ye to stay with her, sir."

"Are you sure? I do not want you to come against your inclinations."

"Women ain't everything, sir."

"Are they not? I think they are . . . a great deal," said my lord wistfully.

"I'm mighty fond o' Mary, but she knows I must go with you."

"Does she? But is it quite fair to her? And I believe I am not minded to drag you 'cross Continent again."

"Ye won't leave me behind, sir? Ye couldn't do that! Sir—ye're never thinking of going by yourself? I—I—I won't let ye!"

"I am afraid I cannot spare you. But if you should change your mind, tell me. Is it a promise?"

"Ay, sir. If I *should* change my mind." Salter's smile was grimly sarcastic.

"I am selfish enough to hope you'll not change. I think no one else would bear with my vile temper as you do. Help me out of this coat, will you?"

"I'll never change, sir. And as to tempers—— As if I minded!"

"No. You are marvellous. My breeches. Thanks."

He shed his satin small-clothes, and proceeded to enter into white buckskins. "Not those boots, Jim, the other pair." He leaned against the table as he spoke, drumming his fingers on a chair-back.

A knock fell on the door, at which he frowned and signed to Jim, who walked across and opened it, slightly.

"Is your master here?" inquired a well-known voice, and at the sound of it my lord's face lighted up, and Salter stood aside.

"Come in, Miles!"

The big Irishman complied and cast a swift glance round the disordered room. He raised his eyebrows at sight of Jack's riding boots and looked inquiringly across at him.

My lord pushed a chair forward with his foot.

"Sit down, man! I thought you were in London?"

"I was. I brought Molly home yesterday, the darlint, and I heard that ye were leaving here this afternoon."

"Ah?"

"And as I'm not going to let ye slip through me fingers again, I thought I would come and make sure of ye. Ye are a deal too slippery, Jack."

"Yet I was coming to see you again whatever happened."

"Of course. Ye are coming now—to stay."

"Oh no!"

O'Hara placed his hat and whip on the table, and stretched his legs with a sigh.

"Sure, 'tis stiff I am! Jim, I've a chaise outside for the baggage, so ye may take it down as soon as may be."

"Leave it where it is, Jim. Miles, 'tis monstrous good of you, but——"

"Keep your buts to yourself, Jack. Me mind's made up."

"And so is mine! I really cannot——"

"Me good boy, ye are coming to stay with us until ye are recovered, if I have to knock ye senseless and then carry ye!"

The lightning smile flashed into Jack's eyes.

"How ferocious! But pray do not be ridiculous over a mere scratch! Recovered, indeed!"

"Ye still look ill. Nay, Jack, take that frown off your face; 'tis of no avail, I am determined."

The door closed softly behind Jim as Carstares shook his head.

"I can't, Miles. You must see 'tis impossible."

"Pooh! No one who comes to Thurze House knows ye or anything about ye. Ye need not see a soul, but come ye must!"

"But, Miles——"

"Jack, don't be a fool! I want ye, and so does Molly. 'Tis no trap, so ye need not look so scared."

"I'm not. Indeed, I am very grateful, but—I cannot. I am going abroad almost at once."

"What?"

"Yes. I mean it."

O'Hara sat up.

"So it has come! I knew it would!"

"What mean you?"

"Ye've found out that ye love Mistress Di."

"Nonsense!"

"And she you."

Jack looked at him.

"Oh, ay! I'm a tactless oaf, I know, and me manners are atrocious to be for trying to break through the barriers ye've put up round yourself. But, I tell ye, Jack, it hurts to be kept at the end of a pole! I don't want to force your confidence, but for God's sake don't be treating me as if I were a stranger!"

"I beg your pardon, Miles. It's confoundedly hard to confide in anyone after six years' solitude." He struggled into his coat as he spoke, and settled his cravat. "If you want to know the whole truth, 'tis because of Diana that I am going."

"Of course. Ye are in love with her?"

"It rather points that way, does it not?"

"Then why the divil don't ye ask her to marry ye?"

"Why don't I ask her? Because I will not offer her a smirched name! Because I love her so much that——" He broke off with a shaky, furious laugh. "How can you ask me such a question? I am a desirable *parti, hein*? *Nom d'un nom!* For what do you take me?"

O'Hara looked up, calmly studying the wrathful countenance.

"Chivalrous young fool," he drawled.

Again the short, angry laugh.

"Is it so likely that I should ask her to marry me, is it not? 'Mademoiselle, you see in me an improvident fool: I began life by cheating at cards, and since then——' Oh, I shall believe it myself ere long! I seem to have told it to so many people. And I lay myself open to the impertinences of——" he checked himself, thinking of the interview downstairs with Mr. Beauleigh.

"Rubbish, Jack."

" 'Tis not rubbish. I have one recommendation—only one."

"Faith, have ye as much? What is it?"

My lord laughed bitterly.

"I dress rather well."

"And fence better, as far as I remember."

"I have reason to. That is but another point to damn me. What woman would marry a fencing-master? Oh, my God! what a mess I have made of my life." He tried to laugh and failed miserably.

"I rather fancy Mistress Di would."

"She will not be asked thus to demean herself," was the proud answer.

"My dear Jack, ye forget ye are the Earl of Wyncham."

"A pretty earl! No thank you, Miles. Richard's son will be Earl—no son of mine."

O'Hara brought his fist down on the table with a crash.

"Damn Richard and his son!"

My lord picked up a jewelled pin and, walking to the glass, proceeded to fasten it in his cravat. The other followed him with smouldering eyes.

"Retired into your shell again?" he growled.

Carstares, with his head slightly on one side, considered the effect of the pin. Then he came back to his friend.

"My dear Miles, the long and short of it is that I am an unreasonable grumbler. I made my bed, and I suppose I must —er—lie on it."

"And will ye be after telling me who helped ye in the making of it?"

Carstares sat down and started to pull on one boot.

"I forsee we shall be at one another's throats ere long," he prophesied cheerfully. "Did I tell you that I informed Mr. Beauleigh of my—er—profession to-day?"

Miles forgot his anger in surprise.

"Ye never told him ye were a highwayman?" he cried.

"Yes, I did. Why not?"

"Why not? Why *not*? God help us all! are ye daft, man? Do ye intend to tell every other person ye meet what ye are? Bedad, 'tis mad ye are entirely!"

Carstares sighed.

"I was afraid you would not understand."

" 'Twould take a wizard to understand ye! Another chivalrous impulse, I doubt not?"

"Chiv——! No. It is just that I could not let him think me an honourable gentleman. He took it well, on the whole, and is now frigidly polite."

"Polite! I should hope so! The ould scarecrow, after ye'd saved his daughter on him, too! And 'twas he made ye so furious?"

Carstares laughed.

"He and myself. You see—he—lectured me—oh! quite kindly—on the error of my ways, and—it hurt."

" 'Tis as well ye are coming to me then, the way things are with ye at present."

My lord opened his mouth to speak, encountered a fiery glance, and shut it again.

"Anything to say?" inquired O'Hara with a threatening gleam in his eye.

"No, sir," replied Jack meekly.

"Ye will come?"

"Please."

O'Hara sprang up joyfully.

"Good lad! Lud! but I was afraid at one time—— Put on your other boot while I go and look for that rascal of yours!" He hurried out of the room to find Jim, who, having foreseen the result of the contest, was already stowing the luggage away on the chaise.

Half-an-hour later, his *adieux* made, Jim and the baggage following, my lord rode out with O'Hara on his way to Thurze House.

For some time there was silence between the two men, with only a perfunctory remark or two on the fineness of the day and the freshness of the mare to break it. Carstares' mind was, as his friend well knew, dwelling on all that he had left behind him. His parting with Diana had been quite ordinary, she at least making no sign that he was anything beyond a chance acquaintance; indeed, it had almost seemed to him that her attitude was slightly aloof, as if she had drawn a little into herself. Her hand when he had kissed it had been lifeless and cold, her smile sweetly remote. He knew that he had held the hand a fraction of a minute longer than was strictly in accordance with the rules of good manners, and he feared that he had clasped it in most unseemly wise, pressing it hard against his lips. He wondered whether she had remarked it. He little guessed that long after he had ridden out of sight, she continued to feel that pressure. If he could have seen her passionately kissing each finger separately for fear her lips might pass over the exact spot his had touched, his heart might have been lighter.

It was true that she had retired into her shell, a little hurt at what she termed his man's blind obstinacy. She had laid her heart bare for him to read; she had offered herself to him as plainly as if she had spoken in terms less general than in the pleasance; she had fought desperately for her happiness, thrusting aside all thought of maiden modesty, and when she afterwards had realised what she had done, and tried to imagine what he must think of her, she had blushed dark, and mentally flayed herself for her lack of proper pride and manners. Terrified that he might think her immodest, overwhelmed with sudden shyness, she had been colder in her attitude towards him than she had intended, even in her anxiety not to appear forward. But in spite of her coldness, how intensely had she hoped that he would sense her love and all that she wanted him to know! Incomprehensible the ways of women!

Not endowed with feminine perspicacity or intuition, how could John hope to understand her dual feelings? He only knew that he had hurt her, and that she had drawn back that she might not lay herself open to more. He could not hope to understand her when she did not fully understand herself.

Reflecting on the swiftness with which love had come to them, he believed that with a like swiftness it might fade, at least from Diana's memory. He told himself that he hoped for that end, but he was honest enough to know that it was the last thing in the world he wanted. The mere thought of Diana indifferent to him, or worse, another man's bride, made him bite on his underlip and tighten his hold on the rein.

O'Hara cast many a surreptitious glance at the stern young profile beside him, wondering whether his lordship would last out the tedious ride or no. He knew enough of Carstares' indomitable courage to believe that he would, but he feared that it would prove too great a strain on him in his present weakened condition.

Very wisely he made no attempt to draw Carstares out of his abstraction, but continued to push on in silence, past fields knee-deep in grass, soon to be hay, with sorrel and poppies, growing apace, along lanes with hedges high above their heads on either side, over hill and down dale—always in silence.

Presently O'Hara fell a little to the rear that he might study his friend without palpably turning to do so. He thought he had never seen Jack's face wear such a black look. The fine brows almost met over his nose with only two sharp furrows to separate them; the mouth was compressed, the chin a little prominent, and the eyes, staring ahead between Jenny's nervous ears, seemed to see all without absorbing anything. One hand at his hip was clenched on his riding-whip, the other mechanically guided the mare.

O'Hara found himself admiring the lithe grace of the man, with his upright carriage and splendid seat.

Suddenly, as if aware that he was being studied, my lord half turned his head and met O'Hara's eyes. He gave a tiny shrug and with it seemed to throw off his oppression. The frown vanished, and he smiled.

"I beg your pardon, Miles. I am a surly fellow."

"Mayhap your shoulder troubles you," suggested O'Hara tactfully.

"N-no, I am barely conscious of it. I've no excuse beyond bad manners and a worse temper."

From thence onward he set himself to entertain his friend, and if his laugh was sometimes rather forced, at least his wit was enough to keep O'Hara in a pleasurable state of amusement for some miles.

By the time they arrived at Thurze House, Carstares was suspiciously white about the mouth, and there was once more a furrow—this time of pain—between his brows. But he was able to greet my Lady O'Hara with fitting elegance and to pay her at least three neat, laughing compliments before O'Hara took him firmly by the arm and marched him to his room, there to rest and recover before the dinner hour.

Shortly after, Jim arrived, highly contented with his new surroundings, and able to give a satisfactory verdict on Jenny's stalling. He had quite accepted O'Hara as a friend, after some jealous qualms, and was now well pleased that his master should be in his house instead of roaming the countryside.

At five o'clock, as the gong rang, my lord descended the stairs resplendent in old gold and silver trimmings, determined to be as gay and light-hearted as the occasion demanded, as though there had never been a Diana to upset the whole course of a man's life.

Not for nothing had he fought against the world for six long years. Their teaching had been to hide all feeling beneath a perpetual mask of nonchalance and wit; never for an instance to betray a hurt, and never to allow it to appear that he was anything but the most care-free of men. The training stood him in good stead now, and even O'Hara wondered to see him in such spirits after all that had passed. Lady Molly was delighted with her guest, admiring his appearance, his fine, courtly manners, and falling an easy victim to his charm.

O'Hara, watching them, saw with content that his capricious little wife was really attracted to my lord. It was a high honour, for she was hard to please, and many of O'Hara's acquaintances had been received, if not with actual coldness, at least not with any degree of warmth.

At the end of the meal she withdrew with the warning that they were not to sit too long over their wine, and that Miles was not to fatigue his lordship.

O'Hara pushed the decanter towards his friend.

"I've a piece of news I daresay will interest ye!" he remarked.

Carstares looked at him inquiringly.

"Ay. 'Tis that his Grace of Andover has withdrawn his precious person to Paris."

Carstares raised one eyebrow.

"I suppose he would naturally wish to remain in the background after our little fracas."

"Does he ever wish to be in the background?"

"You probably know him better than I do. Does he?"

"He does not. 'Tis always in front he is, mighty prominent. Damn him!"

My lord was faintly surprised.

"Why that? Has he ever interfered with you?"

"He has interfered with me best friend to some purpose."

"I fear the boot was on the other leg!"

"Well, I know something of how he interferes with Dick."

Carstares put down his glass, all attention now.

"With Dick? How?"

O'Hara seemed to regret having spoken.

"Oh, well—I've no sympathy with *him*."

"What has Tracy done to him?"

" 'Tis nothing of great moment. Merely that he and that worthless brother of his seek to squeeze him dry."

"Robert?"

"Andrew. I know very little of Robert."

"Andrew! But he was a child——"

"Well, he's grown up now, and as rakish a young spendthrift as ye could wish for. Dick seems to pay their debts."

"Devil take him! Why?"

"Heaven knows! I suppose Lavinia insists. We all knew that 'twas for that reason Tracy flung you both in her way."

"Nonsense! We went of our own accord. She had but returned from school."

"Exactly. And whose doing was that but Tracy's?"

Carstares opened his eyes rather wide and leant both arms on the table, crooking his fingers round the stem of his wine glass.

"Do the debts amount to much?"

"I can't tell ye that. 'Twas but by chance I found it out at all. The Belmanoirs were never moderate in their manner of living."

"Nor were any of us. Don't be so hard on them, Miles! . . . I knew, of course, that the Belmanoir estate was mortgaged, but I did not guess to what extent."

"I don't know that either, but Dick's money does not go to pay it off. 'Tis all frittered away on gambling and pretty women."

My lord's brow darkened ominously.

"Ye-s. I think I shall have a little score to settle with Tracy on that subject—some day."

Miles said nothing.

"But how does Dick manage without touching my money?"

"I do not know." O'Hara's tone implied that he cared less.

"I hope he is not in debt himself," mused Carstares. " 'Tis like enough he is in some muddle. I wish I might persuade him to accept the revenue." He frowned and drummed his fingers on the table.

O'Hara exploded.

"Sure, 'twould be like you to be doing the same. Let the man alone for the Lord's sake, and don't be after worrying your head over a miserable spalpeen that did ye more harm than——"

"Miles, I cannot allow you to speak so of Dick! You do not understand."

"I understand well enough. 'Tis too Christian ye are entirely. And let us have an end of this farce of yours! I know that Dick cheated as well as you do, and I say 'tis unnatural for you to be wanting him to take your money after he's done you out of honour and all else!"

Carstares sipped his wine quietly, waiting for Miles' anger to evaporate, as it presently did, leaving him to glower balefully. Then he started to laugh.

"Oh Miles, let me go my own road! I'm a sore trial to you, I know." Then suddenly sobering: "But I want you not to think so hardly of Dick. You know enough of him to understand a little how it all came about. You know how extravagant he was and how often in debt—can you not pardon the impulse of a mad moment?"

"That I could pardon. What I cannot forgive is his—unutterable meanness in letting you bear the blame."

"O'Hara, he was in love with Lavinia——"

"So were you."

"Not so deeply. With me 'twas a boy's passion, but with him 'twas serious."

O'Hara remained silent, his mouth unusually hard.

"Put yourself in his place," pleaded Jack. "If you——"

"Thank you!" O'Hara laughed unpleasantly. "No, Jack, we shall not agree on this subject, and we had best leave it alone. I do not think you need worry about him, though. I believe he is not in debt."

"Does he have fair luck with his racing and his——"

O'Hara smiled grimly.

"Dick is a very changed man, John. He does not keep racehorses, neither does he play cards, save for appearance's sake."

"Dick not play! What then does he do?"

"Manages your estates and conducts his wife to routs. When in town," bitterly, "he inhabits your house."

"Well, there is none else to use it. But I cannot imagine Dick turned sober!"

" 'Tis easy to be righteous after the evil is done, I'm thinking!"

My lord ignored this remark. A curious smile played about his mouth.

"Egad, Miles, 'tis very entertaining! I, the erstwhile sober member—what is the matter?—am now the profligate: I dice, I gamble, I rob. Dick the ne'er-do-weel is a saint. He—er—lives a godly and righteous life, and—er—is robbed by his wife's relations. After all, I do not think I envy him overmuch."

"At least, you enjoy life more than he does," said O'Hara, grinning. "For ye have no conscience to reckon with."

Carstares' face was inscrutable. He touched his lips with his napkin and smiled.

"As you say, I enjoy life the more—but as to conscience, I do not think it is that."

O'Hara glanced at him sitting sideways in his chair, one arm flung over its back.

"Will ye be offended if I ask ye a question?"

"Of course not."

"Then—do ye intend to go back to this highroad robbery?"

"I do not."

"What then will you do?"

The shadows vanished, and my lord laughed.

"To tell you the truth, Miles, I've not yet settled that point. Fate will decide—not I."

CHAPTER XVI

Mr. Bettison Proposes

MR. BETTISON could make nothing of Diana of late. Her demeanour, at first so charming and so cheerful, had become listless, and even chilling. She seemed hardly to listen to some of his best tales, and twice she actually forgot to laugh at what was surely a most witty pleasantry. It struck him that she regarded him with a resentful eye, as if she objected to his presence at Horton House, and had no desire to be courted. But Mr. Bettison was far too egotistic to believe such a thing, and he brushed the incredible suspicion away, deciding that her coldness was due to a very proper shyness. He continued his visits until they became so frequent that scarce a day passed without his strutting step being heard approaching the house and his voice inquiring for the Miss Beauleighs. Mr. Beauleigh, who secretly hoped for Mr. Bettison as a son-in-law, would not permit the ladies to deny themselves, and he further counselled Miss Betty to absent herself after the first few moments, leaving the young couple together. Thus it was that it so continually fell to Diana's lot to receive the Squire and to listen to his never-ending monologues. She persistently snubbed him, hoping to ward off the impending proposal, but either her snubs were not severe enough, or Mr. Bettison's skin was too thick to feel them; for not a fortnight after my lord's departure, he begged her hand in marriage. It was refused him with great firmness, but, taking the refusal for coquettishness, he pressed his suit still more amorously, and with such a self-assured air that Mistress Di became indignant.

"Sir," she cried, "it seems you have indeed misread my attitude towards you!"

Mr. Bettison was struck dumb with amazement. It had never entered his brain that Diana could seriously refuse him. He could hardly believe his ears at the quite unmistakable tone of voice, and sat gaping.

"I must beg," continued Diana, "I must beg that you will discontinue your all-too-frequent visits here. Please do not deem me unkind, but your persecution of me—I can call it nothing else—is wearying—and—you will forgive the word —tiresome. I confess I am surprised that you had not perceived your attentions to be distasteful to me."

"Distasteful!" cried Mr. Bettison, recovering after two or three unsuccessful attempts from his speechlessness. "Do you mean what you say, Miss Diana? That you will not wed me?"

She nodded.

"Yes, Mr. Bettison, I do."

"And that my attentions are displeasing to you! Well, Miss Beauleigh! Well, indeed!"

Diana softened a little.

"I am indeed sorry that you should have misconstrued——"

"No misconstruction, madam!" snapped the Squire, who was fast losing control over his temper. "Do you dare aver that you did not encourage me to visit you?"

"I do, most emphatically!"

"Oh, I see what 'tis! You cannot hoodwink me. 'Twas never thus with you before that fellow came!"

"Mr. Bettison, I am entirely at a loss, but I desire you to leave this room before you say aught you may afterwards regret."

He disregarded her.

"You are infatuated by that over-dressed popinjay—that insufferable Carr, who, from all I hear, is but a shady fellow, and who——"

With a sweeping movement Diana had risen and walked to the bell-rope. She now pulled it with such vigour that a great peal sounded throughout the house.

She stood perfectly still, a statue of Disdain, tall, beautiful and furious, with compressed lips and head held high. Mr. Bettison broke off and mopped his brow, glaring at her.

Startled, Thomas appeared at the door.

"Did you ring, madam?"

"Show Mr. Bettison out," was the proud answer.

The Squire got up awkwardly.

"I am sure I apologise if I said aught that was untrue," he mumbled. "I hope you will not take my words amiss——"

"I shall try to forget your insults, sir," she replied. "The door, Thomas!"

Mr. Bettison went out, and his step had lost some of its self-confident swagger.

For a full minute after the great front door had shut behind him, Diana stood where she was, and then the colour suddenly flamed in her cheeks, and she turned and ran out of the room, up the stairs, to her own chamber, where she indulged in a luxurious fit of crying. From this enjoyable occupation she was interrupted by a rap on the door, and Miss Betty's voice desiring to know if she was within.

She instantly started up and with hasty fingers straightened her tumbled curls.

"Pray enter!" she called, trying to sound jaunty. To complete the illusion, she started to hum. Her aunt entered.

"I came to see if you had my broidery. I cannot find it, and I am sure 'twas you brought it in from the garden this morning."

"Yes—oh, yes—I am so sorry! 'Tis in that corner on the chair, I think," replied Diana, keeping her face averted.

Miss Betty cast a shrewd glance at her, and sat down on the sofa with the air of one who meant to stay.

"What is it, my love?" she demanded.

Diana pretended to search for something in a cupboard.

"Nothing, aunt! What should there be?"

"I do not know. 'Tis what I want to find out," answered Miss Betty placidly.

"There is nought amiss, I assure you!" To prove the truth of this statement, Diana essayed a laugh. It was a poor attempt, and wavered pitifully into a sob.

"My pet, don't tell *me*! You are crying!"

"I—I'm n-not!" avowed Diana, hunting wildly for her pocket-handkerchief. " 'Tis a cold in the head I have had these three days."

"Indeed, my love? Longer than that, I fear."

"Yes—perhaps so—I—— What do you mean?"

"I doubt but what you caught it the day that Mr. Carr left us."

Diana started.

"P-pray, do not be ridiculous, auntie!"

"No, my dear. Come and sit beside me and tell me all about it," coaxed Miss Betty.

Diana hesitated, gave a damp sniff, and obeyed.

Miss Betty drew her head down on to her shoulder soothingly.

"There, there! Don't cry, my sweet! What has happened?"

" 'Tis that odious Mr. Bettison!" sobbed Diana. "He—he had the audacity to ask me to m-marry him!"

"You don't say so, my love! I thought I heard him arrive. So you sent him about his business?"

"N-not before he had time to insult m-me!"

"Insult you? Di!"

"He—he dared to insinuate—oh no! he accused me outright of being infatuated by Mr. Carr! Infatuated!"

Over her head Miss Betty opened her eyes at her own reflection in the glass.

"The brute! But, of course, 'tis true?"

No answer.

"Is it not?"

The sobs came faster.

"Of—of course 'tis true, but h-how dared he say so?"

"Di, my love, you really are in love with that boy?"

"I—I—I asked him to marry me—and he wouldn't!"

"Good gracious heavens!" Miss Betty was genuinely horrified. "My dear Diana!"

"N-not outright—b-but he understood—and—he loves me! And I'd do it again to-morrow, if I could—immodest or no! So there!"

"Yes, yes," soothed Miss Betty hastily. "Tell me all about it."

Diana lifted her head.

"That's all. And he loves me—he does—he does!"

"Did he say so?"

"N-no—but I could tell. And I love him"—sob—"and I'd sooner die than live without him, and he won't ask me b-because he has not got a spotless p-past, and he'd be a cur, and horrid things, and my husband must not be an—an—outcast, and—and—and I don't care!"

Her bewildered aunt unravelled this with difficulty.

"He'd be a cur if he asked you to marry him?" she asked, with knitted brows.

"Yes. Because he's a highwayman."

"A highwayman! Then 'twas true what he said? Well, well! I should never have thought it! That nice boy!"

Diana disengaged herself; in her eyes was a threatening gleam.

"Don't dare say a word against him!"

"No, no—of course not! I was only surprised. But I am thankfully glad he did not ask you, for all that!"

"Glad? How can you be so cruel?"

"My dear, you could not possibly marry—a—a——"

"Common felon!" sobbed Diana. "I can—I can!"

"And heaven alone knows what else he may have done! Why, child, he said himself that he had a—a spotty past!"

At this her niece gave a tearful giggle.

"La! What ails you now, Di?"

"H-he never said—spotty."

Miss Betty smiled reluctantly.

"A doubtful past, then."

"I don't believe it!"

Her aunt pursed up her lips.

"I won't believe it. He couldn't be wicked. You forget he saved me!"

Miss Betty relented.

"No, I do not, my love; and, to be sure, I think he is a dear boy, but I also think 'twas very right of him to go away."

She was enveloped in a rapturous embrace.

"Auntie, you know you love him almost as much as I do?"

"No, that I do not!" was the grim retort. "*I* am not like to marry him!"

There was another watery giggle at this, and Diana went over to the dressing-table to tidy her hair.

"I doubt I shall never see him again," she said wretchedly. "Oh, auntie, if you could but have seen his dear, unhappy eyes!"

"Stuff and nonsense! Not see him again, forsooth! He will call upon us in town. 'Tis but common politeness."

"You forget he is a highwayman, and not like to come nigh us again."

"Well, my dear, if he cares for you as you say he does, he will see to it that he takes up some decent occupation. Mayhap, he will go into the army, or what not. Then wait and see if he does not come to you."

"Do you think so?" doubtfully.

"Of course I do, sweetheart! And if he does not try to mend his ways, and you see him no more—why then, snap your fingers at him, my love, for he will not be worth one tear!"

Diana sighed and poured out some water to bathe her face with.

"Is not that sensible?" coaxed her aunt.

She raised her head and looked unutterable scorn.

"I think 'tis remarkable silly," she answered. Then her dignity fell from her. "Oh, are all men such big stupids?" she cried.

"Most of 'em," nodded her aunt.

"But can't he tell that I shall be—oh, so miserable, and that I should not ruin my life if I married him?"

"My dear, once a man gets an idea into his head, 'tis the very devil to get it out of him! Not but what I think Master Jack is right, mind you. And your dear papa and I had looked higher for you. After all—what is Mr. Carr?"

"He is the only man I will ever marry! So you may cease looking higher for me! I suppose you want me to marry that great gaby, Sir Denis Fabian, you are for ever inviting to the house? Or, perhaps, this gallant Mr. Bettison? Or Mr. Everard? How *can* you be so unkind?"

"I am not. But I could not bear to see you throw yourself away on a highwayman, my dear."

Diana ran to her, putting her arms round her neck.

"Dearest auntie, forgive my rudeness! I know you did not mean to be unkind! But you do not understand—I *love* him."

"I always said you'd take it badly," nodded Miss Betty gloomily.

"Take what badly?"

"Love. And no man is worth one tear-drop, sweet."

The confident, tender little laugh that answered this statement made her look at her suddenly changed niece in surprise.

"You don't know," said Diana. Her eyes were soft and luminous. "You just do not know."

Before Miss Betty could think of a suitable retort, a knock fell on the door. It was opened, and Thomas was found to be without.

"My Lady O'Hara is below, madam."

For an instant the two ladies stared at one another. Then:

"La and drat!" said Miss Betty. "With the drawing-room in a muddle after cleaning!"

Diana nodded to the man.

"We will come, Thomas." Then as soon as he had withdrawn, she stared again at her aunt. "Lady O'Hara! But why?"

"I suppose she felt she must call after Sir Miles had been here so often. But why, for goodness' sake, must she choose the one day that the drawing-room is all untidy? Drat again, I say!"

Diana was powdering her little nose, and anxiously looking to see if the tear-stains had quite vanished.

" 'Tis not untidy, Aunt Betty. Oh, I am quite eager to see her—I think she must be charming, from all Sir Miles said. Do hurry, aunt!"

Miss Betty stuck a pin into her hair and smoothed out her dress.

"And me in this old taffeta!" she grumbled.

Diana swirled round, her own peach-coloured silk rustling fashionably.

"Never mind, dear—you look very sweet. But *do* be quick!"

Miss Betty suffered herself to be led to the door.

" 'Tis all very fine for you, my love, with a new gown fresh on to-day! Will you just take a look at my petticoat, though?"

"Nonsense, you are beautiful! Come!"

Together they descended the stairs, and went into the drawing-room.

A dainty, very diminutive little lady arose from a chair at their entry, and came forward with outstretched hands, and such a fascinating smile that Miss Betty's ill-humour vanished, and she responded to her visitor's deep curtsy with one of her best jerky dips.

"I am vastly delighted to welcome you, madam," she said primly. " 'Tis good in you to come this long way to see us."

She drew a chair forward for my lady, and presented her niece. Lady O'Hara gave the girl a swift, scrutinising glance, and curtsied again.

" 'Tis a great pleasure to me to meet you at last, Miss Beauleigh," she smiled. "My husband has told me so much of you, I declare I was all agog to meet you!"

Diana warmed instantly to the little lady's charm.

"Indeed, madam, we, too, have heard much of you from Sir Miles. *We* have wanted to meet *you*!"

Lady O'Hara seated herself and nodded briskly.

"I expect he told you some dreadful tales of me," she said happily. "I must ask your pardon for not having visited you before, but, as I daresay you know, I have been away, and, gracious me, when I returned everything seemed topsy-turvy!" She laughed across at Miss Betty. "I promise you I have had my hands full putting things to rights, Miss Beauleigh!"

Miss Betty drew her chair closer, and in a minute they were deep in truly feminine conversation: the prodigious extravagance of the servants; the helplessness of men-folk when left to themselves; and then London, its shops, its parks, the newest play.

Lady O'Hara was begged to take a dish of Miss Betty's precious Bohea—a very high honour indeed—and when Mr. Beauleigh came into the room he found his sister and daughter seated on either side of a pretty, animated little lady whom he had never before seen, talking hard, and partaking of tay and angel cakes. Whereupon he retired hastily and shut himself up in his library.

CHAPTER XVII

Lady O'Hara Wins Her Point

LADY O'HARA looked across at her sleeping husband with no little severity in her glance. He was stretched in a chair beneath a giant oak, and she was busied with some needle-work a few paces from him. O'Hara's eyes were shut and his mouth open. My lady frowned and coughed. She rasped her throat quite considerably, but it was not without effect; her spouse shut his mouth and opened one lazy eyelid. Immediately my lady assumed an air of gentle mournfulness, and the eye regarding her twinkled a little, threatening to close. Molly looked reproachful, and began to speak in an aggrieved tone:

"Indeed, and I do not think it all kind in you to go to sleep when I want to talk, sir."

O'Hara hastily opened the other eye.

"Why, my love, I was not asleep! I was—er—thinking!"

"Do you say so, sir? And do you usually think with your mouth open—*snoring?*"

O'Hara started up.

"I'll swear I did not snore!" he cried. "Molly, 'tis a wicked tease ye are!"

"Miles, 'tis a big baby you are!" she mimicked. "There is a caterpillar on your wig, and 'tis on crooked."

"The caterpillar?" asked O'Hara, bewildered.

"No, stupid, the wig. I had best straighten it for you, I suppose." She rose and stooped over him, setting the wig and removing the caterpillar by means of two leaves, judiciously wielded. Then she dropped a kiss on her husband's brow and sat down at his feet.

"First, you have never asked me where I was gone to all yesterday afternoon."

O'Hara had been carefully broken in, and he now knew what was expected of him, and put on an expression of great interest.

"Where *did* ye go, my lady?"

"I went to call on Miss Beauleigh and her niece, sir!"

She looked up at him triumphantly and a little challengingly.

"The devil ye did!"

"Certainly, sir. I knew that there was something in the air, and I remembered your letter to me saying that Jack was in love with Diana. So I thought I would go and see her for myself."

Miles looked down at her half indulgently, half vexedly.

"Did you, puss?"

"I did. And I found that she was in love with him as well as he with her—of course."

"Of course?"

"Who could help falling in love with him? He's so monstrous captivating, I would like to marry him myself."

She bent her head to hide the roguish smile that had sprung to her lips.

"I beg your pardon?" asked O'Hara, startled.

My lady traced patterns on his knee.

"Provided, of course, that I had not already married you, Miles."

But O'Hara had seen the smile. He heaved a great sigh, and said in lugubrious tones:

"There is always the river, madam."

My lady's fingers wavered and stopped, and her hand tucked itself away into his.

"That is not a nice joke, Miles."

He laughed, and tweaked one of her curls.

"Sure, and did ye not ask for it, asthore?"

"Of course I did not. But about Jack, dear——"

"I thought it *was* about Jack?"

"Miles, will you be quiet and attend?"

"Yes, m'dear."

"Very well, then. As I told you, I drove over to Littledean yesterday afternoon, and made the acquaintance of the Miss Beauleighs."

"And what did ye think of them?"

"I thought Diana was wonderfully beautiful—such eyes, Miles!—and such hair! Miss Beauleigh is very amiable, and so droll! I drank a dish of tay with them, and I spoke of Jack——"

"Madcap, never tell me ye called him Carstares?"

"No, you great gaby! Of course I did not. As it chanced, Miss Beauleigh mentioned him first, and she called him Mr. Carr. So I did, too. And I noticed that Diana said scarce a word about him, and when she did 'twas of the coolest. That, of course, made me all the more certain that she loved him."

O'Hara was plainly puzzled.

"But why should you be certain if she did not speak of him, alanna?"

" 'Tis what you'll never understand, my dear, because you are but a man. But no matter—I knew. I quite adored Diana, and determined to talk to her alone. So I admired the roses, and she offered to escort me round the garden, which was what I wanted. We went out together. I think Diana must have liked me, for——"

"Nonsense!"

"Be quiet, Miles!—for she dropped her ice and became quite friendly. And I talked a lot."

She was aware of a convulsive movement above her, and a suppressed cough. She raised inquiring eyebrows.

"Well, sir?"

"Nothing, asthore—nothing. Go on with the tale—you were saying——"

"That I talked a lot." She paused, and her eyes dared him; then she dimpled and dropped her lashes over them. "I shan't tell you all I said——"

A relieved sigh interrupted her.

"And if you continue to behave in this disagreeable fashion I shall not say another word about anything!"

Having satisfied herself that he was not going to venture a retort, she continued:

"We had a long chat, and I gathered, from all she said and left unsaid, that Jack, for some foolish reason, will not ask her to marry him."

"Foolish reason, asthore?" he interrupted.

"Oh, I know you consider it a remarkable fine reason, but I tell you, 'tis rank cruelty to that poor child. As if she cared about highwaymen!"

" 'Twas not so much that, I take it, as——"

"Yes, but he could tell her he was innocent—oh, Miles, do not look so provoking! Of course he could! I vow if you had treated me so, I would never have let you go until you had truly repented! I am of a mind to speak to Jack."

" 'Twould be an entertaining sight, but ye'll kindly have a care how you touch him, my lady."

"He does not understand. I *know* she would be proud to marry him——"

"And ye'd think it a fine thing in Jack to ask her, the way things are with him at present?"

"I—oh, I don't know!"

"No, me love. Jack is right: he must first clear his name."

"Then, gracious goodness me, why does he not?" cried Molly, exasperated.

This time it was O'Hara's turn to look superior.

"Well, alanna, that's a question ye cannot hope to understand—because ye are but a woman."

Lady O'Hara ignored the challenge.

"But what is to be done?"

"Nought. He will have to work it out himself. He bound me to secrecy some time ago, or I would be tempted to speak to Richard."

"I quite *hate* Richard!" she cried. "He must be a selfish, unkind person. And now Jack swears he must go away almost at once—and, oh! you should have seen Diana's face of despair when I mentioned that he was going abroad again. Miles, we must keep him here as long as ever we can! Oh, dear! 'tis all very worrying."

She broke off as O'Hara pressed her hand warningly. My lord was coming across the lawn towards them.

"I am in dire disgrace," he said. "I was left with your ferocious baby, Molly, and to quiet him, I gave him a string of beads that you had left on the table."

"My precious Indian wooden beads!"

"Yes—I believe so. Anyway, the paint came off, and when Jane returned, David looked as though he had some horrible disease. She was most annoyed about it." He sat down in Molly's lately vacated chair, and carefully wiped a daub of green from his forefinger.

Molly laughed.

"Poor Jane! She will have such a task to clean him. But you've arrived most opportunely. We were talking of you."

O'Hara groaned inwardly, and tried to frown her down.

"You were? I am flattered! May I ask what you were saying?"

"Why, that we do not want you to go back to France."

O'Hara breathed again.

"That is very kind of you, my lady. I regret the necessity myself."

"Are you sure it is necessary? You might just as well live in a nice place near here, with a dear old woman to keep house for you—and—and Jim—and—lots of pleasant things."

My lord shook his head.

"No, thank you!"

"Yes, yes! And later on you could choose a wife!" she continued audaciously.

"Not at all. There would be no choice; I should be made to marry the dear old woman. You would bully me into it."

She laughed.

"Seriously, Jack, could you not settle down near here?"

"Not with that old woman, Molly."

"Never mind her; won't you consider it? No one need know you—in fact, you need see no one—and—oh, Jack! don't look like that. Miles, is he not ridiculous?"

"Sure, alanna, 'tis a dreary life he'd be leading," chuckled O'Hara.

"I see what it is, Molly. You have planned to make me a recluse, *and* to marry me to my housekeeper. I protest, 'tis great ill-usage!"

Molly eyed him doubtfully.

"Would you *much* object to the life, John?"

"Madam," he replied solemnly, "you would find my corpse in the garden at the end of the first week."

"Of course I should not like that," she pondered. "But I do not see what else we can do for you. Oh, and that reminds me! I drove over to Littledean yesterday—Miles, my love, will you be so kind as to fetch my hat? I protest, the sun——"

"We will move more into the shade," said his disobliging husband.

"Oh, well! 'tis of no account, though I did hear that Brown was wanting to speak to you about the new cob——"

" 'Tis prodigious thoughtful of you, Molly, but I met Brown some time ago."

Lady O'Hara gave it up.

"Well, as I was saying, Jack, I went to call at Horton House. Dear me, what a beautiful girl Diana is, to be sure!"

Carstares tried to think of something to say, and failing, made a non-committal sound.

"Yes. They both sent their kind wishes, and hoped you were better. Goodness! 'tis very close here. I wonder if you would give me your arm round the garden? And would *you* fetch me my hat? I left it in the hall, I think. Thank you very much!"

She waited until he was out of earshot before she turned to her husband.

"Now, Miles, you must please to stay where you are. I am not going to do anything indiscreet."

"Molly, I can't have ye worry him——"

"No such thing! I am going to coax him to stay here instead of going abroad. I feel sure that if we can but persuade him to stay, something will happen."

"What will happen?"

"Something!"

"How do ye know?"

"I don't know; I only feel it."

"Very well, asthore. If you can tease Jack into staying, I'll bless ye."

"That will be most enjoyable, I make no doubt!" she answered, and stepped back out of reach.

"Oh, thank you, John!" She tied the hat over her curls, and placed her hand on my lord's arm. "Lazy Miles is going to sleep again!" she said. "And I so dislike to hear him snore, so let's go a long way away—into the rose garden!"

"Don't go so far as all that!" drawled Miles, closing his eyes. "You will tire yourselves."

"Do you allow him to make these ribald remarks?" inquired Jack, waiting for her to extricate a stone from her shoe.

"Not usually," she answered. "He takes advantage when you are here." She dropped the pebble on top of O'Hara and strolled away with my lord.

As soon as they had rounded a corner in the shrubbery she commenced the attack.

"I want to speak to you of Miles," she confided. "He is so worried."

"Is he, Molly? Faith, I hadn't noticed it!"

She reflected that neither had she, but continued, nothing daunted:

"Ah, but he is!"

"What worries him?"

"You," sighed the lady mournfully. " 'Tis the thought of your leaving us. I feel it myself."

"Why——"

"He had hoped you would be with us for a long time—as I had."

" 'Tis monstrous good of you both, but——"

"I am sure I do not know what I shall do with Miles when you are gone. He was so looking forward to having you with him."

"Molly——"

"And, indeed, it has come as a great disappointment to both of us to hear you talk of leaving. Won't you think better of it?"

"Molly, you overwhelm me. . . . How can I remain here indefinitely?"

"If only you would! You don't know how happy it would make us. I declare Miles will worry himself quite ill if you persist in being so unkind."

"Oh, Molly, you rogue!"

She could not repress a smile, but checked it almost at once.

"I mean it, Jack."

"What! That Miles is worrying himself ill over me? Fie!"

"Perhaps not as bad as that," she admitted. "But, indeed, he is much perturbed . . . and, oh! I wish that you would not make us so unhappy." She dabbed at her eyes with a wispy handkerchief, but managed to watch his face all the same. "David loves you so, the pet! and Miles is so delighted to have found you again—and *I* like you—and—and—and I think 'twill be indeed rude and horrid if you do go—besides being so silly!"

"Do you, Molly? You make me feel I should be an ungrateful boor to refuse——"

The handkerchief was whisked away.

"Then, of course you won't try to refuse! You'll stay? Promise!"

"I cannot thank you enough——"

"Oh, you nice Jack. Till the autumn? Promise!"

"Molly, I really——"

"Promise! I shall cry if you do not!"

"I cannot! How could I prey upon your hospitality for so——"

"What rubbish, Jack! As if Miles had not spent months and months at Wyncham when you were boys——"

"That was different——"

"——when you were boys, and now you are so proud that you refuse to stay three miserable little months with us——"

"No, no, Molly; indeed, 'tis not that!"

"Confess, if Miles were a bachelor, you would not hesitate?"

He was silent, nonplussed.

"You see! And just because he has a wife you are disagreeable and proud. You feel you cannot bear to stay with me——"

"I swear I do not!"

"Then why do you refuse?" she triumphed.

"Molly—really, I——" He broke off, laughing. "You little wretch, you leave me nothing to say!"

"Then you will stay, as I ask?"

"You are quite sure——"

"Quite."

"Thank you very much, I will stay. 'Tis monstrous good of you, I vow. When you are tired of me, say so."

"I will," she promised. "Oh, but we shall do famously! How pleased Miles will be! By the way," she continued, airily, "I asked the Miss Beauleighs to honour us on Wednesday, but, unfortunately, they could not. Still, perhaps some other d——"

She stopped, a little frightened, for he was standing beside her, gripping her shoulders in a very elder-brotherly fashion.

"Listen to me, Molly. I know that you have discovered that I love Diana, and I know that you think to be very kind and to bring us together. But I tell you that 'twill not be kind at all, only very cruel to us both. If you worry her to come here, I must go. Do you see?"

Molly looked into the stern eyes, and her lip trembled.

"I'm very—sorry!" she faltered.

Jack drew her arm through his once more.

" 'Tis nothing to be sorry about; and, indeed, I am very grateful to you for trying to make me happy. But please do not!"

"No, I promise I will not. But—but do you think you are being quite fair to——"

"Molly, tell me this: do you think you are being quite good to disobey your husband?"

The blue eyes were dancing. She smiled doubtfully.

"What do you mean, Jack?"

"Do you tell me that Miles did not expressly forbid you to mention this subject to me?"

She pulled her hand away, her mouth forming a soundless "Oh!"

"Well—well—well, how horrid of you!" she cried, and shook her fist at him. "I'm going now!"

Later, she found her husband in the library, and ran into his arms.

"Do you mind holding me tightly?" she asked. "I've—I've been put in the corner!"

"What?" O'Hara drew her on to his knee.

"Yes—figuratively—by Jack. I think, perhaps, I shouldn't like to marry him after all!"

"What has he done?"

"N-nothing. I'm *afraid*," polishing one of his buttons with an assiduous finger. "I'm *afraid* that it was rather my own fault!"

"Oh!"

"Yes—but I only said *very* little about the Miss Beauleighs, and he suddenly turned into an iceberg and made me feel like a naughty little girl. But he is going to stay, all the same; so kiss me, Miles!"

CHAPTER XVIII

Enter Captain Harold Lovelace

At the end of August, after having spent a moderately quiet summer in the country, Lady Lavinia was again seized with a longing for town and its attractions. She would not listen to Richard's warnings of the atrocious conditions of the roads, declaring that she cared not one jot, and go to London she must. After that one protest he desisted, and promised to take her there the following week, secretly counting himself lucky to have kept her so long at Wyncham in comparative cheerfulness of spirits. Lavinia was overjoyed, kissed him again and again, scolded herself for being such a wicked tease, and set about making her preparations for the journey.

The roads proved even worse than Richard had prophesied, and twice the coach nearly upset, and times without number stuck fast in the mire, causing the inmates much inconvenience. Carstares rode by the side of the heavy vehicle, in which were his wife, her maid, her tiny dog, and countless bandboxes and small parcels. In spite of the worry the constant stoppages entailed, he quite enjoyed the journey, for Lavinia was in excellent spirits and made light of their mishaps, receiving each fresh one with roguish laughter and some witty remark. Even when the chimney of her bedchamber, at one of the inns at which they halted, smoked most vilely, she did not, as Richard quite expected she would, fly into a rage and refuse to spend another moment in the house, but after looking extremely doleful, cheered up and told dear Dicky that she would have his room while he should have hers. Then in the morning she would find him all dried up and *smoked*! In high good humour she went down to dinner with him, voted the partridges excellent, the pasties quite French, and the wine marvellously tolerable for such an out-of-the-way place, and kept him laughing at her antics until bedtime.

The journey was, of necessity, very slow, not only on account of the bad roads, but because whenever my lady caught

sight of wild roses growing on the hedges, she must stop to
pluck some. Then she and Richard would stroll along for
some way, he leading his horse, the coach following at a
walking pace. All of which was very idyllic, and had the
effect of sending Richard to the seventh heaven of content.

When at length they arrived at Wyncham House, Mayfair,
they found that the servants had arrived a week before, and
had made good use of their time. Never, declared Lavinia,
had the house looked so inviting—so spick and span.

One of her black pages proffered a small monkey with
much bowing and grinning, and the murmur of: "Massa's
present."

Lady Lavinia flew to embrace her Dicky. How did he
guess that she had for so long yearned for a monkey! Surely
she had but once or twice mentioned it? Oh, he was the very
best of husbands! She danced off to her apartments in a state
of ecstasy.

The *beau monde* was returning to town, and when, a few
days later, Carstares conducted his wife to Ranelagh, they
found the gardens fairly crowded and very gay. Lamps hung
from tree branches, although it was still quite light; the fid-
dlers scraped away almost without a pause; fireworks shot up
from one end; the summer-houses had all been freshly
painted, and the Pavilion was a blaze of light.

Consciousness of her beauty and the smartness of her
Georgia silk gown, with its petticoat covered in a gold net,
considerably added to Lavinia's enjoyment. Her hair she wore
powdered and elaborately curled down on both sides with
dainty escalloped lace half concealing it, and a grey *capuchin*
over all. Her tippet was gold-laced to match her petticoat,
and to fasten it she wore a brooch composed of clustered rubies. Rubies also hung in her earrings, which last were of
such length that the other ladies turned to stare in envy, and
the bracelets that she wore over her long gloves flashed also
with the great red stones. She was well-pleased with Richard's
appearance, and reflected that, when he chose, he could be
very fashionable indeed. The claret-coloured velvet he was
wearing was most distinguished, and the gold clocks to his
hose quite ravishing.

They had not been in the Gardens ten minutes before a little crowd of men had gathered around them, professing
themselves enraptured to behold the fair Lady Lavinia once

more. One of them fetched her a chair, another a glass of negus, and the rest hovered eagerly about her.

Becomingly flushed with triumph, my lady gave her little hand to Mr. Selwyn, who had been once a very ardent admirer, laughed at his neat compliment, and declared that he was a dreadful flattering demon, and positively she would not listen to him!

Sir Gregory Markham, who brought her the negus, she discovered to have just returned from Paris. On hearing this, she broke off in the middle of a conversation with an enchanted French Chevalier and turned to him, raising her china-blue eyes to his face and clasping tight-gloved hands.

"Oh, Sir Gregory! Paris? Then tell me—please, tell me—have you seen my darling Devil?"

"Why, yes, madam," responded Markham, handing her the glass he held.

She sipped the negus, and gave it to the Chevalier to take care of.

"I declare, I quite love you then!" she exclaimed. "What is he doing, and, oh! *when* will he return to England?"

Sir Gregory smiled.

"How can I say?" he drawled. "I fear *monsieur s'amuse!*"

She flirted her fan before her face.

"Dreadful creature!" she cried. "How dare you say such things?"

"Belmanoir?" inquired Lord D'Egmont, twirling his cane. "Enamoured of the Pompadour, is he not—saving your presence, Lady Lavvy!"

Lavinia let fall her fan.

"The Pompadour! He had best have a care!"

"I believe there has already been some unpleasantness between his Majesty and the fair Jeanne on the subject of Devil. Since then she is supposed to have turned on him a cold shoulder."

"*I* heard 'twas he wearied of madame," said Markham.

"Well, whichever it was, I am glad the episode is closed," decided Lavinia. " 'Tis too dangerous a game to play with Louis' mistresses. Oh, mon cher Chevalier! if I had not forgot your presence! But I am sure you say dreadful ill-natured things of our George, now don't you? Oh, and have you held my negus all this time? How monstrous good of you! There, I will drink it, and Julian shall take the glass away . . . *Voila!*"

She handed it to D'Egmont and rapped Mr. Selwyn's knuckles with her fan, looking archly up at him as he stood behind her chair.

"Naughty man! Will you have done whispering in my ear? I vow I will not listen to your impudences! No, nor laugh at them neither! Sir Gregory, you have given me no answer. When will Tracy return? For the Cavendish rout on Wednesday week? Ah, say yes!"

"Certainly I will say yes, fair tormentor! But, to tell the truth, Tracy said no word of coming to London when I saw him."

She pouted.

"Now I hate you, Sir Gregory! And he has been absent since May! Oh, Julian, back already? You shall escort me to the fireworks then. Oh, my fan! Where is it? I know I dropped it on the ground—Selwyn, if you have taken it—Oh, Dicky, you have it! Thank you! See, I am going with Julian, and you may ogle Mrs. Clive, whom I see walking over there—yes, positively you may, and I shall not be jealous! Very well, Julian, I am coming! Chevalier, I shall hope to see you at the rout on Wednesday week, but you must wait upon me before then."

The Frenchman brightened.

"Madame is too good. I may then call at Wyncham 'Ouse? *Vraiment*, I shall but exist until then!" In a perfectly audible whisper, he confided to Wilding that *"miladi était ravissante! mais ravissante!"*

Lady Lavinia went off on her gratified cavalier's arm, encountering many bows and much admiration as she passed down the walk, leaving her husband not to ogle the beautiful Kitty, as she had advised, but to saunter away in the direction of the Pavilion in company with Tom Wilding and Markham.

D'Egmont guided my lady into one of the winding alleys, and they presently came out on a large lawn, dotted over with people of all conditions. Towards them was coming Lavinia's brother—Colonel Lord Robert Belmanoir—very richly clad and rakish in appearance. When he saw his sister, a look of surprise came into his florid face, and he made her a sweeping leg.

" 'Pon my honour—Lavinia!"

My lady was not fond of her brother, and acknowledged the salutation with a brief nod.

"I am delighted to see you, Robert," she said primly.

"The mere word 'delighted' in no way expresses my sensations," replied the Colonel in the drawling, rather unpleasant voice peculiar both to him and to the Duke. "Your servant, D'Egmont. I imagined, Lavvy, that you were in the country?"

"Richard brought me to town last Tuesday," she answered.

"How unwise of him!" taunted the Colonel. "Or had he no choice?"

She tossed her head angrily.

"If you are minded to be disagreeable, Robert, pray do not let me detain you!" she flashed.

D'Egmont was quite unembarrassed by this interchange of civilities. He knew the Belmanoir family too well to be made uncomfortable by their bickerings.

"Shall we leave him?" he asked Lavinia, smiling.

"Yes," she pouted. "He is determined to be unpleasant."

"My dear sister! On the contrary, I believe I can offer you some amusement. Lovelace is in town."

"Captain *Harold*?" she cried incredulously.

"The same."

"Oh, Bob!" Impulsively she withdrew her hand from Julian's arm, transferring it to the Colonel's. "I must see him at once! To think he is returned after all these years! Quick, Julian, dear lad—go and find him—and tell him 'tis I, Lavinia, who want him! You know him, do you not? Yes—I thought you did. Send him to me at once!—at once!"

D'Egmont looked very crestfallen at having his walk with the goddess thus cut short, but he had perforce to kiss her hand and to obey.

"Yes. I thought you would be pleased," remarked Lord Robert, and chuckled. "Allow me to point out to you that there is a chair—two chairs—in fact, quite a number of chairs—immediately behind you."

She sat down, chattering excitedly.

"Why, 'tis nigh on five years since I saw Harry! Has he changed? Lud! but he will deem me an old woman? Is he like to be in town for long, I wonder?—Dear me, Bob, look at the two ladies over behind that seat!—Gracious! what extraordinary *coifs*, to be sure! And cherry ribbons, too! . . . Tell me, Bob, where did you meet Harry Lovelace?"

The Colonel, who, far from attending to her monologue, had been sending amorous glances across to a palpably embarrassed girl, who hung on her papa's arm while that gentleman stopped to speak to a stout dowager, brought his gaze reluctantly back to his sister.

"What's that you say, Lavvy?"

"How provoking of you not to listen to me! I asked where you met Harold."

"Where I met him? Let me see—where did I meet him? Oh, I remember! At the Cocoa-Tree, a fortnight since."

"And he is altered?"

"Not in any way, dear sister. He is the same mad, reckless rake-hell as ever. And unmarried."

"How delightful! Oh, I shall be so glad to see him again!"

"You must present him to Richard," sneered the Colonel "as an old flame."

"I must, indeed," she agreed, his sarcasm passing over her head. "Oh, I see him! Look! Coming across the grass!"

She rose to meet the tall, fair young Guardsman who came swiftly towards her, curtsying as only Lady Lavinia could curtsy, with such stateliness and coquetry.

"Captain Lovelace!" she put forward both her hands.

Lovelace caught them in his, and bent his head over them so that the soft, powdered curls of his loose wig fell all about his face.

"Lady Lavinia!—Enchantress!—I can find no words! I am dumb!"

"And I!"

"In that case," drawled the Colonel, "you are not like to be very entertaining company. Pray give me leave!" He bowed and sauntered away down the path with a peculiarly malicious smile on his lips.

Lavinia and Lovelace found two chairs, slightly apart from the rest, and sat down, talking eagerly.

"Captain Lovelace, I believe you had forgot me?" she rallied him.

"Never!" he answered promptly. "Not though you well-night broke my heart!"

"No, no! I did not do that. I never meant to hurt you."

He shook his head disbelievingly.

"You rejected me to marry some other man: do you say you did not mean to?"

"You naughty Harry! . . . You never married yourself?"

"I?" The delicate features expressed a species of hurt horror. "I marry? No! I was ever faithful to my first love."

She unfurled her fan, fluttering it delightedly.

"Oh! Oh! *Always*, Harold? Now speak the truth!"

"Nearly always," he amended.

"Disagreeable man! You admit you had lapses then?"

"So very trivial, my dear," he excused himself. "And I swear my first action on coming to London was to call at Wyncham House. Imagine my disappointment—my incalculable gloom (on the top of having already dropped a thousand at faro) when I found the shell void, and Venus——"

She stopped him, her fan held ready for chastisement.

"Sir! You said your *first* action was to call upon me!"

He smiled, shaking back his curls.

"I should have said: my first action of any importance."

"You do not deem losing a thousand guineas important?" she asked wistfully.

"Well—hardly. One must enjoy life, and what's a thousand, after all? I had my pleasure out of it."

"Yes!" she breathed, her eyes sparkling. "That is how I think! What pleasure can one get if one neither hazards nor spends one's money? Oh, well!" She shrugged one shoulder, dismissing the subject.

"Have you seen Tracy of late?"

"He was at a court ball I attended at Versailles, but I did not have a chance of speaking with him. I heard he was very popular at Paris."

"Ay!" she said proudly. "He has the French air. . . . I so desire to see him again, but I fear he does not think of returning. I know he was promised for the Duchess of Devonshire's rout months ago—before even the date was fixed, she so dotes on him—but I do not expect to see him there." She sighed and drummed on the ground with her diamond-buckled shoe. "Harry, I am chilled! Take me to the Pavilion! I doubt they are dancing—and Dicky will be there."

"Dicky?" he repeated. "Dicky! Lavinia, do not tell me there is another claimant to your heart?"

"Wicked, indelicate creature! 'Tis my husband!"

"Your *husband*! Enfin——!"

She cast him a sidelong glance of mingled coquetry and reproof.

"Your mind is at rest again, I trust?"

"Of course! A husband! Pooh, a bagatelle, no more!"

"My husband is not a bagatelle!" she laughed. "I am very fond of him."

"This grows serious," he frowned. " 'Tis very unfashionable, surely?"

She met his teasing eyes and cast down her lashes.

"Captain Lovelace, you may take me to the Pavilion."

"Sweet tormentor, not until you cease so to misname me."

"Harold, I am indeed chilly!" she said plaintively, and snatched her hand from his lips. "No, no! People will stare —look, there is my odious brother returning! I declare I will not stay to listen to his hateful, sneering remarks! . . . Come!"

They walked across the grass together, keeping up a running fire of raillery, punctuated on his side by extravagant compliments filled with classical allusions, all more or less erroneous, and on hers by delighted little laughs and mock scoldings. So they came to the Pavilion, where the musicians fiddled for those who wished to dance, and where most of the company had assembled now that it was growing chilly without. Down one end of the hall, card-tables were set out, where members of both sexes diced and gambled, drinking glasses of burgundy or negus, the men toasting the ladies, and very often the ladies returning the toasts with much archness and low curtsying.

Lavinia cast off her *capuchin* and plumed her feathers, giving a surreptitious shake to her ruched skirts and smoothing her ruffles. She rustled forward with great stateliness, fan unfurled, head held high, her gloved fingers resting lightly on Lovelace's velvet-clad arm. Richard, hearing the little stir caused by her entry, glanced up, and perceived her. He did not recognise her companion, but the sparkle in her eyes and the happy curve to her full lips, were quite enough to tell him that it was someone whom she was very contented to have met. He had ample opportunity for studying Lovelace as the good-looking pair drew near, and he could not but admire the delicate, handsome face with the grey eyes that held a laugh in them, the pleasure-loving, well-curved mouth, and the chin that spoke of determination. Here was not one of Lavinia's lisping, painted puppy-dogs, for in spite of the effeminate curls, it was easy to see that this man had character and a will of his own, and, above all, a great charm of manner. He saw Lavinia blush and rap the Captain's knuckles in answer to some remark, and his heart sank. He rose and came to meet them.

Lady Lavinia smiled sweetly upon him, and patted his arm with a possessive little air.

"Dicky, dear, I have found an old friend—a very old friend! Is it not agreeable? Captain Lovelace—Mr. Carstares."

The two men bowed, Richard with reluctancy, the Captain with easy *bonhomie*.

"Sir, I claim to be a worshipper at the shrine of which you, I believe, are High Priest!" he said impudently, and bowed again this time to my lady.

"You are one of many, sir," smiled Richard.

Lady Devereux came tripping up to them, and kissed Lavinia with a great show of affection.

"My dearest life! My sweet Lavinia!"

Lady Lavinia presented a powdered cheek.

"Dearest Fanny, how charming to see you again!" she cooed. Through her lashes she gazed at her friend's enormous headdress, with its rolls of powdered curls and the imitation flowers perched upon the top of the erection.

"But, my angel!" exclaimed Lady Fanny, stepping back to view her, "Surely you have been ill?"

"How strange!" smiled Lavinia. "I was about to ask you that same question, my dear! 'Tis age, I doubt not. Do we both look such dreadful hags?" She turned her bewitching little countenance to the men, and smiled appealingly.

Compliments showered upon her, and Lady Devereux, who was conscious that her own sallow countenance, in spite of rouge and powder, must appear even more sallow beside Lavinia's pink-and-whiteness, flushed in annoyance and turned away, begging her dearest Lavvy to come to the faro with her. But Lavinia, it appeared, was going to watch the dicing at Richard's table: she vowed she should bring him monstrous good luck.

"I don't doubt it, my dear," replied her husband, "but I am not playing to-night. Will you not take your luck to Bob?" He nodded to where the Colonel was lounging, dice-box in hand.

Lavinia pouted.

"No, I want you to play!"

"'Tis of no avail, Lady Lavinia!" drawled Sir Gregory. "Richard is the very devil to-night."

Selwyn, rattling his dice, paused, and looked round at Markham with a face of innocent surprise. Then he turned slowly and stared at Carstares' grave, almost stern countenance, with even more surprise. He started to rattle the dice again, and shifted back to face his opponent, with pursed lips.

"Is he?" he inquired with studied depression.

Even Lavinia joined in the general laugh, not so much at the wit's words as at his comic expression, and the extreme deliberation with which he had enacted the little scene.

Someone cried a bet to Lovelace, which was promptly accepted, and Lavinia's eyes glowed afresh as she followed the Captain to a table.

Richard went to fetch her some refreshment, and on his return, found her leaning over Lovelace's chair, her hand on his shoulder, eagerly casting the dice on to the table. He was in time to see her clap her hands and to hear her cry of: "My luck! Oh, my luck is in! I will throw again!"

Glancing round she caught sight of her husband, and her face fell.

"Do you *mind*, Dicky?" she pleaded.

He did mind, but he could not appear churlish before all these men; so he laughed and shook his head, and went to her elbow to watch her play.

When she at length ceased, her luck had run out, and she had lost her much-prized ruby earring to Mr. Selwyn, who placed it carefully in his vest pocket, vowing he should wear it next his heart for ever. Then, and then only, did she consent to leave the gaming tables for the dancing hall, and for another hour Richard had the felicity of watching her tread the minuet with various young bloods, but most often with her new-found Harry Lovelace.

CHAPTER XIX

The Reappearance of His Grace of Andover

IT seemed to Richard in the days that followed, that Captain Lovelace was never out of his house. If he went to his wife's boudoir, there was Lovelace, hanging over her while she played upon the spinet or glanced through the pages of the *Rambler*. If Lavinia went to a ball or masquerade, the Captain was always amongst the favoured ones admitted to her chamber for the express purpose of watching her don her gown and judiciously place her patches. If Carstares begged his wife's company one morning, she was full of regrets: Harry was calling to take her to Vauxhall or to Spring Gardens. When he entered his door, the first sight that met his eyes was the Captain's amber-clouded cane and point-edged hat; and when he looked out of the window, it was more often to see a chair draw up at the house and Lovelace alight. After patiently enduring a week of his continued presence, Carstares remonstrated with his wife: she must not encourage her friend to spend all his time at Grosvenor Square. At first she had looked reproachful, and then she inquired his reason. His reluctant answer was that it was not seemly. At that her eyes had opened wide, and she demanded to know what could be more seemly than the visits of such an old friend? With a gleam of humour, Richard replied that it was not Captain Harold's age that he objected to, but, on the contrary, his youth. On which she accused him of being jealous. It was true enough, but he indignantly repudiated the suggestion. Very well, then, he was merely stupid! He must not be cross: Harry was her very good friend, and did not Richard admire the new device for her hair? Richard was not to be cajoled: did she clearly understand that Lovelace's visits must cease? She only understood one thing, and that was that Dicky was marvellous ill-tempered and ridiculous today. And he must not tease her! Yes, she would be very good, but so must he! And now she was going shopping, and she would require at least twenty guineas.

In spite of her promise to "be good", she made no attempt to discourage Lovelace's attentions, always smiling charmingly upon him and beckoning him to her side.

It was the morning of the Duchess of Devonshire's rout that Carstares again broached the subject. My lady was in bed, her fair hair unpowdered and streaming all about her shoulders, her chocolate on a small table at her side and countless *billets doux* from admirers scattered on the sheet. In her hand she held a bouquet of white roses with a card attached bearing, in bold, sprawling characters, the intials "H.L." Perhaps it was the sight of these incriminating letters that roused Richard's anger. At all events, with a violence quite unlike his usual gentle politeness, he snatched the flowers from her hand, and sent them whizzing into a corner.

"Let there be an end to all this folly!" he cried.

Lavinia raised herself on one elbow, astonished.

"H-how *dare* you?" she gasped.

"It has come to that!" he answered. "How dare I, your husband, try to control your actions in any way? I tell you, Lavinia, I have had enough of your antics, and I will not longer put up with them!"

"You—you—— What in heaven's name ails you, Richard?"

"This! I will not countenance that puppy's invasion of my house?" He made a furious gesture towards the wilted bouquet. "Neither will I permit you to make yourself the talk of London through him!"

"I? I? *I* make myself the talk of London? How dare you? Oh! how dare you?"

"I beg you will cease that foolishness. There is no question of my daring. How dare *you* disobey me, as you have been doing all this past week?"

She cowered away from him.

"Dicky!"

" 'Tis very well to cry 'Dicky', and to smile, but I have experienced that before. Sometimes I think you are utterly without heart!—a selfish, vain, extravagant woman!"

The childish lips trembled. Lady Lavinia buried her face in the pillows, sobbing.

Carstares' face softened.

"I beg your pardon, my dear. Mayhap that was unjust."

"And cruel! And cruel!"

"And cruel. Forgive me."

She twined white, satiny arms about his neck.

"You did not *mean* it?"

"No. I mean that I will not allow Lovelace to dangle after you, however."

She flung away from him.

"You have no right to speak like that. I knew Harry long before I ever set eyes on *you*!"

He winced.

"You infer that he is more to you than I am?"

"No! Though you try to make me hate you. No! I love you best. But I will not send Harry away!"

"Not if I order it?"

"Order it? Order it? No! No! A thousand times no!"

"I do order it!"

"And I refuse to listen to you!"

"By God, madam, you need a lesson!" he flamed. "I am minded to take you back to Wyncham this very day! And I promise you that, an you do not obey me in this, to Wyncham you *shall* go!" He stamped out of the room as he spoke, and she sank back amongst her pillows, white and trembling with fury.

As soon as she was dressed, she flounced downstairs, bent on finishing the quarrel. But Carstares had gone out some time since, and was not expected to return until late. For a moment Lavinia was furious, but the timely arrival of a box from her mantua-maker's chased away the frowns and wreathed her face in smiles.

Richard did not return until it was time to prepare for the rout, and on entering the house he went straight to his chamber, putting himself into the hands of his valet. He submitted to the delicate tinting of his finger-nails, the sprinkling of his linen with rose-water and the stencilling of his brows. He was arrayed in puce and gold, rings slipped on to his fingers, his legs coaxed into hose with marvellous clocks splashed on their sides, and a diamond buckle placed above the large black bow of his tie-wig. Then, powdered, painted and patched, he went slowly across to his wife's room.

Lavinia, who had by now quite forgotten the morning's *contretemps,* greeted him with a smile. She sat before the mirror in her under-gown, with a loose *déshabillé* thrown over her shoulders. The *coiffeur* had departed, and her hair,

thickly powdered, was dressed high above her head over
cushions, twisted into curls over her ears and allowed to fall
in more curls over her shoulders. On top of the creation were
poised ostrich feathers, scarlet and white, and round her
throat gleamed a great necklet of diamonds. The room was
redolent of some heavy perfume; discarded ribbons, laces,
slippers and gloves strewed the floor; over the back of a chair
hung a brilliant scarlet domino, and tenderly laid out on the
bed was her gown, a mass of white satin and brocade, with
full ruffles over the hips and quantities of foaming lace falling from the corsage and from the short sleeves. Beside it reposed her fan, her soft lace gloves, her mask and her tiny reticule.

Carstares gingerly sat down on the extreme edge of a chair
and watched the maid tint his wife's already perfect cheeks.

"I shall break hearts to-night, shall I not?" she asked gaily,
over her shoulder.

"I do not doubt it," he answered shortly.

"And you, Dicky?" She turned round to look at him.
"Puce . . . 'tis not the colour I should have chosen, but 'tis
well enough. A new wig, surely?"

"Ay."

Her eyes questioned his coldness, and she suddenly remembered the events of the morning. So he was sulky? Very well!
Monsieur should see!

Someone knocked at the door; the maid went to open it.

"Sir Douglas Faversham, Sir Gregory Markham, Moosso
le Chevalier and Captain Lovelace are below, m'lady."

A little devil prompted Lavinia.

"Oh, la-la! So many? Well, I cannot see all, 'tis certain.
Admit Sir Gregory and Captain Lovelace."

Louisa communicated this to the lackey and shut the door.

Richard bit his lip angrily.

"Are you sure I am not *de trop?*" he asked, savagely sarcastic.

Lady Lavinia cast aside her *déshabillé* and stood up.

"Oh, 'tis no matter—I am ready for my gown, Louisa."

There came more knocking at the door, and this time it
was Carstares who rose to open it.

There entered Markham, heavily handsome in crimson and
gold, and Lovelace, his opposite, fair and delicately pretty in
palest blue and silver. As usual, he wore his loose wig, and in
it sparkled three sapphire pins.

He made my lady a marvellous leg.

"I am prostrated by your beauty, fairest!"

Sir Gregory was eyeing Lavinia's white slippers through his quizzing glass.

"Jewelled heels, 'pon my soul!" he drawled.

She pirouetted gracefully, her feet flashing as they caught the light.

"Was it not well thought on?" she demanded. "But I must not waste time—the dress! Now, Markham—now Harry—you will see the creation!"

Lovelace sat down on a chair, straddle-wise, his arms over the back, and his chin sunk in his hands. Markham leant against the *garde-robe* and watched through his glass.

When the dress was at last arranged, the suggested improvements in the matter of lace, ribbons, and the adjustment of a brooch thoroughly discussed, bracelets fixed on her arms and the flaming domino draped about her, it was full three-quarters of an hour later, and Carstares was becoming impatient. It was not in his nature to join with the two men in making fulsome compliments, and their presence at the toilette filled him with annoyance. He hated that Lavinia should admit them, but it was the *mode,* and he knew he must bow the head under it.

My lady was at last ready to start; her gilded chair awaited her in the light of the *flambeaux* at the door, and with great difficulty she managed to enter it, taking absurd pains that her silks should not crush, nor the nodding plumes of her huge head-dress become disordered by unseemly contact with the roof. Then she found that she had left her fan in her room, and Lovelace and Markham must needs vie with one another in the fetching of it. While they wrangled wittily for the honour, Richard went quietly indoors and presently emerged with the painted chicken-skin, just as Lovelace was preparing to ascend the steps. At last Lavinia was shut in and the bearer picked up the poles. Off when the little cavalcade down the long square, the chair in the middle. Lovelace walked close beside it on the right, and Richard and Markham on the left. So they proceeded through the uneven streets, carefully picking their way through the dirtier parts, passing other chairs and pedestrians, all coming from various quarters into South Audley Street. They were remarkably silent: Markham from habitual laziness, Lovelace because he sensed Richard's antagonism, and Richard himself on account of his extremely worried state of mind. In fact, until they reached Curzon Street no one spoke, and then it was only Markham, who, glancing behind him at the shuttered windows of the great corner house, casually remarked that Chesterfield was still at Wells. An absent assent came from Carstares, and the conversation came to an end.

In Clarges Street they were joined by Sir John Fortescue, an austere patrician, and although some years his senior, a close friend of Richard's. They fell behind the chair, and Fortescue took Richard's proffered arm.

"I did not see you at White's to-day, John?"

"No. I had some business with my lawyer. I suppose you did not stumble across my poor brother?"

"Frank? I did not—but why the 'poor'?"

Fortescue shrugged slightly.

"I think the lad is demented," he said. "He was to have made one of March's supper-party last night, but at four o'clock received a communication from heaven knows whom which threw him into a state of unrest. What must he do but hurry off without a word of explanation. Since then I have not set eyes on him, but his man tells me he went to meet a friend. Damned unusual of him is all I have to say."

"Very strange. Do you expect to see him to-night?"

"I should hope so——! My dear Carstares, who is the man walking by your lady's chair?"

"Markham?"

"The other."

"Lovelace."

"Lovelace? And who the devil is he?"

"I cannot tell you—beyond a captain in the guards."

"That even is news to me. I saw him at Goosetree's the other night, and wondered. Somewhat of a rake-hell, I surmise."

"I daresay. I do not like him."

They were entering the gates of Devonshire House now, and had to part company, for the crush was so great that it was almost impossible to keep together. Carstares stayed by Lavinia's chair, and the other men melted away into the crowd. Chairs jostled one another in the effort to get to the door, town coaches rolled up, and having let down their fair burdens, passed out again slowly pushing through the throng. When the Carstares' chair at last drew near the house, it was quite a quarter of an hour later. The ball-room was already full and a blaze of riotous colour. Lavinia was almost immediately borne off by an infatuated youth for whom she cherished a motherly affection that would have caused the unfortunate to tear his elegant locks, had he known it.

Richard distinguished Lord Andrew Belmanoir, one of a group of bucks gathered about the newest beauty, Miss Gunning, who, with her sister Elizabeth, had taken fashionable London by storm. Andrew wore a mask, but he was quite unmistakable by his length of limb and carelessly rakish appearance.

Wilding, across the room, beckoned to Richard, and on his approach, dragged him to the card-room to play at lansquenet with March, Selwyn and himself.

Carstares found the Earl in great good-humour, due, so Selwyn remarked, to the finding of an opera singer even more lovely than the last. From lansquenet they very soon passed to dice and betting, with others who strolled up to the table. Then Carstares excused himself and went back to the ball-room. He presently found himself by the side of one Isabella Fanshawe, a sprightly widow, greatly famed for her wittiness and good looks. Carstares had met her but once before, and was now rather surprised that she motioned him to her side, patting the couch with an inviting, much be-ringed hand.

"Come and sit by me, Mr. Carstares. I have wanted to speak with you this long time." She lowered her mask as she spoke and closely scrutinised his face with her bright, humorous eyes.

"Why, madam, I am flattered," bowed Richard.

She cut him short.

"I am not in the mood for compliments, sir. Nor am I desirous of making or hearing clever speeches. You are worrying me."

Richard sat down, intrigued and attracted by this downright little woman.

"I, madam?"

"You, sir. That is, your face worries me." Seeing his surprise, she laughed, fanning herself. " 'Tis comely enough, I grant you! I mean there is such a strong likeness to—a friend of mine."

Richard smiled politely and relieved her of the fan.

"Indeed, madam?"

"Yes. I knew—this other gentleman in Vienna, three years

ago. I should judge him younger than you, I think. His eyes
were blue, but very similar to yours. His nose was almost
identical with yours, but the mouth—n-no. Yet the whole
expression——" She broke off, noticing her companion's sudden pallor. "But you are unwell, sir?"

"No, madam, no! What was your friend's name?"

"Ferndale," she answered. "Anthony Ferndale."

The fan stopped its swaying for a moment.

"Ah!" said Richard.

"Do you know him?" she inquired eagerly.

"Many years ago, madam, I was—acquainted with him.
Can you tell me—was he in good spirits when last you saw
him?"

She pursed her lips thoughtfully.

"If you mean was he gay, was he witty—yes. But sometimes I thought—Mr. Carstares, when he was silent, his eyes
were so sad——! Indeed, I do not know why I tell you this."

"You may be sure, madam, your confidence is safe with
me. I had—a great regard for this gentleman." He opened
and shut her fan as he spoke, fidgeting with the slender
sticks. "You, too, were interested in him, madam?"

"I do not think ever anyone knew him and was not, sir. It
was something in his manner, his personality—I cannot explain—that endeared him to one. And he once—aided me—
when I was in difficulties."

Richard remembering scraps of gossip concerning the
widow's past, merely bowed his head.

She was silent for a time, staring down at her hands, but
presently she looked up smiling, and took her fan away from
him.

"I cannot abide a fidget, sir!" she told him. "And I see
Lord Fotheringham approaching. I am promised to him this
dance." She rose, but Richard detained her.

"Mrs. Fanshawe, will you permit me to call upon you? I
would hear more of—your friend. You, mayhap, think it
strange—but——"

"No," she answered. "I do not. Certainly call upon me, sir.
I lodge in Mount Street with my sister—No. 16."

"I protest, madam, you are too good——"

"Again, no. I have told you, I like a man to talk as a man
and not as an affected woman. I shall be pleased to welcome
you."

She curtsied and went away on the Viscount's arm.

At the same moment a voice at Richard's elbow drawled:

"Do I see you at the vivacious widow's feet, my good Dick?"

Carstares turned to face his brother-in-law, Colonel Belmanoir.

"Is not all London?" he smiled.

"Oh, no! Not since the beautiful Gunnings' arrival. But I admit she is a dainty piece. And Lavinia? Will she break her heart, I wonder?" He laughed beneath his breath as he saw Richard's eyes flash.

"I trust not," replied Carstares. "Are you all here tonight?"

"Our illustrious head is absent, I believe. Andrew is flirting with the Fletcher girl in the Blue Salon. I am here, and Lavinia is amusing herself with Lovelace. Yes, Richard, Lovelace! Be careful!" With another sneering laugh he walked on, bowing to Elizabeth Gunning, who passed by on the arm of her partner, his Grace of Hamilton, most palpably *épris*.

At that moment two late-comers entered the room and made their way toward their hostess, who appeared delighted to see them, especially the taller of the two, whose hand she slapped with good-humoured raillery. The shorter gentleman wore no mask, and the Colonel recognized Frank Fortescue. His eyes travelled to the other, who, unlike most of the men who only held their masks, had fastened his across his eyes, and they widened in surprise. The purple domino, worn carelessly open, revealed black satin encrusted with silver and diamonds. The natural hair was raven-black, the nostrils were pinched and the lips thin.

"The Devil!" ejaculated Robert, and strolled over to him.

Fortescue walked away when he saw who approached, and his Grace of Andover turned slowly towards his brother.

"I rather thought you were in Paris," yawned the Colonel.

"I am always sorry to disillusion you," bowed his Grace.

"Not at all; I am transported with joy at seeing you. As is Lavinia, it appears."

Lady Lavinia, on recognising his Grace, had dropped her partner's hand and fled incontinent towards him.

"You, Tracy!" She clasped delighted hands on his arm.

"This is very touching," sneered Robert. "It only needs Andrew to complete the happy reunion. Pray excuse me!"

"With pleasure," replied the Duke gently, and bowed as if to a stranger.

"He grows tedious," he remarked, as soon as the Colonel was out of earshot.

"Oh, Bob! I take no account of *him*! But, Tracy, how is it you have come to-day? I thought——"

"My dear Lavinia, do I wear an air of mystery? I imagined you knew I was promised to Dolly Cavendish to-night?"

"Yes, but—oh, what matters it? I am so charmed to see you again, dear!"

"You flatter me, Lavinia."

"And now that you have come, I want to hear why you ever went? Tracy, take me into the room behind us. I know 'tis empty."

"Very well, child, as you will." He held back the curtain for her and followed her into the deserted chamber.

"You want to know why I went?" he began, seating himself at her side. "I counsel you, my dear, to cast your mind back to the spring—at Bath."

"Your *affaire*! Of course! So the lady proved unkind?"

"No. But I bungled it."

"*You?* Tell me at once!—at once!"

His Grace stretched out his leg and surveyed his shoe-buckle through half-closed lids.

"I had arranged everything," he said, "and all would have been well but for an interfering young jackanapes who chanced along the track and saw fit to espouse Madam Diana's cause." He paused. "He tripped me up by some trick, and then—*que veux-tu?*"

"Who was it?"

"How should I know? At first he seemed familiar. At all events, he knew me. He may be dead by now. I hope he is."

"Gracious! Did you wound him?"

"I managed to fire at him, but he was too quick, and the bullet took him in the shoulder. It may, however, have been mortal."

"And so you went to Paris?"

"Ay. To forget her."

"And have you forgotten?"

"I have not. She is never out of my thoughts. I plan again."

His sister sighed.

"She is then more beautiful than the Pompadour?" she asked meaningly.

Tracy turned his head.

"The Pompadour?"

"Ay! We heard you contrived to amuse yourself in a pretty fashion, Tracy!"

"Really? I had no idea people were so interested in my affairs. But 'amuse' is an apt word."

"Ah? You were not then *épris*?"

"I? With that low-born *cocotte*? My dear Lavinia!"

She laughed at his haughty tone.

"You've not always been so nice, Tracy! But what of your Diana? An you are so infatuated, you had best wed her."

"Why, so I think."

Lady Lavinia gasped.

"Tracy! You do not mean it? Goodness me, but a marriage!"

"Why not, Lavinia?"

"Oh, a respectable married man, forsooth! And how long will the passion last?"

"I cannot be expected to foretell that, surely? I hope, for ever."

"And you'll tie yourself up for the sake of one chit? Lud!"

"I can conceive a worse fate for a man."

"Can you? Well, tell me more? 'Tis monstrous exciting. Do you intend to court her?"

"At this stage of the proceedings? That were somewhat tactless, my dear. I must abduct her, but I must be more careful. Once I have her, I can propitiate Papa."

"Tracy, 'tis the maddest scheme ever I heard! What will the others say?"

"Do you really suppose I care?"

"No, I suppose not. Oh, will not Bob be furious, though!"

"It were almost worthwhile—just for the sake of foiling him. He would so like to succeed me. But I really do not think he must." His elbow was on his knee, his chin in his hand, a peculiar smile on his lips. "Can you imagine him stepping into my ducal shoes, Lavinia?"

"Very easily!" she cried. "Oh, yes, yes, Tracy! Marry the girl!"

"If she will."

"Why, 'tis not like you to underrate your persuasive powers!"

His Grace's thin nostrils wrinkled up in a curious grimace.

"I believe one cannot force a girl to the altar," he said.

"Unless she is a fool, she'll have you."

"Her parent would be influenced by my dukedom, but she, no. Not even if she knew of it."

"Does she not know?"

"Certainly not. I am Mr. Everard."

"How wise of you, Tracy! So you've nought to fear?"

"Fear?" He snapped his fingers. "I?"

The heavy curtain swung noiselessly aside. Richard Carstares stood in the opening.

Tracy turned his head and scrutinised him languidly. Then he put up his hand and removed his mask.

"Is it possible the husband scented an intrigue? It seems I am doomed to disappoint to-night."

Lavinia, smarting from her morning's wrongs, laughed savagely.

"More probable he mistook me for someone else!" she snapped.

Richard bowed, his hand on the curtain. He had shown no surprise at seeing the Duke.

"Far more probable, my dear. I thought you Lady Charlwood! Pray give me leave." He was gone on the word.

Tracy replaced his mask, chuckling.

"Honest Dick grow cold, eh? But what a snub, Lavinia!"

Her little hand clenched.

"Oh, how dare he! How dare he insult me so?"

"My dear sister, in all justice to him, you must admit the boot was rather on the other leg."

"Oh, I know—I know! But he is so provoking!—so jealous!—so unreasonable!"

"Jealous? And why?"

With an impatient twitch at her petticoat she made answer, not looking at him.

"Oh, I do not know! Nor he! Take me back to the ballroom."

"Certainly, my dear." He rose and led her out. "I shall do myself the honour of waiting on you—to-morrow."

"Yes? How delightful 'twill be! Come to dine, Tracy! Richard is promised to the Fortescues."

"In that case, I have much pleasure in accepting your invitation. . . . In heaven's name, who is this?"

Lovelace was bearing down upon them.

"Lavinia! I have been seeking you everywhere!—ah—your servant, sir!" He bowed to his Grace, and took Lavinia's hand.

"Oh—oh, Harold!—you remember Tracy?" she said nervously.

"Tracy! I did not know you masked! I saw you last in Paris."

"Really? I regret I was not aware of your presence. It is a good many years since I had the honour of seeing you."

"Five," nodded Lovelace, and sent a smiling, amorous glance at Lavinia.

"Exactly," bowed his Grace. "You have, I perceive, renewed your acquaintance with my sister."

When they were gone he caressed his chin, thoughtfully.

"Lovelace . . . and Richard is so jealous, so unreasonable. Now I do hope Lavinia will do nothing indiscreet—— Yes, Frank, I was talking to myself; a bad habit."

Fortescue, who had come up behind him, took his arm.

"A sign of lunacy, my dear. Jim Cavendish demands you."

"Does he? May I ask why?"

"He is in the card-room. There is some bet on, I believe."

"In that case I shall have to go. You had best accompany me, Frank."

"Very well. You have seen Lady Lavinia?"

Beneath the mask his Grace's eyes narrowed.

"I have seen Lavinia. Also I have seen an old friend— Lovelace by name."

"The captain with the full-bottomed wig? Your friend, you say?"

"Did I say so? I should correct myself: a friend of my sister's."

"Indeed? Yes, I believe I have seen him in her company."

Tracy smiled enigmatically.

"I daresay."

"And what of you, Tracy?"

"Well? *What* of me?"

"You told me this morning that you had at last fallen in love. It is true? You are honestly in love?"

"Honestly? How do I know? I only know that I have felt this passion for four months, and now it is stronger than ever. It sounds like love."

"Then, an she is a good woman, I hope she will consent to take you, such as you are, and make of you such as she can!"

"Now that is very neat, Frank. I congratulate you. Of course she will take me; as to the rest—I think not."

"Tare an' ouns, Tracy! but an that is the tone you take with her, she'll have none of you!"

"I have never found it unsuccessful."

"With your common trollops, no! But if your Diana is a lady, she will dispatch you about your business! Woo her, man! Forget your own damned importance, for I think you will need to humble yourself to the dust if all that you tell me has passed between you is true!"

They had paused outside the card-room. A curtain shut it off from the ball-room, and with his hand on it, Tracy stared arrogantly down at his friend.

"Humble myself? 'Fore Gad, you must be mad!"

"Belike I am; but I tell you, Tracy, that if your passion is love, 'tis a strange one that puts yourself first. I would not give the snap of a finger for it! You want this girl, not for her happiness, but for your own pleasure. That is not the love I once told you would save you from yourself. When it comes, you will count yourself as nought; you will realise your own insignificance, and above all, be ready to make any sacrifice for her sake. Yes, even to the point of losing her!"

His Grace's lips sneered.

"Your eloquence is marvellous," he remarked. "I have not been so amused since I left Paris."

CHAPTER XX

His Grace of Andover
Takes a Hand in the Game

WHEN the Duke of Andover dined next day at Grosvenor Square, he contrived, by subtle means, to make his sister feel inexplicably ill at ease. He let fall pleasant little remarks concerning her friendship with Captain Lovelace, in which she read disapproval and a sinister warning. She was afraid of him, as she was not of her husband, and she knew that if he ever guessed at the depths of her affection for the old flame, he would take very effective measures towards stopping her intercourse with him. It was, then, entirely owing to his return that she told Lovelace that he must not so palpably adore her. Neither must he visit her so frequently. They were both in her boudoir at the time, one morning, and no doubt Lavinia looked very lovely and very tempting in her wrapper, with her golden curls free from powder and loosely dressed beneath her escalloped lace ruffle. At all events, Lovelace abandoned his daintily bantering pose and seized her in his arms, nearly smothering her with fierce, passionate caresses.

Her ladyship struggled, gave a faint shriek, and started to cry. As his kisses seemed to aggravate her tears, he picked her up, and carrying her to a chair, lowered her gently into it. Then, having first dusted the floor with his handkerchief, he knelt down beside her and possessed himself of both her hands.

"Lavinia! Goddess! I adore you!"

Bethinking herself that tears were ruinous to her complexion, Lady Lavinia pulled her hands away and dabbed at her eyes.

"Oh, Harold!" she reproached him.

"I have offended you! Wretch that I am——"

"Oh, no, no!" Lady Lavinia gave him her hand again. "But 'twas wicked of you, Harry! You must never, never do it again!"

His arm crept round her waist.

"But I love you, sweetheart!"

"Oh! Oh! Think of Dicky!"

He released her at that, and sprang to his feet.

"Why should I think of him! 'Tis of you and myself I think! Only a week ago you vowed he was unkind——"

"You are monstrous wicked to remind me of that! We were both cross—and then we were both sorry. I am very fond of poor Dicky."

"Fond of him! Ay, so you may be, but you do not love him! Not as a woman loves a man—do you?"

"Harold!"

"Of course you do not! You used to love me—no, do not shake your head, 'tis true! You would have married me had it not been for Tracy."

"Oh, Harry! How can you say so? What had he to do with it?"

"What, indeed! Whose fault was it that I was time after time refused admittance at Andover? Whose fault was it that you were induced to marry Carstares?"

"Not Tracy's. 'Twas my own wish."

"Fostered by his influence?"

"Oh, no!"

"You never loved Carstares——"

"I did! I do!"

"You may think so, but I know better. Why he is not even suited to you! You were made for life and pleasure and hazard! With me you would have had all that; with him——"

She had risen to her feet and drawn nearer to him, her eyes sparkling, but now she covered her ears with her hands and stamped pettishly.

"I will not listen! I will not, I tell you! Oh, you are unkind to plague me so!"

Lovelace took her into his arms once more, and drawing down her hands, kissed her again and again. She resisted, trying to thrust him off, but she was crushed against him, and he would have kissed her again, had not there come an interruption.

A knock fell on the door, and the footman announced:

"His Grace of Andover, m'lady!"

The guilty pair sprang apart in the nick of time, she fiery red, he pale, but composed.

His Grace stood in the doorway, his quizzing glass raised

inquiringly. His eyes went swiftly from one to the other and widened. He bowed elaborately.

"My dear Lavinia! Captain Lovelace, your very obedient!"

Lovelace returned the bow with much flourish.

"Your Grace!"

"Dear me, Tracy!" cried Lavinia, advancing. "What an unexpected visit!"

"I trust I have not arrived at an inopportune moment, my dear?"

"Oh, no!" she assured him. "I am quite charmed to see you! But at such an early hour——! I confess, it quite astonishes me!" She brought him to a chair, chattering like a child, and so innocent was his expression, so smiling his attitude towards the Captain, that she imagined that he suspected nothing, and had not noticed her blushes.

It was only when Lovelace had departed that she was undeceived. Then, when his Grace moved to a chair opposite her, she saw that he was frowning slightly.

"You—you are put out over something, Tracy?" she asked nervously.

The frown deepened.

"N-no. I am not 'put out'. I merely anticipate the sensation."

"I—I don't understand. What mean you?"

"At present, nothing."

"Tracy, please do not be mysterious! Are you like to be put out?"

"I trust not, Lavinia."

"But what annoys you?"

Instead of answering, he put a question:

"I hope you amused yourself well—last night, my dear sister?"

She flushed. Last night had been Lady Davenant's masquerade, to which Lord Robert had conducted her. She had danced almost exclusively with Lovelace the whole evening, but as they were both masked, she was rather surprised at the question.

"I enjoyed myself quite tolerably, thank you. You were there?"

"No, Lavinia, I was not there."

"Then how do you kn——" She stopped in confusion, biting her lips. For an instant she caught a glimpse of his eyes, piercing and cold.

"How do I know?" smoothly finished his Grace. "One hears things, Lavinia. Also———" he glanced round the room, "one sees things."

"I—I don't understand you!" she shot out, twisting the lace of her gown with restless, uneasy fingers.

"No? Must I then be more explicit?"

"Yes! Yes! I should be glad!"

"Then let me beg of you, my dear Lavinia, that you will commit no indiscretion."

Her cheeks flamed.

"You mean———"

"I mean that you have grown too friendly with Harold Lovelace."

"Well! What of it?"

His Grace put up his eye-glass, faintly astonished.

"What of it? Pray think a moment, Lavinia!"

" 'Tis not likely that *I* shall be the one to disgrace the name, Tracy!"

"I sincerely hope not. I give you my word I should do all in my power to prevent any foolhardy action on your part. Pray do not forget it."

She sat silent, biting her lips.

"It is, my child, unwise to play with fire. Sooner or later one gets burnt. And remember that your gallant captain has not one half of Richard's wealth."

Up she sprang, kicking her skirts as she always did when angered.

"Money! money!—always money!" she cried. "I do not care one rap for it! And Richard is not wealthy!"

"Richard is heir to wealth," replied his Grace calmly. "And even an you are so impervious to its charms, I, my dear, am not. Richard is extremely useful to me. I beg you will not leave him for any such mad rake as Lovelace, who would be faithful to you for perhaps three months, certainly not longer."

"Tracy, I will not have you speak to me like this! How dare you insult me so? I have given you no cause! I did not say I had any desire to run away with him—and he *would* be faithful to me! He has been faithful all these years!"

His Grace smiled provokingly.

"My dear———!"

"Oh, I know there have been episodes—indiscretions. Do you think I count him the worse for that?"

"Evidently not."

"There has never been another serious love with him! I hate you!"

"You are overfree with your emotions, my dear. So you do indeed contemplate an elopement!"

"No, no, no! I do not! I am *fond* of Dicky!"

"Dear me!"

"Of course I shall not leave him!"

"Why then, I am satisfied," he answered, and rose to his feet. "I shall look to see Captain Lovelace more out of your company." He picked up his hat and cane and stood directly in front of her. One dead white hand, on which blazed a great ruby seal ring, took her little pointed chin in a firm clasp and tilted her head up until she was forced to meet his eyes. They held hers inexorably, scorchingly.

"You understand me?" he asked harshly.

Lavinia's eyes filled with tears and her soft underlip trembled.

"Yes," she fluttered, and gave a tiny sob. "Oh. yes, Tracy!"

The eyes lost something of their menacing gleam, and he smiled, for once without a sneer, and releasing her chin, patted her cheek indulgently.

"Bear in mind, child. that I am fifteen years your senior, and I have more worldly wisdom in my little finger than you have in the whole of your composition. I do not wish to witness your ruin."

The tears brimmed over, and she caught his handkerchief from him, dabbing at her eyes with one heavily-laced corner.

"You do love me, Tracy?"

"In the recesses of my mind I believe I cherish some affection for you," he replied coolly, rescuing his handkerchief. "I used to class you with your deplorable brothers, but I think perhaps I was wrong."

She gave an hysterical laugh.

"Tracy, how can you be so disagreeable. Lud! but I pity Diana an she marries you!"

To her surprise he flushed a little.

"Diana, an she marries me, will have all that her heart could desire," he answered stiffly, and took his leave.

Once outside in the square he looked for a sedan, and not seeing one, walked away towards Audley Street. He went quickly, but his progress was somewhat retarded by two ladies, who, passing in their chairs down the street, perceived

him and beckoned him to their sides. Escaping presently
from them, he turned into Curzon Street, and from thence
down Half Moon Street, where he literally fell into the arms
of Tom Wilding, who had much to say on the subject of
March's last bet with Edgecumbe. His Grace affected interest,
politely declined Wilding's proffered escort, and hurried down
into Piccadilly, walking eastwards towards St. James's Square,
where was the Andover town house. He was fated to be again
detained, for as he walked along Arlington Street, Mr. Walpole was on the point of descending the steps of No. 5. He
also had much to say to his Grace. He had no idea that Belmanoir had returned from Paris. A week ago he had arrived?
Well, he, Walpole, had been out of town all the week—at
Twickenham. He hoped Bel. would honour him with his
company at the small card-party he was giving there on
Thursday. George was coming, and Dick Edgecumbe; he had
asked March and Gilly Williams, but the Lord knew whether
both would be induced to appear! Bel. had heard of Gilly's
absurd jealousy? Wilding was promised, and Markham; several other answers he was awaiting.

Andover accepted gracefully and parted from Mr. Walpole. He made the rest of his journey in peace, and on arriving at his house, went straight to the library, where sat a
sleek, eminently respectable-looking individual, dressed like a
groom. He stood up as his Grace entered, and bowed.

Belmanoir nodded shortly and sat down at his desk.

"I have work for you, Harper."

"Yes, sir—your Grace, I should say."

"Do you know Sussex?"

"Well, your Grace, I don't know as how——"

"Do you know Sussex?"

"No, your Grace—er—yes, your Grace! I should say, not
well, your Grace!"

"Have you heard of a place called Littledean?"

"No, s—your Grace."

"Midhurst?"

"Oh, yes, your Grace."

"Good. Littledean is seven miles west of it. You will find
that out—also an inn called, I think, 'The Pointing Finger'.
There you will lodge."

"Yes, your Grace, certainly."

"At a very little distance from there is a house—Horton
House, where lives a certain Mr. Beauleigh, with his sister

and daughter. You are to watch the comings and goings of these people with the utmost care. Eventually you will become groom to Mr. Beauleigh."

"B-but, your Grace!" feebly protested the astonished Harper.

"You will approach their present groom, and you will insinuate that I, Andover, am in need of a second groom. You will tell him that I pay handsomely—treble what Mr. Beauleigh gives him. If I know human nature, he will apply for the post. You then step in. If Mr. Beauleigh asks for some recommendation, you are to refer him to Sir Hugh Grandison, White's Chocolate House, St. James's Street. When you are engaged I will send further instructions."

The man gaped, shut his mouth, and gaped again.

"Do you fully understand me?" asked Belmanoir calmly.

"Er—er—yes, your Grace!"

"Repeat what I have said, then."

Harper stumbled through it and mopped his brow unhappily.

"Very well. In addition, I pay you twice as much as Mr. Beauleigh gives you, and, at the end, if you serve me well—fifty guineas. Are you satisfied?"

Harper brightened considerably.

"Yes, your Grace! Thank you, sir!"

Tracy laid twenty guineas before him.

"That is for your expenses. Remember this: the sooner the thing is done, the more certain are your fifty guineas. That is all. Have you any questions to ask?"

Harper cudgelled his still dazed brain, and finding none, shook his head.

"No, your Grace."

"Then you may go."

The man bowed himself out, clutching his guineas. He was comparatively a newcomer in his Grace's service, and he was by no means accustomed to the Duke's lightning method of conducting his affairs. He was not sure that he quite appreciated it. But fifty guineas were fifty guineas.

CHAPTER XXI

Mrs. Fanshawe Lights a Fire and O'Hara Fans the Flame

RICHARD CARSTARES very soon availed himself of Mrs. Fanshawe's permission to call upon her, and duly put in an appearance at No. 16, Mount Street. He found the house very
tastefully appointed, the sister elderly and good-natured, and
the widow herself an excellent hostess. The first time he
called he was not the only visitor; two ladies whom he did
not know and a young cousin were already there, and later, a
bowing acquaintance, Mr. Standish, also arrived. Seeing that
he would have no opportunity to talk with the widow on the
subject of his brother, he very soon took his leave, promising
to wait upon her again at no very distant date. When, three
days later, he again sent in his name and was admitted, he
found the lady alone, and was gratified to hear her order the
servant to deny her to all other visitors.

He bowed over her hand and hoped she was well.

Mrs. Fanshawe drew him down beside her on the settee.

"I am very well, Mr. Carstares. And you?"

"Also," he smiled, but his looks belied his words.

She told him so, laughing, and he pleaded a worried week.

"Well, sir. I presume you did not come to talk to me about
your health, but about my friend—eh?"

"I assure——"

"Remember, no vapid compliments!" she besought.

"Then, madam, yes. I want to hear about—Ferndale. You
see, I—like you—took a great interest in him."

She sent him a shrewd glance, and nodded.

"Of course. I will tell you all I know, Mr. Carstares, but it
is not very much, and maybe you will be disappointed. But I
only knew him the short time we were both in Vienna, and
—he was not very communicative."

"Ah!—he did not confide in you, madam?"

"No. If one attempted to draw his confidence, he became
a polite iceberg."

196

"Nevertheless, madam, please tell me all that you know."

"It will not take long, I fear. I met him in '48 at Vienna, in the Prater, where I was walking with my husband, who had come to Vienna for his health. I chanced to let fall my reticule when Sir Anthony was passing us, and he picked it up, speaking the most execrable German." She smiled a little at the remembrance. "Mr. Fanshawe, who had the greatest dislike for all foreigners, was overjoyed to hear the English accent. He induced Sir Anthony to continue his walk with us, and afterwards he called at our lodgings. I think he, too, was glad to meet a fellow-countryman, for he came often, and once when I had been talking with him for some time he let fall—what shall I say?—his reserve—his guard—and told me that he had scarcely spoken his own language for four years. Afterwards he seemed to regret having said even that much, and turned the subject." She paused and looked up to see if her auditor was interested.

"Yes, yes?" urged Richard. "And then?"

"I do not remember. He came, as I said, often, mostly to talk to my husband, who was a great invalid, but sometimes to see me. He would hardly ever speak of England—I think he did not trust himself. He never mentioned any relations or any English friends, and when I spoke of home, he would shut his mouth very tightly, and look terribly sad. I saw that for some reason the subject pained him, so I never spoke of it if I could help it."

"He was a most entertaining companion, Mr. Carstares; he used to tell my husband tales that made him laugh as I had not heard him laugh for months. He was very lively, very witty, and almost finickily well dressed, but what his occupation was I could not quite ascertain. He said he was a gentleman of leisure, but I do not think he was at all wealthy. He frequented all the gaming houses, and I heard tales of his marvellous luck, so one day I taxed him with it, and he laughed and said he lived by Chance—he meant dice. Yet I know, for I once had conversation with his servant, that his purse was at times very, very slender."

"The time he aided you, Mrs. Fanshawe, when was that?" She flushed.

"That was a few months after we first met him. I was—foolish; my married life was not—very happy, and I was—or, rather, I fancied myself—in love with an Austrian nobleman, who—who—well, sir, suffice it that I consented to dine with him one evening. I found then that he was not the *galant homme* I had thought him, but something quite different. I do not know what I should have done had not Sir Anthony arrived."

"He did arrive then?"

"Yes. You see, he knew that this Austrian had asked me to dine—I told him—and he counselled me to refuse. But I—well, sir, I have told you, I was young and very foolish—I would not listen. When he called at our house and found that I was out, he at once guessed where I had gone, and he followed me to the Count's house, gave an Austrian name, and was announced just as the Count tried to—tried to—kiss me. I think I shall never forget the relief of that moment! He was so safe, and so English! The Count was furious, and at first I thought he would have his lackeys throw Sir Anthony out. But when he heard all that Anthony had to say, he realised that it was useless to try to detain me—and I was taken home. Anthony was very kind—he did not scold, neither had he told my husband. Two days after, he and the Count fought a duel, and the Count was wounded in the lung. That was all. But it made me very grateful to him and interested in his affairs. Mr. Fanshawe left Vienna a few weeks after that, and I have never seen my *preux chevalier* since." She sighed and looked steadily across at Carstares. "And you—you are so like him!"

"You think so, madam?" was all he could find to say.

"I do, sir. And something more, which, perhaps you will deem an impertinence. Is Anthony your brother?"

The suddenness of the attack threw Carstares off his guard. He went white.

"Madam!"

"Please be not afraid that mine is the proverbial woman's tongue, sir. It does not run away with me, I assure you. When I saw you the other night for the first time, I was struck by the resemblance, and I asked my partner, Mr. Stapely, who you were. He told me, and much more beside, which I was not at the time desirous of hearing."

"Trust Will Stapely!" exclaimed Richard, and mentally cursed the amiable gossip-monger.

"Among other things he told me of your elder brother—who—who—in fact, he told me the whole story. Of course, my mind instantly leapt to my poor Sir Anthony, despite that in appearance he is younger than you. Was I right?"

Richard rose to his feet and walked away to the window, standing with his back to her.

"Ay!"

"I was sure of it," she nodded. "So that was why he would not speak of England? Poor boy!"

Richard's soul writhed under the lash of her pity.

"So he will always be outcast," she continued. "Alone, unhappy, without friends——"

"No!" he cried, turning. " 'Fore Gad, no, madam!"

"Will society—cruel, hard society—receive him, then?" she asked.

"Society will—one day—receive him, Mrs. Fanshawe. You will see."

"I long for that day," she sighed. "I wish I had it in my power to help him—to repay in part the debt I owe him."

At that he lifted his head.

"My brother, madam, would count it not a debt, but an honour," he answered proudly.

"Yes," she smiled. "You are like him; when you speak like that you might almost be he."

"He is worth a thousand of me, Mrs. Fanshawe!" he replied vehemently, and broke off, staring down at the table.

"And his name?" she asked softly.

"John Anthony St. Ervine Delaney Carstares," he said, "Earl of Wyncham."

"So the Anthony was real! I am so glad, for he would always be Anthony to me."

There was a long silence, broken at last by the lady.

"I fear I have made you sad, Mr. Carstares. You will drink a dish of Bohea with me, before you go? And we will not speak of this again."

"You are very good, madam. Believe me, I am grateful to you for telling me all that you have. I beg you will allow me to wait on you again ere long?"

"I shall be honoured, sir. I am nearly always at home to my friends."

Her sister entered the room soon after, and private conversation came to an end.

Carstares lay awake long that night, hearing the hours toll by and the owls screech in the square. The window's words had sunk deep into his ever-uneasy conscience, and he could not sleep for the thought of John, "alone, unhappy, without friends". . . . Time after time had he argued this question

with himself: John or Lavinia? . . . He fell to wondering
where his brother now was; whether he was still roaming the
South Country, a highwayman. No one would even know
how he, Richard, dreaded each fresh capture made by the
military. Every time he expected John to be among the pris-
oners, and he visited Newgate so often that his friends twitted
him on it, vowing he had Selwyn's love of horrors.

He would argue that the matter rested in John's own
hands: if he were minded to come back to society, he would
do so; but deep within himself he knew that such a decision
was unworthy of one even so debased as was he. Then his
mind went to Lavinia, who alternately enchanted and exasperated him. Only a week ago she had defied him openly in
the matter of her friendship with Lovelace, yet had she not
afterwards apologised, and thrust the Captain aside for his
sake? She was so sweetly naughty, so childishly unreasonable.
Selfish? Yes, he supposed, so, but he loved her! loved her so
greatly that it were a pleasure to him to die for her sake. Yet
John—John was his brother—the adored elder brother, and
by obeying Lavinia he was wronging him, hurting him. If
only Lavinia would consent to the truth being told! It always
came back to that point: if only she would consent. And she
never would. She insisted that, having married her under
false pretences, he had no right to disgrace her now. She was
right, he knew, but he wished she could be for once unselfish.

So he worried on through the night, tossing to and fro in
his great bed, a weight on his mind, a ceaseless ache in his
heart.

Towards dawn he fell asleep and did not wake again until
his chocolate was brought to him. Bitterly he reflected that at
least John had no conscience to prey upon him; he did not
fall asleep with his brain seething with conflicting arguments,
and awake with the decision as far off as ever. To-day his
head ached unbearably, and he stayed in bed for some time
contemplating the grey morning. A fog hung over the square,
and through it the trees, with their withered autumn leaves,
loomed dismally before the windows. There was something
infinitely depressing about the dull outlook, and presently he
rose and allowed his valet to dress him, not able to stand the
inaction any longer. His headache was better by the time he
had visited his wife in her room, and listened to her enthusiastic account of last night's rout, and, going out into the
square, he called a chair, ordering the men to carry him to

White's, where he intended to write two letters. Somehow, Wyncham House was too poignantly full of memories of John to-day, and he was thankful to be out of it.

White's was crowded even at that hour of the morning, and the noise seemed to cut through his head. Men hailed him from all sides, offering him bets; someone tried to tell him some piece of scandal; they would not let him alone, and at last his jagged nerves would no longer support it, and he left the house to go further down the street to his other club, the Cocoa-Tree, which he hoped to find less rowdy. It was fuller than he expected, but many of the men had come as he had, to write letters and to be quiet. Very little gaming was as yet in swing.

Richard wrote steadily for perhaps an hour, and sealed his last letter preparatory to leaving. As he affixed the wafer, he was conscious of a stir behind him, and heard exclamations of:

"Where in thunder did you spring from?"

"Gad, 'tis an age since I've seen you!"

"Lord, 'tis O'Hara!"

Then came the soft Irish voice in answer, and he slewed round in his chair to face them all. Miles O'Hara was the centre of a little group of interested and welcoming clubmen, explaining his arrival.

"Sure, I was in town on a matter of business, and I thought I must come to the club to see ye all while I was here, for 'tis not often I get the chance——"

Richard rose, gathering up his letters and stared across at this man who had been Jack's greatest friend. He took a step towards him. As he did so, O'Hara turned and caught sight of him. Richard was about to hail him. when he suddenly noticed the change in his expression. The good humour died out of the Irishman's eyes and left them hard and scornful. His pleasant mouth curved into a disdainful line. Carstares stood still, one hand on the back of a chair, his eyes riveted to O'Hara's face, reading all the reproach, the redhot anger that Miles was trying to convey to him. O'Hara achieved a sneer and turned his shoulder, continuing to address his friends.

Richard's head swam. O'Hara was ignoring him, would not speak to him. . . . O'Hara knew the truth! He walked blindly to the door, and groped for the handle. . . . O'Hara knew! He was in the passage, on the front steps, in the road, shuddering. O'Hara knew, and he had looked at him as if—

as if—again he shuddered, and seeing an empty chair, hailed it, bidding the men carry him to Grosvenor Square. . . . O'Hara despised him!—reproached him! Then Jack was in trouble? He had seen him and learnt the truth? God, but his brain was reeling! . . .

CHAPTER XXII

Developments

AFTER the encounter with O'Hara, whatever peace of mind Richard had had, left him. He knew not a moment's quiet; all day, and sometimes all night, his brain worried round and round the everlasting question: John or Lavinia? He had quite decided that it must be either the one or the other; the idea that he might conceivably retain his wife *and* confess the truth, never occurred to him. So often had Lavinia assured him that he had no right to expect her to share his disgrace, that now he believed it. He thought that she would elope with Lovelace, whom, his tortured mind decided, she really loved. Any attempt to frustrate such an action would, he supposed wretchedly, be the essence of selfishness. Of course he was not himself, and his brain was not working normally or rationally; had he but known it, he was mentally ill, and if Lavinia had thought to examine him closely she could not have failed to observe the fever spots on each cheek, the unnaturally bright eyes and the dark rings encircling them. Richard wore the look of one goaded beyond endurance, and utterly tired and overwrought. As he told Mrs. Fanshawe, when she exclaimed at his appearance—he could not rest; he must always be moving, thinking. She saw that he was not entirely himself, and counselled him to consult a doctor. His half-angry repudiation of all illness did not surprise her, but she was considerably startled when, in answer to her pleading that he should have a care for himself, he vehemently said: "If I could die, I should be glad!" She wondered what his wife was about not to see his condition, and wished that she might do something. But she was not acquainted with Lady Lavinia, and she felt it would be a piece of gross presumption on her part to speak to her of Richard. If she had thought his malady to be physical, she reflected, she might venture a word, but as she perceived it to be mental, she could only hope that it would pass in time, and that he would recover from his rundown condition.

Lady Lavinia was pursuing her butterfly existence, heeding nothing but her own pleasure, bent on enjoying herself. She succeeded very well, on the whole, but she could not help wishing that Dicky were a little more cheerful and wishful to join in her gaiety. Of late he was worse than ever, and although he supplied her wants uncomplainingly, she would almost rather he had refused her and shown a little life, than give way to her with this dreadful apathy.

Lovelace was out of town for a week, and Lavinia was surprised to find how little she missed him. To be sure, playing with fire was very pleasant, but when it was removed out of her reach, it really made no odds. She missed Harry's adulation and his passionate love-making, for she was one of those women who must always have admiration and excitement, but she was not made miserable by his absence. She continued to flutter round to all the entertainments of the season with one or other of her brothers, and when Lovelace returned he was disturbed by her casual welcome. However, she was undoubtedly pleased to see him, and soon fell more or less under his spell, allowing him to be by her side when Tracy was not near, and to charm her ears with compliments and gallantry.

To do him justice, Captain Harold was really in love with her and was quite ready to relinquish his commission if only she would run away with him. He had private means of his own, and promised her that her every whim should be satisfied. But Lavinia scolded him and shook her head. Apart from any ulterior consideration, Richard was, after all, her husband; he, too, loved her, and she was very, very fond of him, although she did plague him dreadfully.

Lovelace assured her that her husband did not love her nearly as much as he, and when she smiled her disbelief, lost his temper and cried that all the town knew Carstares to be at Mrs. Fanshawe's feet!

Lavinia stiffened.

"Harold!"

"I am only surprised that you have been blind to it," he continued. "Where do you think he goes every day for so long? White's? No. To 16, Mount Street! Stapely called there and met him; another day Lady Davenant saw him with her;

Wilding has also met him at her house. He spends nearly every afternoon with her!"

Lavinia was a Belmanoir, and she had all the Belmanoir pride. Rising to her feet she drew her cloak about her with her most queenly air.

"You forget yourself, Harold." she said haughtily. "Never dare to speak to me of my husband again in that tone! You may take me at once to my brother."

He was very penitent, wording his apology most cleverly, smoothing her ruffled plumage, withdrawing his words, but at the same time contriving to leave their sting behind. She forgave him, yes, but he must never offend her so again.

Although she had indignantly refused to believe the scandal, it nevertheless rankled, and she found herself watching her husband with jealous eyes, noticing his seeming indifference towards her and his many absences from home. Then came a day when she caused her chair to be borne down Mount Street at the very moment when Richard was coming out of No. 16.

That was enough for Lavinia. So he was indeed tired of her! He loved another woman!—some wretched widow! For the first time a real worry plagued her. She stayed at home that evening and exerted all her arts to captivate her husband. But Richard, seeing John unhappy, reproachful, every way he turned, his head on fire, his brain seething with conflicting arguments, hardly noticed her, and as soon as he might politely do so, left her, to pace up and down the library floor, trying to make up his mind what to do.

Lady Lavinia was stricken with horror. She had sickened him by her megrims, as Tracy had prophesied she would! He no longer cared for her! *This* was why he continually excused himself from accompanying her when she went out! For once in her life she faced facts, and the prospect alarmed her. If it was not already too late, she must try to win back his love, and to do this she realised she must cease to tease him for money, and also cease to snap at him whenever he felt at all out of sorts. She must charm him back to her. She had no idea how much she cared for him until now that she thought he did not care for her. It was dreadful: she had always been so sure of Dicky! Whatever she did, however exasperating she might be he would always adore her.

And all the time, Richard, far from making love to Mrs.

Fanshawe, was hearing anecdotes of his brother from her, little details of his appearance, things he had said. He drank in all the information, clutching eagerly at each fresh scrap of gossip, greedy to hear it if it in any way concerned John. His brain was absorbed with this one subject, and he never saw when Lavinia smiled upon him, nor did he seem to hear her coaxing speeches. When she remarked, as she presently did, on his pallor, he almost snapped at her, and left the room. Once she put her arms about him and kissed him on the lips; he put her gently aside, too worried to respond to the caress, but, had she known it—grateful for it.

His Grace of Andover meeting his sister at Ranelagh Gardens, thought her face looked pinched, and her eyes unhappy. He enquired the reason, but Lady Lavinia refused to confide even in him, and pleaded a headache. Andover, knowing her, imagined that she had been refused some kickshaw, and thought no more about it.

He himself was very busy. Only two days before a groom had presented himself at St. James's Square, bearing a missive from Harper, very illegible and illspelt, but to the point:

YR. GRACE,

I have took the liberty of engageing this Man, Douglas, in Yr. Name. I hope I shall soon be Able to have carried out the Rest of yr. Grace's Instructions, and trust my Connduct will meet Yr. Grace's Approvall.

Very Obed'tly,

M. HARPER.

Tracy confirmed the engagement and straightway dispatched the man to Andover, where the head groom would undoubtedly find work for him to do. He was amused at the blind way in which the man had walked into his trap, and meditated cynically on the frailty of human nature, which will always follow the great god of Mammon.

Not three days later came another letter, this time from Mr. Beauleigh, addressed to him at White's, under the name of Sir Hugh Grandison. It asked for the man Harper's character.

His Grace of Andover answered it in the library of his own home, and smiled sarcastically as he wrote Harper down "exceeding honest and trustworthy, as I have always found".

He was in the middle of the letter when the door was unceremoniously pushed open and Andrew lounged into the room.

His Grace looked up frowning. Not a bit dismayed by the coolness of his reception, his brother kicked the door to and lowered his long limbs into a chair.

"May I ask to what I owe the honour of this intrusion?" smiled Tracy dangerously.

"Richard," was the cheerful reply, "Richard."

"As I am not interested in either him or his affairs——"

"How truly amiable you are to-day! But I think you'll be interested in this, 'tis so vastly mysterious."

"Indeed? What is the matter?"

"Just what I want to know!"

Tracy sighed wearily.

"Pray come to the point, Andrew—if point there be. I have no time to waste."

"Lord! Busy? Working? God ha' mercy!" The young rake stretched his legs out before him and cast his eyes down their shapeliness. Then he stiffened and sat up, staring at one white-stockinged ankle.

"Now, damn and curse it! where did that come from?" he expostulated mildly.

"Where did *what* come from?"

"That great splash of mud on my leg. Brand new on this morning, and I've scarce set my nose without doors. Damn it, I say! A brand new——"

"Leg?"

"Hey? What's that you say?"

"Nought. When you have quite finished your eulogy, perhaps you would consent to tell me your errand?"

"Oh, ay! but twenty shillings the pair! Think of it! . . . Well, the point—there is one, you see—is this: it is Richard's desire that you honour him with your presence at Wyncham on Friday week, at three in the afternoon exactly. To which effect he sends you this." He tossed a letter on to the desk. "You are like to have the felicity of meeting me there."

Tracy ripped open the packet and spread the single sheet on the desk before him. He read it through very deliberately, turned it over, as if in search of more, re-read it, folded it, and dropped it into the waste-paper basket at his side. He then picked up his quill and dipped it in the ink again.

"What think you?" demanded Andrew, impatiently.

His Grace wrote tranquilly on to the end of the line.

"What think I of what?"

"Why, the letter, of course! What ails the man? 'Something of great import to impart to us,' forsooth! What means he?"

"Yes, I noticed 'twas very badly worded," commented Tracy. "I have not the vaguest notion as to his meaning."

"But what do you make of it? Lord, Tracy, don't be such a fish! Dick is summoning quite a party!"

"You appear to be in his confidence, my dear Andrew. Allow me to congratulate you. No doubt we shall know more —ah—on Friday week, at three o'clock."

"Oh, you'll go, then?"

"Quite possibly." He went on writing unconcernedly.

"And you've no idea of what 'tis about? Dick is very strange. He hardly listens to what one has to say, and fidget —Lord!"

"Ah!"

"I think he looks ill, an' 'pon my soul, so does Lavvy! Do you suppose there is aught amiss?"

"I really have no idea. Pray do not let me detain you."

Andrew hoisted himself out of his chair.

"Oh, I'm not staying, never fear! . . . I suppose you cannot oblige me with—say—fifty guineas?"

"I should be loth to upset your suppositions," replied his Grace sweetly.

"You will not? Well, I didn't think you would somehow! But I wish you might contrive to let me have it, Tracy. I've had prodigious ill-luck of late, and the Lord knows 'tis not much I get from you! I don't want to ask Dick again."

"I should not let the performance grow monotonous, certainly," agreed the other. "Fifty, you said?"

"Forty-five would suffice."

"Oh, you may have it!" shrugged his Grace. "At once?"

"Blister me, but that's devilish good of you, Tracy! At once would be convenient to *me*!"

His Grace produced a key from his vest pocket and unlocked a drawer in the desk. From it he took a small box. He counted out fifty guineas, and added another to the pile. Andrew stared at it.

"What's that for?" he inquired.

"The stockings," replied Tracy, with a ghost of a smile.

Andrew burst out laughing.

"That's good! Gad! but you're devilish amusing, 'pon rep.

you are!" He thanked his Grace profusely and gathering up the money, left the room.

Outside he gave vent to a low whistle of astonishment. "Tare an' ouns! he must be monstrous well-pleased over something!" he marvelled. "I shall awaken soon, I doubt not." He chuckled a little as he descended the staircase, but his face was full of wonderment.

*   *   *   *   *

Lovelace called nearly every day at Wyncham House, but was always refused admittance, as Lady Lavinia deemed it prudent not to see him. There came a day, however, when he would not be gainsaid, and was ushered into her drawing-room. He kissed her hands lingeringly, holding them for a long while in his.

"Lavinia! Cruel fair one!"

She drew her hands away, not too well pleased at his intrusion.

"How silly, Harold! I cannot have you tease me every day!"

She allowed him to sit by her on the window seat, and he again possessed himself of her hands. Did she love him? She hoped he was not going to be foolish. Of course not. He did not believe her, and started to plead his suit, imploring her to come away with him. In vain Lady Lavinia begged him to be quiet; she had stirred up a blaze, and it threatened to consume her. He was so insistent that, expecting Richard at any moment, and terrified lest there should be a disturbance, she promised to give him an answer next evening, at the threatre. She managed to be rid of him in this way, and, with a relieved sigh, watched him walk down the square. She was very fond of dear Harry, but really, he was dreadfully tiresome at times.

She brought her tiny mirror out from her pocket and surveyed her reflection critically, giving a tweak to one curl, and smoothing another back. She was afraid she was looking rather old this evening, and hoped that Richard would not think so. She glanced up at the clock, wondering where he was; surely he should be in by now? Then she arranged a chair invitingly, pushed a stool up to it and sat down opposite. With a sigh, she reflected that it was an entirely new departure for her to strive to please and captivate her hus-

band, and she fell a-thinking of how he must have waited on
her in the old days, waiting as she was waiting now—hoping
for her arrival. Lady Lavinia was beginning to realise that
perhaps Dick's life had not been all roses with her as wife.

The door opened and Richard came into the room. Deep
lines were between his brows, but his mouth was for once set
firmly He looked sombrely down at her, thinking how very
beautiful she was.

Lady Lavinia smiled and nodded towards the chair she had
prepared.

"Sit down, Dicky! I am so glad you have come! I was
monstrous dull and lonely, I assure you!"

"Were you?" he said, fidgeting with her scissors. "No, I
will not sit down. I have something to say to you, Lavinia.
Something to tell you."

"Oh, *have* you?" she asked. "Something nice, Dicky?"

"I fear you will hardly think so. I am about to make an
end."

"Oh—oh, are you? Of *what*?"

"Of this—this deceitful life I am leading—have been leading. I—I—I am going to confess the whole truth."

"Rich-ard!"

He let fall the scissors and paced restlessly away down the
room.

"I—I tell you, Lavinia, I cannot endure it! I cannot! I cannot! The thought of what John may be bearing is driving me
crazy! I must speak!"

"You—you can't!" she gasped. "After seven years! Dicky,
for heaven's sake——!" The colour ebbed and flowed in her
cheeks.

"I cannot continue any longer this living of a lie—I have
been feeling it more and more ever since—ever since I met
—Jack—that time on the road. And now I can no longer
stand it. Everywhere I go I seem to see him—looking at me—
you don't understand——"

Lavinia cast aside her work.

"No! No! I do not! 'Pon rep., but you should have thought
of this before, Dick!"

"I know it. Nothing can excuse my cowardice—my weakness. I know all that, but it is not too late even now to make
amends. In a week they will all know the truth."

"What—what do you mean?"

"I have requested all whom it concerns to come to Wyncham the Friday after this."

"Good heavens! Dick, Dick *think*!"

"I have thought. God! *how* I have thought!"

"It is not fair to me! Oh, think of your honour—Wyncham!"

"My honour is less than nothing. 'Tis of his that I think."

She sprang up, clutching at his arm, shaking him.

"Richard, you are mad! You must not do this! You must not, I say!"

"I implore you, Lavinia, not to try to make me change my decision. It is of no use. Nothing you can say will make any difference."

She flew into a passion, flinging away from him, her good resolutions forgotten.

"You have no right to disgrace me! If you do it, I will never forgive you! I won't stay with you—I——"

He broke in—this was what he had expected; he must not whine; this was retribution.

"I know. I have faced that."

She was breathless for a moment. He knew! He had faced it! He had taken her seriously—he always expected her to leave him! Oh, he must indeed be tired of her, and wanted her to go. What was he saying?

"I know that you love Lovelace. I—I have known it for some time."

Lavinia sank into the nearest chair. To what depths had her folly led her?

"I shall put no obstacle in the way of your flight, of course. . . ."

This was dreadful! Lady Lavinia buried her face in her hands and burst into tears. It was true then—he did not love her—he loved Mrs. Fanshawe—*she* was to elope. She sobbed pitifully as the full horror of the situation struck her.

The temptation to gather her into his arms almost overmastered Richard, but he managed to choke it down. If he allowed himself to kiss her, she would try to break his resolution—mayhap, she would succeed. So he looked away from her, tortured by the sound of her crying.

Lavinia wept on, longing to feel his arms about her, ready to consent to anything if only he would show that he loved her. But when he made no movement towards her, pride came back, and flicking her handkerchief across her eyes, she rose to her feet.

"You are cruel!—cruel—cruel! If you do this thing I *shall* leave you!"

Now surely he would say something—contradict her!

With an immense effort, Richard controlled himself.

"I am—sorry—Lavinia," he said in a queer, constrained voice.

It was of no avail. She had killed his love, and he was longing to be rid of her. She walked to the door, and turned.

"I see that you do not love me," she said, with deadly calmness. "I understand perfectly." Then, as she wrenched the handle round: "I hate you!" she cried, and fled, her silken skirts rustling furiously down the corridor. A door slammed in the distance, and there was silence.

Carstares stood very still, staring down at her crumpled broidery. Presently he stooped to pick it up, and her violet scent was wafted up to him. He carried it to his lips, passionately.

If Lavinia had been able to see him, it would have changed the whole state of affairs; as it was she locked herself into her room and continued her cry in private. When she had no more tears to shed, she sat up and tried to think that she wanted to elope. Harold would be very good to her, she was sure, and she would doubtless lead a very exciting life, but—somehow the more she thought of it, the less she wanted to elope. Then she remembered Dicky—why had she never realised how much she cared for him?—was in love with some horrid widow, and did not want her to remain with him. The idea was not to be borne, she was not going to be the un-wanted wife. She would have to go away, though not with Lovelace. Dicky should *not* force her to elope with another man. She would go somewhere alone—she had forgotten—she had no money. The dowry that had been hers was spent years ago. She was utterly dependent on her husband. That settled it: she *must* elope with Harry!

"Oh, was anyone ever so beset!" she sobbed as her misery swept in upon her with full force. "Why should I run away if I don't want to?"

CHAPTER XXIII

Lady Lavinia Goes to the Play

RICHARD was away from home all next day, and his wife had plenty of time in which to meditate upon her situation. She had quite come to the conclusion that she must elope with Lovelace, and was only waiting for to-night to tell him so. She would never, never ask Richard to let her stay with him now that she knew he loved another. Truly a most trying predicament. The Carstares were going to-night to Drury Lane to see Garrick play one of his most successful comedies: the *Beaux' Strategem*. The *monde* that would flock to see the inimitable Archer was likely to be a very distinguished one, especially as the cast held the added attraction of Mrs. Clive, and ordinarily Lady Lavinia would have looked forward with much excitement to seeing the piece. To-day, however, she felt that she would far rather go to bed and cry. But Lovelace had to be answered, and besides that, she had invited two cousins, new come from Scotland, to accompany her, and she could not fail them.

So that evening saw her seated in her box, wonderfully gowned as usual, scanning the house. Behind her stood her husband—when she thought that this was the last time she would ever go with him to the theatre she had much ado to keep from bursting into tears before them all—and in the chair at her side was the cousin, Mrs. Fleming. Mr. Fleming stood with his hands behind his back, exclaiming every now and then as his kinsman, young Charles Holt, pointed out each newcomer of note. He was a short, tubby little man, dressed in sober brown, very neat as regards his wrists and neckband, but attired, so thought Lavinia, for the country, and not for town. His dark suit contrasted strangely with Mr. Holt's rather garish mixture of apple-green and pink, with waistcoat of yellow, and Richard's quieter, but far more handsome apricot and silver. His wig, too, was not at all modish, being of the scratch type that country gentlemen affected. His wife was the reverse of smart, but she was loud

213

in her admiration of her more affluent cousin's stiff silks and laces.

She had married beneath them, had Mrs. Fleming, and the Belmanoirs had never quite forgiven the shocking *mésalliance*. William Fleming was nought but a simple Scotsman, whose father—even now the family shuddered at the thought—had been a farmer!

Lavinia was not over-pleased that they should have elected to visit London, and still less pleased that they should evince such an affection for the Hon. Richard and his wife.

"Well, to be sure, Lavvy, 'tis pleasant to sit here and admire all the people!" exclaimed Mrs. Fleming, for perhaps the twentieth time. "I declare I am grown positively old-fashioned from having lived for so long in the country!—yes, my dear, positively old-fashioned! . . . I cannot but marvel at the great hoops everyone is wearing! I am sure mine is not half the size of yours, and the lady down there in the stage-box has one even larger!"

Lavinia directed her gaze towards the box in question. At any other time she would have been annoyed to see that the occupant was Lady Carlyle, her pet rival in all matters of fashion. Now she felt that nothing signified, and merely remarked that she considered those absurd garlands of roses on the dress quite grotesque.

Behind, Holt was directing Mr. Fleming's attention to a box at the back of the house.

" 'Pon my soul, William! 'Tis the Duchess of Queensbury and her son—March, you know. I assure you there is no one more amiable in town. When I last visited her——"

"Charles knows well-nigh everyone here," remarked Mrs. Fleming ingenuously, and wondered why her cousin laughed.

When the curtain rose on the first act, Lovelace was nowhere to be seen, and Lavinia tried to interest herself in the play. But it is difficult to be interested in anything when one's whole mind is occupied with something else far more overwhelming. She was not the only one of the party that Garrick failed to amuse. Richard sat wretchedly in the shadow of the box, thinking how, in a short while, he would never again conduct his wife to the theatre and never again sit at her side watching her every change of expression.

In the first interval Lovelace had still not arrived, but many other acquaintances had arrived and called to see the Carstares. Markham, Wilding, Devereux, Sir John Fortescue —all came into the box at different times, paid homage to

Lavinia, were introduced to Mrs. Fleming, laughed and cracked jokes with the men, and drifted away again.

How was it that she had never before realised how much she enjoyed her life? wondered Lavinia. She settled down to listen to the second act, and Garrick's skill caught her interest and held it. For a moment she forgot her woes and clapped as heartily as anyone, laughing as gaily.

The next instant she remembered again, and sank back into unutterable gloom.

But Richard had heard her merry laugh, and his heart was even gloomier than hers. There was no help for it: Lavinia was delighted at the thought of leaving him.

As the curtain fell, Mrs. Fleming suddenly demanded if it was not Tracy seated in the box over on the other side. Lavinia turned to look. In the box, alone, sat his Grace, seemingly unaware of her presence.

"Is it not Tracy?" persisted Mrs. Fleming. "I remember his face so well."

"Yes," nodded Lavinia, and waved to him.

Andover rose, bowed, and left his box. In a few moments he was in their own kissing his cousin's hand.

Lavinia now caught sight of Lovelace standing on the floor of the theatre looking up at her. He, too, disappeared from view, and she guessed that he was coming to speak with her. He had evidently failed to perceive the Duke, who was just a little behind her in the shadow.

Richard and Mr. Fleming had left the box, and only Charles Holt remained, engaging Mrs. Fleming's whole attention. If only Tracy would go! How was she ever to give Lovelace her answer with him sitting there so provokingly.

Captain Lovelace knocked at the door. Carelessly she bade him enter, and affected surprise on seeing him. His Grace looked at her through narrowed lids, and shot a swift glance at Lovelace, whose discomfiture at finding him there was palpable. Not a trace of emotion was visible on that impassive countenance, but Lavinia felt her brother's attitude to be sinister, as if he divined her wishes and was determined to frustrate them. She watched him smile on Lovelace and beg him to be seated. Whether by accident or design, she was not sure which, he had so placed the chairs that he himself was between her and the captain. Skilfully he drew Mrs. Fleming into the conversation, and re-arranged his stage.

Lavinia found herself listening to the amiable Mr. Holt,

and out of the tail of her eye observed that Lovelace had
fallen a victim to her cousin. She could find no way of speaking to him, and dared not even signal, so adroitly was his
Grace stage-managing the scene. Lavinia was now quite certain that he was managing it. Somehow he had guessed that
she had arranged to speak to Lovelace to-night, and was determined to prevent her. How he had found out, she could
not imagine, but she was too well acquainted with him to be
surprised. He would never let her disgrace herself if he could
help it—she knew that. In whatever manner he himself might
behave, his sister's conduct must be above reproach; he
would find some means of separating them until he could
cause Lovelace to be removed. She did not in the least know
how he would contrive to do this, but she never doubted that
he could and would. And then she would have to stay with
Richard—Richard, who did not want her. If only Tracy
would go! Ah! he was rising!

His Grace of Andover begged Captain Lovelace to bear
him company in his box. He would brook no refusal. He
bore his captive off in triumph.

A minute later Mr. Fleming re-entered the box. The third
act had just begun when Richard re-appeared, and softly took
his seat. On went the play. Neither Tracy nor Lovelace came
to the box during the next interval, and from her point of
vantage Lavinia could see that Andrew had been introduced
to the latter. She could guess how cleverly his Grace was
keeping the Captain by him. . . .

Lord Avon, who had only a week ago returned from Bath,
came to pay his respects. He had much to tell dear Lady Lavinia. How Cholmondely and Falmouth had dared to fight a
duel in Crescent Fields, and had been arrested. How furious
the Beau was, but how his age was beginning to tell on him,
and how it was whispered that his power was waning. All of
which at any ordinary time would have interested my lady
quite prodigiously, but now bored and even annoyed her.

On went the play. Scrub and Boniface kept the house in a
roar; all but Richard and his wife were enthralled. The in-
comparable Kitty failed to hold Lavinia's attention. Would
Lovelace manage to speak to her in the last interval? A solicitous enquiry from Mrs. Fleming roused her, and she had perforce to smile—to own to a slight headache, and to evince
some interest in the play. One more interval: would he come?

She became aware of a hand laid on her shoulder. Richard's voice, gravely courteous, sounded in her ears.

"You are heated, my dear. Will you walk outside a little?"

She felt a mad desire to cling to his hand, and suppressed it forcibly. She rose, hesitating. Mrs. Fleming decided the point.

"The very thing. How considerate of you, Mr. Carstares! I shall like to walk amongst all the people, to be sure! Here is Charles offering to escort us, too! What say you, Lavvy?"

"I—oh, I shall be pleased to do what suits you best, cousin," she answered.

"Then let us go, my love. Charles has an arm for each, so we may leave our husbands to chat."

They went out into the broad passage and walked towards the foyer. There Lord March espied Lavinia, who was always a favourite with him, and came forward, offering his arm. Lavinia took it, thankful to escape from Mr. Holt's vapid conversation. She let March conduct her to where his mother was sitting, with Mr. Selwyn at her elbow. Someone fetched her a glass of ratafie, and Montagu came to talk to her.

Stepping out of his box, Richard fell into the arms of his Grace of Andover.

"Ah! Dick!"

Richard eyed him coldly.

"You wanted me?"

Tracy saw Mr. Fleming approaching.

"Only to ask if I may return with you to Grosvenor Square. I have something important to say."

"Certainly," bowed Richard, and turned aside.

Lovelace who had succeeded in escaping from the Belmanoir claws, hurried in search of Lavinia. Not finding her in her box. he gathered she must be in the foyer, and made his way towards it. As soon as she saw him coming she set down her glass and rose to her feet.

"Oh, Captain Lovelace! Have you come to fetch me back to my seat? I have scarce set eyes on you this evening. No, Markham, you may *not* come! No, nor you, my lord! Madam——" She curtsied low to the old Duchess and walked away on Harold's arm.

When they were once in the deserted passage behind the boxes, he turned eagerly towards her.

"Well, my dearest? Well?"

Lady Lavinia's mouth drooped miserably.

"Yes," she said, "I shall have to come with you."

The tone was damping, to say the least of it, but he did not seem to notice it.

"Lavinia! You mean it?"

"Yes," she assented, still more dejectedly.

"My beautiful love! You will really come? When? At once?"

"At—— Oh, no, no!"

"Darling, the sooner the better. I understand 'tis a great step to expect you to take in a hurry, but I assure you 'tis wisest. Can you come to-morrow?"

Her big eyes dilated.

"No! No! I—oh, I cannot leave Dicky so soon!" She ended with a sob.

"But, Lavinia, my dearest! You surely do not want to *stay* with him?" he cried.

"Yes I do!" she answered. "I—I don't want ever to leave him!"

This blighting speech left him gasping.

"You—but—heavens! what are you saying? You love *me*!"

"No, I don't!" she contradicted. "I always s-said I d-didn't. I love my husband!"

"You are distraught!" he exclaimed. "If you love him, why do you consent to elope with me?"

She looked at him reproachfully.

"There is no one else," she said mournfully.

"Good Lord! What——"

"I have to elope with someone—because—Dick—d-doesn't love me any more—you see. I will come with you, and I will try to be good."

He kissed her hand quickly.

"Sweetheart! . . . I still think you are not yourself. You will think differently to-morrow—you do not really love Carstares."

She shut her mouth obstinately, tilting her regal little head.

He watched her anxiously.

"If you really do love him, 'tis ridiculous to elope with me," he said.

Her fingers tightened on his wrist.

"But I must! You don't understand, Harry! You *must* take me! Don't you want me?"

"Of course I do, but not if you are longing to be some-where else all the time. The whole thing seems preposterous!"

" 'Tis all dreadful!—dreadful! I have never been so un-happy in my life! I—oh, I wish I had not been so heedless and selfish!"

Lovelace pondered for a moment, as they stood outside her box; then, seeing that people were returning to their seats, he opened the door and took her in.

"Listen, dear! This is the maddest scheme ever I heard; but if you are determined, you shall carry it through. Come to my lodgings to-morrow evening! Bring as little baggage as possible; I will have all ready, and we will post at once to Dover. Then in time I hope you will forget Richard and come to care for me a little."

"You are very, very good, Harry! Yes, I will do just as you say—and, oh, I am sorry to put you out like this! I am nought but a plague to everyone, and I wish I were dead! You don't really love me, and I shall be a burden!"

"I do indeed love you!" he assured her, but within himself he could not help wishing that he had not fallen quite so pas-sionately in love with her. "I'll leave you now, sweet, for your husband will be returning at any moment." He kissed her hands lightly. *"A demain,* fairest!"

How she sat through the last act Lavinia could never after-wards imagine. She was longing to be at home—so soon to be home no longer—and quiet. Her head ached now as Rich-ard's had ached for weeks. More than anything did she want to rest it against her husband's shoulder, so temptingly near, and to feel his sheltering arms about her. But Dick was in love with Isabella Fanshawe, and she must sit straight and stiff in her chair and smile at the proper places.

At last the play was ended! The curtain descended on the bowing Archer, and the house stamped and clapped its appre-ciation. The curtain rose again—what! not finished yet? Ah, no! it was but Garrick leading Mrs. Clive forward. Would they never have done?

Mrs. Fleming was standing; she supposed they were going, and got up. Someone put her cloak about her shoulders; Richard—for the last time. Mr. Holt escorted her to her coach, and put her and her cousin into it. He and Mr. Flem-ing had their chairs, so only Richard and Tracy went with the ladies. The Flemings were staying with friends in Brook

Street, just off Grosvenor Square, so that when they had put
Harriet down, only a few more yards remained to be covered.

Lavinia wondered dully why Tracy had elected to come
with them. What did he want? Was he going to warn Dick of
her intended flight? He little knew the true state of affairs!

At the foot of the staircase at Wyncham House she turned
to say good-night.

She merely nodded to Tracy, but to Dick she extended her
hand. He took it in his, kissing it, and she noticed how cold
were his fingers, how burning hot his lips. Then he released
her, and she went slowly up the stairs to her room.

His Grace watched her through his eyeglass. When she was
out of sight he turned and surveyed Richard critically.

"If that is the way you kiss a woman, Lavinia has my sympathies," he remarked.

Richard's lips tightened. He picked up a stand of lighted
candles and ushered his Grace into the drawing-room.

"I presume you did not come to tell me that?" he asked.

"Your presumption is correct, Richard. I have come to
open your eyes."

"You are too kind."

His Grace laid his hat on the table, and sat down on the
arm of a chair.

"I think perhaps I am. It may interest you to hear that Lavinia intends to elope with our gallant friend the Captain."

Richard bowed.

"You knew it?"

"Certainly."

Andover looked him over.

"May I ask what steps you are taking to prevent her?"

"None."

His Grace's expression was quite indescribable. For a moment he was speechless, and then he reverted to heavy sarcasm.

"Pray remember to be at hand—to conduct her to her
chair!" he drawled. "Upon my soul, you sicken me!"

"I am grieved. There is a remedy," replied Carstares significantly.

Tracy ignored the suggestion.

"I suppose it is nothing to you that you lose her? No. It is
nothing to you that she disgraces her name? Oh, no!"

"*My* name, I think."

LADY LAVINIA GOES TO THE PLAY

"Our name! Is it possible for her to disgrace yours?"

Richard went white and his hand flew instinctively to his sword hilt.

Tracy looked at him.

"Do you think I would soil my blade with you?" he asked very softly.

Richard's hand fell from the hilt: his eyes searched the other's face.

"You know?" he asked at last, quite calmly.

"You fool," answered his Grace gently. "You fool, do you think I have not always known?"

Richard leaned against the mantel-shelf.

"You never thought I was innocent? You knew that night? You guessed?"

The Duke sneered.

"Knowing both, could I suspect other than you?" he asked insultingly.

"Oh, my God!" cried Carstares suddenly. "Why could you not have said so before?"

The Duke's eyes opened wide.

"It has chafed you—eh? I knew it would. I've watched you." He chuckled beneath his breath. "And those fools never looked beneath the surface. One and all, they believed that John would cheat. John! They swallowed it tamely and never even guessed at the truth."

"You, at least, did not believe?"

"I? Hardly. Knowing you for a weak fool and him for a quixotic fool, I rather jumped to conclusions."

"Instead, you tried to throw the blame on him. I would to God you had exposed me!"

"So you have remarked. I confess I do not understand this heroic attitude. Why should I interfere in what was none of my business? What proof had I?"

"Why did you raise no demur? What motive had you?"

"I should have thought it fairly obvious."

Richard stared at him, puzzled.

"Gad, Richard! but you are singularly obtuse. Have I not pointed out that John was a quixotic fool? When did I say he was a weak one?"

"You mean—you mean you wanted Lavinia to marry me —because you thought to squeeze me as you willed?" asked Carstares slowly.

His Grace's thin nostrils wrinkled up.

"You are so crude," he complained.

"It suited you that Jack should be disgraced? You thought I should seize his money. You—you——"

"Rogue? But you will admit that I at least am an honest rogue. You are—er—a dishonest saint. I would sooner be what I am."

"I know there is nothing on God's earth more vile than I am!" replied Carstares violently.

His Grace sneered openly.

"Very pretty, Richard, but a little tardy, methinks." He paused, and something seemed to occur to him. " 'Tis why you purpose to let Lavinia go, I suppose? You confess the truth on Friday—eh?"

Richard bowed his head.

"I have not the right to stop her. She—chooses her own road."

"She knows?" sharply.

"She has always known."

"The jade! And I never guessed it!" He paused. "Yes, I understand your heroic attitude. I am sorry I cannot pander to it. In spite of all this, I cannot permit my sister to ruin herself."

"She was as effectually ruined an she stayed with me."

"Pshaw! After seven years, who is like to care one way or the other which of you cheated? Play the man for once and stop her!"

"She *loves* Lovelace, I tell you!"

"What of it? She will recover from that."

"No—I cannot ask her to stay with me—'twould be damnably selfish."

His Grace appeared exasperated.

" 'Fore Gad, you are a fool! Ask her! *Ask* her! Force her! Kick Lovelace from your house and abandon the heroic pose, I beg of you!"

"Do you suppose I want to lose her?" cried Carstares. " 'Tis because I love her so much that I will not stand in the way of her happiness!"

The Duke flung round and picked up his hat.

"I am sorry I cannot join with you in your heroics. I must take the matter into my own hands, as usual, it seems. Lord, but you should have learnt to make her obey you, my good Dick! She has led you by the nose ever since she married you, and she was a woman who wanted mastering!" He went over to the door and opened it. "I will call upon you to-morrow, when I shall hope to find you more sane. They do not propose to leave until late, I know, for Lovelace is promised to Mallaby at three o'clock. There is time in which to act."

"I shall not interfere," repeated Richard.

His Grace sneered.

"So you have remarked. It remains for me to do. Goodnight."

CHAPTER XXIV

Richard Plays the Man

LADY LAVINIA'S frame of mind when she awoke next morning was hardly befitting one who contemplated an elopement. A weight seemed to rest on her chest, hopeless misery was gathered about her head. She could not bring herself to drink her chocolate, and, feeling that inaction was the worst of all, she very soon crawled out of bed and allowed her maid to dress her. Then she went with dragging steps to her boudoir, wondering all the time where Richard was and what he was doing. She seated herself at her window and looked out on to the square, biting the edge of her handkerchief in the effort to keep back her tears.

Richard was in no more cheerful mood. He, too, left his chocolate untouched, and went presently down to the breakfast table and looked at the red sirloin with a feeling of acute nausea. He managed to drink a cup of coffee, and immediately afterwards left the room and made his way to his wife's boudoir. He told himself he was acting weakly, and had far better avoid her, but in the end he gave way to his longing to see her, and knocked on one white panel.

Lavinia's heart leapt. How well she knew that knock!

"Come in!" she called, and tried to compose her features.

Richard entered and shut the door behind him.

"Oh—oh—good-morning!" she smiled. "You—wanted to speak with me—Dick?"

"I—yes—that is—er—have you the Carlyles' invitation?"

It was, perhaps, an unlucky excuse. Lavinia turned away and fought against her tears.

"I—I believe—'tis in my—escritoire," she managed to say. "I—I will look for it."

She rose and unlocked the bureau, standing with her back to him.

"'Tis no matter," stammered Carstares. "I—only—'twas but that I could not find it. Pray do not disturb yourself!"

"Oh—not—at all," she answered, scattering a handful of letters before her. "Yes—here 'tis." She came up to him with the note in her hand, extending it.

Carstares looked down at the golden head, and at the little face with its eyes cast down, and red mouth set so wistfully. Heavens, how could he bear to live without her! Mechanically he took the letter.

Lavinia turned away, and as she stepped from him something snapped in Richard's brain. The luckless invitation was flung down.

"No, by God you shall not!" he cried suddenly.

Lavinia stopped, trembling.

"Oh—oh, what do you mean?" she fluttered.

The mists were gone from his mind now, everything was clear. Lavinia should not elope with Lovelace. In two strides he was at her side, had caught her by the shoulders and swung her to face him.

"You shall not leave me! Do you understand? I cannot live without you!"

Lavinia gave a little cry full of relief, joy and wonderment, and shrank against him.

"Oh, please, please forgive me and keep me with you!" she cried, and clung to the lapels of his coat.

Carstares swept her right off the ground in the violence of his embrace, but she did not mind, although the crushing was ruinous to her silks. Silks were no longer uppermost in her brain. She returned his kisses eagerly, sobbing a little.

When Carstares was able to say anything beyond how he loved her, he demanded if she did not love him?

"Of course I do!" she cooed. "I always, always did, only I was so selfish and so careless!"

He carried her to the sofa and sat down with her on his knee, trying to look into her face. But she had somehow contrived to hide it on his shoulder, and he did not succeed.

"Then you never loved that puppy?" he asked, amazed.

One hand crept up to his other shoulder.

"Oh, Dicky, no! And—and you—you don't love that horrid Mrs. Fanshawe, do you?"

He was still more amazed.

"Mrs. Fanshawe? Great heavens, no! You never thought that, surely?"

"I did—I did! Since you were always at her house, and so cold to me—how could I help it?"

"Cold to *you*? My dearest, surely not?"

"You were—you truly were—and I was so miserable—I
—I thought I had been so unreasonable and so horrid that
you have ceased to l-love me—and I did not know what to
do. And—and then you told me that you were going to—to
confess—and I lost my temper and said I would n-not stay
with you—— But I never, never meant it—and when you
seemed to expect me to go—I—I did not know what to do
again!"

He patted her shoulder comfortingly.

"Sweetheart, don't cry! I had no idea of all this—why, I
was sure that you loved Lovelace—I never doubted it—why
in the world did you not tell me the truth?"

She sat up at that, and looked at him.

"Why, how could I?" she demanded. "I was quite certain
that you loved Isabella Fanshawe. I felt I had to go away,
and I could not do it alone—so—so—so, of course I had to
elope. And I told Harold last night that I would go with him
—and I'm afraid he didn't quite want me when he heard that
I loved you. Oh, Dicky darling, you'll tell him that I won't go
with him, won't you?"

He could not help laughing.

"Ay, I'll tell him. 'Pon rep., sweetheart, I can find it in me
to be sorry for him!"

"Oh, he will not mind for long," she said philosophically.
"He loves so *easily*, you see! But you, Dick—why did you go
so often—so *very* often to see Mrs. Fanshawe?"

His face grew solemn.

"She knew—Jack—in Vienna—— I—I wanted to hear all
she could tell me of him—I could think of nothing else."

"Oh, Dicky! How—how wickedly foolish I have been! And
'twas that that made you so cold—and I thought—oh, dear!"

He drew her head down on to his shoulder again.

"My poor love! Why 'tis the kindest lady imaginable, but
as to loving her——!" He kissed her hand lingeringly. "I love
—and always have loved—a far different being: a naughty,
wilful, captivating little person, who——"

Lady Lavinia clasped her arms about his neck.

"You make me feel so very, very dreadful! I have indeed
been naughty—I——"

"And you'll be so many times again," he told her, laughing.

"No, no! I—will—try to be good!"

"I do not want you good!" Richard assured her. "I want you to be your own dear self!" . . . Lady Lavinia disengaged herself with a contented little sigh, and stood up.

"How charming it is to be happy again, to be sure!" she remarked naïvely. "To think that only half an hour ago I was wishing to be dead!" She went over to the glass and straightened her hair.

Richard looked at her rather anxiously.

"Lavinia—you—you quite understand, I am going to tell everyone the truth—next Friday?" he asked.

"Yes, I do, of course—'tis dreadfully disagreeable of you, but I suppose you will do it. I do *hope* people will not refuse to recognise us, though."

"No one would ever refuse to recognise you, dearest."

She brightened.

"Do you really think so? Well, perhaps after all, 'twill not be so *very* horrid. And—and you will like to have Jack again, won't you? Yes—I knew you would. Oh, 'twill all be quite comfortable after a little while, I make no doubt!"

*   *   *   *   *

His Grace of Andover arose betimes, and early sallied forth into the street. He called a chair, and drove to an address in the Strand, where lodged a certain Colonel Shepherd. Half-an-hour did he spend with the Colonel, and when he at length emerged from the house the curl of his lip betokened satisfaction. He did not at once hail a chair, but walked along in the direction of St. James's, entering the Park in company with one Dare, who, seven years before had given a certain memorable card-party.

Dare was pleasantly intrigued over Richard's latest oddity.

"Have you an idea what 'tis about, Belmanoir?" he inquired. "Has he written you to come as well?"

"I believe I did receive some communication from Carstares; yes—I remember, Andrew brought it."

"Well, what does it mean? Fortescue is bidden, and Davenant. 'Tis very curious."

"My dear Dare, I am not in Richard's confidence. We shall doubtless hear all that there is to hear at the given time. Mysteries do not interest me. But 'twill be a pleasant reunion. . . . Fortescue and Davenant, you say? Strange! I have heard that Evans and Milward have also received their sum—invitations. It should be most entertaining."

" 'Tis prodigious curious," repeated Dare. "No one can imagine what 'tis all about!"

"Ah?" His Grace's thin lips twitched.

Midway through the afternoon he repaired to Wyncham House and was ushered into the library.

Richard sat writing, but rose on seeing him, and came forward.

It struck his Grace that Carstares was looking quite happy. "You seem cheerful, Richard!"

"I am," smiled his brother-in-law.

"I am much relieved to hear it. I have seen Shepherd."

"Shepherd?" interrogated Carstares.

"Lovelace's colonel, my dear Richard. You may count on Captain Harold's departure—on an important mission—in, say, forty-eight hours."

"You may count on Captain Harold's departure in very much less, Tracy," said Carstares, a twinkle in his eye.

The Duke started forward.

"She has gone?" he almost hissed.

"Gone? No! She is in the drawing-room with him."

"With Lovelace! And you permit it? You stand by and watch another man——"

"Say farewell to my wife. But I am not watching it, as you see."

The anger died out of his Grace's eyes.

"Farewell? Do you tell me you at last came to your senses?"

"We found that we both laboured under a delusion," replied Carstares pleasantly.

"I am delighted to hear you say so. I hope you will for the future keep a stricter hold over Lavinia."

"Do you?"

"I do. I think I will not undo what I have done; Lovelace were perhaps better out of the way for a time."

"Why, I have no objection to that," bowed Richard.

His Grace nodded shortly and picked up his hat.

"Then there remains nothing more to be done in the matter."

He looked piercingly across at Carstares. "She did not love him?"

Richard gave a happy little sigh.

"She loves me."

The heavy lids drooped again.

"You cannot conceive my delight. If she indeed loves you, she is safe. I thought she had not got it in her. Pray bear my respects to her." His hand was on the door-knob, when something seemed to occur to him.

"I take it my presence at Wyncham on Friday will not be necessary?" he said cynically.

Richard flushed.

"It will not be necessary."

"Then I am sure you will excuse me an I do not appear. I have other, more important affairs on hand. . . . But I shall be loth to miss the heroics," he added pensively, and chuckled. "*Au revoir*, my good Richard!"

Richard bowed him out thankfully.

Presently the front door opened and shut again, and looking out of the window he saw that Captain Harold Lovelace had taken his departure.

He was now awaiting Mr. Warburton, whom he had sent in search of John some days ago. He should have been here by now, he thought, but perhaps he had been detained. Richard was aching to hear news of his brother, longing to see him once more. But at the same time he was dreading the meeting; he shrank from the thought of looking into Jack's eyes, cold—even scornful. It was not possible, so he reasoned, that Jack should feel no resentment. . . .

"Mr. Warburton, sir."

Carstares turned and came eagerly forward to greet the newcomer.

"Well? Well?"

Mr. Warburton spread out deprecating hands.

"Alas! Mr. Carstares."

Richard caught his arm.

"What mean you? He is not—dead?"

"I do not know, sir."

"You could not find him? Quick! Tell me?"

"Alas! no, sir."

"But the Chequers—he said—— Surely they knew something?"

"Nought, Mr. Carstares." Out came Mr. Warburton's snuff-box. Very deliberately he took a pinch, shaking the remains from his finger-tips. "The host, Chadber—an honest man, though lacking in humour—has not set eyes on my lord

for well-nigh six months. Not since I went to advise my lord
of the Earl's death."

"But Warburton, he cannot be far? He is not dead! Oh,
surely not that?"

"No, no, Master Dick," soothed the lawyer. "We should
have heard of it had he been killed. I fear he has gone
abroad once more. It seems he often spoke of travelling
again."

"Abroad? God! don't let me lose him again!" He sank into
a chair, his head in his arms.

"Tut! I implore you, Mr. Carstares! Do not despair yet.
We have no proof that he has left the country. I daresay we
shall find him almost at once. Chadber thinks it likely he will
visit the inn again ere long. Calm yourself, Master Dick!" He
walked up to the man and laid a hand on one heaving shoulder. "We shall find him, never fear! But do not—I know
'twould grieve him to see you so upset, Master Dick—pray,
do not——!"

"If I could only make amends!" groaned Richard.

"Well, sir, are you not about to? He would not wish you to
distress yourself like this! He was so fond of you! Pray, pray
do not!"

Carstares rose unsteadily and walked to the window.

"I crave your pardon, Mr. Warburton—you must excuse
me—I have been—living in hell—this last week."

Warburton came over to his side.

"Master Dick—I—you know I have never cared for you
—as—well—as——"

"You cared for him."

"Er—yes, sir, exactly!——and of late years I may, perhaps, have been hard. I would desire to—er apologise for any
unjust—er—thoughts I may have harboured against you. I—I
—possibly, I never quite understood. That is all, sir."

He blew his nose rather violently, and then his hand found
Richard's.

*   *   *   *   *

Richard Carstares had plenty to occupy him for the rest of
the week. Arrangements had to be made, a house acquired
for Lavinia, Wyncham House to be thoroughly cleaned and
put in order, awaiting its rightful owner. Once she had made
up her mind to face the inevitable, Lavinia quite enjoyed all

the preparations. The new house in Great Jermyn Street she voted charming, and she straightway set to work to buy very expensive furniture for it, and to superintend all the alterations. In her present penitent mood she would even have accompanied her husband to Wyncham on Monday, to stand by him on the fateful Friday; but this he would not allow, insisting that she remain in town until his return. So she fluttered contentedly from Grosvenor Square to Jermyn Street, very busy and quite happy.

Carstares was to travel to Wyncham on Monday, arriving there the following evening in company with Andrew, whom he was taking as far as Andover. His lordship had lately embroiled himself in a quarrel over a lady when deep in his cups, and owing to the subsequent duel at Barn Elms and the almost overpowering nature of his debts, he deemed it prudent to go into seclusion for a spell. Tracy disappeared from town in the middle of the week, whither no one knew, but it was universally believed that he had gone to Scotland on a visit.

Monday at length dawned fair and promising. After bidding his wife a very tender farewell, and gently drying her wet eyelashes with his own handkerchief, Richard set out with his brother-in-law in the big travelling chaise soon after noon. Andrew had quite recovered his hitherto rather dampened spirits, and produced a dice-box from one pocket and a pack of cards from the other wherewith to beguile the tedium of the journey.

CHAPTER XXV

His Grace of Andover Captures the Queen

DIANA stood in the old oak porch, riding-whip in hand, and the folds of her voluminous gown over her arm. Miss Betty stood beside her, surveying her with secret pride.

Diana's eyes seemed darker than ever, she thought, and the mouth more tragic. She knew that the girl was, to use her own expression, "moping quite prodigiously for that Mr. Carr". Not all that she could do to entertain Diana entirely chased away the haunting sadness in her face; for a time she would be gay, but afterwards the laughter died away and she was silent. Many times had Miss Betty shaken her fist at the absent John.

Presently Diana gave a tiny sigh, and looked down at her aunt, smiling.

"You would be surprised how excellently well Harper manages the horses," she said. "He is quite a godsend. So much nicer than that stupid William."

"Indeed, yes," agreed Miss Betty. "Only think, my dear, he was groom to Sir Hugh Grandison—I saw the letter Sir Hugh writ your Papa—a remarkable elegant epistle, I assure you, my love."

Diana nodded and watched the new groom ride up, leading her mount. He jumped down, and, touching his hat, stood awaiting his mistress's pleasure.

Diana went up to the cob, patting his glossy neck.

"We are going towards Ashley to-day, aunt," she said. "I am so anxious to find some berries, and Harper tells me they grow in profusion not far from here."

"Now, my dear, pray do not tire yourself by going too far —— I doubt it will rain before long and you will catch your death of cold!"

Diana laughed at her.

"Oh, no, aunt! Why, the sky is almost cloudless! But we

232

shall not be long, I promise you. Only as far as Crossdown Woods and back again."

She gave her foot to the groom just as Mr. Beauleigh came out to watch her start.

"Really, my dear, I must ride with you to-morrow," he told her. " 'Tis an age since we have been out together."

"Why, Papa, will you not accompany me this afternoon?" cried Diana eagerly. "I should so like it!"

It struck her aunt that Harper awaited the answer to this question rather anxiously. She watched him, puzzled. However, when Mr. Beauleigh had refused she could not see any change in his expression, and concluded that she must have been mistaken.

So with a wave of her hand, Diana rode away, the groom following at a respectful distance. Yet somehow Miss Betty was uneasy. A presentiment of evil seemed to touch her, and when the riders had disappeared round a bend in the road she felt an insane desire to run after them and call her niece back. She gave herself a little shake, saying that she was a fond old woman, over-anxious about Diana.

Nevertheless, she laid a detaining hand on her brother's arm as he was about to go indoors.

"Wait, Horace! You—you *will* ride with Di more frequently, will you not?"

He looked surprised.

"You are uneasy, Betty?"

"Oh—uneasy——! Well, yes—a little. I do not like her to go alone with a groom, and we do not know this man."

"My dear! I had the very highest references from Sir Hugh Grandison, who, I am sure, would never recommend anyone untrustworthy. Why, you saw the letter yourself!"

"Yes, yes. Doubtless I am very stupid. But you *will* ride with her after to-day, will you not?"

"Certainly I will accompany my daughter when I can spare the time," he replied with dignity, and with that she had to be content.

Diana rose leisurely along the lane, beside great trees and hedges that were a blaze of riotous colour. Autumn had turned the leaves dull gold and flame, mellow brown and deepest red, with flaming orange intermingled, and touches of copper here and there where some beech tree stood. The lane was like a fairy picture, too gorgeous to be real; the trees, meeting overhead, but let the sunlight through in patches, so that the dusty road beneath was mottled with gold.

The hedges retained their greenness, and where there was a gap a vista of fields presented itself. And then they came upon a clump of berries, black and red, growing the other side of the little stream that meandered along the lane in a ditch. Diana drew up and addressed her companion.

"See, Harper—there are berries! We need go no further." She changed the reins to her right hand and made as if to spring down.

"The place I spoke of is but a short way on, miss," ventured the man, keeping his seat.

She paused.

"But why will these not suffice?"

"Well, miss, if you like. But those others were a deal finer. It seems a pity not to get some."

Diana looked doubtfully along the road.

" 'Tis not far?"

"No, miss; but another quarter of a mile, and then down the track by the wood."

Still she hesitated.

"I do not want to be late," she demurred.

"No, miss, of course not. I only thought as how we might come back by way of Chorly Fields."

"Round by the mill? H'm.". . .

"Yes, miss. Then as soon as we get past it there is a clear stretch of turf almost up to the house."

Her eye brightened.

"A gallop? Very well! But let us hurry on."

She touched her cob with her heel, and they trotted on briskly out of the leafy canopy along the road with blue sky above and pasture land around. After a little while the wood came in sight, and in a minute they were riding down the track at right angles to the road. Harper was at Diana's heels, drawing nearer. Half unconsciously she quickened her pace. There was not a soul in sight.

They were coming to a bend in the road, and now Harper was alongside.

Choking a ridiculous feeling of frightened apprehension, Diana drew rein.

"I do not perceive those berries!" she said lightly.

"No, miss," was the immediate response. "They are just a

step into the wood. If you care to dismount here I can show you."

Nothing could be more respectful than the man's tone. Diana shook off her nervous qualms and slipped down. Harper, already on the ground, took the cob's rein and tied both horses to a tree.

Diana gathered her skirts over her arm and picked her way through the brambles to where he had pointed.

The blackberry hedges he held back for her entrance swung back after they had passed, completely shutting out all view of the road. There were no berries.

Diana's heart was beating very fast, all her suspicions springing to life again, but she showed no sign of fear as she desired him to hold the brambles back again for her to pass out.

"For there are no berries here, as you can see for yourself."

She swept round and walked calmly towards the bushes.

Then, how she could never quite remember, she was seized from behind, and before she had time to move, a long piece of silk was flung over her head and drawn tight across her mouth, while an arm, as of steel, held and controlled her.

Fighting madly, she managed to get one arm free, and struck out furiously with her slender crop. There was a brief struggle, and it was twisted from her grasp, and her hands tied behind her, despite all her efforts to be free.

Then her captor swung her writhing into his arms, and strode away through the wood without a word.

Diana was passive now, reserving her strength for when it might avail her something, but above the gag her eyes blazed with mingled fright and fury. She noticed that she was being carried not into the wood, but along it, and was not surprised when they emerged on to the road where it had rounded the bend.

With a sick feeling of terror, she saw a coach standing in the road, and guessed, even before she knew, what was her fate. Through a haze she saw a man standing at the door, and then she was thrust into the coach and made to sit down on the softly-cushioned seat. All her energies were concentrated in fighting against the faintness that threatened to overcome her. She won gradually, and strained her ears to catch what was being said outside.

She caught one sentence in a familiar, purring voice:

"Set them loose and tie this to the pummel." Then there was silence.

Presently she heard footsteps returning. An indistinguishable murmur from Harper, and the door opened to allow his Grace of Andover to enter the coach. It gave a lurch and rumbled on.

Tracy looked down with a slight smile into the gold-flecked eyes that blazed so indignantly into his.

"A thousand apologies, Miss Beauleigh! Allow me to remove this scarf."

As he spoke he untied the knot, and the silk fell away from her face.

For a moment she was silent, struggling for words wherewith to give vent to her fury; then the red lips parted and the small, white teeth showed, clenched tightly together.

"You cur!" she flung at him in a panting undertone. "Oh, you cur!—you coward! Undo my hands!"

"With pleasure." He bowed and busied himself with this tighter knot.

"Pray accept my heartfelt apologies for incommoding you so grievously. I am sure that you will admit the necessity."

"Oh, that there were a *man* here to avenge me!" she raged.

His Grace tugged at the stubborn knot.

"There are three outside," he answered blandly. "But I do not think they are like to oblige you."

He removed her bonds and sat back in the corner, enjoying her. His eyes fell on her bruised wrists, and at once his expression changed, and he frowned, leaning forward.

"Believe me, I did not mean that," he said, and touched her hands.

She flung him off.

"Do not touch me!"

"I beg your pardon, my dear." He leaned back again nonchalantly.

"Where are you taking me?" she demanded, trying to conceal the fear in her voice.

"Home," replied his Grace.

"Home!" Incredulously she turned to look at him, hope in her eyes.

"Home," he reiterated. "*Our* home."

The hope died out.

"You are ridiculous, sir."

" 'Tis an art, my dear, most difficult to acquire."

"Sir—Mr. Everard—whoever you are—if you have any spark of manliness in you, of chivalry, if you care for me at all, you will this instant set me down!"

Never had she seemed more beautiful, more desirable. Her eyes shone with unshed tears, soft and luminous, and the tragic mouth pleaded, even trying to smile.

"It would appear that none of these attributes belongs to me," murmured his Grace, and wondered if she would weep. He had never a taste for a weeping woman.

But Diana was proud. She realised that tears, prayers and all would avail her nothing, and she was determined not to break down, at least in his presence. Tracy was surprised to see her arrange her skirts and settle back against the cushions in the most unconcerned manner possible.

"Then, since you are so ungallant, sir, pray tell me what you purpose doing with me?" The tone was light, even bantering, but with his marvellous, almost uncanny perspicacity, he sensed the breathless terror behind it.

"Why, my dear, I had planned to marry you," he answered, bowing.

The knuckles gleamed white on her clenched hand.

"And if I refuse?"

"I do not *think* you will refuse, my dear."

She could not repress a shiver.

"I do refuse!" she cried sharply.

The smile with which he received this statement drove the blood cold in her veins.

"Wait. I think you will be glad to marry me—in the end," he drawled.

Her great eyes were hunted, desperate, and her face was very white. The dry lips parted.

"I think—you will be—very sorry—when my father—comes."

The indulgent sneer brought the blood racing back to her cheeks.

"And he will come!"

His Grace was politely interested.

"Really? But I do not doubt it, Diana, an he knows where to come."

"He will find a way, never fear!"

She laughed with a confidence she was far from feeling.

"I do not fear—not in the least—I shall be delighted to

welcome him," promised his Grace. "I do not anticipate a refusal of your hand from him."

"No?" Diana, too, could sneer.

"No, my dear. Not after a little—persuasion."

"Who are you?" she shot at him.

His shoulders shook in the soundless laugh peculiar to him.

"I am several people, child."

"So I apprehend," she retorted smoothly. "Sir Hugh Grandison amongst them?"

"Ah, you have guessed that?"

"It rather leaps to the eye, sir." She spoke in what was almost an exact imitation of his sarcastic tone.

"True. It was neatly done, I flatter myself."

"Quite marvellous, indeed."

He was enjoying her as he had rarely enjoyed a woman before. Others had sobbed and implored, railed and raved; he had never till now met one who returned him word for word, using his own weapons against him.

"Who else have you the honour to be?" she asked, stifling a yawn.

"I am Mr. Everard, child, and Duke of Andover."

Then she turned her head and looked at him with glittering eyes.

"I have heard of you, sir," she said, evenly.

"You are like to hear more, my dear."

"That is as may be, your Grace."

Now she understood the elaborate hilt of the mysterious sword with the coronet on it, wrought in jewels. She wondered whether Jack had it still, wherever he was. If only some wonderful providence would bring him to her now in her dire need! There was no one to strike a blow for her; she was entirely at the mercy of a ruthless libertine, whose reputation she knew well, and whose presence filled her with dread and a speechless loathing. She felt very doubtful that her father would succeed in finding her. If only Jack were in England! He would come to her, she knew.

His Grace leaned towards her, laying a thin, white hand on her knee.

"My dear, be reasonable. I am not such a bad bargain after all."

The tenderness in his voice filled her with horror. He felt her shrink away.

"Take your hand away!" she commanded throbbingly. "Do not touch me!" He laughed softly, and at the sound of it she controlled her terrors and dropped again to the mocking tone she had adopted. "What? Ungallant still, your Grace? Pray keep your distance!"

The pistol holster on the wall at her side caught her attention. Instantly she looked away, hoping he had not observed her. Very little escaped his Grace.

"I am desolated to have to disappoint you, my dear. It is empty.

She laid a careless hand on the holster, verifying his statement.

"This? Oh, I guessed it, your Grace!"

He admired her spirit more and more. Was there ever such a girl?

"My name is Tracy," he remarked.

She considered it with her head tilted to one side.

"I do not like your name, sir," she answered.

" 'There was no thought of pleasing you when I was christened,' " he quoted lazily.

"Hardly, sir," she said. "You might be my father."

It was a master stroke, and for an instant his brows drew together. Then he laughed.

"Merci du compliment, mademoiselle! I admire your wit."

"I protest I am overwhelmed. May I ask when we are like to arrive at our destination?"

"We should reach Andover soon after eight, my dear."

So it was some distance he was taking her?

"I suppose you had the wit to provide food for the journey?" she yawned. "You will not wish to exhibit me at an inn, I take it?"

He marvelled at her indomitable courage.

"We shall halt at an inn certainly, and my servant will bring you refreshment. That will be in about an hour."

"So long?" she frowned. "Then, pray excuse me an I compose myself to sleep a little. I am like to find the journey somewhat tedious, I fear."

She shifted farther into the corner, leaned her head back against the cushions and closed her eyes.

Thus outwitting his Grace. For it is impossible to be passionate with a girl who feigns sleep when she should be struggling to escape from you. So Tracy, who, whatever else he might lack, possessed a keen sense of humour, settled himself in his corner and followed her example. So they jogged on. . . .

Arriving at length at the inn, the coach pulled up slowly. Diana opened her eyes with a great assumption of sleepiness.

"Already?" she marvelled.

"I trust you have slept well," said his Grace suavely.

"Excellently well, I thank you, sir," was the unblushing reply.

"I am relieved to hear you say so, my dear. I had thought you unable to—your mouth kept shut so admirably. Doubtless you have schooled your jaw not to drop when you sleep sitting up? I wish I might do the same."

The triumph in his voice was thinly veiled. She found nothing to say.

He rose.

"With your leave, I will go to procure you some refreshment, child. Do not think me uncivil if I remind you that a servant stands without either door."

"I thank you for the kind thought," she smiled, but her heart was sick within her.

He disappeared, returning a few moments later with a glass of wine and some little cakes.

"I deplore the scanty nature of your repast," he said. "But I do not wish to waste time. You shall be more fittingly entertained when we reach Andover."

Diana drank the wine gratefully and it seemed to put new life into her. The food almost choked her, but rather than let him see it, she broke a cake in half and started to eat it, playing to gain time: time in which to allow her father a chance of overtaking them before it was too late. She affected to dislike the cake, and rather petulantly demanded a 'maid of honour'.

Tracy's eyes gleamed.

"I fear I cannot oblige you, my dear. When we are married you can go to Richmond, and you shall have maids of honour in plenty."

He relieved her of her glass, taking it from hands that trembled pitifully.

The rest of the journey was as some terrible nightmare. She felt that she dared no longer feign sleep. She was terrified at what his Grace might do, and kept him at arm's length by means of her tongue and all her woman's wit. As a matter of fact, Andover had himself well in hand, and had no intention of letting his passion run away with him. But as the time went on and the light went, some of Diana's control seemed to slip from her, and she became a little less the self-possessed woman, and a little more the trapped and frightened child. When they at last reached Andover Court, and his Grace assisted her to alight, her legs would barely carry her up the steps to the great iron-clamped door. She trembled anew as he took her hand.

On the threshold he paused and bowed very low. "Welcome to your future home, my queen," he murmured, and led her in, past wooden-faced footmen, who stared over her head, to his private room, where a table was set for two. He would have taken her in his arms then, but she evaded him and slipped wearily into a chair.

"I protest," she managed to say, "I protest, I am faint through want of food."

Andover, looking at her white lips, believed her. He took a seat opposite.

Two footmen came to wait on them, and although her very soul was shamed that they should see her there, she was thankful for their restraining presence.

CHAPTER XXVI

My Lord Rides to Frustrate His Grace

MY LORD yawned most prodigiously and let fall the *Spectator*. His eyes roved towards the clock, and noted with disgust that the hands pointed to half after five. He sighed and picked up the *Rambler*.

His host and hostess were visiting some miles distant, and were not likely to be back until late, so my lord had a long dull evening in front of him, which he relished not at all. Lady O'Hara had tried to induce him to accompany them, promising that he would meet no one he knew, but he had for once been prudent and refused steadfastly. So my lady, after pouting crossly at him and assuring him that he was by far the most obstinate and disagreeable man that she had ever come across, not excepting her husband, who, to be sure, had been quite prodigiously annoying all day, relented, told him she understood perfectly, and even offered to kiss him to make up for her monstrous ill-humour. Jack accepted the offer promptly, waved farewell to her from the porch, and returned to the empty drawing-room to while away the time with two numbers of the *Spectator* and his own thoughts till dinner, which was to be later than usual to-day, on account of an attack of vapours which had seized the cook.

His thoughts were too unpleasant to be dwelt on; everything in his world seemed to have gone awry. So he occupied himself with what seemed to him a particularly uninteresting number of the *Spectator*. The sun had almost disappeared, and very soon it became too dark to read; no candles having been brought as yet, my lord, very unromantically, went to sleep in his chair. Whether he would have eventually snored is not known, for not more than a quarter of an hour afterwards the butler roused him with the magic words:

"Dinner is served, sir."

Carstares turned his head lazily.

"What's that you say, James?"

242

"Dinner is served, sir," repeated the man, and held the door wide for him to pass out.

"Faith! I'm glad to hear it!"

My lord rose leisurely and pulled his cravat more precisely into position. Although he was to be alone, he gave his costume a touch here and there, and flicked a speck of dust from one great cuff with his elegant lace handkerchief.

He strolled across the old panelled hall to the dining-room, and sat down at the table.

The curtains were drawn across the windows, and clusters of candles in graceful silver holders were arranged on the table, shedding a warm light on to the white damask and the shining covers. The footmen presented a fish, and my lord permitted a little to be put on his plate. The butler desired to know if Mr. Carr would drink claret or burgundy, or ale? Mr. Carr would drink claret. A sirloin of beef next made its appearance, and went away considerably smaller. Then before my lord was spread an array of dishes. Partridges flanked one end, a pasty stood next, a cream, two chickens, a duck, and a ham of noble proportions.

My lord went gently through.

The butler desired to know if Mr. Carr would drink a glass of burgundy? He exhibited a dusty bottle. My lord considered it through his eyeglass and decided in favour. He sipped reflectively and waved the ham away.

Sweetmeats appeared before him and a soup, while plump pigeons were uncovered at his elbow.

One was whipped deftly on to his plate, and as he took up his knife and fork to carve it, a great scuffling sounded without, angry voices being raised in expostulation, and, above all, a breathless, insistent appeal for Mr. Carr or Sir Miles. My lord laid down the knife and fork and came to his feet.

"It appears I am demanded," he said, and went to the door. It was opened for him at once, and he stepped out into the hall to find Mr. Beauleigh trying to dodge the younger footman, who was refusing to let him pass. At the sight of Carstares he stepped back respectfully. Mr. Beauleigh, hot, distraught, breathless, fell upon my lord.

"Thank God you are here, sir!" he cried.

Carstares observed him with some surprise. Mr. Beauleigh had been so very frigid when last they had met.

"I am glad to be at your service, sir," he bowed. "You have commands for me?"

"We are in terrible trouble," almost moaned the other. "Betty bade me come to find you, or failing you, Sir Miles, for none other can help us!"

Carstares' glance grew sharper.

"Trouble? Not—— But I forget my manners—we shall talk more at ease in here." He led Mr. Beauleigh into the morning room. Beauleigh thrust a paper into his hands.

"Diana went riding this afternoon, and only her horse returned—with this attached to the pommel! Read it, sir! Read it!"

"Diana!" Carstares strode over to the light, and devoured the contents of the single sheet, with eager eyes.

They were not long, and they were very much to the point:

Mr. Beauleigh may haply recall to mind a certain "Mr. Everard", of Bath, whose Addresses to Miss Beauleigh were cruelly repulsed. He regrets having now to take the Matter into his Own Hands, and trusts to further his Acquaintance with Mr. Beauleigh at some Future Date, when Miss Beauleigh shall, He trusts, have become "Mrs. Everard".

Jack crumpled the paper furiously in his hand, grinding out a startling oath.

"——insolent cur!"

"Yes, yes, sir! But what will that avail my daughter? I have come straight to you, for my sister is convinced you know this Everard, and can tell me where to seek them!"

Carstares clapped a hand on his shoulder.

"Never fear, Mr. Beauleigh! I pledge you my word she shall be found this very night!"

"You know where he has taken her? You do? You are sure?"

"Back to his earth, I'll lay my life; 'tis ever his custom." He strode to the door, flung it wide and shot clear, crisp directions at the footman. "See to it that my mare is saddled in ten minutes and Blue Devil harnessed to your master's curricle! Don't stand staring—go! And send Salter to me!"

The footman scuttled away, pausing only to inform my lord that Salter was not in.

Carstares remembered that he had given Jim leave to visit his Mary at Fittering, and crushed out another oath. He sprang up the stairs, Mr. Beauleigh following breathlessly.

In his room, struggling with his boots, he put a few questions.

Mr. Beauleigh related the whole tale, dwelling mournfully on the excellent references for Harper he had received from Sir Hugh Grandison.

Jack hauled at his second boot.

"Tracy himself, of course!" he fumed, adjusting his spurs.

"Pray, Mr. Carr, who is this scoundrel? It is true that you know him?"

"Andover," answered Jack from the depths of the garderobe. "Damn the felow, where has he put my cloak?" This to the absent Jim, and not the Duke.

"Andover! Not—surely not the Duke!" cried Mr. Beauleigh.

"I know of none other. At last!"

He emerged and tossed a heavy, many-caped coat on to the bed.

"Now, sir, your attention for one moment."

He was buckling on his sword as he spoke, and not looking at the other man.

"Tracy will have borne Di—Miss Beauleigh off to Andover Court, seven miles beyond Wyncham, to the southwest. Your horse, I take it, is not fresh" (he knew Mr. Beauleigh's horse). "I have ordered the curricle for you. I will ride on at once by short cuts, for there is not a moment to be lost——"

"The Duke of Andover!" interrupted Mr. Beauleigh. "The Duke of Andover! Why, do you think he purposes to marry my daughter?"

Jack gave a short, furious laugh.

"Ay! As he married all the others!"

Mr. Beauleigh winced.

"Sir! Pray why should you say so?"

"I perceive you do not know his Grace. Perchance you have heard of Devil Belmanoir?"

Then the little man paled.

"Good God, Mr. Carr, 'tis not he?"

Carstares caught up his hat and whip.

"Ay, Mr. Beauleigh, 'tis indeed he. Now perhaps you appreciate the necessity for haste?"

Mr. Beauleigh's eyes were open at last.

"For God's sake, Mr. Carr, after them!"

" 'Tis what I intend, sir. You will follow as swiftly as possible?"

"Yes, yes, but do not wait for anything! Can you reach Andover—in time?"

"I reach Andover tonight," was the grim answer. "And you, sir? You know the road?"

"I will find out. Only go, Mr. Carr! Do not waste time, I implore you!"

Jack struggled into his riding coat, clapped his hat on to his head, and with his Grace of Andover's sword tucked beneath his arm, went down the stairs three and four at a time, and hurried out on to the drive, where the groom stood waiting with Jenny's bridle over his arm. Carstares cast a hasty glance at the girths and sprang up. The mare sidled and fidgeted, fretting to be gone, but was held in with a hand of iron while her master spoke to the groom.

"You must drive Mr. Beauleigh to Andover Court as fast as you can. It is a matter of life and death. You know the way?"

The amazed groom collected his wits with difficulty.

"Roughly, sir."

"That will do—Mr. Beauleigh will know. Drive your damnedest, man—Sir Miles won't mind. You understand?"

Jack's word was law in the O'Hara household.

"Yes, sir," answered the man, and touched his hat.

On the word, he saw the beautiful straining mare leap forward, and the next moment both horse and rider were swallowed in the gloom.

"Well I'm—darned," exploded the groom, and turned to fetch the curricle.

Across the stretch of moorland went Jack at a gallop, Jenny speeding under him like the wind, and seeming to catch something of her master's excitement. Low over her neck he bent, holding the Duke's sword across his saddlebows with one hand and with the other guiding her. So he covered some three miles. He reined in then, and forced her to a canter, saving her strength for the long distance ahead of them. She was in splendid condition, glorying in the unrestrained gallop across the turf, and although she was too well-mannered to pull on the rein, Carstares could see by the eager twitching of her ears how she longed to be gone over the ground. He spoke soothingly to her and guided her on to the very lane where Diana had ridden that afternoon. She fell into a long, easy stride that seemed to eat up the ground. Now they were off the lane, riding over a field to join another road, leading west. A hedge cut them off, but the mare gathered her legs beneath her and soared over, alighting as gracefully as a bird, and skimming on again up the road.

Her responsive ears flickered as he praised her, and pulled her up.

"Easy now, Jenny, easy!"

She was trembling with excitement, but she yielded to his will and trotted quietly for perhaps another half-hour.

Carstares rose and fell rhythmically in the saddle, taking care to keep his spurred heels from her glossy sides. He guessed the time to be about seven o'clock and his brows drew together worriedly. Jenny was made of steel and lightning, but would she manage it? He had never tested her powers as he was about to now, and he dared not allow her much breathing space. Every minute was precious if he were to reach Andover before it was too late.

Assuming that Tracy had captured Diana at four, or thereabouts, he reckoned that it should take a heavy coach four hours or more to reach Andover. Jenny might manage it in two and a half hours, allowing for short cuts, in which case he ought to arrive not long after the others.

He was tortured by the thought of Diana at the mercy of a man of Tracy's calibre; Diana in terror: Diana despairing. Unconsciously he pressed his knees against the smooth flank and once more Jenny fell into that long, swift stride. She seemed to glide over the ground with never a jar nor a stumble. Carstares was careful not to irk her in any way, only keeping a guiding, restraining hand on the rein, and for the rest letting her go as she willed. On and on they sped as the time lagged by, sometimes through leafy lanes, at others over fields and rough tracks. Not for nothing had Carstares roamed this country for two years; almost every path was familiar to him; he never took a wrong turn, never swerved, never hesitated. On and on, past sleeping villages and lonely homesteads, skirting woods, riding up hill and down dale, never slackening his hold on the rein, never taking his eyes off the road before him, except now and then to throw a glance to the side on the look-out for some hidden by-path. After the first hour a dull pain in his shoulder reminded him of his wound, still troublesome. He set his teeth and pressed on still faster.

The mare caught her foot on a loose stone and stumbled. His hand held her together, the muscles standing out like

ribbed steel, his voice encouraged her, and he made her walk
again. This time she did not fret against the restraint. He
shifted the sword under his bridle hand, and passed the right
down her steaming neck, crooning to her softly beneath his
breath.

She answered with a low, throbbing whinny. She could not
understand why he desired her to gallop on, braving unknown terrors in the dark; all she could know was that it was
his wish. It seemed also that he was pleased with her. She
would have cantered on again, but he made her walk for,
perhaps, another five minutes, until they were come to a
stretch of common he knew well. It was getting late, and he
pressed her with his knee, adjuring her to do her best, and
urging her to a gallop, leaning right forward, the better to
pierce the darkness ahead. A gorse bush loomed before them,
and Jenny shied at it, redoubling her pace.

With hand and voice he soothed her, and on they sped. He
judged the time to be now about half-past eight, and knew
that they must make the remaining miles in an hour. Even
now the coach might have arrived, and beyond that he dared
not think.

Another half-hour crept by, and he could feel the mare's
breath coming short and fast, and reined in again, this time
to a canter. He was off the moor now, on a road he remembered well, and knew himself to be not ten miles from Wyncham. Five more miles as the crow flies. . . . He knew he
must give Jenny another rest, and pulled up, dismounting and
going to her head.

Her legs were trembling, and the sweat rolled off her satin
skin. She dropped her nose into his hand, sobbingly. He
rubbed her ears and patted her, and she lipped his cheek lov-
ingly, breathing more easily.

Up again then, and forward once more, skimming over the
ground.

Leaving Wyncham on his right, Carstares cut west and
then north-west, on the high road now, leading to Andover.
Only two more miles to go. . . .

Jenny stumbled again and broke into a walk. Her master
tapped her shoulder, and she picked up her stride again.

She was almost winded, and he knew it, but he had to
force her onwards. She responded gallantly to his hand, although her breath came sobbingly and her great, soft eyes
were blurred.

At last the great iron gates were in view; he could see them through the dusk, firmly shut. He pulled up and walked on, looking for a place in the hedge where Jenny might push through.

CHAPTER XXVII

My Lord Enters By the Window

His Grace of Andover made a sign to the footmen, and with a sinking heart Diana watched them leave the room, discreetly closing the door behind them. She affected to eat a peach, skinning it with fingers that were stiff and wooden. Tracy leaned back in his chair, surveying her through half-shut eyelids. He watched her eat her peach and rise to her feet, standing with her hand on the back of the high, carved chair. She addressed him nervously and with would-be lightness.

"Well, sir, I have eaten, and I protest I am fatigued. Pray have the goodness to conduct me to your housekeeper."

"My dear," he drawled, "nothing would give me greater pleasure—always supposing that I possessed one."

She raised her eyebrows haughtily.

"I presume you have at least a maidservant," she inquired. "If I am to remain here, I would retire."

"You shall, child, all in good time. But do not be in a hurry to deprive me of your fair company." He rose as he spoke, and taking her hand, led her dumbly to a low-backed settee at the other end of the great room.

"If you have aught to say to me, your Grace, I beg that you will reserve it until to-morrow. I am not in the humour to-night."

He laughed at her.

"Still so cold, child?"

"I am not like to be different, sir."

His eyes glinted.

"You think so? I shall show you that you are wrong, my dear. You may loathe me, you may love me, but I think you will lose something of that icy indifference. Allow me to point out to you that there is a couch behind you."

"I perceive it, sir."

"Then be seated."

"It is not worth the while, sir. I am not staying."

He advanced one step towards her with that in his face that made her sink hurriedly on to the couch.

He nodded smiling.

"You are wise, Diana."

"Why so free with my name, sir?" This with icy sweetness.

Tracy flung himself down beside her, his arms over the back of the settee and the fingers of his drooping hand just touching her shoulder. It was all the girl could do to keep from screaming. She felt trapped and helpless, and her nerve was in pieces.

"Nay, sweet! An end to this quibbling. Bethink you, is it worth your while to anger me?"

She sat rigid and silent.

"I love you——ay, you shudder. One day you will not do that."

"You call this love, your Grace?" she cried out, between scorn and misery.

"Something near it," he answered imperturbably.

"God help you then!" she shivered, thinking of one other who had loved her so differently.

"Belike He will," was the pleasant rejoinder. "But we wander from the point. It is this: you shall retire to your chamber at once—er—armed with the key—an you will swear to marry me to-morrow."

Very white, she made as if to rise. The thin fingers closed over her shoulders, forcing her to remain.

"No, my dear. Sit still."

Her self-control was slipping away from her; she struggled to be free from that hateful hand.

"Oh, you brute, you brute! Let me go!"

"When you have given me your answer, sweetheart."

"It is no!" she cried. "A thousand times no!"

"Think. . . ."

"I have thought! I would rather die than wed you!"

"Very possibly. But death will not be your lot, my pretty one," purred the sinister voice in her ear. "Think carefully before you answer; were it not better to marry me with all honour than to——"

"You devil!" she panted, and looked wildly round for some means of escape. The long window was open, she knew, for the curtain blew out of the room. But his Grace was between it and her.

"You begin to think better of it, child? Remember, tomorrow will be too late. This is your chance, now. In truth," he took a pinch of snuff, "in truth, it matters not to me whether you will be a bride or no."

With a sudden movement she wrenched herself free and darted to the window. In a flash he was up and had caught her as she reached it, swinging her round to face him.

"Not so fast, my dear. You do not escape me so."

His arm was about her waist, drawing her irresistibly towards him. Sick with fear, she struck madly at the face bent close to hers.

"Let me go! How dare you insult me so? Oh, for God's sake let me go!"

He was pressing her against him, one hand holding her wrists behind her in a grip of iron, his other arm about her shoulders.

"For my own sake I will keep you," he smiled, and looked gloatingly down at her beautiful, agonised countenance, with its wonderful eyes gazing imploringly at him, and the sensitive mouth a-quiver. For one instant he held her so, and then swiftly bent his head and pressed his lips to hers.

She could neither struggle nor cry out. A deadly faintness assailed her, and she could scarcely breathe.

"By God, it is too late!" he swore. "You had best give in, madam—nought can avail you now."

And then the unexpected happened. Even as in her last desperate effort to free herself she moaned the name of him whom she deemed hundreds of miles away across the sea, a crisp voice, vibrating with a species of cold fury, sounded directly behind them.

"You delude yourself, Belmanoir," it said with deadly quiet.

With an oath Tracy released the girl and wheeled to face the intruder.

Framed by the dark curtains, drawn sword in hand, murder in his blue eyes, stood my lord.

Tracy's snarl died slowly away as he stared, and a look of blank amazement took its place.

Diana, almost unable to believe her eyes, dizzy with the suddenness of it all, stumbled blindly towards him, crying:

"Thank God! Thank God! Oh, Jack!"

He caught her in his arms, drawing her gently to the couch.

"Dear heart, you never doubted I should come?"

"I thought you in France!' she sobbed, and sank down amongst the cushions.

Carstares turned to meet his Grace.

Tracy had recovered from the first shock of surprise and was eyeing him through his quizzing glass.

"This is an unexpected pleasure, my lord," he drawled with easy insolence.

Diana started at the mode of address and looked up at Carstares, bewildered.

"I perceive your sword in the corner behind you, your Grace!" snapped Jack, and flung over to the door, twisting the key round in the lock and slipping it into his breeches pocket.

To Diana he was as a stranger, with no laugh in the glittering blue eyes, and none of the almost finicking politeness that usually characterised his bearing. He was very white, with lips set in a hard straight line, and his nostrils slightly expanded.

His Grace shrugged a careless refusal.

"My dear Carstares, why should I fight you?" he inquired, seemingly not in the least annoyed by the other's intrusion.

"I had anticipated that answer, your Grace. So I brought *this*!"

As he spoke Jack drove the sword he held into the wood floor, where it stayed, quivering.

Nonchalantly Tracy took it in his hand and glanced at the hilt.

His fingers tightened on it convulsively, and he shot a piercing glance at Jack.

"I am entirely at your service," he said very smoothly, and laid the sword on the table.

Some of the glare died out of my lord's eyes, and a little triumphant smile curved the corners of his mouth. Quickly he divested himself of his fine velvet coat, his waistcoat and his scabbard, and pulled off the heavy riding boots, caked with mud. He proceeded to tuck up his ruffles, awaiting his Grace's convenience.

As one in a dream, Diana saw the table pushed back, the paces measured, and heard the ring of steel against steel.

My lord opened the attack after a few moments' cautious circling, lunging swiftly and recovering, even as the Duke countered and delivered a lightning *riposte en quinte*. My lord parried gracefully in tierce, and chuckled softly to himself.

With parted lips and wide eyes the girl on the couch watched each fresh lunge. A dozen times it seemed as though Carstares must be run through, but each time, by some miraculous means, he regained his opposition, and the Duke's blade met steel.

Once, indeed, thrusting in *quarte,* Tracy's point, aimed too high, flashed above the other's guard and ripped the cambric shirt at the sleeve. My lord retired his foot nimbly, parried, and *riposted* with a straight thrust, wrist held high, before Tracy could recover his opposition. The blades clashed as forte met foible, and my lord lunged straight at his opponent's breast.

Diana shut her eyes, expecting every moment to hear the dull thud of Tracy's body as it should fall to the ground. It did not come, but instead there sounded a confused stamping and scraping of blades, and she looked again to find the Duke disengaging over my lord's supple wrist and being parried with the utmost ease and dexterity.

Carstares knew that he would not be able to last long, however. His shoulder, fretted by the long ride, was aching intolerably, and his wrist seemed to have lost some of its cunning. He was conscious of a singing in his head which he tried, in vain, to ignore. But his eyes glowed and sparkled with the light of battle and the primitive lust to kill.

The Duke was fencing with almost superhuman skill, moving heavily and deliberately, seemingly tireless.

Carstares, on the other hand, was as swift and light as a panther, grave in every turn of his slim body.

He feinted suddenly inside the arm, deceiving the parade of tierce. His Grace fell back a pace, parrying in *quarte,* and as John with a quick twist changed to *quarte* also and the blades crossed, Tracy lunged forward the length of his arm, and a deep red splash stained the whiteness of my lord's sleeve at the shoulder.

Diana gave a choked cry, knowing it to be the old wound, and the Duke's blade came to rest upon the ground.

"You are—satisfied?" he asked coolly, but panting a little.

My lord reeled slightly, controlled himself and brushed his left hand across his eyes.

"On guard!" was all he replied, ignoring a pleading murmur from the girl.

Tracy shrugged, meeting Carstares' blade with his, and the
fight went on.

Tracy's eyes were almost shut, it appeared to Diana, his
chin thrust forward, his teeth gripping the thin lower lip.

To her horror she saw that Carstares was breathing in
gasps, and that his face was ashen in hue. It was torture to
her to sit impotent, but she held herself in readiness to fly to
his rescue should the need arise. Suddenly my lord feinted on
both sides of the arm and ripped open the Duke's sleeve,
causing a steady trickle of blood to drip down on to the floor.

Tracy took no notice, but countered so deftly that John's
blade wavered, and he staggered back. For an instant it
seemed as though the end had come, but somehow he stead-
ied himself, recovering his guard.

Diana was on her feet now, nearly as white as her lover,
her hands pressed to her breast. She saw that John's point
was no longer so purposeful, and the smile had gone from his
lips. They were parted now, the upper one rigid, and a deep
furrow cut into his brow.

Then, startling in the stillness of the great house, came the
clanging of a bell, pulled with some violence.

Carstares' white lips moved soundlessly, and Diana, guess-
ing it to be her father, moved, clinging to the wall, towards
the door.

A moment later along the passage came the sound of steps;
a gay, boisterous voice was raised, followed by a deeper,
graver one.

His Grace's face became devilish in its expression, but
Carstares took no notice, seeming not to hear. Only he thrust
with such skill that his Grace was forced to fall back a pace.
The loud voices demanded to know what was toward in the
locked room, and Diana, knowing that my lord was nearly
spent, beat upon the panels.

"Quickly, quickly!" she cried. "Break through, for heaven's
sake, whoever you are! 'Tis locked!"

"Good Gad! 'tis a woman!" exclaimed the voice. "Listen,
Dick!—why—why—'tis a fight!"

"Oh, be *quick*!" implored poor Diana.

And then came the deeper voice: "Stand away, madam, we
will burst the lock."

She moved quickly aside, turning her attention once more
to the duel by the window, as Andrew flung his shoulder
against the stout wood. At the third blow the lock gave, the

door flew wide, and Lord Andrew was precipitated into the room.

And the two by the window fought on unheeding, faster and faster.

"Well, I'm damned!" said Andrew, surveying them. He walked forward interestedly, and at the same moment caught sight of Jack's face. He stared in amazement, and called to Richard.

"Good Lord! Here! Dick! Come here! Surely it's—*who* is that man?"

Diana saw the tall gentleman, so like her lover in appearance, step forward to the young rake's side. The next events happened in a flash. She heard a great cry, and before she had time to know what he was doing, Richard had whipped his sword from its scabbard and had struck up the two blades. In that moment the years rolled back, and, recognising his brother, Jack gasped furiously:

"Damn—you—Dick! Out—of—the way!"

Tracy stood leaning on his sword, watching, his breath coming in gasps, but still with that cynical smile on his lips.

Richard, seeing that his brother would fly at the Duke again, closed with him, struggling to wrest the rapier from his weakened grasp.

"You fool, John, leave go! Leave go, I say!"

With a twist he had the sword in his hand and sent it spinning across the room as without a sound my lord crumpled up and fell with a thud to the floor.

CHAPTER XXVIII

In Which What Threatened to Be Tragedy Turns to Comedy

WITH a smothered cry Diana flew across the room to where my lord lay in a pitiful little heap, but before her was Richard. He fell on his knees beside the still figure, feeling for the wound.

Diana, on the other side, looked across at him.

" 'Tis his shoulder, sir—an old wound. Oh, he is not—he cannot be *dead*?"

Richard shook his head dumbly and gently laid bare the white shoulder. The wound was bleeding very slightly, and they bound it deftly betwixt them, with their united handkerchiefs and a napkin seized from the table.

" 'Tis exhaustion, I take it," frowned Richard, his hand before the pale lips. "He is breathing still."

Over her shoulder Diana shot an order:

"One of you men, please fetch water and cognac!"

"At once, madam!" responded Andrew promptly, and hurried out.

She bent once more over my lord, gazing anxiously into his face.

"He will live? You—are sure? He—he must have rid all the way from Maltby—for me!" She caught her breath on a sob, pressing one lifeless hand to her lips.

"For you, madam?" Richard looked an inquiry.

She blushed.

"Yes—he—we—I——"

"I see," said Richard gravely.

She nodded.

"Yes, and—and the Duke—caught me, and—brought me here—and—and then *he* came—and saved me!"

The air blowing in from the window stirred the ruffles of my lord's shirt, and blew a strand of her dark hair across Diana's face. She caught it back and stared at Richard with a puzzled air.

"Pardon me, sir—but you are so like him!"

"I am his brother," answered Richard shortly.

Her eyes grew round with surprise.

"His *brother*, sir? I never knew Mr. Carr had a brother!"

"Mr.——who?" asked Richard.

"Carr. It is not his name, is it? I heard the Duke call him Carstares—and—my lord."

"He is the Earl of Wyncham," answered Richard, stretching out a hand to relieve Andrew of the jug of water he was proffering.

"Good—gracious!" gasped Diana. "B-but he said he was a highwayman!"

"Quite true, madam."

"True? But how—how ridiculous—and how like him!"

She soaked a handkerchief in the water, and bathed my lord's forehead.

"He is not coming to in the least," she said nervously. "You are sure 'tis not—not——"

"Quite. He'll come round presently. You said he had ridden far?"

"He must have, sir—I wish he were not so pale—he was staying with the O'Hara's at Maltby."

"What? The O'Hara's?"

"Yes—and he must have ridden from there—and his wound still so tender!" Again she kissed the limp hand.

Over by the window his Grace, his breath recovered, was eyeing Andrew through his quizzing-glass.

"May I inquire what brings you here?" he asked sweetly. "And why you saw fit to bring the saintly Richard?"

"I came because it suited me to do so. I never dreamed you were here——'Pon my soul, I did not!"

"Where then did you think I was?"

"Never thought about you at all, my dear fellow. I'm not your squire."

"Why is Richard here?"

"Lord, what a catechism! He is here because he brought me with him on his way to Wyncham. Have you any objection?"

"It would be useless," shrugged Tracy. "Have I killed that young fool?"

Andrew looked him over in disgust.

"No, you have not. You have barely touched him, thanks be."

"Dear me! Why this sudden affection for Carstares?"

Andrew swung round on his heel, remarking over his shoulder:

"He may be a cheat, but he's a damned fine fellow. By Gad! he nearly pinked you as I entered!" He chuckled at the memory of that glorious moment.

"He nearly pinked me a dozen times," replied Tracy, binding his arm round more tightly. "He fights like ten devils. But he was fatigued."

He followed Andrew across the room and stood looking down at his unconscious foe.

Diana's eyes challenged him.

"Stand back, your Grace! You have no more to do here!"

He drew out his snuff-box and took a pinch.

"So that is how the matter lies, my dear. I did not know that."

"You pretend that it would have made a difference in your treatment of me?"

"Not the slightest, child," he replied, shutting the box with a snap. "It has merely come as a slight surprise to me. It seems he has the luck this round." He walked away again as another great bell-peal sounded through the house.

Andrew, pouring cognac into a glass, paused with bottle held in mid-air.

"Thunder and turf! We are like to be a party! Who now?" He set the glass down and lounged out of the room bottle in hand. They heard him give an astonished cry and a loud laugh, and the next moment O'Hara strode into the room, booted and spurred and enveloped in a heavy surcoat. He came swiftly upon the little group about my lord and went down on one knee beside him. His eyes seemed to take in everyone at a glance. Then he looked across at Richard.

"Is he alive?"

Richard nodded, not meeting the hard, anxious gaze.

O'Hara bent over his friend.

"He has been wounded?"

Diana answered this.

"Only slightly, Sir Miles, but 'twas his shoulder again. He was tired after the ride—Mr. Carstares thinks he has fainted from exhaustion."

O'Hara very gently slipped one arm beneath my lord's shoulders and the other under his knees, rising with him as easily as if he were carrying a baby. He walked over to the couch, lowering his burden on to the cushions that Diana placed to receive him.

"He will be easier there," he said, and looked across at her. "Ye are quite safe, child?"

"Quite—quite——He came just in time—and fought for me." She dabbed openly at her eyes. "I—I love him so, Sir Miles—and now I hear that he is an Earl!" she sighed.

"Well, child, 'twill make no difference, I take it. I hope he'll make ye happy."

She smiled through her tears very confidently.

O'Hara turned and faced Richard, who was standing a little in the rear, watching his brother's face. He met O'Hara's scathing look squarely.

"Well?"

"Nought," answered the Irishman cuttingly, and walked over to where Lord Andrew was arguing hotly with his brother.

Carstares returned to my lord's side and stood looking silently down at him.

Diana suddenly gave a little joyful cry.

"He is coming round! He moved his head! Oh, Jack, my dear one, look at me!" She bent over him with eyes alight with love.

My lord's eyelids flickered and opened. For a moment he stared at her.

"Why—Diana!"

She took his head between her hands and kissed him full on the mouth. Then she raised his head to look into the blue eyes.

My lord's arm crept round her and held her tight against him. After a moment she disengaged herself and stood aside. Jack's eyes, still a little bewildered, fell upon his brother. He struggled up on his elbow.

"Am I dreaming? Dick!" His voice was full of a great joy.

Richard went quickly to him, trying to put him back on the cushions.

"My dear Jack—no, no—lie still!"

"Lie still?" cried my lord, swinging his feet to the ground. "Not a bit of it! I am well enough, but a trifle dizzy. How in thunder did you come here? Surely 'twas you knocked up my sword? Yes? Interfering young cub! Give me your arm a minute!"

"But why do you want to get up?" pleaded a soft voice in his ear.

"So that I can take you in my arms, sweetheart," he answered, and proceeded to do so.

Then his glance, wandering round the room, alighted on the heated group by the table; Andrew vociferously indignant, Tracy coolly sarcastic, and O'Hara furious.

"Tare an' ouns!" ejaculated my lord. "Where *did* they all spring from?"

"I don't know!" laughed Diana. "Sir Miles came a few minutes ago—the other gentleman came with Mr. Carstares."

"Ay, I remember him—'tis Andrew, eh, Dick? Zounds! how he has grown! But what in the world are they all fighting over? Miles! Miles, I say!"

O'Hara wheeled round, surprised.

"Oho! Ye are up, are ye." He crossed to his side. "Then sit down!"

"Since you are all so insistent, I will. How did you come here?"

O'Hara went round to the back of the couch to arrange a cushion beneath the hurt shoulder, and leaned his arms upon the back, looking down with a laugh in his eyes.

"Faith, I rode!"

"But how did you know? Where——"

" 'Twas all on account of that young rascal David," he said. "Molly fretted and fumed all the way to the Frasers, vowing the child would be neglected, and what not, and we'd not been in the house above an hour or so, when up she jumps and says she knows that *something* has happened at home, and nothing will suffice but that I must drive her back. We arrived just as Beauleigh was setting out. He told us the whole tale, and of course I had Blue Peter saddled in the twinkling of an eye and was off after ye. But, what with taking wrong turns and me horse not happening to be made of lightning, I couldn't arrive until now."

"You cannot have been so long after me," said Jack. "For I wasted full half-an-hour outside here, trying to find an opening in the hedge for Jenny to get through. She is now stalled in a shed at the bottom of the lawn with my cloak over her. I'll swear she's thirsty, too."

"I'll see to that," promised O'Hara.

Andrew came across the room and bowed awkwardly to my lord, stammering a little. Carstares held out his hand.

"Lord, Andy! I scarce knew you!"

After a moment's hesitation, Andrew took the outstretched hand and answered, laughingly. But my lord had not failed to notice the hesitation, short though it had been.

"I—beg your pardon. I had forgot," he said stiffly.

Andrew sat down beside him, rather red about the ears.

"Oh, stuff, Jack! I'm a clumsy fool, but I did not mean that!"

Richard stepped forward into the full light of the candles.

"If you will all listen to me one moment, I shall be greatly obliged," he said steadily.

Lord John started forward.

"Dick!" he cried warningly, and would have gone to him, but for O'Hara's hand on his shoulder, dragging him back.

"Ah, now, be aisy," growled Miles. "Let the man say it!"

"Hold your tongue, O'Hara! Dick, wait one moment! I want to speak to you!"

Richard never glanced at him.

"I am about to tell you something that should have been told—seven years ago——"

"Once and for all, I forbid it!" snapped my lord, trying to disengage himself from O'Hara's grip.

Miles leant over him.

"See here, me boy, if ye don't keep a still tongue in your head, it's meself that'll be gagging you, and that's that!"

My lord swore at him.

Diana laid a gentle hand on his arm.

"Please, John! Please be still! Why should not Mr. Carstares speak?"

"You don't know what he would do!" fumed Jack.

"In fact, Miss Beauleigh, Sir Miles and Andrew are completely in the dark," drawled the Duke. "Shall I tell the tale, Richard?"

"Thank you, I shall not require your assistance," was the cold rejoinder. "But I must ask you to be quiet, John."

"I will not! You must n——"

"That will do," decided O'Hara, and placed a relentless hand over his mouth. "Go on, Carstares!"

"For the sake of Miss Beauleigh, I will tell you that seven years ago my brother and I went to a card-party. I cheated. He took the blame. He has borne it ever since because I was too much a coward to confess. That is all I have to say."

" 'Twas for that ye wanted to see me on Friday?" shot out O'Hara.

Richard nodded, dully.

"Yes, I was going to tell you then."

"H'm! I'm glad ye had decided to play the man's part for once!"

With a furious oath Jack wrenched himself free and rounded on his friend.

"You take too much upon yourself, O'Hara!"

He rose unsteadily and walked to Richard's side.

"Dick has told you much, but not all. You none of you know the reasons we had for acting as we did. But you know him well enough to believe that it needed very strong reasons to induce him to allow me to take the blame. If anyone has aught to say in the matter, I shall be glad if he will say it to me—now!" His eyes flashed menacingly as they swept the company, and rested for an instant on O'Hara's unyielding countenance. Then he turned and held out his hand to his brother with his own peculiarly wistful smile.

"Can you bear to speak to me?" muttered Richard, with face averted.

"Gad, Dick, don't be ridiculous!" He grasped the unwilling hand. "You would have done the same for me!"

Andrew pressed forward.

"Well, I can see no use in raking up old scores! After all, what does it matter? It's buried and finished. Here's my hand on it, Dick! Lord! I couldn't turn my back on the man I've lived on for years!" He laughed irrepressibly, and wrung Richard's hand.

My lord's eyes were on O'Hara, pleading. Reluctantly the Irishman came forward.

" 'Tis only fair to tell you, Richard, that I can't see eye to eye with Andrew, here. However, I'm not denying that I think a good deal better of ye now than I did—seven years ago."

Richard looked up eagerly.

"You never believed him guilty?"

O'Hara laughed.

"Hardly!"

"You knew 'twas I?"

"I had me suspicions, of course."

"I wish—oh, how I wish you had voiced them!"

O'Hara raised his eyebrows, and there fell a little silence. His Grace of Andover broke it, coming forward in his inimitable way. He looked round the room at each member of the company.

"One, two, three—four, five——" he counted. "Andrew, tell them to lay covers for five in the dining-room."

"Aren't you staying?" asked his brother, surprised.

"I have supped," replied Tracy coolly.

For a moment O'Hara's mouth twitched, and then he burst out laughing. Everyone looked at him inquiringly.

"Ecod!" he gasped. "Oh, sink me an I ever came across a more amusing villain! 'Lay covers for five!' Oh, damme!"

" Or should I have said six?" continued his Grace imperturbably. "Am I not to have the honour of Mr. Beauleigh's company?"

O'Hara checked his mirth.

"No, ye are not! He was content to let me manage the business, and went back to Littledean."

"I am sorry," bowed his Grace, and turned to my lord, who, with his arm about Diana's waist, was watching him arrogantly.

"I see how the land lies," he remarked. "I congratulate you, John. I cannot help wishing that I had finished you that day in the road. Permit me to say that you fence rather creditably."

My lord bowed stiffly.

"Of course," continued his Grace smoothly, "you also wish you had disposed of me. I sympathise. But, however much you may inwardly despise and loathe me, you cannot show it —unless you choose to make yourself and me the talk of town—not forgetting Mistress Diana. Also I abhor bad tragedy. So I trust you will remain here tonight as my guest—er, Andrew, pray do not omit to order bed-chambers to be prepared—— Afterwards you need never come near me again —in fact, I hope that you will not."

My lord could not entirely repress a smile.

"I thank your Grace for your hospitality, which I fear," he glanced down at Diana's tired face, "I shall be compelled to accept. As to the rest—I agree. Like you, I dislike bad tragedy."

Diana gave a tiny laugh.

"You are all so stiff!" she said. "*I* shall go to bed!"

"I will take you to the stairs then," said Jack promptly, and led her forward.

She stopped as they were about to pass his Grace, and faced him.

Tracy bowed very low.

"Good-night, madam. Carstares will know which room I had assigned to you. You will find a servant there."

"Thank you," she said steadily. "I shall try to forget the happenings of this day, your Grace. I see the truth in what you say—we cannot afford to let the world see that we are at enmity, lest it should talk. And, I confess it freely, I find it less hard to forgive you the insults of—of to-day, since they brought—Jack—to me. An I had not been in such dire straits, I might never have seen him again."

"In fact," bowed his Grace, "everything has been for the best!"

"I would not say that, sir," she replied, and went out.

For a moment there was silence in the room. No one quite knew what to say. As usual, it was Tracy who came to the rescue, breaking an uncomfortable pause.

"I suggest that we adjourn to the dining-room," he said. "I gather we may have to wait some time before his lordship reappears. O'Hara, after you!"

"One moment," replied Miles. "Jack's mare is in a shed somewhere. I said I would see to her."

"Andrew!" called his Grace. "When you have finished superintending the laying of the supper, give orders concerning Carstares' mare!"

A casual assent came from outside, and immediately afterwards Lord Andrew's voice was heard shouting instructions to someone, evidently some way off.

On the whole, the supper-party passed off quite smoothly. His Grace was smilingly urbane, Andrew boisterous and amusing, and O'Hara bent on keeping the conversation up. Richard sat rather silent, but my lord, already deliriously happy, soon let fall his armour and joined in the talk, anxious to hear all the news of town for the last six years.

O'Hara was several times hard put to it to keep from laughing out loud at his thoughts. The humour of the situation struck him forcibly. After fighting as grimly as these men fought, and after all that had transpired, that they should both sit down to supper as they were doing, appealed to him strongly. He had quite thought that my lord would incline to tragedy and refuse to stay an instant longer in the Duke's house.

It was not until midnight, when everyone else had gone to bed, that the brothers came face to face, alone. The dining-room was very quiet now, and the table bore a dissipated look with the remains of supper left on it. My lord stood absently playing with the long-handled punch spoon, idly stirring the golden dregs at the bottom of the bowl. The candles shed their light full on his face, and Richard, standing opposite in the shadow, had ample opportunity of studying it.

It seemed to him that he could not look long enough. Unconsciously his eyes devoured every detail of the loved countenance and watched each movement of the slender hand. He found John subtly changed, but quite how he could not define. He had not aged much, and he was still the same laughter-loving Jack of the old days, with just that intangible difference. O'Hara had felt it, too: a slight impenetrability, a reserve.

It was my lord who broke the uncomfortable silence. As if he felt the other's eyes upon him, he looked up with his appealing, whimsical smile.

"Devil take it, Dick, we're as shy as two schoolboys!"

Richard did not smile, and his brother came round the table to his side.

"There's nought to be said betwixt us two, Dick. 'Twould be so damned unnecessary. After all—we always shared in one another's scrapes!"

He stood a moment with his hand on Richard's shoulder; then Richard turned to him.

"What you must *think* of me!" he burst out. "My God, when I realise——"

"I know. Believe me, Dick, I know just what you must have felt. But pray forget it! It's over now, and buried."

There was another long silence. Lord John withdrew his hand at last, and perched on the edge of the table, smiling across at Richard.

"I'd well-nigh forgot that you were a middle-aged papa! A son?"

"Ay—John—after you."

"I protest I am flattered. Lord, to think of you with a boy of your own!" He laughed, twirling his eyeglass.

At last Richard smiled.

"To think of you an uncle!" he retorted, and suddenly all vestige of stiffness had fled.

*   *   *   *   *

Next morning Richard went on to Wyncham, and Diana, Jack and O'Hara travelled back to Sussex. Jack would not go home yet. He protested that he was going to be married first, and would then bring home his Countess. But he had several instructions to give his brother concerning the preparation of his house. The last thing he requested Richard to do was to seek out a certain city merchant, Fudby by name, and to rescue a clerk, Chilter, from him, bearing him off to Wyncham. All this he called from the coach window, just before they set off.

Richard led Jenny, whom he was to ride home, up to the door of the vehicle, and expostulated.

"But what in thunder am I to do with the man?"

"Give him to Warburton," advised Jack flippantly. "I know he needs a clerk—he always did!"

"But perhaps he will not desire to come——"

"You do as I tell you!" laughed his brother. "I shall expect to find him at Wyncham when I arrive! *Au revoir!*" He drew his head in, and the coach rumbled off.

CHAPTER XXIX

Lady O'Hara Is Triumphant

AFTER spending a restless night, starting at every sound, and hearing the hours strike slowly away, Lady O'Hara arose not a whit refreshed and considerably more ill at ease than she had been before.

During the night she had imagined all sorts of impossible horrors to have befallen her husband, and if, when the reassuring daylight had come, the horrors had somewhat dispersed, enough remained to cause her an anxious morning as she alternated between the hall window and the gate.

No less worried was Jim Salter. He had returned from Fittering last night to find his master and Sir Miles gone, Lady O'Hara in a state of frightened bewilderment, and the house in a whirl. No one, least of all poor Molly, seemed to know exactly where the two men had gone. All she knew was that they had come back upon a scene of turmoil, with Mr. Beauleigh in the midst of a small crowd of excited servants. Her husband had elbowed his way through, and into his ears had Mr. Beauleigh poured his story. Then O'Hara seemed to catch the excitement, and she had been hurried into the house with the hasty explanation that Jack was off after Devil, who had caught Diana, and he must to the rescue. Ten minutes after, she had an alarming vision of him galloping off down the drive, his sword at his side and pistols in the saddle-holsters. The poor little lady had sent an imploring cry after him, checked almost before it had left her lips. Afterwards she wished it had never been uttered, and rather hoped that it had escaped O'Hara's ears.

Salter arrived not half-an-hour later, and his feelings when told that his beloved master had ridden off in search of a fight, may be more easily imagined than described. He was all for setting out in his wake, but her ladyship strongly vetoed the plan, declaring that Sir Miles would be rescue enough, and she was not going to be left entirely without pro-

tectors. Jim was far too respectful to point out that there
were five able-bodied men, not counting himself, in the
house, but as his master had left no instructions for him, he
capitulated.

He proved nought but a Job's comforter next day, for
when my lady pessimistically premised that both Carstares
and her husband were undoubtedly hurt, he did not, as she
expected he would, strive to reassure her, but gave a gloomy
assent. Whereupon she cast an indignant glance in his direction, and turned her back.

At four in the afternoon they were both in the hall, anxiously watching the drive.

"To be sure, 'tis monstrous late!" remarked Molly, with
wide, apprehensive eyes.

"Yes, my lady."

"If—if nought were amiss, they should have been back by
now, surely?"

"Yes indeed, my lady."

Lady O'Hara stamped her foot.

"Don't say *yes*!" she cried.

Jim was startled.

"I beg pardon, m'lady?"

"You are not to say yes! After all, they may have gone a
long way—they—er—they may be tired! Jenny may have
gone lame—anything—anything may have happened!"

"Yes, m'—— I mean certainly, your ladyship!" hastily
amended Jim.

"In fact I should not be surprised an they were not at all
hurt!"

He shook his head despondently, but luckily for him the
lady failed to notice it, and continued with airy cheerfulness:

"For my husband has *often* told me what an excellent
swordsman Mr. Carstares is, and——"

"Your ladyship forgets his wound."

What she might have been constrained to reply to this is
not known, for at that moment came the sound of coach-
wheels on the gravel. With one accord she and Salter flew to
the door, and between them, wrenched it open, just as a gentleman's travelling coach, postillioned by men in gold and
black, and emblazoned with the Wyncham arms, drew up at
the door.

My lady was down the steps in the twinkling of an eye,
almost before one of the grooms had opened the door to

offer an arm to my lord. Carstares sprang lightly out followed by O'Hara, seemingly none the worse for wear.

Molly ran straight into her husband's arms, regardless of the servants, hugging him.

Jim Salter hurried up to my lord.

"Ye are not hurt, sir?" he cried.

Carstares handed him his hat and cloak.

"Nought to speak of, Jim. But 'Everard' well-nigh finished me for all that!" He laughed at Jim's face of horror, and turned to Molly, who, having satisfied herself that her husband was quite uninjured and had never once been in danger of his life, had come towards him, full of solicitude for his shoulder.

"Oh, my dear Jack! Miles tells me you have hurt your poor shoulder again! And pray what has been done for it? I dare swear not one of you great men had the wit to summon a doctor, as indeed you should have, for——"

"Whist now, asthore!" adjured her husband. " 'Tis but a clean scratch after all. Take him into the house and give him something to drink! I'll swear 'tis what he needs most!"

Molly pouted, laughed and complied.

Over the ale Jack related the whole escapade up to the moment when he had parted from Diana at Littledean. Then O'Hara took up the tale with a delightful chuckle.

"Sure, Molly, ye never saw anything to equal poor old Beauleigh when his daughter had told him Jack's name! Faith, he didn't know what to do at all, he was so excited! And Miss Betty I thought would have the vapours from the way she flew from Di to Jack and back again, in such a state of mind as ye can't imagine!"

Molly, who had listened with round eyes, drew a deep ecstatic breath. Then she bounced up, clapping her hands, and proclaiming that she was right after all!

"What will ye be meaning, alanna?" inquired O'Hara.

"Pray, sir, did I not say *over* and *over* again that if I could induce Jack to stay with us everything would come right? Now, Miles, you know I did!"

"I remember ye said something like it once," admitted her spouse.

"Once, indeed! I was always sure of it. And I did coax you to stay, did I not, Jack?" she appealed.

"You did," he agreed. "You assured me that if I was churlish enough to leave, Miles would slowly sicken and pine away!"

She ignored her husband's ribald appreciation of this.

"Then you see that 'tis all owing to me that——" She broke off to shake O'Hara, and the meeting ended in riotous hilarity.

When he went to change his clothes, Carstares found Jim already in his room awaiting him. He hailed him gaily, and sat down before his dressing-table.

"I require a very festive costume to-night, Jim. Rose velvet and cream brocade, I think."

"Very good, your lordship," was the prim reply.

Jack slewed round.

"What's that?"

"I understand your lordship is an Earl," said poor Jim.

"Now who was the tactless idiot who told you that? I had intended to break the news myself. I suppose now, you know my—story?"

"Yes, si—my lord. I—I suppose ye won't be requiring my services any longer?"

"In heaven's name, why not? Do you wish to leave me?"

"Wish to——! No, sir—my lord—— I—I thought ye'd maybe want a smarter valet—and—not me."

My lord turned back to the mirror and withdrew the pin from his cravat.

"Don't be a fool."

This cryptic remark seemed greatly to reassure Jim.

"Ye mean it, sir?"

"Of course I do. I should be lost without you after all this time. Marry that nice girl at Fittering, and she shall maid my lady. For I'm to be married as soon as may be!"

"Ay, s—my lord! I'm sure I'm very glad, s—your lordship. Rose, sir? With the silver lacing?"

"I think so, Jim. And a cream—very pale cream waistcoat, broidered in with rose. There is one, I know."

"Yes, sir—your lordship."

My lord eyed him despondently.

"Er—Jim!"

"Yes—your lordship?"

"I'm sorry, but I cannot endure it."

"I beg pardon, my lord?"

"I can't have you call me 'your lordship', after every second word—I really cannot."

"Why, sir—may I still call you 'sir'?"

"I would much rather you did."

"Ah, sir—thank you." . . .

In the middle of tying the bow to his master's wig, Jim paused, and in the mirror Jack saw his face fall.

"What's amiss now? And what have you done with my patches?"

"In that little box, sir—yes—that one. I was just thinking —there's the haresfoot, sir—that I shall never be able to see ye hold up a coach now!"

My lord, striving to affix the patch in just the right spot at the corner of his mouth, tried to control his features, failed, and went off into a peal of laughter that reached O'Hara in the room across the landing, and caused him to grin delightedly. He had not heard that laugh for many a long day.

Epilogue

HIS GRACE OF ANDOVER sat at the window of his lodgings at Venice, looking down at a letter in his hand. The writing was his sister's. After a moment he drew a deep breath and broke the seal, spreading the sheets out upon the broad sill.

My very dear Tracy,

So you have gone again with no Farewell to yr. poor Sister, sir! I am indeed very offended, but I understand yr. Reason. As soon as I sett mine eyes on Diana I knew the Truth and recognised yr. dark Beauty. I am monstrous grieved for you, dear. I quite love her myself, altho' she is very tiresomely lovely, but perhaps as she is dark and I am fair, we shall not clash.

The Home-coming was prodigious exciting. Andrew was present, Dicky, of course, and me. Mrs. Fanshawe, too, was there, for she knew Jack Abroad, and a monstrous queer Old Man, who was vastly fidgetty and overcome to see Jack. Then Sir Miles and his wife came, who I thought quite agreeable nice People, and Diana's Father and Aunt, rather Bourgeois, but, on the whole, presentable.

Everyone knows the truth now, but most People have been prodigious kind and I scarce notice a difference in our Reception. Dearest Dicky is gayer than he was wont to be and more darling, and I almost enjoy being a Social Outcast.

When Diana is properly gowned, as should suit her position (but I grieve to say that she prefers to dress plainly), she will make a prodigious Elegantt Countess. I have promised to connduct her to my own Mantua Maker, which is very sacrificing, as I am sure You will agree. I know London will go Crazy about her, and, indeed, those who have already seen her, which is Avon and Falmouth, are positively Foolish. I make no doubtt 'twill be very mortifying, but I suppose it must be borne.

She and Jack are prodigious happy together; it is most

273

Unfashionable, but so am I happy with Dick, so there are
a Pair of us, and we had best *sett* Fashion.

Pray, return soon, my dear Tracy, you cannot conceive
how I miss you. I was surprised you went away with Mr.
Fortescue, I had no Notion you were so friendly.

With dearest Love,
Yr. Sister,

LAVINIA.

P.S.—'Twill interest you to hear that Miss Gunning is
to marry Coventry. 'Tis all over Town this last Week.

Slowly his Grace put the sheets together and handed them
to Fortescue, who had just come into the room.

"These, from my sister, may possibly interest you, Frank."

Fortescue read the letter through, and at the end folded it
and handed it back in silence. Tracy laid it down on the table
at his elbow.

"I began—wrongly," he said.

"Yes," assented his friend. "She was not—that kind of
girl."

"But having begun wrongly—I could not undo the wrong."

"So you made it worse," said Fortescue gently.

"I would have married her in all honour——"

"In your own arrogant fashion, Tracy."

"As you say—in my own arrogant fashion, Frank. If I
could go back a year—but where's the use? I am not whin-
ing. Presently I shall return to England and make my bow to
—the Countess of Wyncham. Possibly, I shall not feel one
jealous qualm. One never knows. At all events—I'll make
that bow."

"You will?" Frank looked sharply down at him.

"Nothing more, Tracy! You do not purpose——"

"Nothing more. You see, Frank—I love her."

"I crave your pardon. Yes—she would not take you, but
she has, I think, made you. As I once told you, when love
came you would count yourself as nought, and her happiness
as everything."

For a moment his Grace was silent, and then back came
the old smile, still cynical, yet with less of the sneer in it.

"How very pleasant it must be, Frank, to have one's proph-
ecies so happily verified!" he purred. "Allow me to felicitate
you!"

Bantam Book Catalog

It lists over a thousand money-saving best-sellers originally priced from $3.75 to $15.00 —bestsellers that are yours now for as little as 60¢ to $2.95!

The catalog gives you a great opportunity to build your own private library at huge savings!

So don't delay any longer—send us your name and address and 25¢ (to help defray postage and handling costs).